She will reveal everything...
everything but her secrets.

P9-CQA-547

The Virgin's Secret

"As you don't remember my name, I think it's only right that you should have to earn that knowledge. Perhaps if we were to dance again . . ."

"Or kiss in the moonlight."

"Perhaps," she said softly.

He lowered his lips to hers.

"But I never kiss anyone a second time who cannot recall kissing me a first time."

"A dance then," he said quickly. "At least allow me the opportunity to recall a dance."

She considered him. "Very well. But I would prefer that we leave the library separately."

"Then I will meet you on the terrace?"

"You may count on it." With that she swept from the room, leaving him to stare at the door she'd closed in her wake.

By Victoria Alexander

THE VIRGIN'S SECRET
SEDUCTION OF A PROPER GENTLEMAN
THE PERFECT WIFE
SECRETS OF A PROPER LADY
WHAT A LADY WANTS
A LITTLE BIT WICKED
LET IT BE LOVE
WHEN WE MEET AGAIN
A VISIT FROM SIR NICHOLAS
THE PURSUIT OF MARRIAGE
THE LADY IN QUESTION
LOVE WITH THE PROPER HUSBAND
HER HIGHNESS, MY WIFE
THE PRINCE'S BRIDE
THE MARRIAGE LESSON
THE HUSBAND LIST
THE WEDDING BARGAIN

Coming Soon

BELIEVE

VICTORIA ALEXANDER

The
Virgin's Secret

AVON
An Imprint of HarperCollins Publishers

AVON BOOKS
An Imprint of HarperCollins*Publishers*
10 East 53rd Street
New York, New York 10022-5299

Copyright © 2009 by Cheryl Griffin
ISBN 978-0-06-144947-5
www.avonromance.com

First Avon Books paperback printing: May 2009

Avon Trademark Reg. U.S. Pat. Off. and in Other Countries, Marca Registrada, Hecho en U.S.A.
HarperCollins® is a registered trademark of HarperCollins Publishers.

Printed in the U.S.A.

10 9 8 7 6 5 4 3 2 1

*The book is dedicated with affection and thanks
to Mariah Stewart
for the loan of Alistair McGowan and Shandihar;
to Amy Mayberry,
who tries her best to keep me on track;
and to my friend Irene Mercatante,
who is Most Excellent in so many ways.*

sponsible brother, as Miss Thompson often said in an approving manner; as befit the future Earl of Wyldewood, she would add.

Sterling was the one who took the blame when things went awry. He said it was his duty, although why anyone would want to take the blame made no sense to Nathanial. It was another one of those things he assumed he'd probably understand when he was older.

When Nathanial had suggested they grow frogs in the bathtub on the third floor, Sterling claimed it was his idea when maids found a tub full of squirming tadpoles. Girls certainly did make a fuss over things like that. When the boys lost a ball down the old well in the back garden, Quinton was the one who proposed lowering Nathanial into the well to retrieve it because he was the smallest. Nathanial never would have told his brothers that it was much darker in the well than he had expected, and more than a bit scary. But it was Sterling who told Father it was his idea, and Sterling who was punished, even if Quinton did then come forward.

Miss Thompson said that at least the scamp had a conscience, whatever that was, although she apparently thought it was a good thing. And when the governess read them a story about a Greek boy who tried to fly with wings made of feathers and wax, it was Sterling who scoffed and said they should have used glue. But it was Quinton who managed to find the glue and feathers and sticks they needed to build their own wings.

It had taken them nearly a week. When they finished, they used an old rose trellis to climb to the roof of the gardener's cottage. Nathanial, of course, was picked to make the flight. Being the youngest and smallest did have its drawbacks. If they hadn't tied a rope around his waist—to make certain he didn't fly away—he might have been hurt. As it was, he ended up dangling from the roof in need of adult rescue. They were all punished for that adventure. The trellis had now been removed, bathtubs were only to be used for bathing, and the well had been filled in. But Nathanial would still follow his older brothers anywhere.

"It's rather too dark to see anything," he said now, as if stating a fact and not at all bothered by the dark.

The rain thrummed against the roof of Harrington House, a sound not nearly as ominous on the lower floors. If he had been alone, Nathanial might have found the dim, cavernous attic a little frightening. On a sunny day, the garden of the family's London home and the parks nearby provided ample opportunity for adventure, but it had been raining off and on for three days now, and the boys were confined to the house. As was Miss Thompson. Perhaps it was that last prank they pulled that had been the final straw. Miss Thompson was the only girl they knew who didn't seem at all bothered by frogs, but finding one in her desk drawer today did seem to upset her, oddly enough. She'd sent the boys off with orders to read, and then retreated to her private sitting room. She did that on occasion. Usually when it rained.

"So." Quinton surveyed the attic, holding the candle high. He already looked like a pirate, and as soon as they found pirate clothes, they all would. "Where should we begin?"

"The trunks," Sterling said. "There will be pirate clothes in the trunks." He led the way toward the far recesses of the attic, a rather dark and scary place, Nathanial thought, if truth were told. But his brothers were with him so he needn't worry.

"Which one?" Sterling studied the various assorted trunks that looked exactly like pirate treasure chests. Only bigger.

"The biggest of course." Quinton flashed a grin at his younger brother. "The biggest always has the best treasure."

"Very well." Sterling lifted the lid on the largest trunk and the boys peered inside.

"There's only clothes in there." Nathanial grimaced. He had rather hoped they would indeed find treasure.

"These aren't just clothes." Quinton handed Nathanial the candle, then reached into the trunk and pulled out a red coat that looked like one on their painted tin soldiers. "These are clothes for pirates and knights."

"And adventurers," Sterling said. "And explorers."

"I want to be an explorer," Nathanial said quickly. "Or an adventurer."

"Look at this." Sterling pulled something else out of the trunk.

Quinton grimaced. "It's a book."

"It's a journal." Sterling moved closer to the candle and flipped through the journal. "It's great-grandmother's."

"It's still just a book," Quinton said.

"I know," Sterling murmured. "But it might be a good book."

Quinton scoffed. "How good can a book be?"

"You like books about pirates," Nathanial offered.

"This one is about smugglers." Sterling paged through the journals.

Quinton brightened. "Great-grandmother knew smugglers?"

"I think," Sterling said slowly, "Great-grandmother might have been a smuggler."

"Read it," Nathanial said.

"Very well." Sterling nodded.

The boys sat cross-legged on the floor. Sterling took the candle from Nathanial and positioned it to cast the best light on the pages. For the next hour or so he read to his brothers of the adventures of their great-grandmother, who apparently was indeed a smuggler, pursued by a government agent—a previous Earl of Wyldewood.

At last it stopped raining and Sterling closed the journal. "I don't think we should tell Mother about this," he said firmly.

"Because then we'd have to tell her we were in the attic?" Nathanial asked.

"No." Quinton scoffed. "Because she might not like having a smuggler in the family."

"Oh." Nathanial thought it was rather interesting to have a smuggler in the family. It might be rather interesting to be a smuggler. "Let's be smugglers instead of pirates."

"We can't today," Sterling said. "Miss Thompson will be wondering what became of us. But we can come up here again and read and play smuggler perhaps."

"Can we have smuggler names as well?" Eagerness rang in Nathanial's voice.

"Smuggler names." Quinton laughed. "What are smuggler names?"

"They're like pirate names only for smugglers," Nathanial said in a lofty manner. "And I shall be Black Jack Harrington."

The two older brothers traded glances. Sterling shook his head. "We don't think that's quite right for you."

"Why not?"

"Because your real name isn't Jack, for one thing. We're not just playing you know," Quinton explained with the superiority of an older brother. "It's quite a serious thing to have new names. Even smuggler names. Your smuggler name has to make sense with your real name."

"Nate," Sterling said abruptly. "Sounds like a smuggler, and you can be Quint."

Quinton frowned. "It's not very exciting." He thought for a moment. "What about Peg Leg Quint or Quint the Wicked?"

"More likely Quint the Scamp." Sterling smirked.

"And who will you be?" Nathanial—now Nate—asked. "What will your smuggler name be?"

"I shall remain Sterling."

Quint snorted. "Not much of a name for a smuggler."

"Oh, I shan't be a smuggler." Sterling grinned. "I shall be the intrepid Earl of Wyldewood, agent of the crown, fearless hunter of smugglers. And I shall be the rescuer of the fair maiden, her hero."

"Girls can't play," Nate said firmly. "They're girls."

"Then I shall be Quint." Quinton planted his fists on his hips and puffed out his chest. "Daring, bold King of the Smugglers."

"Who am I to be?" Nate looked from the intrepid earl to the king of the smugglers. It wasn't at all fair. No matter what the game, he always had the last choice.

"Very well." Sterling heaved a long suffering sigh. "I shall give up fearless. You may be the Fearless Smuggler Nate."

"I'd rather like to keep 'daring,' but I shall give you 'bold.'" Quint grinned. "You are now the Fearless Smuggler, Nate the Bold."

The Fearless Smuggler Nate the Bold. He quite liked it.

"We shall have a grand time playing smuggler and smuggler hunter," Sterling said in a most serious manner, as if it were in fact a most serious matter. "And we shall amass great treasures and have grand adventures and rescue fair maidens."

"And wander the world and discover new places," Quint added.

"And . . . and . . . " Nate couldn't think of anything. Once again he was last. But it didn't matter. He too could have grand adventures and wander the world.

"We need a pact, I think," Sterling said thoughtfully. "A smugglers' pact."

Nate frowned. "Do smugglers have pacts?"

"I don't know." Quint shrugged. "You mean like musketeers? One for all and all for one?"

"That's a motto." Sterling scoffed. "Besides, we're brothers. We'll always be one for all and all for one."

Nate studied him. "Forever and ever?"

"As we ever have and ever will be." Sterling nodded in a solemn manner, as if he were making a promise that would indeed last forever. "Brothers one for the other."

"One for the other," Quint murmured.

"One for the other." Nate grinned.

It was a very good pact.

One

They had the look of men who would have disregarded society entirely if they could. If they did not enjoy its comforts and its pleasures. No, not merely society but civilization itself. They shared a similarity of appearance that marked them as brothers, but it was more in the look in their eye and the set of their chin and the confidence in their walk than the coloring of their hair or the breadth of their shoulders or their taller than ordinary height.

There was a look in the eye of the youngest, of intelligence and amusement. Even the least sensible woman knew, upon meeting his gaze, that here was a man who was more than he might at first appear. And knew as well that he was a man who might steal the heart of even the most resistant woman.

But oh, what a lovely theft.

Reflection of a female observer upon meeting
Nathanial Harrington and his brother

London, 1885

It appears the natives are particularly restless this year." Nathanial Harrington gazed over the crowd below from his vantage point on the mezzanine balcony.

"It is spring, after all," his older brother, Quinton, said, an amused note in his voice. "The mating rituals have begun."

"I daresay the cream of London society would not be at all pleased at your referring to the season's festivities as mating rituals," Nate said wryly.

"As accurate as the observation might be."

"Accuracy has never played a significant role in the activities of society." Nate glanced at his brother. "Nor, fortunately for you, has punctuality."

Quint shrugged. "I am merely fashionably late."

"You left Egypt a full fortnight before I did, and yet I've been back in London for five days now." Nate eyed his brother. "What kept you? Where have you been?"

"Here and there. As for what kept me, it's remarkable, the number of—" Quint grinned in the wicked manner that had been the downfall of more than one unsuspecting woman. "—'diversions' a man without the accompaniment of his conscience might encounter."

Nate raised a brow. "When you say 'conscience,' are you referring to me?"

"Absolutely, little brother." Quint chuckled. "You are my conscience, the custodian of my morals, the guardian of my virtue, the—"

Nate laughed. "I don't seem to do a very good job of it."

"And for that I am eternally grateful."

"As am I." As much as he hated to admit it, given that trouble seemed to nip incessantly at Quint's heels, Nate knew his life would have been extraordinarily dull were it not for his brother's penchant for adventure.

When Nate had finished his studies, it was Quint who suggested that he join him on his travels and quests for the lost treasures of the ages. Together they had been to lands and places Nate never dreamed he'd see with his own eyes. The day might find them in Egypt or Persia or Asia Minor, where the Nile or the Tigris or the Euphrates flowed. Wherever men had once lived and built cities and aspired to forever.

If truth were told, he'd rather expected to spend his days in the dusty bowels of museum libraries or the hallowed halls of one university or another. He had anticipated his life would consist of merely searching for the knowledge of the ancients. Instead, he now studied yellowed manuscripts and carved stone fragments for clues to finding the tangibles left behind by history. For Nate, the artifacts and antiquities he and his brother found breathed life into long dead civilizations and made them real. Quint was more concerned with the fine price they would bring from museums or collectors. Yet despite their differences in philosophies, or perhaps because of them, they made an excellent and accomplished team.

"Did you . . . " Quint paused, the question unasked, but then it didn't need to be said aloud.

Nate cast his brother a resigned look. "The fines were paid, the permits arranged for the appropriate—if fictitious—dates to avoid further fines, all necessary authorities received the usual—and in a few cases, more generous than usual—bribes. And the French counsel is now certain it was not you seen leaving his wife's rooms. Attention was diverted toward one of the Americans." Nate shook his head. "It's a pity really. I rather liked them."

"I daresay their morals in matters of this nature are no better than mine. And certainly no better than the

French counsel's wife." Quint flashed him an unrepentant smile. "Your help is most appreciated, you know."

"I do." Nate sighed. "However, you should be prepared for Mother's ire. I can't help you there. She was concerned that you wouldn't make it home at all."

"Come now, I would never miss our little sister's coming out ball." Quint adjusted the cuffs at his wrists. He had the look of a man who'd dressed in a hurry, as he no doubt had. "Reggie would cut my heart out, as would Mother and, probably, Sterling as well."

"It does seem a requirement to have all family members present when launching a sister on the seas of society." Nate gazed over the crowd below them. "When did you finally arrive in London?"

"What time is it now?" Quint grinned. "Obviously, I haven't missed anything of importance, nor does it sound as if I missed anything of interest in Alexandria."

"Not really." Nate paused. "Oh, there was someone asking about you."

Quint's grin widened. "Someone is always asking about me."

"Yes, well, this was not a suspicious husband or outraged father. Do you recall Enrico Montini?"

Quint shrugged. "Vaguely."

"Surely you remember him. He claimed to have discovered a seal, ancient—Akkadian, if I remember—that made reference to the Virgin's Secret, the lost city of Ambropia. He was very cautious and wouldn't show us the seal itself, only the clay impression made by the seal." Nate stared at his brother. Quint had worked with the professor who was the leading authority on Ambropia years ago. "You can't possibly have forgotten. It was a remarkable find."

"Yes, of course."

"Apparently he died rather suddenly a few months ago."

"How unfortunate," Quint murmured.

"Indeed. His brother, odd little fellow, accosted me a few days after you left. He was quite irate and accused us, really you—"

"Me?"

"Your reputation precedes you." Nate grimaced. While he worked hard to keep their activities legitimate, there had been incidents before he joined Quint that had been, at the very least, questionable. "Montini's brother suspects someone substituted a seal of lesser quality and age for his, which he then unknowingly presented to the Antiquities Society Validation Committee. Needless to say, they were not amused."

"Very little does amuse them," Quint said under his breath.

"Montini was discredited. His brother claims the shattering of his reputation somehow led to his death, and he wants to find those responsible."

The Validation and Allocation Committee of the London Antiquities Society was charged with determining the significance of the finds of its members who hunted for artifacts in the far corners of the world as well as evaluating proposals for future work. The society's board used the committee's decisions to determine whether to lend support to an expedition. Support that might be as minimal as the use of the society's influential name or as consequential as financial backing.

"You should know I told his brother you had left Egypt for Turkey. I suspect he intended to follow you."

"Most appreciated."

"One does what one can for one's brother." Nate shook his head. "Pity about Montini, though."

"No doubt he simply made a mistake," Quint said.

"Still, if I recall the impressions he showed us—"

"Such things happen all the time. You and I have on occasion believed a find to be more significant than it was." Quint paused, nodded at the gathering below them and abruptly changed the subject. Not that it really mattered. "Whose idea was it to have this ball out of doors?"

Nate chuckled. "Who do you think?"

"And Mother allowed it?"

"She fretted all week about the possibility of rain and what would we do then? But you know how Reggie is when she sets her mind on something." Nate shrugged. "And this is, after all, her party."

Even at age eighteen, Regina Harrington had a strength of character that would be some poor man's undoing one day. Their sister was the youngest child and only girl, and neither her mother nor her brothers had ever managed to say no to her. Reggie had gotten it into her head that it would be a grand idea to have dancing on the terrace under the stars and reserve the ballroom for tables for dinner and conversation. She had ignored her mother's concerns with the blithe confidence known only to young women in their first season. Besides it wouldn't dare rain on Lady Regina Harrington's coming out ball, and it hadn't. It was a perfect spring night.

Nate leaned on the balustrade and studied the crowd. "When was the last time we were in England in the spring?"

"I'm not sure." Quint thought for a moment. "This

time last year we were in Persia, and the year before
that Egypt, I think, or perhaps Turkey. I really can't say
but it's been a long time."

It had been at least six years by Nate's estimation
since he and his brother had resided for more than a
handful of months at a time in England, at their family's London home or their country estate. They were
more likely to be found searching for a lost city in
Turkey or a pharaoh's vanished tomb in Egypt or a
forgotten temple in Persia and the treasure that would
surely accompany such a find. These days they were
more at home sleeping under the stars than dancing
under them. Nate tugged at the scratchy, starched collar
imprisoning his neck. And they'd be far more comfortable as well. Still, it was good to be home.

"As much as I hate to admit it, I have rather missed
the London season," Quint said thoughtfully.

Nate scoffed. "I find that hard to believe. I thought
you hated all this."

"Nonsense, brother dear." Quint scanned the crowd
below them. "I've never especially liked the unrelent-
ing rules governing it all. The 'You must do this' and
'You absolutely cannot do that.' But the array of English
beauty on display during the season is unmatched. It's
a grand feast and well worth the effort."

Nate chuckled. "A feast?"

"Absolutely." Quint rested his forearms on the balustrade, clasped his hands together and scanned the
gathering. He nodded toward a group of fresh-faced,
hopeful young females in white gowns.

Nate followed his brother's gaze but his eye caught
on a dark-haired young woman. She wore a dress the
deep color of ripe apricots and casually circled the ter-

race as if she were looking for something or someone.

"There you have the debutantes, those in their first season. They are a first course, light and teasing to the appetite. No more than a suggestion of the offerings to come."

"And the second course?" The woman carried herself with the self-assurance borne of beauty, but Nate had the most absurd notion that she was somehow out of place. It was a silly thought. He didn't know half the guests in attendance and wouldn't have known who belonged here and who didn't. Nor did he care.

"There." Quint indicated another group of pastel-clad young ladies. "This is no doubt their second or third season or more. They are somewhat more substantial to the palate but again nothing more than a prelude. As for the main course . . . " He narrowed his gaze thoughtfully. "Presentation of a plate, its appeal to the eye, is as important as flavor. One wouldn't be tempted by an offering that did not whet one's appetite." He continued to study the crowd. "Those in more vibrant colors are married or widows many years out of mourning. Here, brother, you must make your selection of which dish to sample carefully. While an unhappily married woman makes an excellent main course, an outraged husband does tend to produce unpleasant aftereffects."

"Indigestion?" Nate said absently, still watching the unknown lady meander around the perimeters of the terrace. He couldn't clearly make out her features but had the oddest sense of familiarity. Had he met her before? Years ago perhaps? Or on one of his rare visits home? Nonsense, from the balcony he couldn't clearly see her face.

"At the very least. But a widow who is content in her

widowhood and has no desire to become a wife again can be a most substantial and satisfying—" Quint grinned. "—dining experience."

"Very tasty," Nate murmured.

Quint slanted him a suspicious glance. "Are you listening to me?"

"What? Yes, of course," Nate said quickly, and straightened. "I am hanging on every word. I believe you have come to—" He cleared his throat. "—dessert."

"A most important and delightful addition to a meal." Quint shrugged. "Although dessert is entirely dependent upon one's taste. A light and frothy confection of spun sugar and air—"

"Similar to the first course?"

Quint nodded. "Quite. While tasty upon the tongue, such a sweet can lead to a permanent diet, which I personally prefer to avoid. And a heavier offering, say a pudding, can be thoroughly enjoyable as long as one is careful not to develop a taste for it."

"Or one might find oneself eating pudding for the rest of one's life?"

"Exactly. And as much as I might like pudding, I can't imagine having it every day until I breathe my last."

"Nor can I." Although Nate suspected he would be ready for a steady diet of pudding long before his brother was. Not that he was ready for pudding—or rather, marriage—as of yet. Still, the idea was not nearly as repugnant to him as it was to Quint. He himself was confident he would know the right woman when she stepped into his life. Until then, he was more than willing to try whatever desserts were offered.

"It appears Sterling has noted my arrival," Quint

said out of the corner of his mouth, directing a smile and a brief wave to their brother, who stood off to one side of the terrace beside their mother. The Earl of Wyldewood's annoyed glare was as unyielding as the legendary beacon from the long vanished Pharos of Alexandria. "Shall we join the others?"

"I don't think we can avoid it." Nate chuckled.

Quint stepped through the door onto the mezzanine that overlooked the ballroom. Nate cast a last glance over the crowd below, then followed his brother. He had lost the woman in the apricot dress but had no doubt he would find her. He smiled to himself, noting the same sense of anticipation he always had at the start of any quest, be it for the lost treasures of an ancient people or an intriguing female. Would this be a find of great importance? Or like that poor wretch Montini, would it be nothing more than a dreadful mistake?

Regardless, he had always been fond of apricots.

It wasn't as if she'd never been to a ball before. Why, when her brother had been in London, they always attended the annual ball of the Antiquities Society and on occasion others hosted by organizations affiliated with a university or museum.

She wandered along the edges of the crowd on the terrace in as casual a manner as she could muster, as if she belonged here, her confidence bolstered by the knowledge that she looked her best. Her gown was the latest French fashion and something of an extravagance, even if she could well afford it. Regardless, her world did not demand an excess of fashionable gowns. Still, it did enhance her appearance, and she had just

enough vanity to appreciate that. She was well aware
that she was considered pretty, with her dark hair and
deep blue eyes, although it had never been of particular
concern.

Gabriella Montini smiled and nodded at people she
had never met nor ever expected to meet. Certainly,
this would be easier if she'd ever before attended a ball
given by an earl. And considerably less, well, awkward
if she had actually been invited instead of quietly slipping in through the back garden gate.

This was the home of those vile Harrington brothers,
and this was where she hoped to find evidence that one
or, more likely, both of them had stolen the Ambropia
seal from her brother. Not that she had any real proof
yet, but they were at the top of Enrico's list of possibili-
ties and an excellent place to start. She stepped through
the tall French doors thrown open to the terrace and
walked into the ballroom. Should the opportunity ever
present itself, she would have to thank whoever had the
odd idea to have the dancing out of doors. It made her
task much less difficult. And this time she had a plan.

Gabriella accepted a glass of punch from a passing
footman and inquired as to the location of the ladies'
retiring room. Not that she had any intention of retiring, but it would provide an excellent excuse should
she be discovered. All part of her plan. Admittedly, it
wasn't an excellent plan, but it was far better than the
last, which hadn't involved the least bit of sensible fore-
thought and could have had disastrous consequences.
Disaster was inevitable when one acted on emotion and
impulse rather than rational thought.

She should have learned that lesson years ago, and

thought she had. But she'd never anticipated how sorrow and anger could build inside a person for months, until it banished sanity from even the most sensible head. Still, it was something of an adventure, and ended without serious incident, though it was not especially successful. It had been years since she'd had any kind of adventure whatsoever that could not be found between the pages of aged, dusty manuscripts and the yellowed notebooks of long dead explorers. And she did so long to get away from books. For that alone it was perhaps worth the deception involved.

"Emma, my dear girl!" An older woman swept up to her in a flurry of satin skirts and exuberance. "How are you? It's been simply forever since we've seen one another. I heard you and your mother were in Paris."

Gabriella ignored the panic twisting her stomach. The lady had obviously mistaken her for someone else, and it seemed wise not to correct her. The last thing she needed was for anyone to realize she didn't belong here. She forced her brightest smile. "It has been a long time."

"You are as lovely as always. At least I think you are." The older woman squinted her eyes and peered at Gabriella. "Do forgive me, my dear, I have misplaced my spectacles once again." She heaved a dramatic sigh. "It's one of the banes of growing older. All sorts of things that used to work quite well no longer perform even adequately. I won't bore you with a long list. Suffice it to say eyesight and forgetting where I've put something are among them."

The woman couldn't clearly see her? Relief and a touch of gratitude for this stranger washed through Gabriella. Not enough, however, to tell her that her spectacles dangled from a jeweled broach pinned to her expansive bosom. "Nonetheless, you do appear well."

"Oh, I am. Quite well, thank you. And I have always been dreadful about misplacing my things so I really can't blame that on age." She leaned closer and laid a hand on Gabriella's arm in a confidential manner. "Age is a lovely excuse, you know. One is allowed to be eccentric rather than merely scatterbrained." She straightened and glanced around the room, which was rather pointless Gabriella thought. "Is your charming husband with you this evening?"

"Yes, of course. He's . . . " She paused. Not having a husband, she wasn't at all sure where one might be found. But she did know where she wished to put her plan in motion. "In the library, I believe. Yes, I think that's what he said. Do you know where it is?"

"Through the main doors into the corridor and then just a few doors down."

Just past the ladies' receiving room. How convenient. "I really should find him."

"Yes, indeed, you should be getting back to him." The older woman shook her head. "I wouldn't let a husband as handsome as your Lord Carpenter wander about freely. I should find my husband as well. Not as handsome as yours and certainly not as young, but age looks better on him then it does on me."

"I can't believe that."

"Neither can I." She laughed. "Do pay a call on me soon, my dear. It has been far too long." She smiled, nodded, and took her leave.

Gabriella did hope someone would tell her the location of her spectacles. Preferably after Gabriella had left the ball. She headed toward the library and hoped she didn't run into anyone's husband, or anyone at all for that matter. Fortunately, there was no one in the corridor. She found the library door, pressed her ear against it, heard nothing, then drew a deep breath and pushed it open as if she had every right to be there. As if she was simply another invited guest.

She stepped into the room and closed the door behind her. Thankfully, the library was indeed empty and well lit. She would hate to have had to stumble around in the dark. Antique swords and pistols were mounted on the walls on either side of the doors. A large desk sat at the far end of the room. Flanked by floor-to-ceiling windows, it was the dominant feature in the room, as she imagined the desk of an earl would be. The remaining walls were covered with tall book-lined shelves interspersed with portraits of long dead ancestors. She sniffed in disdain. Pirates and thieves the lot of them, no doubt. A smaller desk, probably for use of the earl's secretary, was placed off to one side of his lordship's.

She crossed the room to the smaller desk and wondered where to begin. It had been remarkably easy to learn that the earl's secretary also handled whatever paperwork his younger brothers' activities required. A few casual conversations with some of the older members of the Antiquities Society bemoaning how terribly complicated verification of finds and requests for funding had become. And hadn't it been so much easier in those long ago days when they were the ones uncovering the artifacts and treasures of forgotten civilizations? Why, one could scarcely accomplish anything these days without hiring clerical help, which certainly was a financial burden unless one was independently wealthy. Or had a clever sister who could handle such matters, or an earl for a brother who was willing to provide the services of his own secretary.

If the Harrington brothers had Enrico's seal, there could well be correspondence regarding it. It was a fabulous find. One of the few pieces ever discovered that might lend credence to the existence of the legendary city of Ambropia, if properly authenticated, of course. The discoverer of such an artifact would reap great fame, his reputation and his future assured.

The muscles in her jaw tightened. A reputation and a future that should have been her brother's, that would have been had not someone stolen the seal. It was a little more than a year ago that Enrico had returned to London with the seal. She had lived with her half brother since she was ten years old, after he found her residing in Italy with distant relatives of their father, two years after his death. But she couldn't recall ever seeing Enrico more excited about a discovery. Not that he had shown her the piece, only the impression made by rolling the cylindrical seal over wet clay. Her brother was remarkably superstitious about such things. He'd said it would be bad luck to reveal the seal prematurely. After all, Ambropia was clouded in mystery and legend, which included a curse placed by the city's virgin goddess protector on the heads of those who would disturb its sleep. Now she wondered if he hadn't been right.

When Enrico had unwrapped the seal in front of the Antiquities Society's Verification and Allocation Committee, he found a seal of far lesser significance. His claims that someone had stolen his seal and replaced it with a relatively common one did not sway the committee. Especially as Enrico had lost his temper and charged the society itself with trying to ruin him.

Her brother was never the same after that. Recovering the lost seal had consumed him. Competition for an artifact such as this was intense, and Enrico was certain that one of his rivals had stolen the Ambropia seal. He left London to pursue those he'd suspected responsible. His letters to her had detailed his progress as well as listed the names of the men he thought might have taken the seal or hired someone to steal it.

But the letters grew progressively less rational, less lucid, even a touch mad, although Gabriella had refused to see them that way at the time. A mistake she later deeply regretted. If he had taken Xerxes—the manservant who usually accompanied him—or if she had gone with him herself, perhaps . . . But she hadn't accompanied her brother on an expedition of any kind for years, not since what she thought of as the "incident," and she knew then he would never have allowed her to do so.

Then, six months ago, she received word that he'd died in Egypt, allegedly of a fever. The impersonal notice from a minor British foreign officer was accompanied by a crate containing her brother's possessions. She'd been devastated, of course. Enrico was twenty years older than she and as much father as brother. Aside from relatives of her English mother, whom she'd never met, he was the only family she had. She'd vowed then to find those who were responsible and restore her brother's reputation.

Now, the answers might be within reach. Absently, she chewed on her lower lip and studied the desk. It was probably locked. Damnation, she should have thought of that and come prepared. This plan was not going substantially better than the last one, and was probably not much smarter.

It wasn't until after Enrico's death that Gabriella had discovered they were far better off financially than she'd ever suspected. She was shocked to learn that their father had left the bulk of his significant fortune to her. Indeed, from the statements she had seen, it appeared it was her money that provided not only her support, but funding for Enrico's work as well. Enrico had never mentioned any of this, nor was it necessary for him to do so. As he was away more often than he was in London, his solicitor handled their finances. The solicitor arranged payment of all their expenses, including the fees for her initial schooling, the costs of continuing her studies at Queen's College, the modest London house where she resided, and the salary of Miss Henry. Florence Henry served as companion, chaperone, and friend, and had been by Gabriella's side since she first took up residence in London.

But her discoveries weren't merely financial. She had also found a packet of letters addressed to her mother—the mother who had died giving her birth. She thought they might prove useful someday to find her English relations, should she ever be so inclined. But as they had never sought her out, why should she look for them? Still, one letter in particular might prove useful. Her newfound wealth certainly had.

Though not exorbitantly rich, Gabriella now found herself in command of a sizable fortune. She wasn't at all used to having money. While it was nice to realize she could afford to do whatever she wished, the very idea of frivolous expenditures brought on a queasy feel-

ing in the pit of her stomach. Even so, the now impressive state of her finances made it that much easier when
anger and grief prompted her to impulsively travel to
Egypt to confront the Harringtons. She was still bothered by twinges of guilt about having deceived Florence on that score. Regardless, it couldn't be helped,
and what Florence didn't know wouldn't upset her.
Florence believed that she had spent those few months
coming to grips with her grief in the peaceful, contem-
plative setting of a convent in France. And believed as
well that Xerxes and his wife, Miriam, had enjoyed
a much deserved holiday, waiting for Gabriella in a
nearby village rather than on a futile quest to Egypt.

Gabriella wished Xerxes was with her now. Among a
number of unique abilities, Xerxes Muldoon could open
any lock. She had no idea how he had acquired such a
skill, but it was a useful one to have. Still, it was one thing
for her to slip into this party alone, and quite another to
be accompanied by Xerxes. The product of an Egyptian
mother and an Irish father, he was tall and powerfully
built, with an exotic look about him. He would not have
gone unnoticed. At this very moment Xerxes was waiting with her carriage near the back gate.

No, she would have to do this by herself. She tried the
desk drawers; they were indeed locked. It was pointless
to look for a key. People who locked drawers would
certainly not leave a key lying around in plain sight.
There was scarcely anything on the desk at all save an
inkstand, complete with inkwell, several pens, and a
letter opener with an Egyptian faience scarab affixed
to the handle. A gift from the brothers, no doubt, and
probably stolen. Gabriella picked up the letter opener
and hefted it in her hand. It would prove useful.

She knelt down and studied the center drawer. There was a keyhole in the middle that more than likely released the locks on all the drawers. If she could wedge the letter opener in the thin crack between the drawer and the desk itself, perhaps she could pop the lock and—

"May I be of some assistance?"

Two

Only the top half of her face was visible over the edge of the desk but her blue eyes widened in surprise.

Good. Nate liked surprising a woman, it gave him the upper hand. He had spotted her leaving the ballroom and had assumed she was headed to the ladies' receiving room. He had planned to wait by the door for her return, but glanced down the corridor to see the library door closing and decided this was the opportunity to make her acquaintance. If, of course, she wasn't meeting someone else in the library.

He stepped toward her. "May I help you?"

"No, but thank you." She straightened. She was taller than he had thought when he first saw her but not overly so. She stood about half a head shorter than he, the perfect height.

"May I ask what you are doing in here?"

"What I'm doing in here?" She shrugged graceful shoulders left bare by the apricot gown. "As you have caught me, I suppose I must confess."

He smiled the slow, slightly wicked smile that had

always served him well. While not quite as accomplished as Quint when it came to the fairer sex, Nate had no lack of confidence in his own ability to charm. And this particular smile was his most effective weapon. "Oh, I am fond of confession. Especially when it comes from a beautiful woman."

She stared at him for a moment, then laughed. "I'm afraid you'll be disappointed." She moved around the desk, a letter opener in her hand. "It's not an especially exciting confession."

His gaze slipped over her. He knew little about fashion, but thanks to the ravings of his mother and sister since his return home, he could see her gown was French and in the latest fashion. The silk of the dress molded nicely to curves no doubt enhanced by a corset. Even so, the swell of her breasts revealed by the low cut of her bodice needed no enhancement. Thank God for the French. "I can't imagine anything you say to be less than exciting."

She cast him a seductive smile of her own and his mouth went dry. "What a delightful thing to say."

"Oh, I can say any number of delightful things." He moved toward her. "I can say how the color of that dress is most becoming with the color of your eyes."

"My, that is delightful."

"I can do better. I can say—" His glance fell to the letter opener in her gloved hand. "What are you doing with that?"

She shifted it in her hand, and for the oddest moment he thought she intended to use it as a weapon. "I saw it on the desk and wanted a closer look. Clumsy fool that I am, I dropped it and it fell under the desk." She handed it to him. "Is the scarab real?"

"As real as something purchased in a market in Cairo can be." He turned it over in his hand. "I picked it up last year as a gift for my brother's secretary."

"Then you are thoughtful as well as charming?"

He laughed. "I can be." He tossed the letter opener on to the desk. "But you promised me a confession as to why you are here in the library."

"I have changed my mind." She raised a shoulder in a casual shrug. "It doesn't seem quite fair for me to confess to you without you confessing to me in return." Her eyes narrowed slightly. "Surely you have something to confess? Some misdeed that has weighed heavily on your conscience?"

"Nothing that comes to mind." He grinned. "Although I will confess I hope you are not here for a clandestine liaison with another gentleman."

She paused, then heaved a dramatic sigh. "You have found me out. How very embarrassing, especially as it appears he is not coming."

"But how fortunate for me." He took her hand and drew it to his lips, his gaze meshing with hers.

"Do you think so?"

"I do." He kept her hand in his and studied her. "Forgive me but have we met? You look remarkably familiar."

"You don't remember?" An odd note sounded in her voice. Nate wasn't sure if she was offended or relieved.

"My apologies." He shook his head. "I can't imagine not remembering you but—"

She pulled her hand from his. "I must say this isn't the least bit delightful."

"I am sorry—"

"You don't remember dancing together?"

"No, I'm afraid—"

"A few flirtatious moments during a walk in a garden very much like yours?"

"I can't recall—"

"A kiss stolen in the moonlight?"

He swallowed hard. "I must be an idiot."

"Yes, you must." She flipped open the fan dangling from her wrist and studied him thoughtfully. "Although I suppose you have danced with many women, had many flirtations in gardens, stolen many kisses in the moonlight. It must be difficult to recall every incident, every woman."

"Yes. No!" Indignation washed through him. "I have never once forgotten—"

She raised a brow.

"Until now." He huffed. "You have me at a distinct disadvantage."

"Do I?" she laughed, the sound engaging and infectious. "Now that is delightful."

He smiled reluctantly. "Who are you?"

"Now, now, if I told you it would quite spoil my fun. And as you don't remember my name, I think it's only right that you should have to earn that knowledge." Amusement glittered in her eyes. "Perhaps if we were to dance again . . . "

"Or walk in the garden." He moved closer and gazed into her eyes. "Or kiss in the moonlight."

"Perhaps," she said softly.

He lowered his lips to hers.

"But I never kiss anyone a second time who cannot recall kissing me a first time." She stepped out of his reach and started toward the door.

"A dance, then," he said quickly. "At least allow me the opportunity to recall a dance."

She glanced over her shoulder and considered him. "Very well. But I would prefer that we leave the library separately. I should hate to be the subject of gossip."

"Then I will meet you on the terrace?"

She cast him a brilliant smile, and his heart shifted in his chest. "You may count on it."

With that she swept from the room, leaving him to stare at the door she'd closed in her wake.

Who was she? She did seem familiar, but for the life of him, he couldn't place her. Surely he would remember a woman that lovely. He had always been fond of pretty women with dark hair and blue eyes, especially if they were intelligent. And there was no doubt she was clever. She certainly wasn't one of this year's new crop of debutantes. Her manner was far too assured. Besides, she looked only a few years younger than he. Perhaps he had met her on his travels. There was the vaguest suggestion of an accent in her voice. It—She was indeed delightful. No, he would remember kissing her in the moonlight.

And with any luck at all, he'd soon have another kiss in the moonlight. And this one he would not forget.

Good Lord, what had come over her?

Gabriella hurried down the corridor, forced herself to adopt a calm air and stepped into the ballroom. She mingled with the crowd, staying toward the perimeter of the room until she reached the open doors to the terrace.

Certainly she had flirted with men before, but never with such abandon. She hadn't planned to flirt with Nathanial Harrington, it simply happened, almost of its own accord. It wasn't as if she liked the man. She

despised him and his brother. Still, she couldn't deny
he was charming and handsome, with his dark hair
streaked by the sun, the devilish glint in his brown
eyes, and his broad shoulders. He had the sort of wicked
smile that made a woman wonder exactly what wicked
things he was thinking. And wonder as well why those
improper thoughts were most intriguing.

Nor had she planned to speak to him at all. In truth
she hadn't considered what she might say if she were
discovered in the library. The letter opener provided
the perfect excuse. If he had come in a moment later
she would have been trying to pry the lock open. And
that she would have been unable to explain.

She slipped through the doors and out onto the terrace, then began making her way to the steps that led to
the garden. He thought she looked familiar, which was
disturbing. Hopefully all that nonsense about dancing
and kisses in the moonlight would divert his attention.
It wouldn't do for him to realize she was the one who
had accosted him in Egypt. He had thought then that
she was a man, her brother's brother, and she preferred
he continue to think that.

She reached the stairs to the garden and paused, stepping back to allow a young couple who obviously had
improper thoughts of their own to pass. The worst part
of the encounter with Mr. Harrington was that she had
enjoyed it. There had been an element of danger in their
meeting that was intoxicating. And toying with him had
been great fun. The uncomfortable look in the man's eyes
when she said they had once kissed was most satisfying.
And didn't he deserve it? Hadn't he told her his brother
had gone to Turkey? She'd had every intention of going

after him when Xerxes learned that both brothers were separately headed back to England. Regardless, that venture had proven no more successful than tonight's.

"Was I mistaken?" Nathanial Harrington emerged from the crowd. "Were we to rekindle my memory with a walk in the garden rather than a dance?"

"I think a walk in a garden with a man who can't remember a lady's name would be rather dangerous." Damnation, she should have left when she had the chance. Still, there was no harm in a single dance. A tiny voice in the back of her head suggested that's why she had lingered. Nonsense. Gabriella brushed aside the thought that she might well want to dance with him.

"Yes, of course." He nodded. "A lady would truly be foolish—"

"I was thinking dangerous for the gentleman." Lord help her, this was fun.

He stared at her, then chuckled. "Very well, then." He gestured at the dance floor. "Shall we?"

"I do so love to waltz," she murmured, and took his arm. It was the most honest thing she'd said to him thus far. He led her onto the floor, and a moment later she was lost.

She did indeed love to waltz. Loved how the music wrapped around her soul and swept her away to a place and time and a life that existed only in her dreams. And only for people like Regina Harrington, who had an earl for a brother and a family willing to do whatever necessary to assure her future, her happiness, and a place where she belonged. Not for people like Gabriella Montini, who had been lost among relatives who cared nothing for her until she was found by a brother who dragged her from one expedition to another, one treasure hunt to the next.

Not that she'd minded. She had loved the life she lived with Enrico. Relished dressing like a boy for safety and being treated like one. She had hated it when her brother realized that his life was no life for a young lady. He had abandoned her in England while he went on with his work, although it was as much her fault as his. And abandoned was not entirely accurate. He had provided for her needs, arranged for her schooling and her expenses. If she had no real home and a family that consisted only of two longtime servants and a paid companion, it was her lot in life, and she'd never been especially discontent. Why it bothered her at this moment, she couldn't say, save to blame it on the waltz. On the promises inherent in the melody and the rhythm and the warmth of the man whose arm encircled her and who held her hand in his.

And hadn't she made the best of it? Hadn't she spent these past nine years studying languages and ancient civilizations, all with an eye toward eventually rejoining her brother? And hadn't whoever destroyed his life destroyed her future as well?

"I fear you are very far away." The firm pressure of Harrington's hand against her back increased and her gaze jumped to his. "Although I daresay I deserve it."

"My apologies, Mr. Harrington," she said lightly. "You may blame it on the music."

"Blame it on the Blue Danube?" He grinned down at her. "Excellent. I would much prefer to think your pensive state is attributable to the beauty of the waltz rather than the dullness of my character."

"I can't imagine any lady considering your character dull."

"Ah, but I suspect you are not just any lady, are you?"

"No." She smiled up at him. "I am the one you cannot remember."

His brows drew together and he studied her face. "I assure you, it will come to me." They executed a perfect turn. "We dance well together."

"As if we have danced together before?"

"Exactly." He shook his head. "I cannot believe I have met the woman of my dreams and I cannot remember her name."

"The woman of your dreams?" Her breath caught but she forced a teasing smile. She had no desire to be the woman of his dreams, not that she thought for a moment that his words were sincere. They came far too easily. "No doubt in the course of your travels there have been many dreams and many women."

"They pale in comparison." He gazed into her eyes, the moment between them at once fraught with unspoken meaning and promise. Dear Lord, he *was* dangerous.

"The dreams or the women?" she said without thinking.

"Both."

She drew a deep breath and ignored the tremulous feeling inside her brought on by his words and the gleam in his eye. "You are an adventurer, sir, a treasure hunter. Such men are not to be trusted."

"I assure you, I can be quite trustworthy," he said in a lofty manner.

"I admit you can be charming and even perhaps thoughtful, but trustworthy? I doubt that." She shook her head. "Besides, it's been my experience that trust needs to be earned."

"I think I would like the opportunity to prove that I can indeed be trusted." He stared down at her, the look in his eyes abruptly serious.

She ignored it. "I suspect the opportunity you seek has nothing to do with trust."

A slow smile spread across his face. "You are a beautiful woman and a mystery, even if perhaps of my own making. Do you blame me for seeking any opportunity whatsoever?"

"Not at all." She cast him a pleasant smile. "Your reputation, and that of your brother, precedes you. You are a scoundrel, Mr. Harrington, and scoundrels are rarely worthy of trust."

His hand tightened around hers. "Was I a scoundrel when I kissed you in the moonlight?"

"Never more so than then." The music ended and he led her off the dance floor. "Well?"

"Well?"

"Has our dance restored your memory?"

"No." Frustration sounded in his voice. "Will you give me another chance? If you will not walk in the garden, then do allow me another dance."

She raised a brow. "You are a persistent sort."

"Indeed I am." He grinned, and she steeled herself against the charm of it. "It's one of my better qualities."

"I'm not sure I would boast about that."

"It's not boasting, it's simply a fact." He leaned close and spoke softly. "I will remember, you know. I promise you that."

"You shouldn't make promises you can't keep."

"I never do."

"We shall see." She stepped away from him. "I find I am rather parched. Would you fetch me a glass of punch?"

"Only on the condition that when I return, you give me at least a hint as to where we have met before."

She shrugged. "I will consider it."

"Very well, then." He took her hand and raised it to his lips. His gaze locked with hers and for the briefest moment she wondered what might happen next if they had indeed met before, if he had once kissed her in the moonlight. If she were part of his world. Would this then be the beginning of something extraordinary and not merely a game she played? He released her hand. "I shall be but a moment."

She smiled but said nothing.

He turned and made his way across the terrace. She watched him for a few seconds, ignored the oddest feeling of regret, then quickly slipped down the stairs and headed toward the back garden gate. Within a minute she was back at her carriage.

"Well?" Xerxes assisted her into the vehicle.

She shook her head. "The desks were locked. I shall have to return when the household is asleep."

"Tonight?"

"A ball like this will go on for hours. Tomorrow, I think, or the day after would be best."

"It's not a good idea, girl." Xerxes fairly growled the words. From the time she had first come to live with her brother, Xerxes had called her "girl." She had long thought it was his effort to remind her that she was one. It was most endearing.

"And yet, it's the only one I have, so it shall have to do." She settled back against the cracked leather seat, and Xerxes closed the door, muttering something she couldn't quite make out. Which was probably for the best. He had agreed to tonight's endeavor reluctantly and only because he had no better plan himself, save beating the truth out of Harrington and his brother. Gabriella preferred to avoid that, at least until they had some sort of proof as to who had taken the seal.

While she was no closer, tonight's excursion hadn't been a complete failure. At least she knew the arrangement of the earl's library. And her flirtation with Nathanial Harrington had been, well, fun and surprisingly exhilarating. Still, it would never happen again, she would not allow it. Why, just in their brief encounter tonight, the man made her want things she could never have, long for what would never happen. He was indeed dangerous. To her purpose and possibly her heart.

The worst thing wasn't that she had found him so charming. That, she should have expected. But rather that she had found herself so very charmed.

Nate rested his hip against the terrace balustrade and surveyed the crowd. He wasn't the least bit surprised that the lady with the blue eyes of an angel wasn't where he had left her. Indeed, he would have been surprised if she had. She did seem familiar, but while he may well have forgotten a dance, he would never have forgotten a kiss. He had no idea what seductive little game she'd been playing, but he was more than willing to play. Tonight and whenever they next met.

He chuckled to himself and sipped her punch. There

was no doubt in his mind that her game was indeed seductive, and most effective as well. Seduction had crackled in the air between them. Nor did he doubt that he would see her again. And when next they met, she would not be the only one playing.

Nor would she be the victor.

Three

abriella's heart thudded in her chest. Most annoying, as she'd always considered herself quite courageous. Still, she'd never stolen into someone's house in the middle of the night before, and a certain amount of trepidation was to be expected, even if all was going well.

She flattened her back against the wall and inched her way down the corridor toward the library. A window at the far end glowed faintly with starlight but the corridor remained heavily shadowed and she took each step with care.

She and Xerxes had decided that the best way to proceed was to retrace her steps from the night before last, starting at the back garden gate. Once again that lock had proven no challenge. They had then made their way through the garden, grateful for the numerous trees, shrubs, and other plantings, to provide hiding spots should the need arise. It was far easier now than it had been when she'd worn a gown. Tonight she had donned the men's clothes she wore in Egypt, her hair tucked up under the same worn felt hat. She had grown up wearing men's clothing and, in spite of the circumstances, loved the sense of freedom they gave her.

Thus far it appeared the household was fast asleep. Save for a few lamps lighting windows here and there, the house was dark. Xerxes assured her, thanks to his surveillance in advance of the ball, there were always a few lamps left burning in the house. A dreadful waste of money in her opinion.

They had decided to enter by way of the French doors leading from the terrace to the ballroom. Xerxes was confident the locks there would prove no greater obstacle than the one on the gate. A check of all the doors had found two in such disrepair that they scarcely kept the doors closed. Perhaps if the Harringtons weren't squandering their money on lamps burning all night . . .

However, Xerxes wasn't at all happy when Gabriella insisted that he remain outside. She pointed out that, if caught, the earl would be much more likely to turn him over to the authorities than he would her, and Xerxes could scarcely argue with that. Especially when Gabriella enlightened his lordship regarding the legitimate complaint she had with his brothers. From the little she'd heard of the earl, he was known to be an honorable man. Pity his brothers weren't more like him.

Aside from all else, Gabriella was half British and far less imposing than Xerxes. And while she hadn't mentioned it to him, she had a weapon he knew nothing about, which she thought might prove useful.

Regardless, at this particular moment she regretted not letting Xerxes take on this task. She reached the library door, paused for a moment to gather her faltering courage, then slowly pushed the door open and stepped into the room. A small gas lamp glowed faintly on the earl's desk. She sniffed in disdain at the extravagance, although it did serve her purposes.

Gabriella closed the door quietly, crossed the room and took the lamp, then moved it to the secretary's desk. She did need to see what she was doing, after all. She pulled a long thin piece of flexible metal hooked on one end, similar to a flattened crochet needle, from where it was tucked into the lining of her coat. Xerxes had spent much of the day teaching her how the insignificant tool could be used to open a lock. It was a handy skill to have.

It took her but a minute or two to trip the lock. She grinned with satisfaction. This had been surprisingly easy. She slipped the metal tool back in its hiding place and pulled open the center drawer. It was filled with neatly arranged pens and stationary and the other accoutrements a man who dealt in the correspondence and business of an earl might need, but there was nothing of significance. She pulled open the larger of two drawers on the right. Here were files, well organized, tidy and clearly labeled. Her confidence surged. Thank God the earl had the intelligence to hire an efficient secretary.

She flipped through the files. They all had to do with the earl's affairs. None of the precisely labeled files indicated anything regarding the work of the younger Harringtons. Perhaps she would have better luck with the drawers on the other side of the desk. She shut the open drawer, reached for the next—

"Sterling?" The door swung open. "Are you still—"

Gabriella jerked her head up and met the startled gaze of Regina Harrington.

"Good Lord!" Lady Regina called to a point behind her. "Come quick! We're being robbed!"

Gabriella's heart lodged in her throat. One thing they hadn't planned was an escape route. But then she hadn't planned on being caught either. She raced for the nearest window.

"Help! He's getting away!" the girl screamed.

Gabriella fumbled with the window sash.

"Oh no you're not!" Lady Regina yanked an ancient broadsword off the wall.

"Oh yes I am." Damnation, why wouldn't it open?

"Don't think you can break into my home, take whatever you wish and waltz off! Not bloody likely!"

"Your language, Lady Regina," Gabriella muttered, pounding on the sash. It was bad enough to be caught, but to be caught by a spoiled brat was an added insult. "Your mother would be appalled."

"My mother would do exactly what I'm doing," Lady Regina said staunchly, struggling to brandish the heavy sword with both hands. "Apprehending a brigand!"

"Oh, for goodness sakes." And stupid as well as spoiled. "Aren't you afraid?" Gabriella tugged at the window sash. It wouldn't budge. "I could be dangerous."

"I doubt that." Lady Regina scoffed, lowering the sword, which seemed too much for her. "You're no more than an inch or so taller than I and you're a rather frail looking sort."

"I'm not the least bit frail," Gabriella said under her breath, and beat her fist against the sash. "But I am desperate."

"Nonetheless, someone will be here at any moment to assist me." The faintest trace of unease sounded in the girl's voice. "A servant or my brothers or someone."

She glanced over her shoulder. "Nathanial and Quinton were right behind me."

"Well, they're not behind you now, and I suspect most of your servants are asleep." For the first time, Gabriella noticed the girl was wearing a ball gown. "Are you just now coming in? At this hour?"

Miss Harrington stared. "I was accompanied by my brothers. It's not at all uncommon for a ball to last— that's none of your concern! You're a common thief!"

"I'm not the least bit common." Gabriella sniffed, and tried the window once more.

"There will be no escape that way. That window sticks."

"Regardless, unless you are willing to stand aside and allow me to leave by the door, I am going out the window." Gabriella looked around for something with which to break the glass.

"It's a nasty drop to the ground," Lady Regina warned, still gripping the sword handle, but making no effort to lift it. "You'll likely break your neck."

"I shall take my chances." She spotted a poker by the fireplace and started toward it.

"Stay right where you are!" The girl's voice rose.

"You'll have to run me through to stop me." Gabriella reached the fireplace, grabbed the poker, and turned just in time to see the girl hurl a vase at her. She ducked. The vase skimmed past her head, knocked off her hat, and shattered on the mantel behind her.

Lady Regina gasped. "You're a woman!"

"Yes, I'm a woman!" Gabriella snapped, and started back toward the window.

The girl advanced. "If you don't drop that this very instant, I assure you, I shall indeed run you through!"

"Hah. You can barely lift that sword, let alone wield it." Gabriella gripped the poker in both hands and pointed it at the younger woman. "And I assure you, I have a fair amount of skill with a . . . a poker."

Lady Regina narrowed her eyes. "Do I know you?"

"No." Lady Regina gestured with the poker. "Now stand back."

The girl studied her closely. "You look very much like Emma—Lady Carpenter, that is."

"Obviously, I'm not." Who *was* this Emma person?

"No." Miss Harrington shook her head. "Your hair is much darker. The light in here is weak but you do bear a striking—"

"As much as I hate to interrupt you, I must be on my way." Gabriella clenched her teeth. She didn't have much time before the rest of the household finally responded to the young woman's calls. It was something of a miracle no one had come yet. "I am going to break this window, so I suggest you stand back."

"I cannot allow you to do that!"

"You cannot stop me." Gabriella turned away from the girl, aimed the poker, and drew it back.

"But I can." A familiar male voice rang through the room. "Drop the poker! Now!"

Gabriella sucked in a hard breath. This was it, then. Even if she broke the window, she would never be able to climb through it before he grabbed her. She released the poker and let it clatter to the floor, then turned to meet Nathanial Harrington's gaze.

He gasped. "You!"

Gabriella resisted the urge to drop a sarcastic curtsy. "We meet again, Mr. Harrington."

"And again in the library." He had taken the broadsword from his sister, and for a fraction of a second she saw him as a knight of old. Strong and powerful and menacing. And for an even briefer moment, regretted that he was her enemy. He studied her through narrowed eyes. "How very interesting."

"Where have you been?" his sister snapped. "Why didn't you come when I called? I could have been murdered, assaulted, kidnapped!"

"I'm very dangerous, you know." Gabriella stared at him with a bravado she didn't quite feel.

"Oh, I am well aware of that," he said coolly. He addressed his words to his sister, but his gaze remained on Gabriella. "One of the servants thought he saw someone on the grounds. Quint and I went with him to look but he was mistaken. We found no one."

Gabriella fought to keep relief from showing on her face. At least Xerxes was safe. At once her confidence returned. She could take care of herself, she always had. She smiled in a pleasant manner. "I assure you, I am quite alone."

Harrington raised a brow. "Forgive me if I find anything you say to be less than trustworthy under the circumstances."

"I say, what is going on here?" Quinton Harrington stepped into the room, followed closely by a woman Gabriella recognized as his mother, the Countess of Wyldewood, and his older brother, the earl.

"What is all the commotion about?" Lady Wyldewood asked. She and the earl were both dressed in nightclothes and had obviously just awakened. "And who is this?"

"That's the question, isn't it?" The earl stepped forward to stand beside his brothers. Even in a dressing gown and with his hair disheveled, there was an air of command about him. "Who are you and what are you doing in my library?"

Under other circumstances, Gabriella might have found the three Harrington brothers—all sharing a similarity of height and build, and all undeniably handsome and dashing—to be an enticing display of the best of British manhood. If only two of them weren't the scoundrels she knew them to be.

"She's a thief and I caught her." Regina smirked, and nodded at Nathanial. "And he knows her."

"All I know," Nathanial said slowly, his gaze locked with Gabriella's, "is that I have never kissed her in the moonlight."

"Pity." A half smile curved Quinton Harrington's lips, and his gaze traveled over Gabriella in a most improper manner. She'd never especially considered how revealing men's clothes were before, but now had the uneasy feeling he was seeing her without benefit of any clothing at all. "I would have."

"Quinton," his mother said sharply. "This is not the time for your nonsense. And do light some additional lamps so that we may see her properly."

"I saw her rather well," Quinton said under his breath, and proceeded to comply with his mother's request.

"Now, then," the earl began. "Who are you and what are you doing here?"

Gabriella hesitated. Apparently her courage wasn't entirely up to this task, after all. She squared her shoulders and met the earl's gaze firmly. "I am here to find proof that your brothers stole an artifact of no little significance from my brother. That theft ultimately led to his death." She drew a deep breath. "My name is Gabriella Montini."

Nathanial stared. "That's why you look so familiar. You bear a striking resemblance to your brother."

"Don't be absurd." Quinton snorted. "She doesn't look the least bit like Enrico Montini. He was a good twenty years older and considerably darker in coloring than she."

"Montini," Lady Wyldewood murmured, more to herself than the others, the oddest look on her face.

"Not that brother." Nathanial waved off Quinton's comment. "The brother who confronted me in Egypt."

Good Lord, he still didn't realize she *was* the brother who had confronted him. Gabriella sent a silent prayer of gratitude heavenward. "The brother you lied to and sent on a wild goose chase to Turkey?"

"You what?" The earl glared at his younger brother.

"I was protecting *my* brother," Nathanial said sharply.

Quinton shrugged. "Not necessary but appreciated nonetheless."

"Regardless, she looks exactly like that brother," Nathanial said. "Are you twins?"

"We are . . . like one," Gabriella said, ignoring a twinge of conscience. It wasn't exactly a lie but it certainly wasn't the truth.

Regina glanced toward her mother. "I thought she looked remarkably like Lady Carpenter."

"Yes, of course," the older woman said thoughtfully.

"I fear, Miss Montini," the earl said in the cool tone of someone used to being obeyed without question, "that I require a more detailed explanation for your presence here tonight. Unless you would prefer that I send for the authorities."

"You can't have her arrested," Nathanial said without warning.

Surprise widened Gabriella's eyes. "Why not?"

The earl stared at his brother. "Why not indeed?"

"She has a legitimate complaint. Not with us," Nathanial added quickly. "We did not take the seal. But someone did and has caused her irreparable harm. It doesn't seem quite right to have her arrested."

Regina scoffed. "She did break into the house."

"Frankly, my lord, I would prefer to avoid arrest," Gabriella added.

"What seal?" Impatience rang in the earl's voice. "I want to know what this is all about, and then I shall decide what should be done with her." He turned to Gabriella. "Miss Montini, if you will."

She nodded, then paused to gather her thoughts. "My brother, Enrico, spent his life engaged in the same sort of work as your brothers. The study of archeology and the search for the lost treasures of the ancients."

"Is this going to be a long story?" Regina said under her breath.

"Perhaps it would be best if we adjourned to the parlor, where we could all be seated." Lady Wyldewood smiled at Gabriella. "I find my mind works much better at this time of night if I am not shifting from foot to foot."

"Yes, of course," Gabriella murmured.

Within a few minutes they were all seated in a large parlor, somewhat extravagant but tastefully furnished. A hastily dressed servant the earl addressed as Andrews, who Gabriella assumed was a butler, appeared with brandy. Lady Wyldewood and her daughter settled on one sofa, Gabriella sat on another. The earl and Nathanial each took a chair. Quinton remained standing, leaning idly against the mantel piece.

Once everyone was served, the earl glanced at Gabriella. "Miss Montini, if you will continue."

"Very well." She thought for a moment. "My brother found an ancient Akkadian seal, made of greenstone I believe. This sort of seal is cylindrical in shape. It's incised with symbols. They were quite common in the ancient world. When rolled across wet clay, the carving produces an impression. It can be a message or a story or have religious significance."

The earl nodded. "I am familiar with them. My father had a collection. It's in a case here somewhere."

"The seal Enrico found made a reference to the Virgin's Secret, and had a symbol carved in it for the lost city of Ambropia," Gabriella continued. "While it's been mentioned in the writing of the ancient Greeks, there has never been solid evidence of its existence. The very name means 'immortal place,' and even that is a Greek interpretation of a far older name that has since been lost. It has long been thought to be nothing more than a legend or a myth."

"As much as Troy or Atlantis or Shandihar have been or still are believed to be nothing more than stories," Nathanial said.

"But Enrico believed his seal went beyond merely being the oldest discovered written reference to Ambropia." She leaned forward and addressed the earl. "He thought it was one of a set of seals that together would reveal the location of the city itself."

"The Virgin's Secret," Nathanial said softly.

Lady Wyldewood raised a brow.

"The city was said to be under the protection of an

ancient virgin goddess," Nathanial explained. "Her name too has been lost." He shrugged. "Until now, it's only been a story."

"That is a find," the earl murmured.

"Is there a great deal of treasure in this city?" Lady Regina asked.

"The treasure, dear sister, is in the knowledge of history to be obtained," Nathanial said firmly.

Gabriella stared. Was it possible that she had misjudged him?

"Although gold and jewels and items that will fetch small fortunes are always nice." Quinton grinned and sipped his brandy.

Obviously she had not misjudged that brother.

"Go on, Miss Montini," Lady Wyldewood said.

"When Enrico went to present the seal to the Antiquities Society," Gabriella said, and took a bracing sip of her brandy, "he discovered it had been stolen and a seal of no great significance substituted." She paused. "It was most distressing."

The earl nodded. "I can well imagine."

"From what I heard of the story," Quinton said, "Montini became somewhat enraged. Made all sort of wild charges and accusations." He shook his head and looked at Gabriella. "The members of the Verification Committee do not take that sort of thing well."

"No, they don't." She blew a long breath. "His behavior, coupled with the fact that the seal in his possession was not as he had claimed . . . well, his reputation was shattered. He became determined to find whoever had taken the seal and recover it."

She got to her feet and paced the floor, absently wringing her hands. "That was over a year ago. Enrico left London for Egypt, Turkey, Persia, wherever those few he had told about the seal might be found."

"Including my brothers?" the earl asked.

"Yes, among a handful of others. His letters grew . . . " She hesitated. Was it disloyal to reveal just how odd Enrico's letters had become? Or, at this point, was it necessary? Perhaps it no longer mattered. "They became less and less rational. His search consumed him. Then six months ago I learned he had died."

"Do you suspect foul play?" the earl asked.

"I was told he died of a fever, but yes, I suspect everything," Gabriella said simply. "I have become a most suspicious person." She resumed her seat. "Now, it is up to me to recover the seal and restore my brother's reputation."

Regina scoffed. "But you're a woman."

"Regardless," Lady Wyldewood said, "I suspect Miss Montini is up to the task."

Gabriella's gaze met the older woman's. "It is my responsibility."

"I see," the earl said thoughtfully, then glanced at Nathanial.

"I can assure you, I have stolen nothing." Sincerity rang in Nathanial's voice. Even so, it was her experience that the very best liars were those who sounded sincere.

The earl's gaze, along with that of everyone else in the room, shifted to Quinton.

"Why are you all staring at me? I did not steal Montini's seal. I haven't stolen anything." Quinton sipped his drink, then added in a low voice, "Recently."

"Sterling." Lady Wyldewood turned to her oldest

son. "Can't you do something about this? You're on the board of the Antiquities Society."

The earl shook his head. "It's little more than an honorary position, Mother. And only because Father held it before me. Were it not for the significant funding we provide, as well as the possibility of funding in the future, my welcome on the board would be limited."

"Well, we should do something to help her," Lady Wyldewood said firmly.

Gabriella drew her brows together. "Why?"

Nathanial studied her. "Yes, Mother, why?"

"It seems to me that until this situation is resolved, and the reputation of Miss Montini's brother restored, it hangs over all our heads. The longer Miss Montini continues her efforts, the more likely it is that her brother's suspicions as to the possible identity of the thief or thieves will become common knowledge. The Antiquities Society would not look kindly upon that." Lady Wyldewood met Nathanial's gaze. "While you are not dependent upon the society for funding, you do need to remain in its good graces for reasons of credibility. Your own reputations are at stake." She shifted her gaze to Quinton. "And yours has never been entirely spotless."

Quinton shrugged.

"Aside from the especially unwise decision to try to find information in our house in the middle of the night—"

Unexpected heat washed up Gabriella's face.

"—and being discovered—"

"Not part of the plan," Gabriella said quickly.

Lady Wyldewood pinned her with a firm gaze. "And

yet it may well work to your advantage." She addressed the others. "As I was saying, Miss Montini strikes me as an intelligent young woman. If I were her, I would use a weapon I don't believe she realizes she has to ensure our assistance."

The earl's brow furrowed. "What weapon, Mother?"

"If it were to become publicly known that two of the members of this family are suspected of thievery, it would bring scandal down upon us all." Lady Wyldewood shook her head. "It is in our best interest to resolve this quickly. Even a hint of something like this would have a devastating effect."

Lady Regina gasped. "It would ruin my prospects for a good marriage! My very life! We would all be disgraced!"

"I see." The earl considered Gabriella for a moment. "Would you accept our help? It would be an uneasy truce, of course. I very much doubt that you trust us, and I cannot say we trust you."

Gabriella shook her head. "Quite honestly, my lord, I don't know what to say. I did not expect such an offer."

"Let me ask you this, my dear," Lady Wyldewood said. "Was Enrico your sole financial support?"

"Yes," Gabriella said without thinking. Again, it was neither an actual lie nor the complete truth.

The older woman studied her. "You have no other family?"

"No." Aside from English relations she'd never so much as heard from, that, at least, was the truth.

"Except for the brother I encountered in Egypt," Nathanial said.

"And I have had no word from him since then," Gabriella quickly said. "He is no doubt still in Turkey. Although he too may be . . . " She paused. She'd always considered herself an honest sort. Yet the lies that fell from her lips came with surprising ease. " . . . gone forever."

Suspicion glittered in Nathanial's eyes. He obviously wasn't stupid. It was only a matter of time before he realized the truth about their first meeting. What would he think of her then? She ignored the annoying question. Nathanial Harrington's opinion of her was of no consequence.

"Then it's agreed." Lady Wyldewood nodded. "As they are the ones most affected, Quinton and Nathanial will assist Miss Montini to find the seal and restore her brother's good name."

Quinton scoffed. "I have better things to do than help her."

"I don't," Nathanial said, then shook his head. "I do, but I can't think of anything more important than recovering an artifact of such significance. To prove Ambropia actually existed would be to rewrite history." He blew a long breath. "It's the stuff careers and reputations are made of."

"My brother's reputation," Gabriella pointed out.

Nathanial met her gaze. "Without question. It is his find."

"I suspect such an artifact would have a great monetary value as well," the earl said in an overly casual manner. "It would bring a small fortune from museums or collectors."

"Yes, it would." Gabriella bristled. "But I fully intend to donate it to the collection of the Antiquities Society."

"Very admirable, my dear," Lady Wyldewood said, "and I have no intention of trying to convince you otherwise, but I am well aware of the precarious nature of the finances of men who follow the path your brother did. Unless they have independent wealth or family money, as my sons do, they depend upon grants and funding from museums or organizations like the Antiquities Society." Concern shone in Lady Wyldewood's eyes. "With one brother dead and another missing, your finances must be uncertain at best."

"I will admit . . . " Gabriella chose her words with care. " . . . my discovery of the state of our finances after Enrico's death did come as something of a shock."

"I'm not surprised." The older woman nodded. "My husband was not merely a patron of the society, but he had a passion for the study and the artifacts of ancient man as well. Many a dinner here included men like your brother and long discussions late into the night about their work and their adventures. It has been my observation that such men are more concerned with the past than the present and give little thought to financial stability. I doubt that your brother was substantially different.

"Therefore. . . " Lady Wyldewood cast her children a decided look. "I propose that until this situation is resolved and the seal recovered, Miss Montini stay here as our guest."

"What?" the earl's brow rose.

Lady Regina scoffed. "How absurd."

"Insane but interesting," Quinton said.

Nathanial nodded slowly. "I think it's an excellent idea. We don't trust her, she doesn't trust us. How better to keep an eye on one another than if we resided in the same house?"

"How better indeed," Quinton said under his breath.

Gabriella scarcely heard him. The very idea of living in the same house with Nathanial Harrington—who danced as if he had been her partner always, and brought out a flirtatious demeanor in her she hadn't known she had, and made her wish, if only for a moment, that they were not on opposite sides—struck her as exceptionally dangerous. "I don't know . . . "

"Mother." The earl's brow furrowed. "I can't believe you're inviting a complete stranger to stay in our home."

"She's not exactly a complete stranger, Sterling." Lady Wyldewood's gaze met Gabriella's. "I knew your mother."

Gabriella lifted her chin. "I know."

"Did you?"

Gabriella nodded. "After my brother died, I found a packet of letters written to my mother. One was from you."

"I was so sorry to learn of her death, and then your father's."

"It was a very long time ago," Gabriella said with a shrug, as if it didn't matter.

The countess's expression remained serene, but there was the tiniest glimmer of amusement in her eyes. "You should have come to me directly about all this, you know, rather than resort to the clandestine methods you employed tonight."

Gabriella had the good grace to blush. "My apologies."

"I look forward to having a long talk with you about your mother. I suspect you have a lot of questions."

A lump formed in Gabriella's throat. She hadn't considered that Lady Wyldewood might want to talk about the mother who had died giving her birth. She rarely thought about her mother at all, and only dimly remembered a portrait her father had that, along with the rest of his furnishings and possessions, vanished among his relations after his death. The only thing his relatives had no use for was a little girl. She swallowed hard. "That would be most appreciated."

"It is decided, then." Lady Wyldewood rose to her feet, and the others followed suit.

Living with the Harringtons hadn't been part of her plan, but it would certainly serve her purposes. What better way to find the secrets of scoundrels than to live among them? Although, she amended the thought, Lady Wyldewood was very likely as genuinely nice as she appeared.

"The hour is late and I for one would like to retire," the countess said. "I will have a room prepared for you. You may send for your things in the morning." She cast an appraising glance over Gabriella. "I assume you have more appropriate clothing?"

Gabriella nodded. "But I should send a note now. The . . . lady I have been residing with is a very old friend . . . of my brother's." Which was, at least, partially true. "She will worry if she finds me missing in the morning."

"Most thoughtful of you, my dear." The countess nodded approvingly, then glanced at her daughter. "Are you coming?"

"Yes, Mother." Lady Regina followed her mother out of the room.

"We should retire as well," the earl said. "You will find paper and pens in Mr. Dennison's desk, although apparently you have already discovered that."

Gabriella smiled weakly.

"Quinton?" The earl glanced at his brother.

Quinton downed the rest of his brandy, set the glass on the mantel, and stepped to Gabriella. "Miss Montini." He took her hand and raised it to his lips. "It has been a most enlightening evening." His gaze never left hers, in precisely the same polished manner as his brother's had when he'd kissed her hand. And yet, with this brother it was nothing more than overly practiced. "I look forward to many more." He released her hand and started for the door.

"Andrews will see you to your room when you're ready," the earl said. "Good evening, Miss Montini."

"Lord Wyldewood," she murmured.

He traded glances with Nathanial, and the younger brother followed him out of the room. A moment later Nathanial returned. "You should write your note, Miss Montini," he said coolly.

She moved to the secretary's desk—Mr. Dennison's desk—sat down in the chair and opened the top drawer, knowing full well Nathanial watched her every move, and ignoring a distinct twinge of embarrassment. After all, she wouldn't know where the paper and pens were if she hadn't broken into the desk.

She would write two notes. One to Xerxes and Miriam assuring them that all was well, and another to Florence. She'd put both notes in the same envelope. Xerxes was no doubt watching the house, and he would certainly intercept her notes and make certain Florence saw only what she should.

She would tell Florence the truth: she had been invited to stay with an old friend of her mother's. It struck her that, at this point, her lies might well be at an end.

Aside from the true state of her finances, and that nonsense about a second brother, there was little left to lie about.

She scribbled a quick message to Xerxes, then took a fresh sheet of paper and started the note to Florence.

"You're writing rather a lot, aren't you?"

She resisted the urge to look at him. "I have rather a lot to say. I don't want her to worry."

"Then I imagine you're not telling her you broke into my house."

"No," she said sharply. It was remarkably difficult to concentrate on her writing, knowing his unflinching gaze was fixed on her. "Are you going to keep staring at me?"

"I assure you, Miss Montini," he said smoothly, "I don't intend to let you out of my sight."

Four

"Excellent," Miss Montini murmured, her gaze still on the papers before her. "That will save me the effort of keeping you in my sight."

It was obvious, even from where Nate stood, that she was writing more than one note. He could question her about that, again, but she would no doubt evade his question. Again. "I do not appreciate being lied to."

She folded her notes, slid them into an envelope and sealed it. "I would imagine few people do."

Still, her dishonesty made her no less attractive, and somewhat more intriguing. Odd, as he had always thought he valued honestly above all else. Apparently not as much as he valued deep blue eyes and a nicely curved figure.

"We have never met before, have we?" It was a statement more than a question.

She addressed the envelope. "I never said we did. You said I looked familiar and asked if we had met. I asked if you remembered, and you did not."

"I didn't remember because there was nothing to remember." Hah. He had her there.

"Regardless." She finished writing the address with a refined flourish, set the pen down and looked up at him. "You didn't realize that. You thought you had kissed me and couldn't recall it. It was most insulting."

"How could it possibly be insulting?" He stared. "I couldn't remember because it didn't happen."

"If it had and you couldn't remember, I would have been insulted."

"If it had, I would have remembered!"

"No doubt," she said in a tone that indicated she had a great many doubts about his ability to remember the women he'd kissed. She didn't know anything about him but had made assumptions based on nothing more than her own suspicious nature. Although admittedly the fact that her dead brother had named himself and Quint among those who might have stolen the find of a lifetime from him could have adversely influenced her opinion.

She held out the envelope. "Given the lateness of the hour, it would be best if this were delivered to Mr. Muldoon. He and his wife have been in my—in Miss Henry's—employ for years. He is most discreet and trustworthy and will see that she receives it in the morning. I should hate to wake her up at this time of night, and I'm certain Mr. Muldoon will be awake."

Nate glanced at the address. It was in a respectable if not especially fashionable neighborhood. "I suspect the footman I send with this might well arrive before he does."

She smiled in a pleasant manner. "Oh?"

"Come now, Miss Montini, you strike me as an intelligent woman. And an intelligent woman would not roam the streets of London alone late at night."

He waved the envelope. "Therefore it is logical to assume the trustworthy, discreet Mr. Muldoon accompanied you."

"I assure you, Mr. Harrington," she said smoothly, "I am quite alone."

He raised a brow. "Are you?"

"I have never been more alone in my life than I am at this very minute." She rose to her feet and continued as if she had just said nothing of significance, rather than made a comment as enigmatic as it was perhaps revealing. There was a great deal more to Gabriella Montini than met the eye. "If you have no objections, I should like to retire now." But what met the eye was most desirable. "It has been an eventful evening."

He raised a brow. "Then I take it you do not attempt to rob houses every night?"

"Not every night," she said in a casual manner. "No."

"Or ever before?"

"Or ever before." She sighed. "There now, are you reassured that robbing houses is not my chosen profession?"

"I never imagined for a moment that you were a skilled burglar. A professional would not have been caught by a mere girl."

"A random act of circumstance." She met his gaze directly. "You may be confident, the next time I attempt to rob a house I shall take additional precautions against discovery."

Was that a slight hint of amusement in her eye or was she mocking him? He bit back a smile of his own. "That is good to know, since the next time we might well be working together."

"Do you foresee our breaking into houses?"

"I suspect making any prediction regarding you and I would be a mistake." He stepped to the door and opened it. "Now, I would be happy to escort you to your rooms."

"I thought the earl said the butler would show me to my rooms?" She swept past him into the corridor with the same aplomb as if she wore a ball gown rather than somewhat shabby men's attire. He had never before considered just how enticing men's clothing might be on the right woman. While not an improper inch of skin was revealed anywhere—although the mere nature of the trousers themselves were improper—there was something about the vague suggestion of what the loosely fitting clothing concealed that was distinctly . . . exciting.

"We thought it would be best if I accompanied you rather than a servant." He started off, confident she would stay by his side.

"So that you may keep an eye on me?"

He paused for a moment, then nodded. "Exactly."

She smiled in a superior manner, as though somehow this had been her plan all along, but said nothing. He could well imagine what she might be thinking. Miss Montini did not appear to be the kind of woman to take well to anything less than total victory.

He led her up the stairs to the next floor. While his mother had told Andrews to prepare a room in the wing where she and Regina and Sterling had their rooms, Nate and his older brother had thought it better to put her into the unoccupied rooms next to Quint and across the hall from Nate. It was an excellent idea, he thought now, in so many ways.

He stopped at the door to her rooms and opened it. "I hope this will be satisfactory."

She glanced inside. "It's lovely."

"A footman will be here in the morning to escort you to breakfast."

Miss Montini slanted him an annoyed look. "Will a servant be stationed at my door all night as well?"

He raised a brow. "Is that necessary?"

"I wouldn't think so." Her tone was sharp. "Unless I am to be considered a prisoner."

"Not at all, Miss Montini. You are our guest." He narrowed his eyes. "And I fully expect you to behave like one."

"I do know how to behave properly, Mr. Harrington."

"Oh, so these past few days of house breaking and attending parties you have not been invited to were an aberration?"

"I believe I have already said that." Her jaw clenched. "My actions were necessary."

"No, in truth they weren't. You could have come to my mother or Sterling. You could have come to me. I would have listened to you."

"You didn't listen in Egypt."

"Perhaps not. And when I next see your brother, he shall have my apologies." He paused. "I'm sure you will hear from him soon."

"Yes, well, he's never been very good about that sort of thing." She shrugged as if her brother's lack of communication didn't worry her.

"Miss Montini, if we are to work together, it's not too soon to develop a certain level of trust between us. I suggest, in the morning, you tell me all of your older brother's suspicions as well as everything regarding his search for the seal." He thought for moment. "It might also be wise if I took a look at the letters you received from him. In spite of their questionable nature, there might be something you have overlooked."

"Very sensible." She stared at him thoughtfully. "I must confess, I had the same thought. I requested his letters be sent along with my things."

He waved the sealed note in his hand. "I shall have this delivered at once."

"Thank you. Mr. Harrington?"

"Yes?

She pulled the door closed and leaned her back against it, as if concerned that he might be overcome by the mere sight of a bed and ravish her on the spot. With a little encouragement he would be more than willing to try. He brushed the intriguing thought from his mind. "Might I ask you a question?"

"Go on."

"Why are you doing this?"

He shrugged. "It is an exceptionally large house, and as I assume you did not explore the entire building—"

"No, I didn't mean escort me to my rooms." She huffed in disdain. "I understand why your mother might wish to help me. She wishes to avoid even a hint of scandal, and I suspect that her tentative connection to my mother plays a part as well. But you." She shook her head. "Why would you want to help me?"

"A number of reasons." At least one of which had to do with her blue eyes and the curve of her shoulder in an apricot dress. "To begin with, I have worked far too hard to improve my own brother's reputation to have speculation damage it now. Nor do I wish to have my own honesty in question. Secondly, we are talking about a discovery of immense importance. I should like to play a role in that." He rested his shoulder against the door frame and gazed down at her. "And because I wish to know you better."

She studied him suspiciously. "Do you?"

"I do indeed."

"Why?"

"Because I have thought of nothing but you since we first met. You see, Miss Montini, you made a rather serious error the other night."

"Did I?" Her eyes widened.

"You did. You made me think, however briefly, that we had shared a kiss. The thought that I couldn't recall such a kiss was driving me mad. However," he leaned closer, "even before you vanished from the ball, I realized we had never met because I would never have forgotten kissing you."

"Nonsense," she said weakly.

"And I cannot get the idea of kissing you out of my head."

She swallowed hard. "Are you thinking of kissing me now?"

"I can think of little else."

"Why?"

"Surely, Miss Montini, you have looked in a mirror. You are quite lovely. The delicate curve of your cheek is only emphasized by the defiant tilt of your chin. I appreciate defiance almost as much as intelligence in a woman. Your eyes flash with fire, Miss Montini, when you're angry or indignant or trapped. And your lips . . ." His gaze dropped to her mouth, then back to her eyes. " . . . beg to be kissed. Often and quite thoroughly. In short, Miss Montini, you are entirely . . . " He lowered his mouth to hers. " . . . irresistible." His lips brushed across hers, and for a moment she stilled.

Then she laughed. "Good Lord, is that really effective with women?"

He straightened slowly. "What?"

"All that 'your eyes shimmer like stars and your lips are like cherries' nonsense."

"I don't believe I mentioned stars or cherries." He smiled slowly.

"You would have if you had thought of it."

"Probably."

Her eyes narrowed. "But you didn't answer my question. Do you find that sort of thing is successful with women?"

"Quite often, yes."

She shook her head. "They must be very stupid women."

"I'll have you know I don't like stupid women. I find them . . . " He searched for the right word. " . . . stupid. And not the least bit enjoyable."

"Oh?" She raised a brow. "Are you the type of man who likes a bit of a challenge in his carnal pursuits, then?"

"Yes. No." He paused. She had him so confused he had no idea what he meant. "I'm afraid however I answer that now will be wrong. But do tell me, Miss Montini, do you intend to be a challenge?"

"I do not intend to be the object of your pursuit, if that's what you're asking. Furthermore, if by some wild alignment of the stars and the disappearance of all rational behavior in this world I were to become said object, I am not a challenge you can overcome with pretty words." She crossed her arms over her chest, and he was compelled to step back. "Poor Mr. Harrington. Apparently you have never before encountered a woman who is not merely not stupid, but of an intelligence superior to yours."

"Nor have I done so now," he said with a shrug, although he wasn't entirely sure she might not be as intelligent as he.

She scoffed. "We shall see."

"Indeed we shall."

"You do need to understand and acknowledge this, Mr. Harrington—I am not here to be your friend, and I am certainly not here to be your . . . your lover." Again her eyes flashed at her words. It was most fetching. "We are uneasy allies in the pursuit of justice. We are together for the express purpose of recovering the seal. Nothing more than that."

"Yes, of course." His gaze drifted to her lips once again. They did indeed beg to be kissed. "Yet it seems to me one relationship does not preclude the other."

"Nor does one ensure the other."

"You do owe me a kiss, you know." He bent closer. "Preferably in the moonlight."

"I see no moonlight at the moment."

"Save that in your eyes."

"I thought there was fire in my eyes."

He chuckled. "They are most remarkable eyes."

"Ah, Mr. Harrington." She rested her hand on his cheek and her voice softened. "You are a scoundrel, but a charming scoundrel. I can well imagine your words would make any number of women melt at your feet. Fortunately . . . " She gazed into his eyes, and his breath caught. " . . . I am not one of them." She dropped her hand and pushed open the door. "Good evening."

"Miss Montini." He grabbed her hand and pulled it to his lips. "You should know I am not the type of scoundrel to easily accept defeat. Be it the pursuit of artifacts . . ." He kissed her palm, then met her gaze firmly. "Or the pursuit of something far more exciting." He released her hand and stepped back. "You may consider that fair warning."

"I shall consider it as nothing more than it was. A frivolous statement from an admitted scoundrel. As such, I see no need to take your warning as anything other than the inconsequential comment that it was." She nodded. "Good evening." She stepped into her room and closed the door firmly in his face. He heard the lock click into place.

He knocked sharply on the door. "I did not admit to being a scoundrel."

Her voice on the other side of the door was faint. "You did not deny it."

"You do realize I fully intend to kiss you in moonlight or elsewhere."

"I wouldn't wager on it, Mr. Harrington."

"Regardless, you do owe me a kiss."

Muffled laughter was the only response.

He stared at the closed door for a moment, then smiled slowly. This—She—was no doubt going to be far more than he had bargained for. But there was time enough to consider her, and all that went with her, in the morning.

At the top of his list of items needing consideration was his brother's role in all this. He needed to make certain Quinton had had no part in this theft. Not that he didn't believe his brother's denial, but Quint had a habit of twisting facts to suit his own purposes. He wouldn't put it past Quint to know more about this than he had said thus far.

Regardless of his brother's involvement or lack thereof, he felt that odd sense of anticipation, of impending excitement, that he always had at the beginning of a new adventure.

Still, he couldn't help but wonder what would be the greater adventure. The quest or the woman?

And ultimately, which would be the greater find?

Gabriella pressed her ear against the door, She heard his footsteps retreat, then another door opened. Apparently, Nathanial Harrington's rooms were directly across the hall. Not that it mattered. He could be sleeping in the next bed for all the good it would do him.

She blew a long breath and looked around. The room was far larger than her own and far more luxurious. There was something to be said for immense wealth. She moved to the bed and saw that nightclothes had been laid out for her. They no doubt belonged to the Lady Regina, who probably wasn't at all pleased about the loan of them.

Gabriella changed quickly, extinguished the lamp, and climbed into bed. And stared unseeing at the ceiling.

Well, this hadn't turned out as she had planned. The plan, as ill-conceived as it now appeared, was simply to find some sort of proof of the Harringtons' involvement with the seal. Now, she had agreed to accept their assistance, and was furthermore installed in their home as a guest. Which, admittedly, could prove to her advantage.

She had not anticipated Lady Wyldewood's response to her situation. Not her insistence that the family provide their help, and certainly not the countess's intention to talk to her about her mother. In truth, she had thought the fact of that long ago friendship might well prove a valuable weapon to keep her out of the hands of the authorities. Lady Wyldewood surely wouldn't have the daughter of an old friend arrested. It was the one thing Gabriella hadn't revealed to Xerxes about tonight's plot.

Admittedly, on occasion, she'd wondered about her mother. Who she had been and who her family was. The letters she'd found gave no clue, even though nearly all the notes were from her mother's sisters. They were the kind of letters sisters wrote to one another, bits of gossip and that sort of thing. One mentioned a necklace her mother had apparently left in England. But while the letter from Lady Wyldewood had been on her stationary, in the letters from her mother's sisters there were no surnames used, no addresses included, and no clue as to where these sisters might be found. Not that she cared beyond simple curiosity. Her jaw clenched. After all, they had had no interest in their sister's only child, so why should she have any interest in them?

Gabriella closed her eyes and willed herself to sleep. How different her life might have been if her aunts had taken her in after her father's death. She would have grown up as a proper English lady in a proper English home, rather than the Gypsylike existence she had lived with Enrico. Not that she would have changed any of it, she amended quickly. Her years of traveling with her brother, sharing his work, had been the grandest of adventures. Still, it would be nice to feel one had a permanent place in the world. A home, a family, people who cared if you existed or not. She had lived in London for nearly a decade now yet still felt out of place. She did not belong here, not really, and there was nowhere she did belong.

She couldn't help but wonder if her mother had lived whether she would be like Lady Wyldewood—kind, generous, and very nice. She rather hoped so, not that it made any difference now. It was pointless to consider what might have been. Her thoughts tonight, here in the dark, were probably attributable to seeing the bond shared by the countess and her family, and of no more significance than that. But if her mother hadn't died or if her aunts had taken her in and she'd been raised as a proper English lady . . .

She would be the perfect match for Nathanial Harrington.

Where on earth had that come from? It was absurd. She huffed, rolled over and punched the pillow, then curled up and tried to push the annoying thought from her head. No doubt it was all his fine words that had made her think such a ridiculous thing in the first place. She had never wanted to be a proper English lady. She had accepted long ago that she would never be *any* man's wife, let alone the wife of the son of a noble family. No matter what path Nathanial's life took, he would always be the brother of an earl, and she was not part of that world. She simply did not belong and never would.

And if she had wondered, if only for an instant, when he'd held her in his arms to dance, how lovely it would be to dance with him always, it was a ridiculous notion. And if, when he had kissed her hand, she felt the oddest longing deep within her, if just for a second, for him to keep her hand in his forever, it was an absurd thought. And if, when he'd come so very close to kissing her tonight, she'd wanted him, if for no more than a moment, to truly kiss her, often and quite thoroughly, it was insanity and best forgotten.

No, Nathanial would be . . . well, he would be her partner in this quest, and when it was done, they would go on with their separate lives. Even if, at the moment, she had no idea what hers might entail and no plans beyond recovering the seal. She had more than enough time to decide her future when Enrico's legacy was assured. Right now, that was all that was important and the only thing she wanted.

And in that last moment before sleep claimed her, when all rational thought had faded and dreams beckoned, the oddest thought drifted through her head. Just possibly Nathanial Harrington might well be all she'd ever wanted.

Five

There was indeed a servant waiting to escort her to breakfast. Gabriella wondered briefly if he had been outside her room all night, then discarded the idea. It made no difference, after all. She had no intention of leaving the house and had been far too tired to resume any kind of search last night.

No more than a minute or two after she climbed out of bed, a maid had appeared at her door bearing a fashionable dress and appropriate undergarments. No doubt these too were Lady Regina's. The maid, a young woman named Edith, helped Gabriella dress. In spite of the look of curiosity in her eye as to who this stranger was who had taken up residence in the middle of the night, Edith was apparently too well trained to speak unless spoken to. And this morning Gabriella had no desire to explain herself again.

Morning sun flooded the elegant breakfast room. It was already half past nine, far later than Gabriella usually slept. Even so she found herself alone save for the butler—Andrews, if she recalled correctly—and a maid who was leaving as she arrived. Andrews filled her plate from an enticing array of dishes laid out on the sideboard and set it before her.

"Will there be anything else, miss?" the butler said, pouring her a cup of tea.

"No, thank you." Gabriella stared at the heaping offering. There were kippers and kidneys, coddled eggs, bacon and toast, and far more than she was used to. "This will do, I think."

"Very well, miss."

She took a bite of the eggs and realized just how hungry she was. She had been too nervous last night to eat much of anything, and this was delicious. She finished half her plate before she realized she was eating entirely too quickly. In spite of concealing the true state of her finances, she wouldn't want anyone to think she was starving.

"Mr. Andrews?" She glanced at the butler.

He had taken up his position beside the breakfast room door. "Just Andrews, miss."

"Andrews, then." She nodded. "I rarely sleep this late. Am I the last to come down for breakfast?"

"No, miss."

"Oh." Apparently he was also too well trained to offer information that had not been requested. "Who else is about this morning?"

"His lordship rides in the park every morning. Today, Master Nathanial joined him."

"And Lady Wyldewood?"

"She has not yet come down."

"And the others?"

"It was an exceptionally late evening, miss." A hint of chastisement so vague she might have been mistaken sounded in his voice. "Neither Lady Regina nor Master Quinton have yet arisen."

"I see." Gabriella slathered some jam on a piece of toast. "Will they return soon? Lord Wyldewood and his brother, that is."

"I cannot say, miss. However, Master Nathanial suggested you might enjoy waiting for his return in the library. The collection includes a great number of books regarding ancient civilizations he thought you might appreciate." The butler paused. "He also requested that I remind you of your position here as a guest."

"Tell him—" She bit back the words. Andrews was nothing more than a messenger, and it really wasn't fair to take any annoyance triggered by Nathanial's comments out on the butler. She forced a pleasant smile. "I shall tell him myself."

"As you wish, miss."

Obviously, Master Nathanial had no intention of allowing her to forget for a moment that while she was to be considered a guest, she was certainly not to be trusted. Nor, if truth were told, could she blame him. If the circumstances were reversed—if he had been caught trying to find evidence of her wrongdoing in her own home—she would be hard-pressed to trust him.

She took a bite of her toast and considered exactly what she'd gotten herself into. She was now committed to searching for the seal with a man she didn't trust who didn't trust her. In that respect it did seem a fitting partnership. And admittedly, it would work to her advantage. While she was familiar with some of the older members of the Antiquities Society, as well as the director and his wife, she didn't know those men who followed the same path as her brother had. Like Enrico, they were more likely to be found perched on the back of a camel or sleeping beneath the stars than on the streets of London. For most of them, their infrequent return to the seat of the civilized world was a chore to be avoided as long as possible. Necessary only to acquire funding or negotiate with museums or consult with scholars. Even though she'd spent a great deal of time in the society's library, she had never so much as seen any of the men, save one, that her brother suspected of having the seal.

Besides, as much as she hated to admit it, as a man, Nathanial had entrée to places she did not, and could move about far more freely than she as well. It was at times like this that she longed for the days of her childhood when she had dressed as a boy and Enrico treated her as one. It could have gone on forever had her waist not narrowed and her chest blossomed, and had a young man not much older than she discovered that Enrico's little brother was in truth his sister.

She brushed aside the faintest touch of regret. There was no point in looking backward. Life unfolded as it would, as it was meant to be. The ancients knew that. Even in the Bible it said there was a season for everything. Which didn't mean, of course, that one should sit back and wait for life to happen. One needed to pursue one's destiny. Even if one was female.

Gabriella finished her breakfast and a footman led her to the library. As irritating as it was to be accompanied everywhere, she had to admit, if grudgingly, that this was an exceptionally large house and she would have been lost if left to find her own way through its many twists and turns.

The footman opened the library door. She stepped inside and pulled up short. "My apologies, I didn't realize anyone was in here."

A gentleman sitting behind the secretary's desk rose to his feet. "Miss Montini, I presume?"

She walked toward him. "And you must be Mr. Dennison."

The earl's secretary was not especially handsome, yet not unattractive either. Rather, he was one of those unassuming men one might pass on the street and never notice. He nodded in a curt manner. "I have been instructed to give you whatever assistance you require."

"How very accommodating of his lordship."

Mr. Dennison pulled open the drawers on one side of his desk, then the other, and indicated them with a wave of his hand. "Perhaps you would like to go through my files? Again."

Heat washed up her face and she ignored it. "A very thoughtful offer, Mr. Dennison, and most appreciated."

"Would you care to look through the drawers of the earl's desk, then?"

"I'm not sure at this point it's necessary," she murmured.

"It most certainly is not. I can assure you, Miss Montini, I am not aware of any correspondence, documentation, or anything else in reference to the Montini seal."

She raised a brow. "The Montini seal?"

"That's what Mr. Harrington called it."

"I see." *The Montini seal.* "Nathanial Harrington, you mean?"

"Of course."

"Well, isn't that a surprise," she said under her breath. Apparently the man had meant it when he had assured her that credit for finding the seal would go to her brother. Again she wondered if Nathanial might be a far better man than she had expected.

"While I do handle all manner of paperwork for Mr. Harrington and his brother, as I was saying, I had never heard of this seal before this morning." His eyes narrowed. He no longer appeared the least bit unassuming, but rather, looked very much like a man one would not want to cross. "However, you may certainly search through both desks, as well as anywhere else in the library."

"That's not necessary, Mr. Dennison," she said in as contrite a manner as she could muster. It wouldn't do to continue to irritate the earl's secretary. He could prove an ally at some point. Although given the way he glared at her, that did not seem likely. "I wouldn't dream of questioning your word."

Mr. Dennison snorted in disdain. No, she and Mr. Dennison would probably not be friends.

"Now then, Miss Montini—"

A knock sounded at the door, and it opened without pause. Andrews stepped into the room and cast her an almost apologetic look. "Miss Montini, you have a—"

"Stand aside, my good man." Florence prodded him out of her way with the umbrella she routinely carried—because one could never be too prepared—and stormed into the room. "Gabriella Montini, what do you have to say for yourself?"

"Good morning, Florence?" Gabriella said weakly.

"It's not the least bit good. It's confusing and more

than a little upsetting." Florence's gaze slid to the earl's secretary. "And who are you?"

"Edward Dennison, miss." Mr. Dennison drew himself up straighter. "Secretary to the Earl of Wyldewood."

"Hmph." Florence cast him a disdainful look, then turned back to her. "Gabriella, I insist you tell—"

"And you are?" Mr. Dennison cut in.

"I am Miss Florence Henry. Miss Montini's com—"

"Friend," Gabriella said quickly. "She is a very old and very dear friend. She has been so good as to allow me to live with her."

Florence glared at her, then huffed. "Yes, I am her *friend*." She fixed Gabriella with a firm look. "Now then, Gabriella, tell me what on earth is going on here."

"What is going on, Miss Henry," Mr. Dennison said coolly, "is that your *friend* was caught breaking into the house in the middle of the night like a common criminal."

Gabriella winced.

Florence stepped toward Mr. Dennison like a lioness defending her cub. "I can scarcely believe that. Furthermore, Miss Montini is not now, nor has she ever been, a criminal of any sort, let alone common!"

"Florence . . . " Gabriella started.

Mr. Dennison crossed his arms over his chest. "Ask her for yourself, then."

Florence glared at the secretary but directed her words to Gabriella. "Is what this man says true?"

"Didn't I mention that in the note?" Gabriella said under her breath.

"You most certainly did not." Florence continued to

stare at Mr. Dennison. "Regardless of the inappropriate nature of her actions, I am certain she had good cause for her behavior."

Mr. Dennison snorted. "Her criminal behavior, you mean."

"Her necessary behavior to uncover the criminal activity of others!" Florence aimed her umbrella at him. "Activity you, no doubt, had a hand in!"

Gabriella leaned toward Andrews. "Perhaps you should send for help."

"Before they kill one another, you mean?" Andrews shook his head. "Mr. Dennison is a gentleman, he'd never strike a lady."

"I wasn't worried about Mr. Dennison's behavior but his safety," Gabriella murmured. She should do something to stop this, but the sight of dear, mild-mannered Florence filled with fury directed at the heretofore unassuming Mr. Dennison was so unimaginable that she couldn't seem to do more than stare.

Florence's eyes narrowed. "You—"

Mr. Dennison glared. "You—"

"You are the most sanctimonious man it has ever been my displeasure to meet! You, sir, are—are—" Florence raised her chin. "—no gentleman!"

Gabriella gasped. In Florence's view of the world, not being a gentleman was the ultimate failing.

"And you," Mr. Dennison's eyes narrowed, "are probably the most overbearing and irritating female I have ever encountered."

"I have never seen anyone so—so—" Florence shook her umbrella at him.

"And I have never seen . . . " Mr. Dennison grabbed the umbrella and, as Florence would never surrender her umbrella, her along with it. He stared down at her. "I have never seen . . . "

"What, Mr. Dennison?" Florence snapped. "What have you never seen?"

"I—" He huffed. "I don't believe I have ever seen—" He squared his shoulders. "—eyes quite as remarkable as yours, Miss Henry."

"Flattery, Mr. Dennison, will not win my favor," Florence said in a lofty manner. "However, oddly enough, I was thinking the very same thing about your eyes."

They stared at each other for a long moment as if there was no one else in the room. The initial tension between them changed abruptly, to something far more . . . intimate. It was distinctly uncomfortable.

At last Mr. Dennison drew a deep breath and released her umbrella. "Miss Henry."

"Mr. Dennison," Florence said coolly.

"You may wish to speak with Miss Montini privately, so I shall take my leave." He paused. "Regretfully."

"That would be most appreciated, Mr. Dennison." The tiniest hint of a smile curved the corners of Florence's lips. Gabriella wasn't sure she had ever seen a smile like that from Florence. "And equally regretted."

Good Lord, Florence was flirting!

Mr. Dennison flushed.

"I should need someone to escort me to my carriage when I am finished speaking with Miss Montini. If you would be so good as to return in a few minutes?"

"It would be my honor." Mr. Dennison nodded a bow and left the room. Andrews followed, obviously stifling a smile.

Gabriella stared at Florence. "What on earth was that all about?"

"I'm not sure." A smug smile danced on Florence's lips. "Did you see that? From the moment I stepped through the door, that man was flirting with me."

"He was arguing with you."

"Call it what you will, he was extremely flirtatious."

"You were extremely flirtatious!"

"Yes, I was, wasn't I?" A twinkle sparked in Florence's eye. "I've never been flirtatious before and I certainly didn't intend to be so now. Quite honestly, I didn't know I knew how. But apparently I find a battle of wills to be rather . . . stimulating."

"Florence!"

"He was quite dashing, don't you think?"

"Mr. Dennison? I think . . . " In truth, the gentleman who had been ordinary only a few minutes ago now did seem rather dashing. "Yes, I think he was. And I think he was quite taken with you."

"Well, well, fancy that," Florence murmured.

Gabriella stared. Enrico had hired Florence when Gabriella began living in London, to be both chaperone and companion. Florence had shared Enrico's—now her—modest London house for more than nine years. A mere ten years older than her, Florence was very much the sister—the family—she had never had. But in all their years together, Gabriella had never seen sparks between Florence and any man.

"It simply indicates that Mr. Dennison has extremely good taste," Gabriella said firmly.

"My dear Gabriella." Florence turned a knowing eye on the younger woman. "Your flattery will work no better than Mr. Dennison's."

"I thought his worked rather well."

"Which will not help you." Florence settled in one of

the wing chairs positioned before the desk. "Your note said you were staying at a friend of your mother's?"

Gabriella nodded. "Lady Wyldewood knew my mother."

"Did you know that when you attempted to rob her house?"

"Yes." Gabriella sank into the other chair.

"I cannot approve of your methods. However," reluctance sounded in Florence's voice, "that was excellent knowledge to have at hand."

Gabriella studied her. "You don't sound very angry."

"Oh, I am furious with you. But I should have expected something of this nature. You have never been the sort of person who would let sleeping dogs lie, as it were."

"No, I can't. This is something I and I alone have to do."

Florence raised a brow. "A quest, then?"

"Exactly. I have to . . . to right this wrong." It was indeed a quest, as noble as any of those of the knights of old. "Someone ruined my brother, destroyed his life's work."

"And your hopes for the future."

Gabriella started. "You know?"

"You've never admitted it but I have long suspected your plans."

"My hopes were absurd, and more so now of course with Enrico's death. But still, I suppose the important word there is hope." She shrugged. "Hope that until the moment came that Enrico actually said I could not rejoin him and share in his work—"

"His adventures, you mean?"

"Yes, I suppose I do. I am not so foolish as to think

convincing Enrico to take me with him would have been easy. In recent years I tried to subtly encourage him to come to the realization on his own that I could be of great help to him. That's why I studied and learned and worked—to become indispensable." For a moment, a sense of loss, for her brother and for herself as well, threatened to overwhelm her. She ignored it, as she always did. "I was so sure that the discovery of the seal would be the start of a hunt for Ambropia itself and that he would need me."

"I am so sorry, Gabriella." Florence reached over and patted the younger woman's hand. "Tell me, my dear." She straightened and fixed her with a steady gaze. "As you went to all this trouble, rightly or wrongly, did you find anything of significance?"

"No." Gabriella blew a resigned breath. "They all swear they have no knowledge of the whereabouts of the seal."

"And do you believe them?"

"Certainly I believe Lady Wyldewood and the earl. Mr. Dennison, as well, has assured me he has no information about the seal and has offered—really encouraged—me to search through his files myself."

Florence nodded. "He seems an honest man to me."

Gabriella resisted the urge to comment on Florence's assessment of the dashing Mr. Dennison. Files could be removed; his offer meant little. "Both Quinton and Nathanial Harrington say they know nothing about the seal's disappearance. I am not certain about the older of the two, but Nathanial—"

"Nathanial?" Florence's brow rose.

"I believe I can trust him, to a point at any rate." She

met Florence's gaze. "He is going to help me find the seal."

"Is he now?" Florence considered her curiously. "I'm surprised that you don't find that suspicious."

"It was his mother's idea. She fears that the longer I continue my efforts to find the seal, the more likely it is that others will learn of my search. Which could bring suspicion and then scandal upon the entire family."

"I see." Florence thought for a moment. "Perhaps you should tell me everything that has occurred thus far, as I am, after all, your *friend*."

"My dearest friend," Gabriella said in a firm manner. "Yes, well, perhaps I should." She quickly related all that had happened: her appearance at Lady Regina's ball, and the details of what had transpired last night, leaving out the nonsense about kisses in the moonlight or dancing with Nathanial or the odd, longing way he made her feel.

"I see," Florence said when she was finished. "That matches what Xerxes told me, although he didn't have all the pieces."

Gabriella's eyes widened. "You already knew all of this?"

"I just said Xerxes didn't have all the pieces. Goodness, Gabriella, after all these years, you don't think I can't tell when something is amiss?" Florence snorted. "I knew the minute I read your note this morning that all was not quite right. And when I read the one you wrote to Xerxes—"

"You read the note I wrote to him?"

"Did you think I wouldn't? Did you think I wouldn't demand to read it after I read mine?"

"What I didn't think was that you would know I'd written a note to Xerxes in the first place."

"Then you should have arranged for him to be present when the note arrived." Florence shook her head. "When a servant arrives in the wee hours of the morning and says he bears a note from Miss Montini—"

Gabriella winced.

"I don't care whose name is on it, I will read it." Florence rose to her feet. "Gabriella, when we began this journey together you were sixteen and I was a governess without a position. Admittedly, that was due in part to my not being overly fond of small children." She shuddered as she always did when the subject of small children reared its head. "Regardless, your brother thought you and I would suit, as you were nearly an adult."

"And I always thought you were the only one willing to accept the position."

"There was that, of course. My point is that with your brother's death, I am now in your employ."

"We don't need to talk about this now."

"We haven't discussed it at all, and we do need to talk about it. Especially as you are about to embark on something—well, on this quest of yours. You are twenty-five years of age and now of independent means. Your brother hired me to be your chaperone, companion, and in many ways guardian, as, Lord knows, he was so infrequently in London. I had hoped that you would be married long before now."

"I have never planned to marry."

Florence ignored her. "Your failure to do so is as much my fault as it is yours. I did think, though, that amidst those libraries and museums you would find someone who would suit. It's not too late, of course—"

"Florence," Gabriella said firmly. "Marriage is not in my future. It never has been."

Again Florence paid her no mind. But then, she'd always dismissed Gabriella's opinion of her prospects for marriage. "However, until that time comes—"

"It won't."

"Or the time comes that you no longer desire my services—"

"Never," Gabriella said staunchly. "You are as much my family as Enrico was. As Xerxes and Miriam are now."

Florence shook her head. "It's a poor excuse for a family, but I suppose it is better than nothing."

"It's not nothing." For a moment, panic flashed through her at the very thought of being without Florence, Xerxes, and Miriam, who in many ways were more of a family to her than her half brother had ever been. Gabriella pushed the disloyal thought away. Enrico had been a wonderful brother.

Florence smiled. "We love you too, dear. But as I was saying," her voice hardened, "as long as I remain in your employ I shall do all in my power to keep you from harm. To continue to attempt to guide you along a path that will keep you from total disaster and, God willing, to avoid scandal." She shook her head. "Since your brother's death, you have not made it easy."

"I daresay you wouldn't like easy." Gabriella grinned. "I seem to recall liking easy quite a lot."

"That wouldn't be any fun at all for you."

"Fun, my dear girl, is relative." Florence huffed. "I

see no particular difficulty with you staying here. As long as Lady Wyldewood is in residence, you will be well chaperoned. However, I do not intend to leave you here alone."

Gabriella drew her brows together. "You're not planning on staying here—"

"Don't be absurd."

"Then what do you mean?"

"You shall see." Florence cast her a pleasant smile, but there was a determined look in her eye. "You are not the only one who can devise clever plans."

"What are you—"

"Furthermore, I expect a note from you daily and a visit every other day. You shall come to the house or I shall come here. To ensure that, I have brought only enough of your things for a few days."

"And Enrico's letters?"

"I brought those as well." Florence nodded. "Do be careful, my dear. And do attempt to be as honest and forthright as possible."

"Of course," Gabriella said in an overly innocent manner.

Florence studied her skeptically. "The ends do not always justify the means, Gabriella. Remember that. But you will follow your heart, I suppose. You always have."

"You have always encouraged me to do so."

"Yes, well, that might have been my mistake." She gave Gabriella a quick hug and started toward the door. "I shall see you soon, my dear." She paused and looked back. "And try not to refer to the younger Mr. Harrington by his given name."

"It's simply a way to distinguish one brother from another," Gabriella said, shrugging in an offhand manner. "It has no particular significance."

"No?" A skeptical smile creased Florence's lips.

"No," Gabriella said firmly. "It means nothing at all. I don't trust the man completely and I certainly don't like him. Admittedly, I will have to spend a great deal of time in his company, but it . . . " She set her chin. " . . . it can't be helped."

"A necessary evil, then?"

"Exactly."

"Yes, of course, he would be," Florence murmured. "Always the worst kind."

"What do you mean by that?"

"Nothing of significance. I shall see you soon, and I expect to receive a note from you tomorrow." Florence pulled the door open. "Mr. Dennison, how good of you to . . . " The door closed behind her.

Well, that was certainly a surprise. All of it. From Florence's reaction to her flirtation with Mr. Dennison to her mention of a plan of her own. But then hadn't the last two days been fraught with surprise?

Gabriella sighed and sank down in the nearest chair. Nothing was quite as she'd expected. Lady Harrington was very nice. The earl was suspicious and rather stodgy but not unkind. As for his youngest brother— Nathanial Harrington was the greatest surprise of all. He wasn't at all what she'd expected.

And she had no idea if that was good or very, very bad.

Six

"What did you do to Mr. Dennison?" Nate strode into the library, his tone far harder than he had intended.

"I didn't do anything to Mr. Dennison," Miss Montini said coolly. She sat at the secretary's desk as if she owned it, which in and of itself might well annoy Mr. Dennison, but certainly wouldn't disconcert him in any way.

"Someone did." Nate drew his brows together. "He looks both preoccupied and puzzled."

"Does he?" Miss Montini's tone was noncommittal and she continued examining what appeared to be letters arrayed before her on the desk.

"It is not like him to be either." Nate narrowed his eyes. "I have never known Mr. Denison to be anything other than competent and assured. And I have never seen him the least bit disconcerted."

"To every thing there is a season," she said under her breath, her gaze still on the papers on the desk. No doubt these were the letters from her brother.

She was ignoring him, that's what she was doing. Oh

certainly she was responding, but in nothing more than a cursory manner. And with biblical quotes, no less. In truth, she was paying him no attention whatsoever. It was most annoying.

Admittedly, his mood was already somewhat foul. He wasn't sure how it was her fault—he hadn't even seen her today—but clearly it was. Usually when he joined his older brother on his morning ride, it was an excellent way to start the day, invigorating and refreshing. There was nowhere on earth as green and lush as England in the spring, even here in London. Today, Sterling had been full of questions about the legend of the Virgin's Secret and what scant factual evidence existed about Ambropia.

In and of itself, Nate enjoyed detailing what little was known of the lost city. But he knew that the Earl of Wyldewood was nothing if not thorough. It was just a matter of time before he would want to know about Enrico Montini. Which might well lead to Miss Montini learning more about her brother than he suspected she knew, or at least that was his impression, given the passion of her quest. He had the oddest desire to protect her from that knowledge. Absurd, of course, since he barely knew her.

He drew a deep breath and forced a cordial note to his voice. Regardless of the circumstances, she was still their guest. "I trust you slept well?"

"Quite."

He had scarcely slept at all, and even the most rational man could indeed place the blame for that squarely at the feet and well-turned ankles of Miss Montini. He had tossed and turned all night. In those few moments when he had dozed, he dreamed of kisses shared with blue-eyed beauties in the moonlight. Little wonder he awoke in a foul mood.

"Your rooms were acceptable, then?"

"More than acceptable."

If they were to accomplish anything together, he should probably set aside all thoughts of kissing the delectable Miss Montini, as difficult as that might be.

"And breakfast? Was it satisfactory?"

"It was excellent."

Still, even now with her hair pinned neatly into place, wearing a gown that was more than proper—indeed one might even call it virginal—her attention focused firmly on the letters before her, he had the most insane desire to vault over the desk, yank her to her feet, pull her into his arms and press his lips to hers. Lips he had no doubt would be firm and warm and pliant beneath his and would respond to his ardor with immediate enthusiasm as her shapely, seductive body pressed—

"And the weather, Mr. Harrington?"

"What?" His attention jerked back to reality, and in his mind she reluctantly slipped out of his arms.

"The weather, Mr. Harrington." She turned over a page then lifted her gaze to his. "I assume that was the next inconsequential topic."

"Inconsequential?" He stared. What was it about this woman that made him want to at once kiss her and turn her over his knee?

A slight, knowing smile touched the corners of her mouth as if she knew exactly what he had been thinking. Damnable creature. Well, two could play at that game.

"I'd scarcely call a fine spring day such as this inconsequential, Miss Montini."

She shrugged. "It is a spring day like any other."

"Not at all. It could be cloudy or rainy or blustery. But today the sun shines, the birds sing, and flowers are in bloom, their fragrance wafted about on the mere caress of a breeze." He propped his hip on the desk and smiled at her. "Indeed, Miss Montini, 'What is so rare as a day in June?'"

"Poetry, Mr. Harrington?" She scoffed. "I would not have suspected you were a poetic sort of man."

"I daresay, there are many things about me you do not suspect." He wagged his brows at her in a wicked manner.

"And many that I do." She settled back in her chair and studied him. "For example, I suspect you are a man who does not let minor inconsistencies like facts stand in your way."

"And why do you suspect that?"

"For one thing," she smiled in a smug manner, "it's only May."

"Are you not impressed, then?" He forced a mock serious note to his vote. "That I can bend the months of the year to suit my purposes?"

"You did no such thing. What you did was quote a line of poetry in hopes of impressing me because any number of women would fall at the feet of poetry spouting, handsome, exciting men who make their living in the pursuit of treasure and adventure."

He grinned. "You think I'm handsome?"

Her eyes widened in obvious dismay at what she'd said and the most delightful blush swept up her face. She leaned forward and directed her attention back to the letters on the desk. "Goodness, Mr. Harrington," she said under her breath. "A mirror would tell you no less, and I cannot imagine you are surprised."

"It's not the observation." He laughed. "It's the observer that has shocked me."

"Hmph."

"I am flattered that you think so highly of me."

"I don't think highly of you," she muttered, her gaze still on the papers before her. "I don't think of you at all."

"You think I'm handsome."

"It was an observation, Nathanial," she said with a shrug. "Nothing more significant than that."

His grin widened. "You think I'm exciting as well."

"I didn't say that." She glanced up at him, her expression again composed and cool. "I was speaking in general terms about men who make their living as you do."

"Nonsense, Gabriella." He laughed. "You think I'm handsome and exciting."

"I most certainly—"

"As we are making confessions." He leaned toward her. "I find you exciting as well as quite lovely."

"I am not the least bit exciting."

He grinned. "But you will not protest my observation as to your beauty?"

"It seems rather pointless; I am well aware of my appearance. Not that it matters."

"It matters to most women."

"I am not most women."

"No, you are not." He chuckled. "Most women would not treat a compliment as though it were an insult."

"You're right." She heaved an exasperated sigh. "It was rude of me of me. Thank you for the compliment, Mr. Harrington, it was very nice of you. Why, I am flattered beyond words."

He snorted back a laugh.

She pushed away from the desk and rose to her feet.

"You have no idea how wonderful it is to know that a gentleman"—she cast him a skeptical look, as if questioning whether he was worthy of the title—"thinks you are lovely."

"Quite lovely." He nodded in a somber manner and slipped off the desk to his feet.

She crossed her arms over her chest. "Why, it has *quite* made my life worth living."

"Well." He shrugged modestly. "One does what one can."

Her eyes narrowed. "I daresay I should weep into my pillow each and every night if you did not think I was lovely."

He grinned. "There's no need for sarcasm."

"I cannot imagine a worse fate than not being lovely in your eyes."

He laughed, and she ignored him.

"Now then, I suggest we dispense with discussion of the fire in my eyes or the tilt of my chin, as I recall they were thoroughly discussed last night." She waved at the papers on the desk. "These are my brother's letters. I have read them countless times but you should go through them. You might see something I've missed. The letters contain the names of four men, including you and your brother—what are you staring at?"

"Your lips, Gabriella." His gaze flicked to her eminently kissable lips and back to her eyes, which did indeed flash with at least annoyance if not fire. "We have not discussed your lips."

"The lips that beg—" She bit her bottom lip as if to hold back the words.

He bit back a smile of his own. "That beg to be kissed? Yes, those lips."

She stared at him, then rolled her gaze toward the heavens. "Very well, then." She stepped toward him, closed her eyes and raised her chin. "Go on."

He grinned down at her. "Go on what?"

Her eyes remained closed but her shoulders heaved with a resigned sigh. "Kiss me. It's what you want. Go on, then."

He bit back a laugh. "Now?"

"Yes, of course now." Her eyes snapped open. "It seems to me we will never get anything at all accomplished if all you can think about is kissing me."

"That's not entirely all I'm thinking about," he said under his breath.

She cast him a glance designed to wither the confidence of even the most arrogant man. "That, Mr. Harrington, is not my problem."

"You called me Nathanial a moment ago."

She paused. "Did I?"

"Indeed you did, and I liked it."

"It was a slip of the tongue." She shrugged. "Not the least bit important. I certainly didn't intend for you—"

"There's nothing like hearing your given name from the lips of a beautiful woman. Lips I might add that are—"

"Yes, yes, begging to be kissed." She waved off his words with an impatient gesture.

"Regardless, I believe it would be most expedient for our purposes if we dispense with formalities altogether. You may call me Nathanial, I shall call you Gabriella."

"Mr. Harrington," she said firmly.

He raised a brow.

"Very well, then, I suppose it does make a certain

amount of sense. And I have already been thinking of you as Nathanial. But only to differentiate you from your brother," she added quickly.

"Exactly as I thought."

"And it shall be no more importance that that of a . . . a . . . sister—yes that's it—a sister calling a brother by his given name. Not the least bit significant. Now, then." She again closed her eyes and raised her chin. "If you would be so good as to kiss me, we can put this nonsense behind us."

"Behind us?"

"This too is a matter of expediency. Nothing more."

"Expediency." He nodded. "And efficiency too, I would imagine?"

"Yes, yes." Impatience sounded in her voice. Her shoulders stiffened. "Go on with it."

"It's tempting," he said in a low voice, and stared down at her. This was indeed an opportunity. But one only a fool would take. "I daresay I cannot remember when last I encountered anything this . . . irresistible."

"I am flattered," she said in a cool voice that none-theless sounded just a touch breathless. Her chin rose another notch.

"But I think not."

Her eyes snapped open. "What do you mean—you think not? How could you possibly think not?"

"It might have been that business about you calling me by my given name in the manner of a sister." He shook his head. "For future reference, Gabriella, when asking a man to kiss you, you should not put him in mind of his sister. It does tend to spoil the mood."

"I did not ask you to kiss me!"

"No." He shrugged. "You told me. That too tends to

destroy the ambience of the moment. A man likes to believe—even if it's not true—that he is in command of such things."

She stared in disbelief. "Then you are not going to kiss me?"

"Oh, I am most certainly going to kiss you, but not at this particular moment."

"Don't be absurd. This is your opportunity, and I warn you, Nathanial, there shall not be another. Now." She huffed, stepped toward him and once more closed her eyes and lifted her chin. "Let's get this over and done with."

He bit back a laugh. "My dear Gabriella, a kiss is not something one gets over and done with. It is not a foul tasting medicine one is forced to take."

Her eyes opened. "I do know—"

"Surely you have been kissed?"

"Of course I have been kissed," she said sharply. "Any number of times."

He raised a brow. "Have you?"

She blushed yet again, and he noted how there was something quite compelling about an intelligent, confident woman who blushed so easily. "I am not a child."

Still, he'd wager his next big find that she had not been kissed often and probably not well. "And were those previous kisses such that you simply wished for them to be over and done with?"

"Well, ye—no!" She forced an awkward laugh. "Each and every kiss was quite enjoyable. Really, very nice."

"Very nice?" He shook his head in a somber manner. "A kiss, Gabriella, should never be merely nice."

She opened her mouth to protest.

"Even *very* nice is not good enough," he said before

she could utter a word. It did seem best. "First of all, a kiss is . . . an overture, if you will, to the grander symphony to come. A prologue to the rest of the story." He clasped his hands behind his back and slowly circled her. Her wary gaze followed him. "A taste of the banquet yet to be savored."

"Mr. Harrington—Nathanial." She jerked her gaze back to a point directly in front of her and squared her shoulders. "There will be no symphony, no story, and certainly no banquet."

Nate smiled. "You are taking my words in a manner in which they were not intended. I am explaining the nature of a kiss in general terms, not the nature of our kiss." He paused. "Unless, of course, you see our kiss as the first step toward you joining me in my bed."

She shot him a look of disdain over her shoulder. "I most certainly do not! And would you stop circling me. I feel like a chicken being marked by a fox."

"Regardless." He casually moved to stand in front of her. "A kiss is still a beginning. As well as a turning point. A kiss should make you feel as if it were the first moment of something wonderful."

She snorted.

"You don't agree?"

"No." Her foot twitched as if she were resisting the urge to stamp it. "A kiss is . . . "

"Yes?" His brow rose.

"It's . . . " She raised a shoulder in an offhand shrug. "It's a momentary loss of control of one's senses. Yes, that's it. It's nothing more than an instant of surrender to one's baser instincts."

"Oh dear, Gabriella." He shook his head in a mournful manner. "You may have been kissed but you have obviously not been well or properly kissed. And you have never been kissed by me."

"Come now, Nathanial."

"Do you doubt me?"

"I do not doubt your arrogance."

"A kiss is not something one closes one's eyes and braces oneself for as if one were England preparing for a Viking invasion." He cast her a slow, wicked smile. "A women who has been well kissed does not think of a kiss as merely a kiss."

She stared for a moment then accepted his challenge. "A woman who has kissed you, you mean?"

He shrugged in a modest manner. "I have yet to hear a complaint."

"Very well, then." She smiled pleasantly. "Prove yourself."

He hadn't quite foreseen that. Caution edged his voice. "What do you mean?"

"I mean, Nathanial, I have offered you a kiss for the one you feel I owe you. And even I can understand how you might have a legitimate claim. Therefore, as I can see you will be like a dog with a bone and not let this go, I shall give you another chance." She crossed her arms over her chest, a gleam of triumph in her eye. "Kiss me."

"I don't know that I should." He shook his head slowly. "A kiss—especially a first kiss—is to be savored and enjoyed. And remembered always."

She raised a brow. "Not up to the challenge, then?"

"Oh I am certainly up to the challenge," he murmured, and studied her for a moment. "I'm simply not certain if I wish to be commanded to kiss you."

She shrugged. "It remains your choice."

"Indeed it does." He paused. "And were I to kiss you, I should begin by stepping very close to you." He moved closer and stared down at her, close enough to see the satisfaction in her eyes fade to uncertainty. "So that I may take you in my arms."

"No doubt. Go on."

He wrapped his arms around her and gently drew her closer. "I would then gaze into your eyes, your endless blue eyes that could hold a man, even a man of strength, spellbound. Lost, if you will."

"Nonsense," she said weakly. "They're simply blue."

"There's nothing simple about them. They are the color of a mountain lake, the calm waters before the storm. Eyes that carry within them secrets, and promises of something wonderful for a moment or forever."

"Utter rubbish." Nonetheless her arms slipped around his neck and he bit back a smile

"Then my gaze would slip to your lips." He glanced at her mouth. She bit her bottom lip in the nervous manner he had already noticed, and his stomach tightened. "Just for a moment, just long enough to anticipate the soft, ripe warmth of them against my own. To wonder at the taste of you. Will you taste of bold, erotic spices or will you taste as sweet and delicious as new picked berries? Or as intoxicating as champagne? Anticipation, Gabriella." His gazed shifted and locked with hers. "Anticipation in a first kiss is most important."

She swallowed hard. "How absurd."

"And then I would lean closer, until my senses are awash with the scent of you." He angled his head toward hers until his lips were no more than a breath from hers.

"Fresh and vaguely like lavender, with the merest touch of something more. Something exotic, unknown as yet but exciting and completely irresistible."

"Oh . . . " The word was no more than a sigh, the merest breath of air against his lips. Her eyes drifted closed.

"It would be very nearly perfection itself."

"Yes . . . " Her body pressed closer to his with a movement so slight he doubted she was aware of it. But he was. "Perfection . . . "

He had her now. She wanted to kiss him as badly as he wanted to kiss her. And he couldn't remember ever wanting to kiss a woman more. But as much as he wanted this, he knew one kiss with Gabriella Montini would never be enough.

"Very nearly." Nate drew a deep breath and summoned every bit of self-control he possessed. "But without moonlight, it is not the kiss you promised." He straightened and released her, ignoring the stunned look on her face. He moved around the desk and settled in the chair. "Now then, we should get on with these."

She sucked in a sharp breath and glared. There wasn't a doubt in his mind, he would pay for this.

He grinned to himself. He couldn't wait.

Seven

Y ou—You—You—" Gabriella sputtered as if she couldn't quite catch her breath. As if she'd been hit in the face with a pail of cold water. Not that she was going to let him know how shocked and, well, possibly disappointed she was. As if she had wanted him to kiss her, which she certainly hadn't and never would. Regardless, his behavior was nothing short of dastardly. "Nathanial Harrington, you are an arrogant ass!"

"My, my, Gabriella, your language." He shuffled through the letters on the desk, his gaze firmly on the papers in front of him as if she hadn't said a word. As if she wasn't there!

There was nothing to be done about it. She was going to have to kill him. Slowly.

"Your brothers have obviously been a bad influence on you."

My brother and men exactly like you. She bit back the words and drew a deep calming breath. It hadn't been easy to discard the manners, or rather, lack of manners, she acquired in the years spent with her brother. Propriety, especially when it came to language, had always been something she'd had to work at, much like any of her other studies.

"One would have thought one was back among his comrades in the deserts of Egypt," Nathanial said mildly.

She clenched her fists by her side. "My apologies, Nathanial."

"Accepted."

"I am eternally sorry—"

He smiled in a benevolent manner. "Not at all."

"—that you are such an arrogant ass."

He glanced up at her, his eyes wide with feigned innocence. "I don't know why you're glaring at me like that, it's not as if you wanted to kiss me."

"I'm not glaring," she said in a clipped tone.

"My dear Gabriella, if looks could kill, I would be lying on the floor dead by now, shot through the heart by your gaze alone."

"That would be a very great pity." She sniffed.

"I'm glad you think so."

"It would be entirely too fast." Gabriella braced her hands on the desk and leaned toward him. "No, you deserve something much, much slower. Tied to stakes and stretched out over a hill of African ants perhaps."

He rose to his feet. "Tied, did you say?"

"Under the hot, blistering tropical sun."

He planted his hands on the desk, mirroring her stance, a distinctly wicked smile on his lips. "Naked, no doubt?"

Naked? Why on earth did he have to use the word naked? At once the image of a naked Nathanial Harrington staked over an ant hill popped into her mind.

Not that she knew exactly what an adult male would look like in that position, but between her limited experience and the paintings and sculptures she'd seen, well, she did have a fairly vivid imagination. She pushed the thought firmly aside.

"Or perhaps torn from limb to limb by savages in the jungles of South America."

"Savages who have first ripped my clothes to shreds, do you think?" The gleam in his eye matched his smile.

Again a naked Nathanial Harrington filled her head, savages pulling on every limb, tattered remnants of his clothes dripping off him like icing from a cake. She winced and shook her head. "Or . . . or . . . eaten by cannibals. Yes, that's exactly what you deserve."

"Boiled alive probably." He nodded in a solemn manner belying the look in his eye. "Naked, of course."

"Would you stop that!" A naked Nathanial Harrington sat in a large iron pot over a fire surrounded by cannibals. She straightened with a jerk. "Stop that this minute!"

He raised a brow. "Stop what?"

"Stop using that word!"

"What word?"

"You know what word!"

He shook his head and grinned. "I have no idea what you're talking about."

She huffed. "Naked, Nathanial!" Good Lord, had she just used *naked* and *Nathanial* in the same sentence? Aloud and in front of him? "The word is naked! Naked, naked, naked!" And she couldn't seem to stop. "As you well know."

His grin widened. "The examples were yours."

"Not the way you embellished them with . . . with . . ."

She closed her eyes and sent a quick prayer heaven-ward to beg for calm and to give thanks that she wasn't armed. "It was highly improper, most suggestive, en-tirely too . . . too intimate and . . . and . . . " *Erotic, exciting, seductive.* She drew a deep breath and met his gaze. "Uncomfortable."

"Come now, Gabriella. You can't—" Realization dawned on Nathanial's face and his smile vanished. "You are embarrassed, aren't you? Why, you're blush-ing again."

"Yes, well . . . " The ease with which she blushed was the bane of her existence, and there didn't seem to be anything she could do about it. But of course she was embarrassed. Not as much by his words as by the explicit images her own mind had created. Even so, it was his fault.

"I am sorry." He winced. "I didn't intend—I had no idea that you—that is to say—"

"No idea? And why not?" The words came without thinking. "Because women who break into houses and pretend to be someone they're not and are every bit as clever as you, who want to restore the good name of their family and have a sense of honor, would, of course, not be the sort to be embarrassed by crass, im-proper comments? That such women do not deserve the common courtesies you would give to a lady on the street? Because my family, my background, my cir-cumstances are not such that they warrant respect?"

It was his turn to look as if he'd been dashed by cold water. "I assure you, Gabriella, my intent was only to tease—flirt, if you will. I never meant—"

"Enough, please." She pushed out her hand to stop him. Where had her outburst come from? In truth she was far more annoyed than embarrassed. Just like her tendency to blush, not keeping her mouth shut when she was angry had always been another unfortunate character flaw. "Now, I must apologize." Certainly, the differences between her family and his, her life and his, had been brought home to her last night. And yes, she might have felt a twinge of what could possibly be called resentment or even jealousy. But it was absurd. Life was what one made of it regardless of the hand one had been dealt. "Your family has been nothing but kind and generous to me, far more so than I deserve. My remarks were uncalled for."

"No, I am to blame. I baited you, and for that I must beg your forgiveness. I am most sorry. I lost my head." He took her hand. "In my defense, Gabriella, you should know . . . " He raised her hand to his lips, his gaze never leaving hers. " . . . you were not the only one who was disappointed."

"I wasn't—" She paused, then drew a deep breath. "Your apology is accepted. I would prefer that we never bring this incident up again."

"Oh I agree," Nathanial said somberly, but the wicked twinkle had returned to his eye.

She stared for a moment. "I can't trust you at all, can I?"

"Of course you can. In most matters, I can be most trustworthy. Now, then." He gestured at the letters. "Where do you suggest I begin?"

"Here." She stepped to the desk, of necessity standing far too close to him than was proper. Still, they were going to work together, and her standards of what was and was not acceptable would have to change, or at least bend. She reached in front of him, her arm brushing against his. Without warning the feel of being in his arms washed through her. She firmly set it aside. Now was not the time, nor, she amended at once, would there ever be a time. She arranged the letters in chronological order. "There are only seven. The first few came rather quickly, and as you will see, are the most lucid of the lot. The last . . . " She shrugged. "I suggest you read them in order."

"Very sensible." He sat down and picked up a letter. "This is the first?"

She nodded. He started reading, then glanced up. "Do you plan to watch me read every word?"

"Not every word."

"It makes me most uncomfortable." He grimaced. "This is a library, Gabriella. I would think you could find something to read. There are a great many reference works here that you might enjoy. Or better yet, a novel."

She scoffed. "I never read novels."

"That explains a great deal," he said under his breath.

"What do you mean?" She drew her brows together. "What exactly does that explain?"

"Your manner. Your attitude toward life, as it were."

"My attitude is just fine."

"You, Gabriella Montini, take the world entirely too seriously."

"You don't know that. You don't know me."

"Nonetheless." He shrugged. "This was not difficult to ascertain."

"Just because a woman doesn't leap into your arms, doesn't long for your embrace, doesn't ache to feel your lips upon hers—"

He arched a brow.

She ignored him. "Does not mean she takes the world too seriously."

"If you say so."

She huffed. "The world is a serious place, Nathanial Harrington."

"Indeed it is."

"And my life is a serious matter. My brother is dead, his reputation is shattered. I have no real family save a handful of serv—friends. And the one thing I truly wanted in my life is now—" She blew a resigned breath. "—out of the question."

He settled back in the chair and studied her. "What is the one thing you truly wanted?"

"It scarcely matters." She waved off his question and wandered to a bookshelf. "As you think a novel will somehow make my manner more frivolous—"

He laughed. "I never used the word frivolous."

She cast him a haughty glance. "It was implied."

"I should have said . . . lighthearted. Yes, that's it."

"My heart is anything but light at the moment, nor has it ever been."

"What a shame," he said softly.

"Not at all, Nathanial. It's simply how life is." She turned back to the shelves. "Do you have a recommendation? As to a novel, that is?"

"Come now, Gabriella, there must be some author's works you like? You cannot tell me you've never read a novel? Not even in a youthful misspent moment perhaps?"

"My youth was not especially misspent." Unless one considered being dressed as a boy and accompanying your brother from one exotic location to another on a quest for antiquities misspent.

"Still, you must have a favorite?"

"I don't think so," she said under her breath. Now that she thought about it, she couldn't remember ever having read an account of fiction, although surely she must have. Her brother had taught her to read, but in that employed the use of the manuals and historical references he routinely carried with him, and the Bible, of course. When she began her schooling in England, she had been made to memorize a great deal of poetry, and recalled studying the plays of Mr. Shakespeare, but not a single work of narrative fiction came to mind.

"Not Mr. Dickens? Or Mr. Trollope or Miss Austen?"

"Apparently my education has lacked in that respect." She perused the titles on the shelf. "Besides, I've never had the time."

"How do you spend your time?"

"I study, Nathanial. I study ancient civilizations, history, archeology, myths, legends, and anything else that might prove useful for my brother's work. I have earned certificates at Queen's College, have already been awarded one university degree, and I continue my studies. I have as well committed to memory most of the books and papers in the Antiquities Society library and archives." She glanced at him over her shoulder. "I have an excellent memory."

"I'm not surprised."

She arched a brow. "A compliment, Nathanial? One that has nothing to do with the tempting nature of my lips or the hypnotic quality of my eyes?"

"I don't know what came over me." He grinned. "I shall try not to let it happen again."

In spite of herself, she returned his smile. The man was quite engaging. "In addition, I am fluent in nine languages, including Coptic, Persian, Turkish, and Arabic."

He stared. "Nobody speaks Coptic. It's extinct."

"Not entirely. It's still used in the Church of Alexandria."

"Even so, why learn something so obscure?"

"Because it's the closest thing we have to any knowledge of an ancient Egyptian spoken language."

"I suppose it makes sense in a strictly scholarly sense. But why would you learn Turkish, Arabic, Persian? Most women of my acquaintance—even those few engaged in scholarly pursuits—learn French, a smattering of Italian, perhaps German. Even if one wished to travel extensively, that would certainly be sufficient."

"I thought we had already agreed I am not like most women of your acquaintance."

"Still, it seems rather unusual."

"Perhaps it is." She studied him for a long moment. Telling him her plans hardly mattered now. Nothing would come of them. Surely she should trust him enough to tell him this, and trust as well that he wouldn't laugh at her ambitions. She drew a deep breath. "I had hoped to become knowledgeable enough to join my brother in his work. To be indispensable to him."

"I see." He nodded thoughtfully. "I would say it is a farfetched aspiration for a woman, but we have established you are not like most women." He paused and considered her. "This, then, is what you wanted most in your life, isn't it?"

"It's of no consequence now." She shrugged and turned back to the shelf. Somehow, telling him, saying it aloud now twice today when she'd never admitted it to anyone before, made her loss all the more real. "Besides, I'm not sure I ever could have convinced Enrico to let me join him. I had hoped if I learned enough, if I made myself . . . well, essential, important to his work, he would allow me to come with him."

"Those obscure, remote areas of the world where your brother and the rest of us search for the treasures of the past are not places for western women," he said slowly, as if treading lightly.

"I know that."

"And yet that did not deter you?"

"It sounds rather silly, I suppose. I know the proper place of a woman in this day and age. Still, women do travel the world and go all sorts of places not substantially more civilized than those regions you frequent. Besides, I would prefer to be considered an expert in the field of archeology rather than a mere woman."

He chuckled. "There is nothing 'mere' about you."

"Nonetheless, as a practical matter, I am well aware I can do nothing as a woman alone. It doesn't seem especially fair, but it is the way of the world." She didn't have to turn to know he had risen to his feet and crossed the room to stand behind her. "So, my studies, my training, has all been for nothing."

"I am sorry, Gabriella." Genuine regret sounded in his voice. "I can only imagine what it must be like to lose something you had worked for. Something you had wanted."

"And I did," she said softly, "want it very much." For a moment, misery swept through her. She had some time ago laid to rest the grief she'd felt for her brother. This was for her, her dreams, her hopes. She drew a deep breath. Ridiculous, of course. Her dreams never had any chance of coming true. "It was quite foolish to think it was ever a legitimate possibility." She turned to face him. He was less than the width of her hand away. Her heart sped up. She ignored it. "There you have it, Nathanial. My frivolous hope. As fictional as anything one might read in a novel, I suspect. My—" She sighed. "—secret, as it were." She cast him a deprecating smile.

He smiled back as if he did indeed understand. At once it struck her that no matter what else he might be, he was a nice man. A very nice man. The kind of man one might be able to depend on. The kind of man one might possibly trust.

She stared into his brown eyes and abruptly the moment between them changed. Without warning, an odd tension snapped in the air between them, charged with an intensity and awareness as unexpected as it was irresistible.

The kind of man one could love.

He stared at her. "And do you have many secrets?"

Where on earth did that come from? She had no business loving any man, let alone this one. She pushed the thought away and forced a cool note to her voice. "Yes, of course. We all have secrets."

He moved imperceptibly closer, bracing one hand on the shelves to the left of her head. "Any you wish to share?"

"They wouldn't be secrets then, would they?" Her gaze slipped from his eyes to his mouth. Hers weren't the only lips that begged to be kissed, not that she intended to do anything of the sort. "I should hate for you to know everything about me. Where would be the mystery? The excitement? The challenge?"

"I suspect that will not be a problem," he said under his breath.

She could feel the books on the shelves behind her pressing into her back. Still, why not kiss him? Just once. What harm could it do? "You're nicer than I expected you to be."

"Excellent." He smiled in a wicked manner that should have seemed silly or overly dramatic or far too arrogant instead of making her breath catch and her knees week.

"Are you going to kiss me?" She swallowed hard.

"I think I might, yes."

"There is no moonlight now, Nathanial."

"I may be willing to forgo that condition."

"Would you?" She raised her lips toward his.

"I can't seem to help myself." He leaned closer.

"You said a first kiss should be savored and remembered always."

"I shall remember it forever." His lips were within a breath of her own.

"Nathanial?" She fairly sighed his name.

He paused. "Yes?"

She tossed caution aside and brushed her lips lightly across his. "As will I."

"Mmm." He pressed his lips firmly to hers. Her stomach clenched with newfound desire.

"Ahem." Someone cleared his throat at the doorway. "Beg pardon, my lord."

Eight

*D*amnation, she knew that voice.

Nathanial straightened reluctantly, cast her a quick smile and turned toward the new-comer. "Yes?"

Xerxes stood in the door, garbed in the same apparel as every other servant she'd seen thus far in the house-hold, holding a silver slaver bearing a letter. "This just arrived for Miss Montini, sir. I was told to deliver it at once."

"Very well." Nathanial took the letter, glanced at it in passing, and handed it to Gabriella. "Are you new here?" he asked Xerxes. "I was under the impression that John Farrel was the footman on duty in the morning."

"I am serving in John's stead, my lord," Xerxes said smoothly.

Gabriella clenched her teeth.

"I hope nothing is wrong," Nathaniel said.

"He was called to the country on a family matter of some urgency, sir."

A family matter—hah! Gabriella glared. "Was he?"

Xerxes met her gaze firmly. "Yes, miss."

She narrowed her eyes. "How urgent?"

"Gabriella." Nathanial shook his head. "I really don't think—"

"It's his younger sister, miss. My cousin fears she could be getting herself into some difficulty and may need his assistance." Xerxes's gaze locked with hers. "Even perhaps rescue."

Gabriella crossed her arms over her chest. "Is she a child?"

"In spite of her behavior on occasion, no, miss, she is an adult."

"Then I'm sure she's more than competent to handle the situation on her own," Gabriella said.

Nathanial's confused gaze slid between her and the older man. "Gabriella?"

"I've no doubt she thinks she is, miss. However, she has been mistaken about her competence in the past." His eyes narrowed slightly. "The entire family is most concerned." He turned his attention to Nathanial. "Will there be anything else, sir?"

"No, thank you." Nathanial cast an amused glance at Gabriella. "Unless you had something more?"

"Not at the moment," she muttered.

"Then you may go." Nathanial nodded.

Xerxes headed for the door.

"Oh, I don't know your name," Nathanial said.

"John Farrel, sir."

"Like your cousin?"

Gabriella choked back a snort of disgust.

Nathanial glanced at her.

"It's a family name, sir."

"I see." Nathanial nodded, and Xerxes took his leave. "Do you know him?"

"No," she said shortly. "He reminded me of someone— something in his manner, I think." She cast him an apologetic smile. "I seem to be rather on edge today."

"Not surprising, really." He nodded at the letter in her hand. "Aren't you going to read that?"

"Yes, of course." Gabriella opened the letter and scanned it. "It's from my friend, Miss Henry."

"Wasn't she just here?"

"Apparently there were some things she failed to mention." Among them the fact that she, or Xerxes, had paid John the footman to go on a bit of a holiday so Xerxes could take the man's place. Apparently that was the plan Florence had referred to.

"Now that we're alone . . . "

To keep an eye on her. Gabriella's jaw clenched. No one in her household seemed to understand that she was no longer a child.

"Yes?" she said absently. Still, it wasn't a bad idea to have Xerxes within reach should she need his assistance.

Nathanial cleared his throat. "Now that we're alone . . . "

"You said that," she murmured. Indeed she should have thought of it herself. She refolded the note and glanced at Nathanial. "Now that we're alone, did you still want to kiss me?"

"And get it over with, you mean?"

"I didn't mean that at all." Even so, the moment wasn't quite as electric as it had been. The desire to press her lips to his not as urgent, although she was certain it wouldn't take much more than a heated glance for her to again want what she'd never imagined she'd want. Regardless, the opportunity had passed.

"I should . . . " He nodded toward the desk. " . . . finish the letters."

"By all means." She suspected as well that it would not take much to reignite his desire either.

He sat back down and picked up a letter. The first, she noted. He certainly hadn't progressed very far. She crossed her arms over her chest, bookshelf at her back, and watched him read.

"I thought we had established that I find your observation somewhat unsettling," he said without looking up.

She bit back a smile. "Then I suggest you read quickly."

"Hmph."

She probably shouldn't stand here and watch him, but she couldn't seem to help herself. The man was an enigma and not at all as she had expected. She hadn't expected his nature. He was nice and funny and wicked all at the same time. Beyond that, he did seem, well, honest. A man who possibly could be trusted.

She'd never trusted more than a handful of people in her life. And hadn't Enrico told her over and over that men who coveted ancient treasures were, on the whole, an unscrupulous lot and not—no, never—to be trusted? Still, there was something about Nathanial Harrington that made her want to trust him. Want to believe that he would never betray her.

What had this man done to her? She'd always considered herself a completely honest person. But from very nearly the first moment they met, Nathanial had her saying things and doing things she never would have considered doing. As when he caught her in the library and she'd come up with that ridiculous story about his once having kissed her. Which resulted in his insisting she owed him a kiss, preferably in the moonlight, although that no longer seemed a consideration. She ignored the voice in the back of her head that pointed out her actions before then had not been especially legitimate.

And now, God help her, she wanted him to kiss her. Wanted to feel the warmth of his arms around her, the pressing of his body against hers. Wanted the heat of his desire to burn into her very soul. Wanted the—

"Interesting," he said under his breath.

Gabriella blinked in surprise. "Well, yes, that's not quite what I would . . . " She uttered an odd, uncomfortable sort of laugh, heat rushing up her face. Again. "I'm not sure interesting, while somewhat accurate, in that, yes it is indeed interesting if completely unexpected and not at all distasteful, but rather . . . quite . . . "

He grinned.

She stared, then winced. "You're talking about the letters, aren't you?"

"I am indeed." His grin widened as if he knew the answer before he asked the question. "What are you talking about?"

"The letters, of course." She adopted a brisk tone and moved to the chair positioned in front of the desk, a safe distance from him. He certainly couldn't reach across the desk and pull her unresistingly into his arms. Not that she would be the least bit unresisting. Dear Lord, she groaned to herself, what had he done to her? She drew a calming breath. "Well?"

He picked up a pencil and scribbled on a piece of paper. "As you have said, your brother considered only four possible suspects. These were all men to whom he had shown the clay impression made from the missing seal. The list includes an American, Alistair McGowan, and one Javier Gutierrez, a Spaniard." He shuffled through the letters. "Although, he regards Gutierrez only as an agent for Viscount Rathbourne."

She nodded. "Lord Rathbourne is a member of the Antiquities Society and a well-known collector. I have heard of him and I have seen him on occasion, although I have never met him myself."

"His reputation is such that I don't doubt he would sanction whatever means possible to get what he wanted. If Gutierrez took the seal, he has no doubt turned it over to Lord Rathbourne by now. The last two names, of course, are mine and my brother's." He glanced at her. "Have we been taken off the list?"

She hesitated.

His eyes narrowed. "You still suspect me?"

She met his gaze. "Yes."

"I see." He paused. "I thought we agreed to trust one another?"

"I don't remember agreeing to that at all. I recall you saying we should begin to develop trust between us, which was in reference to my brother's letters." She shrugged. "Trust, Nathanial, has to be earned."

He studied her for a long moment. "Indeed it does. On both sides. My name remains, then, and I assume my brother's as well?"

She nodded. "I have not eliminated him, no."

"I daresay I cannot blame you, given Quentin's reputation. However, I am confident he has had nothing to do with this."

She chose her words with care. "And would you know if he had?"

"Perhaps not. But I do know that I will do all that is necessary to recover the seal, regardless of who has it." His voice was hard and she had no doubt he was as good as his word. "Very well, then." He again wrote on the paper, and she could see now it was a list of the men her brother had suspected and included the names of Nathanial and Quinton Harrington. Her stomach twisted.

"You don't need to add your name," she said without thinking.

"Why?"

"If we are to work together, trust is indeed essential. I should give you the benefit of the doubt. Besides, thus far, aside from my brother's suspicions, you have less reason to trust me than I do to trust you." She drew a deep breath. "When it comes to the theft of the seal, I am willing to attempt precisely that."

"Why?" he said again.

"I have no choice, do I?"

"I should think—"

"I can either trust that you are being forthright and honest, that you are truly trying to help me, or I can be suspicious of your every word." She shook her head. "I am by nature suspicious, and no more so than this past year, but I am also practical. If I spend all of my time doubting, we will not accomplish anything. Therefore, in this endeavor, you have my trust, Nathanial Harrington, for good or ill."

"For good or ill." He shook his head. "Not a ringing endorsement."

"Now and again one must take a leap of faith." She met his gaze. "I'm not sure I ever have before."

"Then it is doubly appreciated." He smiled, then with

a flourish crossed his name off the list. "Now, only three names remain, and as I am confident one is innocent, I suggest we concentrate on the other two."

She nodded. "First, the American." She glanced at him. "Do you know him?"

Nathanial shrugged. "Not well but I have made his acquaintance. He seems a decent enough sort."

"But is he the type of man to steal another man's find?"

"It's hard to say. A find like this would tempt even the most honest of men. If McGowan has it . . . " He thought for a moment. "It might well have come into his hands indirectly. He doesn't strike me as a thief."

Gabriella got to her feet and paced the room. "He hasn't arrived in London yet but is expected to arrive any day now."

Nathanial's brows drew together. "Why would McGowan be in London?"

"For the same reason you're in London at this time of year."

"His sister is coming out?"

She rolled her gaze toward the ceiling. "I tend to forget that your family's wealth means you don't have the same concerns as others in your field."

He stared in confusion, then smacked his palm against his forehead. "Of course. The Verification Committee begins its meeting this week. Anyone with any significant finds or proposals for funding will be in London to present their case." He stared at her. "It was a year ago that your brother—"

"Yes," she said simply, and continued, "As McGowan is not yet in London, I propose we start with Lord Rathbourne. I would imagine you know him?"

"To say I know Lord Rathbourne would be an over-statement." Nathanial chose his words with care. "I am aware of his status as a collector. Not merely of artifacts, but of art and other valuables. Beyond that . . . "

"Yes?"

"He married the woman my brother loved."

Gabriella widened her eyes. "The earl?"

He nodded.

"I thought he was a widower?"

"He is, but . . . " Nathanial drummed his fingers on the desk as if deciding how much to tell her. "It's public knowledge for the most part, I suppose, and it's all firmly in the past. It's been, oh, ten years now. Sterling loved Olivia—Lady Rathbourne. It was assumed, at least in this family, that they would marry. Then one day they were no longer seeing one another, the next day she had married Lord Rathbourne, and a few days after that Sterling was engaged to Alice. Which pleased both her family and ours."

"But she died within a year of their marriage."

"Yes." He cast her a suspicious frown. "How did you know that?"

"I probably heard it at the Antiquities Society." She shrugged. "As you said, it is common knowledge."

"I don't think Sterling ever got over it."

She nodded. "His wife's death."

"Yes, of course," he said quickly. "That's what I meant."

Gabriella thought for a minute. "Then you know Lady Rathbourne?"

"I suppose I do, although I haven't spoken to her in years."

"Don't you think it's time, then, to pay a call on her and resume your acquaintance?"

"And what do you propose I say?" He stared at her. " 'Good afternoon, Lady Rathbourne. I trust you're well today. Oh, did you know you broke my brother's heart, he's never quite recovered, and by the way, we are curious as to whether or not your husband—the man you left my brother for—is a thief.' "

"Now you're being absurd, Nathanial," she scoffed. "We wouldn't want to put it quite like that."

"Oh." He raised a brow. "How then would you put it?

"I think we should pay a call on Lady Rathbourne and ask her if her husband's collections include a recently acquired ancient Akkadian cylinder seal." She smiled.

"Are you insane?"

"I don't think so," she said coolly. "You think this is insane?"

"Under what pretext would we say we were calling?" He clenched his teeth. "Aside from the absurd idea of resuming our acquaintance."

"I don't know." She resumed pacing and tried to think. "Surely between the two of us we can come up with something plausible. We are fairly intelligent, after all."

"You don't have a plan, do you?" He rose to his feet, his brow furrowed. "You have no idea how to go about locating this seal at all, do you?"

She winced to herself. "Well, I suppose one might say, if one was particularly concerned with minor details . . . "

"One might say what?"

"One might say," she said slowly, "the answer to that is . . . "

"Yes?"

"No."

"No!" He shook his head as if he couldn't quite believe his ears. "No?"

"I believe I said that," she said under her breath.

"Say it again!" he snapped.

"No, I don't have a plan. There, now are you happy?"

"Ecstatic!" He drew a deep breath. "So you are saying that you have no plan, no idea where to start, nothing beyond a list of possible suspects?"

"I did once have a plan," she muttered.

"Oh?" He crossed his arms over his chest. "Was that the one that involved breaking into my house and searching my brother's library?"

Along with an ill-fated jaunt to Egypt. She shrugged. "Apparently I'm not very good at plans."

"You've just now realized that?"

"One doesn't learn such things about oneself until one attempts them."

"Perhaps we should simply break into Lord Rathbourne's house and see for ourselves if the seal is there. After all, you have experience in such things now."

"There's no need for sarcasm, Nathanial." She paused. "Still, I suppose—"

"Absolutely not!" He circled the desk. "I forbid it!"

"You what?"

"I forbid it." He stepped toward her. "I will not allow you to pull the kind of stunt you pulled here ever again. You could be in jail by now, or worse, shot. People do tend to shoot people they find breaking into their houses in the middle of the night, you know."

He was right, she hadn't thought of that. Regardless, she straightened her shoulders. "I wouldn't have been caught if people were in their beds in the middle of the night instead of finally returning home at a most indecent hour!"

"If you were half as clever as you think you are, you would have been well aware that a majority of the members of this household were still out for the evening!" He stepped to within inches of her and glared.

"Well, then." She planted her hands on her hips. "If we can't break into his house and we can't call on his wife, how do you propose we find out if Rathbourne has the seal? Do *you* have a plan?"

"I didn't say we couldn't call on Lady Rathbourne. I asked what reason we would have for such a . . . " He paused.

She studied him. "You have an idea, don't you?"

He nodded slowly. "Perhaps."

"Possibly a plan?"

"Possibly."

She grinned. "I knew you would come up with something."

His brow rose. "Did you?"

"Well, not until a moment ago."

A reluctant smile curved the corners of his mouth. "And how did you know that?"

"Faith, Nathanial." Her grin widened. "I leapt."

Nine

"I must say, this is all very interesting." Merrill Beckworth narrowed his eyes behind his gold-rimmed glasses and considered them curiously.

Nate slanted a quick glance at Gabriella, seated in the chair beside him. She wore her own clothes today, a dress not quite shabby but certainly well worn, a sensible hat, serviceable gloves, and appeared as poised, serene, and collected as if she sat in the office of the director of the Antiquities Society every day. And why shouldn't she be calm? For her, sitting in front of the massive desk in a room filled with dark woodwork and shadows, surrounded by shelves crammed with books, the odd artifact here and there and the occasional travel souvenir, was not the least bit reminiscent of sitting in front of one's father's desk, waiting for one's duly deserved punishment to be meted out. Nate resisted the urge to squirm in his chair.

"More tea, Miss Montini?" Mrs. Beckworth asked.

"Yes, please." Gabriella held out her cup and the director's wife efficiently refilled it. Still, some of Gabriella's composure might well be attributed to keeping a tight rein on her annoyance with him. She hadn't been at all pleased to discover their destination when they had arrived. He'd hurried her out of the house this morning without telling her, arranging for a maid to accompany them for propriety's sake, but without telling her where they were going. It had taken him nearly two full days simply to arrange the meeting, and he was not about to let any reservations she might have interfere. It wasn't a great idea, but it was better than nothing.

In spite of Gabriella's impatience, the past two days hadn't been a complete waste. She had found any number of things among the library bookshelves of interest to her. She seemed somewhat fond of memoirs. And he had found any number of reasons to stay in the library by her side. He wasn't sure he'd ever met a woman like her. She was lovely, of course, as well as brilliant, not to mention stubborn and headstrong and annoyingly independent. But prying anything of a personal nature out of her was bloody well impossible. He'd never known a female to be so reticent about her life. It was as intriguing as it was frustrating. As was her resistance to all his attempts to kiss her again. Which only made him want her more.

"Mr. Harrington?" Mrs. Beckworth offered the pot.

Nate shook his head. "Thank you but no."

Mrs. Beckworth smiled, refilled her own cup, then settled in a chair a bit behind and off to one side of the director. She was a good twenty years younger than her husband, somewhere in her mid- to late thirties probably. In spite of the severity of her tightly pinned hair and the simplicity of her nondescript gown, Nate suspected that she was the kind of woman who had once been considered a beauty, and even now was still quite lovely. Although there was no accounting for attraction, he couldn't help but wonder what had drawn her to the older, somewhat portly scholar.

"Gabriella, why didn't you come to me before now?" Merrill Beckworth pinned her with a firm look. "Indeed, it seems to me we have seen little of you this past year."

"My studies have kept me busy, sir." She paused then met his gaze directly. "And, frankly, given the nature of my brother's last appearance here . . . "

"My dear girl." Mrs. Beckworth leaned forward in her chair. "No one would ever think ill of you for your brother's behavior."

"My absence is not due to the society's opinion of me under these circumstances," Gabriella said firmly, setting her teacup on the table between them and folding her hands in her lap. "But rather my opinion of the society."

"Oh." Mrs. Beckworth's eyes widened and she sat back in her chair.

Nate winced.

The director chuckled. He directed his words to Nate but his gaze remained on Gabriella. "Were you aware of Miss Montini's outspoken nature?"

"I have noticed it, sir," Nate said wryly.

Gabriella smiled in a polite manner. "I prefer the term 'forthright' to 'outspoken,' sir."

"I have known Miss Montini for some years now. Since she began her studies at Queen's College, I believe." The director cast her an affectionate smile. "Despite her gender, she has one of the finest scholarly minds I have ever run across. She's quite remarkable. Did you know, Harrington, this young woman remembers everything she has ever read?"

Nate glanced at Gabriella. In spite of the ambiguous nature of the compliment, and the blush that colored her cheeks, she remained completely composed. "No sir, but it does not surprise me."

"Then you are more intelligent than you look," Beckworth said in a dismissive manner, and turned his attention back to Gabriella. "I have long thought the manner in which your brother and the society parted company last year was a great shame."

"Such a pity," Mrs. Beckworth said under her breath.

"Indeed, if he had not been quite so . . . irrational—"

Gabriella didn't so much as flinch at the word. There was a great deal about her Nate didn't know, but Beckworth was right, she was remarkable.

"—the situation might well have been salvageable. Still, while Mr. Montini's behavior was not excusable, it was somewhat understandable given the circumstances." Beckworth paused. "You should know, my dear, that once the committee members' ruffled feathers were smoothed—no easy task, I assure you—"

"They can be quite stubborn." Mrs. Beckworth sighed in a long suffering manner.

"There was a great deal of interest in your brother's claim. A find of this magnitude, the possibility that Ambropia might have actually existed, well, you can imagine the excitement." He glanced at Nate. "Once the committee calmed down, of course. Still, there was no proof."

"As it had been stolen," Gabriella said pointedly.

"Now you tell me your brother had several men he

suspected of either taking or engineering the theft of this seal?"

She nodded.

The director's eyes narrowed. "You realize you cannot make charges of wrongdoing without proof of some sort. And, as the only proof that exists is your brother's unsubstantiated claim, and as he was—"

"Not at all, sir," Nate cut in quickly. "I saw the clay impression made by the Montini seal myself."

The older man raised a brow. "The Montini seal?"

Nate nodded. "It appeared quite genuine."

"Still, such things can be fraudulent." The director shrugged. "And, as I imagine you do not have that impression—"

"I do," Gabriella said. "Enrico left it with me."

"There you have it, sir," Nate said, stifling any show of surprise at her announcement, though it was the first time he'd heard of it. She could have mentioned she had the impression. She'd had the opportunity when they'd read and reread her brother's letters, picking them apart word by word to determine if there was anything they had missed. She'd had the chance during dinners with his family when the conversation turned to their search. Most of the talk either centered on the Antiquities Society's annual general meeting and the events associated with that, including the convening of the Verification Committee and the ball, or minor family matters. She'd seemed fascinated by what he considered not at all unusual.

And after dinner each night, when they gathered in the parlor, and later when he escorted her to her rooms and resisted what was fast becoming more of a need than a mere urge to kiss her, again she had the opportunity to tell him about the impression. And again she kept silent. Still, he supposed it scarcely mattered at the moment.

"These ancient cylinder seals were carved by hand," he said to Beckworth now, "and no matter how perfectly crafted, there are always subtle differences between them. If we can find the seal that matches her impression, we have the Montini seal."

"And the thief," Gabriella added.

"My, that is clever," Mrs. Beckworth said under her breath. "I wouldn't have thought of that."

"Regardless." The director shook his head. "Even should you recover the seal, proving whoever has it in his possession is the same man who actually stole it might well be impossible." He glanced at Nate. "You know how difficult culpability would be to prove in a matter like this. And how quickly artifacts might change hands. Furthermore, when you consider that Lord Rathbourne, with his influence and resources, is among—"

"Mr. Beckworth." Gabriella's hands, folded in her lap, tightened, the knuckles white. Abruptly, Nate realized her calm had a price. His heart twisted for her. "I came to the realization some time ago that whoever physically stole the seal—an act which I believe led to my brother's death—will never be punished for that particular crime. As you say, it would be impossible to prove. Then too is the question of jurisdiction, of where it was stolen. England? Egypt? Somewhere in between?"

"Then I don't see—"

"All I want is to recover the seal and prove it is the same one my brother had." She drew a deep breath.

"Thus restoring his reputation. I want him to be credited with the find. Nothing more than that."

Beckworth studied her carefully. "But the seal alone is worth a great deal of money. So is the possibility that it is part of a puzzle that will solve the Virgin's Secret, the location of the lost city itself."

"I don't care," Gabriella said simply.

"Others might."

She shrugged. "Let them."

Beckworth's gaze shifted back to Nate. "This search of yours could prove to be dangerous."

While neither he nor Gabriella had mentioned the idea of danger, Nate was well aware of the possibility. It was among the reasons why he thought coming to the society made sense.

"I fully intend to donate the seal to the society," Gabriella said quickly. "As for the location of the city . . . " She paused, and Nate wondered if she was again letting go of her own dreams. " . . . that is not my concern. And while there may well be some risk involved, that shall not dissuade me. Risk, sir, is always a possibility when one attempts to do what is right."

"What a courageous girl you are," Mrs. Beckworth said softly.

"Not at all." Gabriella sat a little straighter, if possible. "I am simply . . . " She blew a long breath. " . . . angry, I think. I want my brother's legacy restored."

"Understandable, of course." Beckworth considered her thoughtfully. "But I don't see how I can be of help."

"Sir." Nate leaned forward. "We are here today because it strikes me that even something as simple as Miss Montini and I making inquires about the seal is somewhat awkward. We have no authority in the matter other than a personal interest. I thought that perhaps if the society, if you—"

"You want me to make this an official inquiry?" Beckworth's bushy brow rose.

Gabriella cast Nate a sharp look.

"Exactly." Nate nodded. "As Miss Montini fully intends to give the seal to the society should we prove successful, it seems to me the society has a vested interest in its recovery."

"Well, I suppose . . . " the older man said slowly.

"If she and I could act as representatives of the society—agents, if you will—it would ease our way to speak to those who might be involved."

"You plan to talk to those you suspect?" Beckworth scoffed.

"Well, we simply can't break into their lodgings," Gabriella said under her breath.

"Confronting the culprit might well force him to show his hand," Nate went on. "We might then be able to come to an agreement about credit for the find, perhaps even sharing it." Gabriella slanted him a disbelieving glance. "It seems to me, sir, that whoever has the seal will want to present it to the Verification Committee just as Miss Montini's brother planned to do last year. It's worthless otherwise."

"Unless they were planning to use it to find the lost city," Mrs. Beckworth said thoughtfully.

Gabriella shook her head. "My brother believed the seal was one of a set and that there are probably at least two more. He thought together they would somehow reveal the location of the city. One alone would not be sufficient."

"How very interesting," Mrs. Beckworth murmured.

Beckworth ignored his wife. "Why not wait until it is presented to the committee to make your claim? Why go to all this trouble before then?"

"That would be too late," Gabriella replied. "Someone else would have claimed the credit for finding the seal. Regardless," she raised her chin, "I do not intend to let this matter drop. Should the seal be presented and its legitimacy verified, I should be forced to make the circumstances surrounding it public. Such a revelation would certainly create a scandal, at least in scholarly circles, as well as among the society's benefactors. As the society has a reputation of integrity to maintain, and as it is financially dependent upon donations, it would seem to me such a revelation would be most unfortunate."

The director narrowed his eyes. "That sounds suspiciously like blackmail, my dear."

"Not at all, sir. It doesn't 'sound' like blackmail." Gabriella met the older man's gaze directly. "I believe it is blackmail."

Nate stared at her. One never would have imagined the pretty, dark-haired woman with the eyes of an angel and the straight-backed bearing of a proper English lady had it in her. Oh, yes, there was much more to the delectable Gabriella Montini than met the eye. She was definitely a woman with secrets. It was very nearly irresistible.

"I wouldn't have thought it of you, Gabriella." The director settled back in his chair.

The faintest hint of a smile quirked her lips. "I wouldn't have thought it of myself, sir, but one does what one must."

"Very well, then." The director tapped his pen on the desk in a thoughtful manner. "You may consider yourselves agents of the society in respect to this matter, and you may use the society's name accordingly. However," his gaze shifted pointedly to Nate, "should there be any activity of a . . . shall we say, less than lawful nature—"

"Sir!" Nate sat up straighter. "We would never—" At once, Quint's lingering reputation sprang to mind, as well as Gabriella's apparent tendency toward larceny. "You have my assurances—"

"Yes, yes, I'm certain I do." Beckworth waved his comment away. "Nonetheless, should such an incident occur, I would be forced to disavow any knowledge of your actions. Furthermore," his gaze bored into Nate's, "I will hold you personally responsible. Should this quest of Miss Montini's bring any dishonor whatsoever upon this august institution, I will see to it that you and that renegade brother of yours are never allowed to so much as cross the threshold here again."

"Which brother sir?" Nate drew his brows together, although he knew full well which brother. "Surely you're not speaking of the earl? The Earl of Wyldewood?"

"You know exactly which brother I am talking about. I am well aware of the earl's position on the board here, as well as your father's before him. And I am equally aware of your family's financial support. Regardless," Beckworth's eyes narrowed, "this is not an idle threat. If you bring so much as a modicum of disgrace or scandal, not only will I ban you from these premises but I will use every bit of influence at my disposal to make certain no reputable university, museum, or private collector will so much as accept your calling card."

"That's rather harsh, dear," Mrs. Beckworth said.

"Sir." Gabriella's brow furrowed. "Mr. Harrington and his family are assisting me, but this is entirely my endeavor. Therefore, if there are any unforeseen consequences, they should fall entirely on my head. Not Mr. Nathanial Harrington, nor Mr. Quinton Harrington, nor any member of their family."

"Gabriella." Beckworth's expression softened. "In spite of your rather surprising willingness to resort to actions that are beneath you, I fully understand the emotional nature of the situation. As brilliant as I have always thought you to be, you are a member of the fairer sex, after all, and therefore such things—while not condoned—may be overlooked."

Gabriella choked. "I am not—"

"Sir," Nate said quickly, to forestall her saying something they would both regret, or at least he would. "You have my word I shall not do anything to cast this institution in a disreputable light. Nor will I allow Miss Montini to . . . well . . . allow her feminine emotions, as it were, to overrule her head."

Gabriella's jaw clenched.

"And I will do all in my power as well to ensure her safety."

"See that you do." Beckworth gestured at his wife. "Mrs. Beckworth will check our files. We should have information as to where Mr. McGowan will be staying and when he is expected to arrive in London that will prove helpful to you." Mrs. Beckworth nodded and hurried out of the office. "I assume you know where to find Lord Rathbourne?"

"Yes, sir," Nate said.

"He is . . . " The director thought for a moment. " . . . 'ruthless,' I think is the word, when it comes to his collections, and extremely possessive. It's my understanding he does not display them but rather keeps them locked away. There have been any number of rumors through the years regarding the manner of his acquisitions." The older man's gaze met Nate's. "I suspect there are no lengths he would not go to protect what he considers his."

Nate acknowledged the warning in Beckworth's eyes with a nod. Beckworth rose to his feet, Nate and Gabriella following suit.

His wife returned and handed Nate a piece of paper. Her gaze met his. Her eyes were the cool, pale blue color of ice, at odds with the warmth in her voice. "If there is anything else you need, do not hesitate to call on us. We have always been fond of Gabriella."

"If there is nothing else," Beckworth said, "I have a great deal of work to do, what with the Verification Committee as well as the meeting of the general membership bearing down upon us. Mr. Harrington, Gabriella." He cast her an affectionate smile. "Do be careful, my dear."

"And we will see you both in a few days, I assume." Mrs. Beckworth's gaze shifted between Nate and Gabriella in a speculative manner. "At the ball?"

The Antiquities Society Ball marked the beginning of the ten day meeting of the Verification Committee. The committee would adjourn at noon on its final day, the annual general membership meeting following an hour or so later. Reggie and his mother had been talking about the ball ever since he returned home. This would be the first year his sister was old enough to attend. His mother and Sterling, of course, made an appearance every year. Nate couldn't remember the last time he and Quinton had attended.

Gabriella shook her head. "I really don't think—"

"Of course we will." Nate favored the older woman with his most charming smile. "We wouldn't think of missing it." He took her hand and raised it to his lips. Again the look in her eyes struck him as cold. Nonsense, he told himself. It was simply the pale color that made them appear so. "And I do hope you will save a dance for me."

She smiled. "I shall indeed, Mr. Harrington."

Nate grinned. "Good day, then." He nodded at the director. "Sir."

Gabriella murmured a polite farewell. Nate took her elbow and steered her firmly out of the office. The moment they were out of the Beckworths' presence, her jaw tensed, her posture stiffened, and her eyes narrowed. As much as he didn't know about Gabriella Montini, only a man long dead in his grave would fail to recognize the timeless signs of a woman who was not happy, especially with the man at her side. He braced himself.

When they stepped out of the building, she shook off his hand and turned to him, her blue eyes glittering with anger in the sunlight. "What on earth were you thinking?" She glared. "Coming here? To them?"

"You didn't have a plan," he said calmly, and looked down the street for his carriage. "You had no idea where we should begin."

"You could have mentioned this was where we were going! You didn't tell me this was your *plan*." She fairly spat the word.

"You wouldn't have come."

"Of course I wouldn't have come. This is the last place—"

"Gabriella." He met her gaze directly. "We needed a certain amount of authority, credibility. Legitimacy, if you will."

Her eyes narrowed. "My claim is perfectly legitimate."

"I understand that—"

"And as for credibility, even if I am a female without a brain in her head—"

"No one said anything of the sort. In fact, your intelligence was highly praised by Beckworth."

She snorted with disdain. "For a woman."

"For anyone. You needn't be so indignant about Beckworth's appraisal."

"Perhaps I am allowing my feminine emotions to overrule my head!"

"Perhaps you are." He gritted his teeth. "You know full well the limitations on women in this world. You acknowledged them yourself when we talked about your desire to follow your brother's path in life."

"You suggested sharing credit! I have no intention of doing so."

"It was a suggestion, nothing more." Where was his blasted carriage?

"He charged you with my protection! I don't need—"

"You most certainly do." His patience snapped. "You are irrational on this subject. Thus far your actions have been anything but sensible and well thought out."

She gasped.

"Can you deny it?" He grabbed her elbow and stared into her eyes. "You could be in jail right now. First you attempt to search my brother's library at my sister's ball. Then you break into my house—" A thought struck him and he paused. "Have you done anything else I should know about?"

She hesitated for no more than a fraction of a second, but it was enough. He could see there was something she still kept from him. She squared her shoulders. "No, of course not."

He didn't believe her for a second, and vowed to himself to find out what else she might have done in this quest of hers. "Why didn't you tell me that you had the impression?"

"Oh." Her eyes widened. "That."

"Yes, that!"

She shrugged. "You didn't ask."

"So much for trust and leaps of faith," he said sharply.

"It's not that I don't trust you," she said quickly. "It simply slipped my mind, that's all."

"I don't believe you." He released her and waved at his carriage that had just turned onto the street.

Her forehead furrowed. "Why not?"

"As you said, Gabriella." The carriage pulled to a stop in front of them and he jerked open the door. The waiting maid stared at him with widened eyes and slid back into the farthest corner of the carriage. "Trust has to be earned."

He helped her in and snapped the door shut.

"Furthermore I have no intention of attending that ball." She huffed.

"Oh yes you will. It's in your best interests to make an appearance, and you will do so."

She glared. "You cannot order me as if I were—"

"As if you were the woman I could have arrested?"

She sucked in a sharp breath. "Nathanial Harrington, I can't believe you—"

"Would resort to blackmail?" He narrowed his eyes. "One does what one must. I shall see you at home."

She leaned out of the window. "Aren't you coming?"

"No," he said firmly. "I have an errand to attend to."

"What kind of errand?" Suspicion rang in her voice.

"Trust, Gabriella. Try to have a little faith in me. I will not fail you." Nate signaled to the driver and the carriage rolled off. He heaved a frustrated sigh. "You have my word, Gabriella Montini."

He turned and started off down the street. If he had any hope of keeping his word, he needed to know her secrets. His family's solicitor had long employed an excellent and reputable investigation agency. According to Sterling, its operatives were fast and efficient and had proved most useful in the past. Nate had never needed them before, but if ever there was a time, it was now.

With every moment spent in her company, he discovered there was much he didn't know about Gabriella Montini. And much he needed to discover.

hare the credit for discovery of the seal?" Gabriella paced the parlor of her house, noting in the back of her mind how very small it was. Obviously residing with the Harringtons had changed her perceptions. That too was annoying. "Can you imagine such a thing?"

Florence glanced up from the work in her hand. "It seems rather sensible to me."

Gabriella stopped in mid-step and glared. "Sensible?"

"Gabriella." Florence sighed and dropped the pillow cover she'd been embroidering into her lap. "You know as well as I—as well as Mr. Harrington and Mr. Beckworth, apparently—that whoever is in possession of the seal is not necessarily the same person who stole it. Whoever has it now might well have come by it in a relatively legitimate manner. If so, he would be hard-pressed to give up recognition of the find at all, let alone share it."

"I am well aware of that. I simply prefer not to think about it." Gabriella blew a long breath. "Still, to have Nathanial suggest it, well, it smacked of betrayal."

Florence raised a brow. "I thought you said you trusted him?"

"I did. I do. Somewhat." She sighed. "I can't completely. I am trying." She resumed pacing. "It's not that I don't want to trust him. I want to trust him more than anything." The very idea of trusting Nathanial was almost irresistible. Of not having to watch every word she said. Of trusting him with her confidence, her secrets. Maybe even her heart. Although that was absurd.

"I should think it would be a great relief for you to trust someone completely."

Gabriella widened her eyes. "I trust you completely."

"Do you?" Florence said, picking up her embroidery. "Always?"

"Yes, of course." Gabriella ignored the thought of her trip to Egypt. "I trust you implicitly."

"Implicitly?"

"Yes." Gabriella nodded. "Without question."

"Yet you did not trust me enough to tell me anything about your intended misdeeds at Mr. Harrington's home."

"You would have stopped me."

Florence cast her a chastising look. "That is my job."

"And you do it well. Which is why I didn't tell you."

"Hmph." Florence paused, no doubt to compile more examples. "You didn't tell me you have the clay impression of the seal."

"Yes, well . . . "

Florence glanced at her sharply. "Gabriella?"

"That is a bit of a problem," Gabriella murmured.

"A problem?"

"In definition." Gabriella shrugged. "Nothing more significant than that."

Florence narrowed her eyes. "An explanation, if you please."

"The impression is not actually in my possession at the moment." Gabriella held her breath.

"I see." Florence thought for a moment. "Do you know where it might be?"

"I am certain it is in London and probably under our very noses."

"London is a very big place."

"I'm sure it is here in the house," Gabriella said with far more conviction than she felt.

"But you don't know."

"No, but I am fairly confident." She sank down on the sofa beside Florence. "It doesn't make sense for it to be anywhere else. Enrico told me he was leaving it in the one place where he knew it would be safe. Where, he said, he kept everything he valued. It has to be the house, there is nowhere else." She smiled ruefully. "My brother, if you recall, was even less trusting than I."

"I could scarcely forget." Florence paused. "But is there a chance he would have left it in a box at the bank?"

"He had no box, as far as I can determine. I contacted the bank to confirm that."

"After his death." Florence nodded. "Very sensible."

"Actually, before." Heat washed up Gabriella's face. "When his letters began to ramble, it seemed like a good idea to find the impression. I should have known better. Enrico barely trusted the bank with his money." *My money.* "Did you have any idea how much money we had?"

"Not at all." Florence sniffed. "I certainly would have asked for an increase in my wages if I had so much as suspected I wasn't employed by an archeologist who could barely pay his mortgage, but by a treasure hunter with an impressive fortune. He never said a word," she added under her breath. "Your brother was a man of many secrets."

"Yes, I know."

Florence paused for a long moment as if considering her words. "On those rare occasions when he was in London, he and I would frequently have long talks. Sometimes we would talk about you or occasionally about the politics inherent in dealing with museums or the Antiquities Society, but usually we talked about his life, his work. About things he had done or seen in his quest for artifacts. I think I was the only one he could talk to about such things. He had few friends, you know, and few he could confide in. Indeed, there were times when I thought of myself as his father confessor." She drew a deep breath. "There was even a moment once, long ago, when I fancied myself in love with him."

Gabriella stared. "Did you?"

Florence smiled. "As I said, it was a moment and not much more than that. I was wise enough not to lose my heart to a man like your brother."

Florence didn't say it, but then it wasn't necessary to say it aloud. Enrico had a passion for women of all sorts. Even when she was a child there was often a women in his room or his tent. They seemed as necessary to his existence as food and drink. It wasn't until years later that she had understood his behavior in regards to women was not that of an honorable man.

"If anything, your brother and I were friends of a sort. As he had charged me with your care, I believe he felt I was worthy of his trust, although he trusted people even less than you do. I believe it was only his excitement about the seal that led him to ignore his usual guarded nature in such matters and show the impression to the men you now suspect of involvement in its theft."

"I do trust you," Gabriella said firmly. "And I need your help."

"Oh?"

"A prolonged absence from the Harrington household on any given day would surely arouse suspicion. I am only here now because Nathanial, in his arrogance, put me in his carriage, ordered the driver to return me to his house, and assumed I would do so."

"Foolish man," Florence murmured.

Gabriella ignored her. "I need you to search the house. Every nook, every cranny." She got to her feet and resumed pacing. "The impression has to be here. This is the only place it could possibly be."

"It's not an especially big house, Gabriella, but I imagine there are any number of hiding places. If it is here, it might well be impossible to find. However, I shall enlist Miriam's help and we shall do our best." She studied Gabriella thoughtfully. "But why on earth did you say you had it when you didn't?"

"I don't know." Gabriella sighed and brushed an errant stand of hair away from her face. "I needed a way to prove the seal, once found, was Enrico's. The words just seemed to come out of my mouth of their own accord."

"That's the problem with deceit, dear. The first lie is awkward, difficult, and often carries a great deal of guilt. The second is a bit easier, the third easier yet. And eventually . . . " Florence's knowing gaze met Gabriella's. " . . . deceit becomes far easier than truth."

Gabriella crossed her arms over her chest in an effort to disguise her unease. Indeed, the lie about possessing the impression had been remarkably easy, without thought or guilt. "I shall not let that happen."

Florence's cast her a skeptical look.

"I won't," Gabriella said firmly, resolving to at least try. "I have always been an honest sort, it's just that now . . . well, honesty is somewhat awkward."

"It always is, Gabriella." Florence shook her head. "Do remember the ends do not always justify the means."

"You needn't keep saying that."

"Oh but I do. At least until you understand its meaning as more than just a saying embroidered on a pillow." Florence heaved a long suffering sigh. "You come by it naturally, I'm afraid, your brother never understood it."

Gabriella narrowed her eyes in confusion. "What do you mean?"

"Simply what I said. For your brother it was the acquisition that counted, not the method by which it was acquired."

"I don't understand."

"Nor do you need to," Florence said in a firm manner, then deftly changed the subject. "Now, will you wear your new gown to the ball?"

The same gown she had worn to Lady Regina's ball. "I don't particularly wish to go."

"Nonetheless, Mr. Harrington is right. You have nothing to be ashamed of and nothing to hide. My dear, you have gone to that ball for a good six years that I can recall, and as you will be in the company of the Harrington family, there is no reason for you not to go this year."

"But last year . . . " Last year the ball had been glorious. Enrico was excited about presenting his seal to the committee; she had been confident that she could at last convince him to take her with him, and she'd had no end of eager partners. This year . . .

This year there would be Nathanial.

"And should you need another friendly face—"

"Which reminds me," Gabriella interrupted. "I was not at all pleased to see Xerxes—or John, as he is now known at Harrington House. I gather that was the plan you mentioned?"

"Not quite as deceitful as yours, but then I have not had as much practice nor do I seem to have the natural gift for it that you do." Florence fixed her with a firm look. "I am only grateful this tendency of yours did not surface in your younger days."

"It does seem to be recent," Gabriella murmured. She couldn't very well deny it, as much as she might wish to. No, the lies and deceptions did seem to be piling up, although soon there would be no more need for them.

The rules of the Verification Committee were both clear and unyielding. Once an artifact had been presented and ruled on unfavorably, the presenter had only until the end of the next year's meeting to challenge that decision. Last year the committee had decided that Enrico's claim was not legitimate; that the seal he had was not the one for which he presented evidence was considered irrelevant. Only extraordinary circumstances could prompt a reopening of a case after the time limit had passed, and Gabriella knew of few instances where that happened. The committee did not like to reverse itself or admit mistake. No, she had a sure and certain conviction, in her heart, that if the seal wasn't recovered this year for this meeting of the Verification Committee, it never would be. Her chance to restore her brother's good name would be lost forever.

"How do you think Mr. Harrington will respond when he learns of your deceptions?" Florence asked.

"He will understand the necessity of my actions," Gabriella said with a confidence she didn't quite feel. What if he didn't understand? What if her actions disgusted him? Her stomach lurched at the thought that she might lose him. Not that she had him or wanted him or that he mattered at all.

Florence considered her in an assessing manner, as if she knew exactly what Gabriella was thinking. It was—it always was—most unnerving.

Still, Gabriella should at least be honest with herself, if with no one else. In spite of Nathanial's arrogance, the way he seemed to have taken over her life, she had to admit he was indeed beginning to matter. Quite a lot. She was not looking forward to telling him all the truths about herself, all her secrets. When he knew everything . . . She firmly set the thought aside. Now was not the time to dwell on what might—what would—happen then.

"As I was saying, I shall be at the ball as well." Florence glanced at a large bouquet of roses in a vase on a side table that Gabriella had noted but to which she'd paid no attention until now. "Mr. Dennison has invited me to join his sister and her husband's party. They shall accompany me to the ball and I shall see him there."

Gabriella raised a brow. "I gather the invitation came with flowers?"

"No. Mr. Dennison came with flowers." Florence smiled in a decidedly smug manner. "Yesterday evening."

"Oh?"

"We had a lovely chat." A dreamy look drifted across the older woman's face. Gabriella realized that Florence was really quite lovely. She wasn't sure why she'd never noticed before. Florence shook her head as if to clear away thoughts of the dashing Mr. Dennison. "Now then, I will see you at the ball."

"Yes, I suppose." Gabriella sighed and again sank down beside Florence. "Still, the society, those people, treated my brother like—"

"Like a man who made claims he could not substantiate." Florence's voice was surprisingly hard. "Like a man who then behaved like a madman and blamed the very people he hoped to win over for his loss."

"He wasn't mad," Gabriella said quickly

"No dear, just obsessed." Florence studied her closely. "Much as you are with finding the seal."

"I'm not obsessed. It's simply something that is left undone." She drew a calming breath. "It seems to me when one dies, one's loose ends should be tied up."

Florence shook her head. "Life is scarcely as tidy as that. Nor is death."

"Pity it can't be more tidy. More certain, if you will."

"The only thing certain about death is that it is inevitable. As for life . . . " Florence smiled. "I consider its very uncertainty one of the best things about life. One never knows what might happen."

"For the worst, no doubt," Gabriella said darkly.

Florence laughed. "Or for the best. Usually when one least expects it."

"Are you talking about Mr. Dennison?"

"I don't know, Gabriella." Again Florence's eyes took on a far off look. "I rather hope so." Her gaze met Gabriella's. "But then, my dear girl, what would become of you?"

"Of me?" Gabriella laughed. "You needn't worry about me. I shall always have Xerxes and Miriam."

Regardless of her words, she couldn't help but wonder what indeed would become of her. With Enrico's death, any chance she had for the kind of life she'd wanted to lead had vanished. And once the seal was found, she really had no more purpose to her life.

Would she spend the rest of her days poring over old books in the society's library, storing knowledge that she would never put to practical use? Would she grow old in this house, alone save for those who, while more family than servant, still had each other?

"Perhaps a husband," Florence said under her breath.

Gabriella smiled. "I don't think I'm suited for marriage."

"We shall see. Regardless, you shall always have me," Florence said firmly. "Unless of course your Mr. Harrington—"

"He's not my Mr. Harrington." A firm note sounded in Gabriella's voice. "And he never can be."

She ignored the persistent voice murmuring in the back of her head.

But oh, wouldn't she like him to be?

Eleven

They were plying her for information, that's what they were doing.

Nate gritted his teeth and resisted the urge to wring the neck of very nearly every member of his family. Oh, they were subtle enough, if one didn't know them. If one did, their intentions were obvious, and given the nature of their casual inquires, one might have thought they had a coordinated plan of attack. They had attempted it before, but tonight, somehow, they seemed more determined. He ignored the inconvenient fact that only this afternoon he had employed a firm to do very much the same thing, to find out more about Gabriella Montini.

"And you have lived in London, then, for nine years now?" Sterling sipped his wine in an offhand manner.

Gabriella nodded. "It was thought London would be best for my studies. Even though he was by birth Italian, Enrico preferred London, which was sensible given the Antiquities Society, the universities, and museums here." She shrugged. "London had become home for him, as much as anyplace could."

"London is the center of all things stolen," Quint said with a wry smile. "We have been spiriting antiquities away from their countries of origin for generations."

Sterling cast him a chastising look. "It has never bothered you before."

"And it doesn't bother me now." Quint lifted his glass to his brother. "In fact, I should drink most happily to the arrogance of those modern seats of civilization. And not just London, but Paris and Berlin and Vienna, as well as to all the museums and institutions and private collectors who believe the ancient treasures of any country are better off in our care than in their place of origin. And as they are all willing to pay nicely to acquire more, my dear sanctimonious brother, it doesn't bother me in the least."

"That is a discussion for another time." His mother's firm gaze slipped from Quinton to Sterling and then to Nate, no doubt simply for good measure, as he had yet to join in. "I do not wish to open that particular kettle of fish tonight."

It was a ongoing debate within the Harrington household, as well as among scholars and, God help them all, politicians, and it was certainly not new. The continuing question as to whether the treasures of antiquity should be saved by foreigners spiriting away artifacts to institutions far from their point of origin or whether such activity constituted theft of a nation's heritage had been a topic in this house for as long as Nate could remember.

Influenced by intellectual scholarly articles or something as simple as a conversation on a train, current members of the family switched sides of the debate nearly as often as it lifted its head. All except Reggie, of course, who thought it was dreadfully boring and couldn't they talk about something else for a change? Mother had often said the ease with which they all changed their minds and the passion with which they then pursued their new positions had nothing to do with the issue itself, but with their love of a good argument.

Better to argue about something they could do little about, Nate thought, rather than Sterling's continuing failure to find a new wife, or Quint's disregard for anything that smacked of proper behavior, or his own . . . well, whichever flaw of his was uppermost in the others' minds at the moment.

Mother turned to Gabriella. "This particular discussion has been raging in this household for generations."

"A philosophical matter of debate." Regina rolled her gaze toward the ceiling. "That's what they call it."

Mother cast her a chastising look, then continued. "My late husband, Charles, said even in his own childhood the question of Britain's possession of the Elgin marbles had been a subject of heated debate around this very table."

"Said discussion no doubt prompted by our great-grandparents' search for lost gold in Egypt." Nate leaned toward Gabriella. "As we understand it, it was quite an adventure, with kidnappings and murderous suitors and that sort of thing."

"It sounds most exciting," she murmured.

Nate wasn't sure if she was bored by his family's less than perfectly proper demeanor at the dinner table or overwhelmed. It would not have surprised him. Aside from her brothers, she was apparently alone in the world.

"Regardless," Quint continued, returning to the topic at hand, "one would think if countries were truly concerned about the loss of their artifacts, they would make it more difficult to spirit them across borders. Hire civil servants perhaps who did not see bribery as an expected portion of their incomes."

Mother winced. "That is a problem."

"It's simply the way things work in much of the world," Nate said. "A necessary evil, if you will."

Gabriella choked back what sounded like a gasp but was probably just a cough.

"But rest assured, Mother," Quint said. "Nate is keeping me within the confines of legality as well as upright behavior."

"And I am most grateful to him," she replied. "It eases my mind to know that your brother is watching you."

Nate scoffed. "I scarcely watch him, Mother."

"Watch over him then," she continued. "I know Quinton is the older brother and should be the one watching over you—"

Quint cast her his most unrepentant grin.

"—but his nature is not conducive to responsibility of that sort."

Quinton laughed. "Or responsibility of any sort."

She fixed her middle son with a firm look. "I am confident that will change someday."

Reggie snorted in a most unladylike manner.

Mother sighed. "I had once thought my youngest sons would become scholars like their father."

"Like Father?" Sterling smiled. "Father was scarcely more than an amateur scholar, Mother. And there was no one more delighted than he when Quinton first abandoned the path of scholarly pursuit to accompany

Professor Ashworth on his journeys. And delighted too when Nathanial joined him."

"It was the adventure, you understand," his mother said to Gabriella. "I suspect my husband always rather longed for adventure. It was different, you know, in the past. Charles grew up on stories of the Earls of Wyldewood and their exploits." She glanced at Sterling in a speculative manner. "Today, the earl has little opportunity to chase smugglers or battle pirates or rescue fair maidens."

"However, I keep myself busy," Sterling said mildly.

His mother considered her two youngest sons. "At best, this is a questionable business you are engaged in. And, I suspect, often dangerous and certainly disreputable on occasion."

"Can't be helped, Mother," Nate said.

"It certainly has its moments." Quint chuckled and turned toward Gabriella. "That's something your brother no doubt well understood, Miss Montini."

Nate would have kicked him under the table if he could have reached. The last thing he wanted was a discussion of Enrico Montini.

"I beg your pardon?" she said.

"He understood that there was a fine line between a discovery and a theft. A lauded archeologist or a thief." Quint shrugged. "Enrico Montini was certainly not above doing whatever was necessary to acquire what he wanted. He understood that deceit, illegalities, ignoring moral standards, and so forth are often necessary to achieve the ultimate goal."

"In that we all understand as much," Nate said quickly, and cast his brother a warning glance, "that's what he meant."

"Yes." Quint took a sip of his wine. "That's what I meant."

"Has there been any word from your brother, Gabriella?" His mother turned to Gabriella, thankfully changing the subject. "The one Nathanial met in Egypt. What was his name?"

"Antonio," Gabriella said.

"Ah." Mother nodded. "Named for your father then."

"Yes and no, I have not heard from him. But he has never been good about that sort of thing."

"Perhaps tomorrow we can talk about your mother." Mother smiled. "And her family."

"Lady Wyldewood, while I would like to know something of my mother, as I understand it, her family had no use for her, nor for me. Besides, I suspect we will be rather busy for the next few days." Gabriella's tone was polite, but Nate had the distinct impression she wished to avoid that particular chat. "What with our plans and the ball."

"I should have thought of that." His mother looked at her youngest sons. "As you are in London this year, I shall expect you both to attend."

"Wouldn't miss it," Quint said under his breath.

"Come now, Quinton, it's quite exciting," Sterling said in a wry manner. "Upward of six hundred people all discussing the newly excavated ruins of somewhere or other. Most enjoyable."

"It's an obligation, Sterling, as you well know. As a board member and as benefactors of the society it is our duty to make an appearance," Mother said firmly and directed her words to Gabriella. "My oldest son is not overly fond of events like this."

Sterling grimaced.

"In deference to him, we rarely stay very long."

"This year we shall stay longer," Reggie announced. Sterling cast her an annoyed glance. "Well, it's a ball. A grand ball, and I am quite looking forward to it."

"I have always enjoyed the Antiquities Society Ball," Gabriella said with a smile. "My brother and I and Miss Henry have attended every year since I have been old enough to do so."

"Have you? And yet I have never noticed you." His mother winced. "Forgive me, that sounded dreadful."

Gabriella laughed. "Not at all, Lady Wyldewood. The ball is a huge crush, and as you don't stay very long, it's not at all surprising that our paths have never crossed."

"Every year, hmm. Imagine that. And right under my very nose." Mother studied Gabriella thoughtfully. "We shall save our talk about your mother for another time, then. A few more days will scarcely matter."

Gabriella smiled. "I shall look forward to it."

The remainder of the meal was uneventful, and the feeling Nate had had earlier—that his family was trying to glean information from Gabriella—did not recur. Dinner concluded without major incidents, disclosure, or arguments. The ladies retired for the evening, leaving Nate to follow his brothers onto the back terrace for cigars.

The moment they stepped through the doors, Nate turned to Quint.

"What on earth were you thinking?"

"I probably wasn't." Quint took a cigar from the humidor Andrews placed on a table on the terrace every evening. Cigar smoke was not allowed in the house when Mother was in residence. "What, precisely, are you talking about?"

"I'm talking about your comments about Enrico Montini."

Quint trimmed his cigar. "Why shouldn't we talk about Montini?"

"Because I don't think Miss Montini is aware of the type of man he was."

Sterling selected a cigar. "What kind of man was he?"

"Montini was . . . " Nate chose his words with care. "Not well liked."

"He was cold, callous," Quint said, lighting his cigar. "Merciless, as it were, when it came to acquiring what he wanted. My reputation may have once—"

Nate snorted.

"—been 'questionable,' but no one has ever suspected me of resorting to whatever means possible to get what I wanted."

"Whatever means possible?" Sterling said slowly.

Quint nodded, a grim look in his eye. "If this seal was stolen from anyone else, and the alleged owner were dead, Montini would be at the top of my list as a suspect. For theft and murder."

Sterling studied his youngest brother. "Why do you think she isn't aware of her brother's nature?"

"I don't know." Nate plucked a cigar from the humidor. "There's something about the way she talks about him. She adored him—idolized him, I think—and she will do whatever necessary to restore his professional reputation." He shook his head. "I can't imagine she would feel the same if she knew the type of man he was."

"And yet we don't know she isn't exactly like him," Sterling said mildly, lighting his own cigar.

"She isn't the least bit like him," Nate said staunchly.

Quint and Sterling traded glances. Sterling chose his words with care. "Still, we really know nothing about her."

"Mother knew her mother," Nate said quickly, ignoring the fact that he had already come to the same conclusion and was taking steps to learn more about the intriguing stranger in their midst.

Quint lit Nate's cigar. "And yet Mother has said nothing more about that. Don't you find that odd?"

"She is up to something." Sterling's eyes narrowed. "She has been preoccupied since Miss Montini arrived. And she studies her with a look in her eye that is most curious."

"As interesting as that is, it's of no concern at the moment," Nate said firmly. "I would prefer, and request, that there be no more discussion of Miss Montini's brother in her presence."

Quint leaned against the terrace balustrade and blew a perfect smoke ring. "You honestly believe she doesn't know what kind of man her brother was?"

"I do." Nate ignored the niggling thought that he might be wrong. He might be wrong regarding any number of things about the lovely Gabriella. There was a reserve around her that she carried like a shield. Even so, there was something about the woman that called to something deep inside him. From the moment he met her, he had the oddest feeling of inevitability, of anticipation perhaps. The vague sense that something extraordinary and unique and wonderful had stepped into his life. It was an absurd idea with nothing whatsoever to base it on save the ridiculous feeling that washed through him when he so much as thought of her.

There was lust, of course. With the fire in her blue eyes and the fervor to right what she considered a grievous wrong, one couldn't help but wonder what other passions might lie just beneath the surface. He had known lust before, but this was tempered with something as yet unknown. And whereas she would do whatever she had to do to recover the seal, he would do whatever necessary to protect her from harm. Besides, he had given his word.

"It scarcely matters, the man is dead now and we have promised to help her." Nate pinned Quint with a hard look. "The lady has been through a lot this past year. I do not wish to upset her further by discussion of her brother's character."

"Or lack of it," Quint muttered.

"I do have to wonder, though . . . " Sterling blew a stream of blue smoke then met his youngest brother's gaze. " . . . why you are so vehement about this. You scarcely know the woman."

"I was wondering the very same thing." Quint studied Nate, then snorted back a laugh. "You want her! I should have known."

Nate's jaw clenched. "That's enough, Quint."

"You devil." Quint grinned "You want her in your bed."

"I—" Quint had done this to him most of his life. Bait him until he inevitably blurted out whatever truth he was trying to conceal. He had long ago learned there was only one way to handle Quint's teasing. He forced a wicked grin to his face. "Wouldn't you?"

"No, not at all." Quint shook his head. "She's pretty

enough, with those deep blue eyes of hers and that luscious figure and that seductive hint of an accent—"

Nate narrowed his eyes.

"—but she's too bloody damn smart for me. God save me from an intelligent woman. She'd do for you, though." Quint's eyes widened. "Good God you don't just want her—you like her!"

"She's very . . . nice." Nate tried and failed to hide the defensive note in his voice. "She's quite easy to like."

"Really?" Sterling murmured. "I haven't found her particularly easy to like."

"I have spent a great deal of time with her," Nate said. "I have come to know her better than anyone else."

"She's stubborn and independent and has a streak of larceny in her," Quint said. "No man in his right mind would 'like' her." He laughed. "Want her, definitely, but not like her."

"And yet I do," Nate said defiantly, and glanced at Sterling. "You don't think it's too fast, do you? To like her, that is?"

"Admittedly, you still know little about her." Sterling puffed on his cigar thoughtfully. "So yes, in a rational sense it may well be too soon. However, I suspect rational thought has little influence here. I would, however, be cautious if I were you until you know more."

"I would say it all depends on what you have in mind." Quint studied his younger brother. "Seduction and a short but passionate affair is one thing. I know you are familiar with that concept."

Nate gestured with his cigar. "Go on."

"It's quite another if you have in mind something that will last the rest of your life."

Sterling scoffed. "Nonsense."

Nate nodded, the oddest sinking sensation settling around his heart. His brothers were right, of course. "And it's entirely too soon for that."

"In my opinion . . . " Quint paused for a moment. " . . . it's just the opposite."

Sterling stared. "You can't mean that."

"Oh, but I do." Quint nodded. "I have long suspected that if I ever meet the right woman, a woman I would be content to spend the rest of my days with, I will be struck with the certain knowledge that she is right with the efficiency and speed of a bolt of lightning." He met Sterling's gaze. "You know what I mean."

Sterling paused, then nodded.

Abruptly, Quint grinned. "Although I admit it is a somewhat trite and overly romantic idea."

"And unbelievable as well, given its source," Sterling said.

Quint shrugged.

"Take care, little brother." Sterling's gaze met Nate's. "Miss Montini might not be as you see her."

"But then again she might be." Quint blew another smoke ring. "And if so, yes, I think she'd do nicely for you."

"Well, I'm not looking for anyone to do for me," Nate said quickly. "Not at the moment."

"Of course not," Sterling said without an ounce of conviction, and changed the subject. "Have you noticed, by the way, the number of bouquets that have arrived for Reggie in recent days?"

Quint chuckled. "She has certainly made an impression on the eligible young men of society. Still, I suspect Reggie is in no hurry to select a husband. Although I suppose we—and when I say 'we,' I really mean Sterling—should keep a close eye . . . "

The conversation between the brothers droned on until late in the night. Nate told them what little he and Gabriella had thus far uncovered. Usually, they would have joined the ladies when they had finished their cigars. Tonight, however, Mother had said she wished to retire early, and both Gabriella and Reggie had taken that as their cue to do the same. Regretfully so. He had hoped to again escort Gabriella to her room.

In spite of the absorbing nature of the discussion, ranging from Reggie's potential suitors to the current state of politics to the latest scandals, his thoughts returned again and again to Quint's comments about knowing the right woman at once when she came along. He couldn't help but wonder if—as odd as it might seem at first glance, and given the unusual circumstances they found themselves in—Gabriella might well be the right woman for him.

Or if she was very, very wrong.

Twelve

G abriella perched nervously on the edge of a red
velvet sofa. Nathanial stood beside the fireplace
looking substantially less apprehensive than she
felt. And why not? He at least knew Lady Rathbourne.

The parlor they had been shown into was, if possible,
even more elegant than the Harringtons'. Whereas their
home had a feeling of warmth to it, this house seemed
cold and unwelcoming. The parlor was perfectly ap-
pointed, in the height of fashion, but it struck her as
rather more like a stage setting than a place where
living people resided. It was far and away too, well,
perfect. The temperature was warm, but a chill shot
through her.

"Nathanial Harrington." A tall woman glided into
the room and held her hand out to Nathanial. "You
were just a boy when last I saw you."

He chuckled and raised her hand to his lips. "Lady
Rathbourne, you are as beautiful as ever."

She was indeed beautiful, startlingly so. Lady Rathbourne might well have been the loveliest creature Gab-

riella ever seen. She was nearly as tall as Nate, her blond hair meticulously styled, an air of grace and elegance lingering about her. Her gown was in shades of red, the latest in French fashion, and Gabriella had the most absurd feeling that it had been selected to compliment the room.

"Am I?" Lady Rathbourne tilted her head in a manner that might have appeared artificial with anyone else yet was completely natural to her, and studied Nate. "How very kind of you to say so."

Lady Rathbourne was, all in all, perfect. Gabriella didn't like her one bit, and liked even less the way she stared into Nathanial's eyes and held onto his hand. Gabriella rose to her feet and, although she'd never considered herself clumsy, wished she could have done so with a bit more grace.

"Not at all," Nathanial said in a gallant manner. "You have not changed one bit. You are exactly as I remember you."

"Well, you have most definitely changed. You have become quite charming, no doubt dangerously so." Lady Rathbourne studied him for a moment. "You are very nearly a foot taller than when we last we met. Indeed, the boy I remember has become quite a handsome man. You very much resemble . . . " A shadow crossed her face so quickly Gabriella thought she might have been mistaken, "And how is that rascal of a brother of yours, Quinton?"

Nathanial smiled. "Quinton too does not change."

"And . . . the rest of the family? Your mother and Regina? Regina must be grown as well."

"And just launched upon the seas of society." Nathanial shook his head. "One must fear for those hapless unmarried men who have not been forewarned."

"I can well imagine." Lady Rathbourne laughed. It struck Gabriella very much like a laugh not well used, but then this room too seemed like a place that had heard little laughter.

She cleared her throat softly.

"And this is?" Lady Rathbourne smiled at her.

"My apologies," Nathanial said quickly. "Lady Rathbourne—"

"You used to call me Olivia," she chided.

"I was an impertinent scamp." Nathanial grinned. "Olivia, allow me to introduce Miss Gabriella Montini."

Gabriella nodded. "A pleasure to meet you, Lady Rathbourne."

"Do call me Olivia." To Gabriella's surprise, genuine warmth colored the lady's green eyes, warmth at odds with the surroundings. At once she decided that she liked Lady Rathbourne after all. "I don't receive many callers, especially not old friends. I have known Nathanial's family for much of my life, although I have not seen any of them for some time." She waved at the sofa. "Please sit down. I have requested tea for us, it should be here any moment."

"Thank you." Gabriella retook her seat on the sofa. In this room, with this woman, her serviceable blue gown and practical hat seemed both out of place and rather shabby. In the back of her mind she resolved to purchase some new clothes.

Olivia joined her on the sofa and waved Nathanial to a nearby chair. "Now then, your note said you had a matter of some importance to discuss."

"Yes, that." He looked a shade uneasy. "It's a long

story and I'm not sure you can actually be of help. Still, because I knew you . . ."

Olivia raised an amused brow. "Yes?"

"Perhaps I should explain," Gabriella said quickly.

Nathanial nodded with obvious relief.

"Lady Rathbourne—Olivia," Gabriella began. "My brother was an archeologist who discovered a rare, ancient cylinder seal. A seal that made reference to the lost city of Ambropia, the first such reference ever found. But the seal was stolen from him, and while searching for it he died."

"Oh dear," Olivia murmured. "My condolences."

"Thank you." Gabriella drew a deep breath. "Now it is up to me to recover the seal and prove it was his discovery. I intend to donate it to the Antiquities Society, and we have been authorized by the society to use its name in our queries."

"The Antiquities Society? How very prestigious."

Gabriella nodded and winced to herself. Authorized was perhaps not entirely accurate.

Olivia drew her brows together. "And how can I can be of help?"

"One of those my brother suspected of taking the seal was a man named Javier Gutierrez." Gabriella paused. How did one accuse a woman's husband of theft and possibly worse? "He apparently often acted as an agent in the gathering of antiquities for Lord Rathbourne."

"I see," Olivia said coolly, the warmth of her demeanor abruptly gone.

A maid entered bearing a tray with tea and biscuits. Olivia waited until the maid had left the room to continue.

"As much as I wish otherwise, I'm afraid I can't help

you." She poured a cup for Gabriella, handed it to her, then poured one for Nathanial. "I know little about my husband's activities in regards to his collections."

"Olivia." Nathanial leaned forward eagerly. "We were hoping that you might know if he had come into possession of such a seal. If he might have mentioned something that might help us. Or if you had noticed a new acquisition to his collections or—"

"My dear Nathanial." Olivia filled her own cup, her tone offhand, as if she were discussing nothing of particular importance. "I do not share my husband's passion for such things. He never discusses his acquisitions with me and I would not know a seal such as the one you are looking for if it were to sprout legs and walk into the room. Beyond that . . . " The warmth in her eyes had now vanished along with her demeanor, replaced by something hard and resolute. "My husband collects for the joy of acquiring. He particularly enjoys besting another collector or, better yet, a museum or institution. It is something of a game for him, and his fortune is such that he can demand nothing less than total victory, regardless of cost.

"He is not a man to be trifled with." The vague hint of a warning sounded in her voice. "I would permit you to view his collections, to determine if indeed what you seek is there, but that's impossible. His acquisitions— be they of art or sculpture or antiquities—are displayed in a locked room for his eyes alone. I do not have access to them nor do I wish to." She sipped her tea. "I have not seen most of what he has accumulated and I have no interest in doing so. It is, as I said, not something we share."

Disappointment washed through Gabriella at her

words. And more, the oddest feeling of sympathy for this beautiful woman who would appear to have everything yet seemed as well to have nothing. "I see."

"As for your Mr. Gutierrez . . . " Olivia shook her head. "The name is not familiar. I would be surprised if it was. I never meet anyone who has a business arrangement of any sort with Lord Rathbourne. However . . . " She paused. " . . . I would certainly not be surprised to learn that he and my husband were involved in something, shall we say, less than above-board. If this seal is as rare as you say, it is exactly the type of item that would indeed arouse Lord Rathbourne's desire." She shrugged. "His fine hand in this incident would not be unexpected."

"But you don't know," Nathanial said.

"No, I am sorry. And I would not ask him." Olivia hesitated as if choosing her words. "Lord Rathbourne and I essentially live separate lives. Occasionally I appear with him at social events, but for the most part we rarely even share the same dwelling." She smiled at Nathanial. "I say this only because we are old friends and I cannot remember the last time I have had a visit from an old friend. I have always been sentimental about such things and fear I am becoming more so with every passing year."

"I'm sure my mother would enjoy it very much if you were to call on her."

"That's not possible," she said simply. "Nathanial." Her gaze pinned his. "I trust the confidences I have shared with you will go no farther than the three of us?"

"Of course not." Nathanial nodded

"Do I have your word on that?"

"You do."

She glanced at Gabriella, who nodded her agreement as well.

Olivia smiled. "Thank you both. Your discretion is most appreciated."

"Will we see you at the Antiquities Society Ball?" Gabriella said impulsively.

"I'm afraid not. I rarely attend such events in London. I prefer to spend most of my time in the country. When I'm in London, I tend to be something of a recluse." She smiled, but this time it did not reach her eyes. "Someday, in my dotage, I suspect I will be called eccentric. Oh dear." She cast Gabriella a rueful glance. "My future sounds dreadful. I shall be an eccentric as well as a sentimental doddering old creature."

"Never," Gabriella said staunchly.

"You are too kind." Olivia directed her attention back to Nathanial, her tone brisk. "Now, do tell me more of your mother. She had any number of charitable pursuits, if I recall."

They chatted for a few minutes about Lady Wyldewood and Regina, about Nathanial's and Quinton's adventures. Gabriella noted Olivia never asked about Lord Wyldewood nor did Nathanial bring up his oldest brother's name.

A quarter of an hour later they took their leave and settled in the carriage they'd had wait for them, Nathanial sitting on the seat beside her rather than across from her. At her insistence, they'd dispensed with the ever-present maid. It seemed wise, given the nature of their mission. It was most improper and really quite nice.

He blew a long breath. "That was worthless."

"I suppose it was." She shrugged. "Still, we do know the seal is something that would arouse Lord Rathbourne's interest. So we have not eliminated Gutierrez. And we know his lordship's collections are kept in a locked room in the house."

Nathanial raised a brow. "So that if we break in we will know where to look?"

"Don't be absurd." She scoffed. "We don't know where the room is. And as we should have to break in at night, we'd spend most of our time stumbling about in the dark looking for—" She caught Nathanial's grin and sighed. "You're teasing me, aren't you?"

"Yes, I am." His grin widened. "It's the most fun I've had today."

"I'm glad I can provide you with some amusement." She huffed and settled back against the worn leather seat. "I daresay Lady Rathbourne has few amusements."

"You noticed that, did you?"

"It was hard not to."

"Mother says she's rarely seen in public." Nathanial shook his head. "She used to be quite a social creature."

"She said she has known your family for a long time."

He nodded. "Her father's country estate borders ours. Although she and Sterling had known each other most of their lives, it was a casual acquaintance, not at all significant. As I remember, they did not fall in love until she was out in society and they ran into one another at a ball in London. It was as if they had never met before. If you recall, I told you that my family assumed they would marry, but then, abruptly, they were no longer seeing one another, and almost at once she married Lord Rathbourne.

"She is as lovely today as she was then." He paused. "But today, she looked like a woman afraid."

"Not at all." Gabriella shook her head. "She looked

like a woman resigned. She seems as much a possession as anything else her husband has collected."

"I noticed that as well," he murmured.

"In spite of her obvious strength, she seemed very sad to me. She is not happy with the choices she has made in her life."

"And yet they were her choices."

"As far as you know."

He paused, then nodded. "As far as I know."

"What if they weren't?" Gabriella said slowly. "Her choices, I mean."

"It scarcely matters now and we will probably never know." Nathanial sighed. "We all thought she was the love of Sterling's life. That they were fated to be together—soul mates, if you will. But she shattered his heart. I have always thought the speed with which he married Alice was a direct result of that."

Gabriella hesitated. "Perhaps he should know."

"Who should know what?"

"Your brother, the earl. Perhaps he should know how unhappy she is."

Nathanial turned to her, disbelief in his eyes. "Are you mad?"

"Possibly," she murmured.

"What good would that do? For good or ill she has made her choice. She is married and he has gone on with his life. There is nothing to be done about it."

"Still." An odd wistful note sounded in her voice. "It does seem a shame."

Nathanial narrowed his eyes suspiciously. "What?"

"That one might find the love of one's life, one's soul mate, and lose him because of circumstances."

"She lost him because she chose to marry the man

who had the biggest fortune." Nathanial shrugged. "One could argue if she was willing to make such a choice, she could not have been the love of his life after all."

"One could argue as well that one suitor having more money than another is a circumstance." Gabriella had no idea why she was arguing the point at all, why she cared, and yet she did. "Do you think there are such things as soul mates? As two people who are fated to be together against all odds?"

He looked into her eyes in a firm manner. "Yes."

"As strictly a . . . a . . . " She thought for a moment. " . . . a philosophical matter of debate, mind you . . . What if they are from completely different backgrounds?"

"It's of no concern."

"What if they don't trust one another?"

"They need to learn to do so. Leaps of faith and that sort of thing."

"What if one has a large, boisterous family, traditions, and heritage, and the other has no family whatsoever?"

He smiled. "A large, boisterous family very nearly always welcomes an additional member."

"What if she isn't what he thinks she is?" She gazed into his eyes. "What if she can't be what he needs? What he deserves? What he wants?"

His voice was low, measured, and fraught with meaning. His words a statement as much as a question. "What if she already is?"

Her breath caught. Sheer panic warred with the most wonderful feeling of surrender within her.

She swallowed hard. "It was a philosophical matter of debate, Nathanial, nothing more."

"I know." He pulled her into his arms. "Everyone in my family loves a good debate."

"This is not a good idea."

"And I thought it was an excellent idea," he murmured, his lips against the side of her neck.

"Well, that is . . . indeed . . . " Shivers skated down her spine. " . . . excellent."

"I thought so." He angled his mouth over hers, and she lost herself in his kiss. Her mouth tentatively opened to his and his tongue met hers. Desire and need exploded within her and she clung to him. Sensation swept through her, and her toes curled in her sensible shoes.

The most scandalous thought occurred to her. Why not enjoy Nathanial's touch? Why not surrender to him? She had no idea if he was her soul mate, she wasn't even sure she believed in such nonsense. But she did know he made her feel things she had never suspected she could feel. Made her want things she could never have. And she knew as well that Nathanial Harrington, the youngest brother of the Earl of Wyldewood, would never marry Gabriella Montini, who had no family or position and was, in fact, with her brother's death, no one and nothing of note. Even if he could overlook all else, there was one thing he could not overlook. No honorable man could. If she had learned nothing else in her years in England she had learned this. There was no future in his arms.

And when he knew all her secrets, he would know that as well. Her heart would be left broken and she would be alone. Better to stop thinking, hoping, *wanting*, now—before it was too late.

The carriage drew to a stop and she pushed out of his embrace.

"We're here." She scrambled out without waiting for his assistance.

"Yes, I was aware of that." He chuckled, climbed out of the carriage and ambled after her. "Unfortunately."

She turned to him and squared her shoulders. "That cannot happen again. There will be no more kisses shared in carriages or in libraries or at the door to my room."

"I haven't kissed you at the door to your room."

"But you've thought about it."

"Indeed, I have." He grinned in an unrepentant manner. "I find I have a hard time thinking about anything but kissing you."

"It has to stop," she said firmly. "All of it."

His grin widened. "I don't see why."

"No." She steeled her resolve against the need to throw herself back into his arms and forced a collected note to her voice. "I don't suppose you do."

Gabriella turned and walked into the house, leaving him staring after her.

She acknowledged Xerxes standing by the door with a slight nod and ignored the questioning look in his eye. She didn't pause until she reached the sanctity of her room. Closing the door firmly behind her, she rested with her back against it and closed her eyes.

The meeting of the Verification Committee was fast approaching. Either they found the seal and restored Enrico's reputation or they failed and all was lost. Regardless, one way or the other, this would be over then. She would leave this house and this family and Nathanial forever.

The irony of it all hit her. She and Nathanial were

searching for a seal that might reveal the location of the lost city. After centuries it could well disclose the Virgin's Secret, which had been sought by so many for so long. The search had brought her to the one man she would be willing to give up everything for. But it was her own secret that would keep them forever apart.

Apart like the earl and Lady Rathbourne. Through circumstances and bad choices and life-changing decisions one had no say in.

And things that could never be undone.

Thirteen

*J*f I leave to fetch you some refreshment, will you be here when I return?" Nathanial smiled down at her and her heart fluttered.

Gabriella ignored it and favored him with an impersonal smile. "I don't know. I haven't decided yet."

She was in his arms, a waltz was playing, and she had already realized that in spite of her resolve not to encourage his affections—if indeed *affection* was what he harbored for her, and not simply lust—this was the best Antiquities Society Ball she had ever attended. The music was somehow richer tonight, the gowns of the ladies more exquisite, even the flickering gaslight that illuminated the society's ballroom cast an air of magic over the proceedings. In the apricot-colored gown she'd worn to Reggie's ball, she felt like a princess in a fairy tale. In truth, if she had been a more fanciful sort of woman the entire evening would have seemed enchanted.

He laughed and pulled her a bit closer than was proper. "I expect you to be here. I allowed you to vanish from a ball once before, I shall not allow you to do so again."

She raised a brow. "And how would you intend to stop me?"

He cast her a wicked grin.

Gabriella stared in annoyance. She had scarcely seen him at all since they'd returned from Lady Rathbourne's the day before yesterday. She'd begged off dinner one night, claiming a headache. Last night he and his brothers had gone to the earl's club. She heard them return late, more than a little inebriated, she suspected. Today she'd stayed in her room preparing for tonight's ball. No one seemed to think it odd that such a thing would take an entire day. At least no one mentioned it. Nathanial had not sought her out, which was at once a relief and more than a little maddening.

She had spent some of the last few days rereading her brother's letters. She remembered every word, as she always did, but still hoped to see them with a fresh eye. They were, of course, unchanged. The tone gradually shifting from the first to the last. From anger and rational determination to an almost giddy expectation of impending triumph and something rather less than sane. Rantings, actually, in the final letter.

"I want your promise that you will not vanish in the night," Nathanial said.

"Very well, then, I promise."

"Ah, but is it a promise I can trust?"

"Leaps of faith, Nathanial," she said wryly.

He laughed, and she cast him a reluctant smile. The man was incorrigible, his persistence very nearly irresistible. As was the way he held her and gazed into her eyes and made her feel as if they were alone in the ballroom, in the world, with nothing but the music and the magic.

She and Lady Wyldewood, the earl and his sister, had come tonight in a separate carriage from Nathanial and Quinton. She had not seen Nathanial until his arrival a quarter of an hour later. There was something about putting formal attire on a man used to living in the least formal of circumstances that would make the heart of even the most resistant woman skip a beat. And the look in his eye when he saw her had very nearly taken her breath away. She suspected, in her later years, the memory of that look would be like a flower pressed in a book. Something to take out on occasion and remember and savor. She thrust the thought aside, the fragile dried blossom crumbling to dust.

"You paid no attention whatsoever to what I told you, did you?" she said with a resigned sigh.

"That nonsense about not kissing you?" He shrugged. "Not really."

"Well, then heed my words now," she said firmly. Not being with him every minute had strengthened her resolve, but now that she was in his arms, she found it difficult to maintain her determination. Difficult to think of anything but the warmth of his body next to hers, and the hard feel of his shoulder beneath her hand, and the vague scent of something spicy and completely masculine. Nonetheless, she mentally shook her head to clear it. This was for the best. "I have decided from this moment on we should keep our relationship on a strictly professional level. We should be colleagues, if you will."

"Colleagues?"

"Yes." She nodded. "Colleagues."

He laughed. "I don't have any colleagues who look like you."

She sniffed in distain. "My appearance is irrelevant."

"Not to me."

"Nathanial—"

"Nor do I have any colleagues who smell as good as you."

"The way I smell is scarcely—"

"You smell like I imagine heaven would. Of exotic flowers and summer skies and promises left unsaid."

"Most poetic, Nathanial," she said coolly. "Utter nonsense, of course. Summer skies don't smell. As for promises left unsaid . . . " She scoffed. "I thought we had already established I am not the sort of woman who would be swayed by such flowery sentiment."

"No, of course not. You wish to be my colleague. Although I would be remiss in my responsibilities as a 'colleague' if I failed to point out," he gazed into her eyes, "that I have never had a colleague who fit so perfectly in my arms."

"Have you danced with many of them, then?"

He laughed.

"You are not taking this seriously." She sighed. "This is a serious matter. I would appreciate it if you gave it serious attention."

"Oh, but I am. I am taking it most seriously. I simply intend to ignore it."

"We will not get anything accomplished if we— you—are continuously distracted."

"Then, my dear Gabriella, we will not get anything accomplished." He smiled down at her. "You are a most distracting colleague and I cannot help myself."

"Don't be absurd. Surely you are a stronger man than that."

"Ah, but you have weakened me. Sapped my strength.

I am the frailest of men in your presence." He executed a complicated turn, and she followed his lead perfectly.

"Beyond that, I don't want to be your colleague."

"Well, what do you want?" she said before she could stop herself. Before she could realize what a dangerous question it was.

He stared at her and once again the look in his eyes stole her breath, and possibly her heart. "Everything." His hand tightened around hers. "I want everything."

"I have no idea what you mean," she said in a lofty manner. This was dangerous ground. "Besides, that's absurd."

"How can it be absurd if you don't know what I mean?"

"I mean . . . " She huffed. "I don't know what I mean. But I do know what I want and what I don't want."

"Oh?" He smiled. "And what do you want?"

"I want to find the seal."

"That goes without saying." He nodded. "What else do you want?"

I want . . .

"I want you to listen to what I say."

"You wound me deeply, Gabriella." He shook his head. "I listen to every word."

"And then you do precisely as you please."

He grinned in an unrepentant manner. "But I do listen."

"You are a stubborn creature, Mr. Harrington."

"No more so than you. It's one of the things I love about you."

"Now you're being ridiculous. We barely know each other. How can you love anything about me?"

"Oh but I do. I love your passion for justice for your

brother. And the way the least thing makes you blush in a most delightful way. I love the independence of your nature and how you try to be terribly proper even when you're considering acts that are somewhat less than legal."

She steeled herself against the desire to melt against him. "Nonetheless, you shouldn't use words like love unless you—"

"Mean them?" He nodded thoughtfully. "You're absolutely right." The music drew to a close and he escorted her off the dance floor. "Punch?"

That was it, then? He was to fetch her punch as though he hadn't mentioned love? Hadn't implied he had, well, feelings for her? Not that she wanted him to. Not that it made any difference whatsoever. No, it would only make everything more difficult.

She smiled politely. "That would be most welcome."

He chuckled as if he had the upper hand, and she watched him walk off. He was indeed a fine figure of a man, tall and handsome and dashing. The kind of man that made women want . . . She sighed. That simply made women ache with a newfound need for something they couldn't quite put their finger on. Made her want all sorts of things she could never have. That she never imagined she'd want. Most of all . . . him.

She glanced around the ballroom noting that whatever magic might have been here before was gone. The lights were overly bright, the gowns no more than pretty, the music only passable. It was an Antiquities Society Ball like any other. No more special today than it had been in the past.

Still, she acknowledged reluctantly, she had always

loved attending this ball. Perhaps because she attended so very few. Last year she had been filled with hope here. Enrico was in an excellent mood, and she'd been optimistic that she could convince him to allow her to accompany him, to assist him in his work. She had danced very nearly every dance, even though she only knew a handful of people.

It struck her for perhaps the first time that her world was extraordinarily narrow. Limited to acquaintances she had made at the college, the older gentlemen who tended to spend their days in the society's clubroom whose paths she crossed on her way to or from the society library, the director and his wife. She had no friends beyond Florence and Xerxes and Miriam. She'd never noticed before, but her brother had had no real friends either, at least none that she knew of. There had been no letters of condolence, no true expressions of sympathy. It was to be expected, of course. Enrico only had his work and nothing more.

Regardless, he had been a good brother. She bit her bottom lip absently. It would be the height of disloyalty to think otherwise. Still, how many times had she said that to herself? Had she reassured herself that he was a good brother? Not merely since his death, but for years before that. And if he'd never been around, if he had not quite protected her as he should have, if he had not taught her all those things someone should have taught her about proper behavior and temptations and how a single unthinking act could effect the rest of her life, well, it scarcely mattered now.

She raised her chin. Enrico was dead and she was essentially no more alone now than when he was alive.

Once she found the seal, she would go on with whatever life she might manage to find. At least, she thought wryly, she was not poor.

"You appear too pensive for so grand an evening," Florence's voice sounded beside her.

"Do I?" Gabriella forced a light note to her voice and turned toward her hired companion and friend. She cast her a genuine smile. "I can't imagine why. It is indeed a grand evening."

"I thought perhaps you were thinking of last year's ball."

"It's inevitable, isn't it?" Gabriella's gaze wandered idly around the room. As always, the crowd was an odd mixture of those who studied or searched for the treasures of the ancients, and those who provided financial support for their efforts. Society benefactors mingled with professors, archeologists chatted with board members, elderly scholars danced with titled matrons. "Last year held so much promise, so much lay before us. Enrico would present the seal, his reputation would be solidified, and who knows? Even without the other seals, he might have been able to unravel the Virgin's Secret, find the location of the lost city, and—"

"And he would never have allowed you to come along," Florence said in a hard tone.

"I have read everything ever written about Ambropia, not that there is very much. I have studied languages and maps and histories and—" She met Florence's gaze. "I would have been indispensable."

Florence stared at her, then drew a deep breath. "You would have been nothing more than you ever were to him."

A debt to a dead father. An obligation that was

easily met with little inconvenience. A means to control a fortune.

Thoughts she'd preferred for years not to think at all, and the one she'd tried to ignore since his death, throbbed in her head.

Florence's expression softened. "You have facts to face, my dear Gabriella, but now is not the time to do so. This is an evening to put aside all thought beyond enjoyment of the moment." Her eyes twinkled. "I suspect Mr. Harrington is having an agreeable evening. He's scarcely let you out of his sight."

"He's afraid I'll disappear if he does."

"And will you?"

"No." Still, wouldn't that be the easiest way to end whatever it was happening between them? Once they had resolved the question of the seal, she could simply vanish from his life. She certainly had the money to do so.

"I daresay he wouldn't take that well. Not given the way he looks at you."

"Nonsense."

Florence raised a brow.

"I don't know what to do about him." Gabriella shook her head.

"What do you want to do about him?"

I want . . .

"I don't know," she snapped, then sighed. "My apologies. I didn't mean—"

"It's quite all right." Florence chuckled. "I can well see why you might be confused. Mr. Harrington certainly is handsome enough. And from what Mr. Dennison has said, he seems a good sort. Honest, honorable—"

Gabriella scoffed. "Then we are obviously well-matched."

"Your less than completely honest behavior of late is an aberration. It is not your nature." Florence raised a shoulder in a casual shrug. "I suspect a man like Mr. Harrington would understand and overlook this temporary flaw in your character."

"Perhaps he could overlook that." Gabriella shook her head. "But as you said, he is an honorable man. I daresay an honorable man couldn't possibly overlook—"

"Not if you don't give him the opportunity to do so."

"I am . . ." It was hard to even say the words. *Ruined. Fallen. Soiled goods.*

"Gabriella, you were scarcely more than a child. You were fifteen."

"And I should have known better."

"Yes, you should have, and if you had been raised properly instead of being hauled around from one uncivilized place to another, pretending to be a boy, surrounded by men not substantially better than your brother, you would have known better."

"I know better now."

It had come as a shock to her, when she began attending school in England, how a single incident with a boy scarcely older than she would impact the rest of her life. When she realized that by allowing her own seduction—even though she had not comprehended the significance of the act at the time—she would never be an acceptable match for a decent man. When she understood that what she had done with the son of a German archeologist was the same thing she'd heard bandied about in snippets of conversation from men like her brother in lewd and vulgar terms. Shame had filled her then, and she abandoned any thoughts of love and marriage and ever finding someone to trust with her heart.

"But enough about me." She drew a calming breath. "How is your Mr. Dennison this evening?"

"He's not my Mr. Dennison." Florence grinned. "Yet."

Gabriella raised a brow. "Oh?"

"I rather thought any chance I had to marry had passed me by long ago, and I never thought I'd meet a man like Mr. Dennison. He is good and kind and clever. And he makes me feel . . . well, special." Florence sighed. "As if I were the most beautiful, most clever, most special woman in the entire world. And I must confess, when he kissed me—"

"You allowed him to kiss you?"

"Allowed him? My dear child, I encouraged him." Florence leaned toward her in a confidential manner, a smug smile on her lips. "And he did so exceptionally well."

Gabriella laughed.

Florence looked across the room. "I sent him for refreshments and I see he is back. I should return to him." She studied Gabriella for a moment. "Are you all right, my dear?"

"Of course." She mustered her brightest smile. "I am having nearly as lovely an evening as you. You needn't worry about me tonight. Go back to your Mr. Dennison and have a grand time. I shall send you a note tomorrow and tell you all about my evening."

"Are you any closer to finding the seal?"

"Probably not." Gabriella shrugged. "But we are no farther away, at least."

"The Verification Committee begins its meeting tomorrow." A warning note sounded in Florence's voice.

"And concludes in ten days." Gabriella shook her head. "I am well aware of that."

"You don't have much time left."

"I know."

Florence paused. "Might I make a suggestion?"

Gabriella smiled. "Could I stop you?"

"If you don't find the seal, if you cannot present it to the committee . . . " Florence paused and her gaze met Gabriella's directly. "Abandon your quest. Go on with your life. Do not let this haunt you for the rest of your days."

"Florence, I—"

"Enrico is dead. He's gone, and you must lay him to rest. Redeeming his professional reputation will not now change the way he felt about you." Florence laid her hand on her arm. "It will not make him love you."

Gabriella's eyes widened. "What an absurd thing to say. I have no doubt as to my brother's feelings for me. There is no question in my mind whatsoever that he did indeed care for me. Why, he rescued me and provided for my home and my studies and everything."

And did so with my money.

The unspoken charge hung in the air between them. She ruthlessly shoved it aside. It was disloyal and unfair.

"My apologies," Florence murmured. "I don't know what I was thinking to have said such a thing. Of course he cared for you." She leaned close and brushed a kiss across Gabriella's cheek. "Have a lovely time this evening, my dear. I shall see you soon." She cast the younger woman an affectionate smile and took her leave.

Gabriella watched her circle the ballroom until she reached Mr. Dennison. Even from where she stood, she could see the manner in which Florence seemed to light up in the secretary's presence. And the way he lit up in hers.

Gabriella smiled. Florence had apparently found love. *Love*. Her smile faded. How could Florence say such a thing about Enrico? He did love her, of course he did. He *was* a good brother.

As for the money, she was a child when he had found her. She certainly could not have managed her fortune. And if, as she grew up, he never mentioned it to her, it was no doubt because it wasn't important. He'd used it to support them both as well as fund his travels and his work. Besides, even if she had known, she wouldn't have protested. Aside from all else, he was her brother, her only male relative, and in the eyes of society he had every right to use her resources as he saw fit.

Still, it would have been nice to know.

Not that there was anything that could be done about it now. No one knew better than she that the past was the past, and aside from a few artifacts, a few crumbling relics and the occasional memory, it was best to put the past firmly in the past.

"May I have the honor of this dance, Miss Montini?" A voice sounded behind her.

"Certainly," she said with a sigh of relief. A dance would be just the thing to set her spirits right. "I should be delighted."

She turned to face her new partner and froze.

Fourteen

S hall we?" Lord Rathbourne offered his arm.

He was tall and imposing, with dark hair touched by gray at the temples. She'd seen him before, of course, but never this close. He looked younger than she had thought, somewhere in his fifties perhaps. On first glance he would have been considered distinguished and extremely handsome, until one noted the cold look in his eyes.

"Yes, of course," she murmured, and allowed him to escort her onto the dance floor. Words like *ruthless* and *whatever means possible* popped to mind and a chill shivered through her.

They took their place on the floor, and for once the music didn't sweep her away.

"I understand you paid a call on my wife," he said coolly.

"Yes, I did." She forced her most pleasant smile. He knew about their visit, she had no idea what else he might know. "She was gracious enough to talk with me for a few minutes."

"I know."

"She is quite lovely."

He smiled. "I know that too."

"You are a lucky man."

He glanced down at her, the smile on his lips never reaching his eyes. "I do not depend on luck, Miss Montini. With enough money and determination and power, one makes one's own luck."

"Oh." She uttered a weak laugh. "How resourceful of you."

"I am extremely resourceful." He paused. "I understand you are looking for the ancient seal your brother once claimed to have in his possession."

"Yes?"

"Come now, my dear, you needn't look so surprised. Surely you understand what an incestuous community this is—this world of treasures and those who hunt for or study them. The only way to keep a secret is not to share it. You have been asking questions. It has not gone unnoticed."

A frisson of fear skated up her spine. It was absurd, of course. She was safe enough here in the middle of a crowded ballroom. "As you are aware of my search, perhaps you would be so good as to answer one of my questions."

"How wonderfully direct of you, Miss Montini," he said smoothly. "I should be happy to answer any question you have."

"Excellent." She didn't quite believe him. Still, it would do no harm. "Do you have the seal?"

"Alas, to my eternal regret I do not. I had, however, arranged to acquire it."

Her heart sped up. "Oh?"

"I shall not bore you with the details. Suffice it to say, the efforts taken on my behalf—"

"You mean the attempt to steal the seal by a man in your employ," she blurted, indignation in her voice.

He raised a brow. "My, you are direct. I would not have put it so bluntly." He chuckled, a mirthless sound. "My methods may be considered—"

"Nefarious?"

He glanced down at her. "Again not the word I would have chosen. Regardless, my methods have always proved most efficient. This time, unfortunately, that was not the case."

She stared. "Then you admit you tried to have my brother's seal stolen."

"Miss Montini, whether I admit anything or not scarcely matters. I could admit any number of misdeeds—"

"Misdeeds?" She could barely choke out the word.

"Crimes if you prefer, although that does seem an arbitrary term. And might I point out, Miss Montini, that as we are dancing, and dancing is supposed to be an enjoyable activity, you should try very hard not to look as if you are either furious with me or terrified."

She jerked her chin up and adopted her most brilliant smile. "Does this meet with your approval?"

"Not entirely but it will do."

"Do continue, my lord. You were about to confess everything to me."

"What I was about to say is that I could admit any number of transgressions to you here in the middle of this ballroom. And while the world would prefer to believe the word of a beautiful young woman over an aging collector, that is not the way these things work."

He shrugged. "Furthermore, you have no proof of anything. My efforts were futile and I do not have your seal."

She studied him closely. "Why should I believe you?"

"You have no reason to do so, but then I have no reason to lie to you." He pulled her closer and spoke into her ear. "Still, it might be great fun to lie to you."

She shivered but refused to let her unease show. Indeed, this was her opportunity to get information from him. And if a little banter—even flirtatious banter—was required, why not? Besides, here and now she had nothing to fear.

"And what, my lord, would you lie to me about?"

"The usual things one tends to lie about to a lovely woman, I imagine. The extent of my estates. The quality of my stables. The size of my . . . " He smiled. " . . . fortune."

"And would you need to lie about such things?"

"One could always own more land or have a larger fortune." He chuckled. "But no, I have no need to lie about those matters."

"Then the seal remains the only thing to lie about?"

"You are a clever girl. But I have not lied to you about the seal. You have my word, which I rarely give, and never lightly."

"I see." It's not that she trusted him, she had no reason to do that. But he was right when he'd said he could confess nearly anything to her and few would take her word over his. So why go to the bother of lying?

They danced on in silence for a few moments.

"I have a proposition for you, Miss Montini," he said at last.

"Do you, my lord? Dare I ask what such a thing would involve?"

"Nothing *nefarious*, I assure you. It has come to my attention in recent days that many of my acquisitions have not been catalogued as thoroughly they should be. In the past, those I have charged with the care of my collections have been somewhat lax, which is why they did not maintain their positions for any length of time."

She stared. "You're offering me a position?"

"I am indeed."

She narrowed her eyes. "Why?"

"My, you are a suspicious creature, but then I should consider you rather foolish if you weren't. The why is obvious. I have a task that needs to be done."

She shook her head. "But why me?"

"Any number of reasons. First of all you are extremely qualified for a position of this nature. One might think you had been training for it for much of your life."

"Go on."

"One gets to a point in life when one realizes there are more days behind you than before you. In addition, I have recently realized that my friends are far fewer in number than my enemies. Indeed, I am hard pressed to name a true friend. It's nothing new, it has always been that way. I am a difficult person to know and even more difficult to like. It's the price one pays, I suppose, for taking what one wants in life without apology. Still . . . " A hard light shone in his eyes. "If I had to live my days over, I would do exactly the same things again.

"I make no excuses for who I am, Miss Montini. No doubt it is my advancing years that cause me now to take notice of my failings in life in regards to those things other people take for granted—friends, family, and the like." He paused. "But these are treacherous times, my dear girl, for both of us perhaps. You would beware."

She widened her eyes. "What on earth do you mean by that?"

"Only that there are those who search for the same thing you do. Those who would not hesitate to do whatever they deem necessary to acquire your seal."

"Oh." She swallowed hard. It wasn't a completely new thought, of course, but coming from Lord Rathbourne, it seemed somehow less of a possibility and more of a certainty.

"I want my collections put in order so that when the time comes that I am no longer on this earth, they will make a certain amount of sense. I want my genius, if you will, acknowledged."

"My lord," Gabriella said cautiously. "Are you ill?"

"No more so than any man of my age. My collections are priceless, and I intend for them to remain together always regardless of where they might end up. Beyond that . . ." He cast her an assessing look, as if she were a horse he intended to purchase. ". . . I rather like the idea of a beautiful woman among my other possessions."

"Your wife is beautiful."

"But she does not share my interests."

"Nonetheless, I'm not at all sure this is a good idea."

"Allow me to tell you why you cannot pass up this opportunity."

"I can scarcely contain my enthusiasm," she said wryly.

"Sarcasm, Miss Montini, is most unbecoming. I do not permit it among my employees."

"My apologies," she murmured.

"As I was saying, with your brother's death, you cannot help but be at loose ends."

"Not at all," she said staunchly. "I have much to keep myself busy."

"Really? Aside from your search for this seal, may I be so bold as to ask what precisely is filling your days, Miss Montini?"

"No, you may not, my lord." She huffed. He might be a bit frightening but he was not yet her employer, if indeed she decided to accept his offer. She couldn't imagine why she would, although the idea of simply getting to see the art and artifacts he'd collected had an unexpectedly strong appeal. To see all that he had and make certain of what he said he didn't have.

He shrugged. "And I suspect you have considered the fact that, as you will be allowed total access to my collections, you will be able to make certain I have not lied to you. That I do not have the seal you search for."

"I hadn't thought of that," she lied.

"Of course not," he said smoothly.

The music faded to a close. He offered her his arm and escorted her off the floor.

"May I ask you one other thing, my lord?"

"You may ask."

"Other than its intrinsic value as a rare and priceless artifact, why were you interested in the seal?"

"My dear Miss Montini." He cast her a disillusioned look. "I should think you of all people would understand that."

"And if I don't?"

"Now I see. You wish to ascertain exactly what I

know and what I don't know." He cast her a chastising look. "I did expect you to be a bit more subtle than this, however."

"I apologize if I have disappointed you."

"Do not let it happen again."

She stared at him. She could never work for such a man. "Yes, my lord."

"As you know, Ambropia was said to have been a city of great riches, great treasure. Whoever finds the city would claim a treasure beyond measure, not merely in a monetary sense but in terms of antiquities as well." His eyes gleamed. "The finder of the city would have his choice of artifacts, hidden from mortal view for eons. Unique in today's world. Irreplaceable. Priceless. For a collector of any stature, items from the lost city would make his collection the finest in all creation. The finest ever known.

"A legacy of that magnitude, Miss Montini, would make a man of my nature go to nearly any length to acquire it."

"I see."

"Yes, I imagine you do." He considered her closely. "Perhaps, before you make your decision as to whether or not to accept my offer, you might wish to see my collections for yourself."

Behind Lord Rathbourne, she noted Nathanial staring at them, a look of concern on his face. It was absurd. She wasn't an idiot, she could certainly take care of herself. She met the older man's dark gaze directly. "I would like that very much."

"Excellent. Let us say the day after tomorrow, then." A knowing smile curved his lips. "You may bring Mr.

Harrington along, if you wish. If it would make you less apprehensive."

"I am not the least bit apprehensive, my lord," she said firmly, and held out her hand.

"Perhaps you should be." He raised her hand to his lips but his gaze locked on hers. "I understand your brother thought his seal, along with others, might hold the clue to the Virgin's Secret."

"Two additional seals, possibly." She thought for a moment. "His assumption was based on the pattern on the seal he had, although he suspected even with the other seals, the message would still need to be deciphered."

"How very interesting," he murmured.

"Is it?" She studied him carefully. "Why?"

"Because, my dear Miss Montini, from all that I have been able to gather, not having seen your brother's seal for myself, of course, I have one that appears very much to be its mate."

Fifteen

W hat in the name of all that's holy did you
think you were doing?" Nate plastered a
pleasant smile on his face, took Gabriella's
elbow and firmly steered her toward the door.

"And what do you think you're doing?" She smiled at
him through gritted teeth.

"I am getting you out of here so that we may talk privately." He escorted her briskly through the door and
across the corridor.

"Where are we going?"

"The courtyard," he muttered.

It was not the most private place, since anyone could
walk in on them at any time, but he was not familiar
enough with the society's building to think of anywhere
better. He directed her through the French doors, which
had been thrown open to catch the breeze, and down
three steps into the courtyard.

There were benches and potted trees, urns overflow-
ing with flowers and a bit of ancient statuary artistically
placed as if to remind visitors that this was a place dedicated to such things. It was a charming setting and, as

the night was exceptionally mild, would have been the perfect place for a momentary assignation. Indeed, if he hadn't been so angry, that's precisely why he would have brought her here. Thankfully, the courtyard was empty.

She shook off his arm and glared at him. "Explain yourself, Nathanial."

"Explain myself?" He fairly choked on the words. "You want *me* to explain *myself*?"

"I most certainly do." She crossed her arms over her chest, a gesture that emphasized the full, ripe nature of her bosoms. It would have been most distracting if he wasn't so annoyed. "Go on."

"Very well." He clenched his jaw. "What were you doing with Lord Rathbourne?"

"I believe we were dancing." She shrugged in an off-hand manner. "He is an excellent dancer."

"Oh no." He shook his head. "You weren't merely dancing. You were questioning him."

"Have you ever met Lord Rathbourne?"

"No."

"He is not the type of man one questions."

"Regardless, I have known you long enough to recognize that look on your face."

Her brow arched upward. "And what look is that?"

"You know the look."

"I'm afraid I have no idea what you're talking about," she said in a lofty manner.

"This is not a game, Gabriella." He lowered his voice and leaned closer to her. "Lord Rathbourne is a dangerous man."

"I think his reputation is . . . " She raised her chin defiantly. " . . . exaggerated."

"Have you no sense whatsoever?"

"What do you mean by that?"

"Lord Rathbourne is the kind of man who gets what he wants."

"And?"

"And I saw the way he was looking at you. What he wanted on that dance floor was you."

A blush washed up her face. She stared at him for a moment, then laughed. "That's absurd."

"Is it?" He narrowed his eyes. "Do you have any idea how delicious you look in that dress? How the fire of your passion lights up your eyes? How you appear both vulnerable and determined at the same time? Completely irresistible and somehow out of reach?"

"Do you really think—" Her eyes widened. "You're jealous!"

"I most certainly am not." He couldn't possibly be jealous. Jealousy would mean all sorts of things he wasn't prepared to admit. Or perhaps all sorts of things he was afraid to admit. In spite of Quint's comments, it was too soon. Even so, he'd never had his heart broken, but if he knew nothing else, he knew that this was a woman who could do exactly that. "I am concerned for you. For your safety."

"My safety is not your concern."

"It most certainly is." He grabbed her arm and glared down at her. "I have promised to help you find your brother's seal. That promise extends to making certain you come to no harm in the process."

"I shall do exactly what I determine is necessary," she snapped.

"You cannot go off doing precisely as you please without concern for the consequences."

"I danced with him, Nathanial." She shook off his arm. "There is nothing more to it than that." She hesitated. "For the moment."

Apprehension caught at his throat. "What do you mean?"

"Lord Rathbourne has offered to let me see his collections."

"To my knowledge, that is an offer he makes rarely if ever, and never lightly. Don't you find that suspicious?"

"Not at all." She tossed her head back. "It makes perfect sense. He wishes to employ me—"

He drew his brows together. "To do what?"

"To catalogue his collections." A determined light shone in her eye.

"Alone? In his house?"

"I imagine there will be servants about. And Lady Rathbourne."

"Absolutely not. I forbid it."

"You what?"

He glared at her. "I cannot allow you to do something so reckless, so potentially perilous—"

"Nonsense. I know Lord Rathbourne has a certain reputation but I can't imagine I'd be in any real peril. Besides," her eyes narrowed dangerously, "you cannot forbid me to do anything."

"And yet . . ." He crossed his arms over his chest. He knew she would not take this well but it scarcely mattered. Injuring her sensibilities was well worth it to ensure her safety. " . . . I am."

"You have no right. Or are you going to threaten to have me arrested again?"

"If necessary to keep you safe . . . " He nodded. " . . . I would do exactly that."

"I see. So now you show your true colors."

"My true colors?" Anger raised his voice. "Let us speak of truth for a moment." This was treacherous ground but right now he didn't care. "The truth is that no matter what plans you may have had for your life, no man in his right mind who did what your brother did would let you assist him in his work. Go to the places he went. The truth is that while you are brilliant and knowledgeable, you are still a woman. A beautiful woman, which would only be more of a problem, headstrong and stubborn and independent as well, but a mere woman nonetheless, and it's past time you understood that."

She stared at him. "I thought my independent nature was one of the things you loved about me?"

"I was wrong!"

"I suspected as much." She sniffed. "A man like you has no understanding of the word love. You've probably said it hundreds of times to dozens of different women."

He clenched his jaw. "Hundreds."

"What?"

"Hundreds of different women. Why not say that? You barely know me at all but that's what you think of me."

"I know men of your nature." She shrugged. "I have seen any number of men exactly like you. Men who use women as playthings. You are just like—"

"Your brother?"

Shock washed across her face.

"Understand this, Gabriella, there have been any

number of women in my life, but none that didn't want from me exactly what I wanted from them." He grabbed her and pulled her into his arms. "And I have never before used the word 'love' in any manner whatsoever with any of them."

She glared up at him. "Oh?"

"Furthermore, I am not anything like your brother in any number of ways I will refrain from mentioning now. But know this, Gabriella, I would never abandon you."

She gasped. "He didn't—"

"And I would give up my own life before I would allow you to come to any harm." His gaze locked with hers and he watched as her anger faded to acceptance, to belief, and then to something warmer, deeper, more important. His heart thudded in his chest. What had this woman done to him? Damn it all if he didn't indeed love her.

"Gabriella," he moaned, and lowered his mouth to hers.

"He said you could come," she whispered against his lips.

"Now is not the time," he murmured. He had no idea what she meant, nor did he care. All he wanted was to press—

"Lord Rathbourne." She pulled away from him. "He said you could come. To see his collections."

"Excellent . . . " He drew a steadying breath. The last thing he wanted was to talk, but apparently he had no choice. "As I had no intention of allowing you to go alone. As for this alleged position—"

"He told me . . . " She paused as if choosing her words. "He told me he had arranged to have my brother's seal stolen."

"He told you that?" The admission caught him unawares. Obviously Rathbourne would never have admitted such a thing if he had the seal.

She nodded.

"By Javier Gutierrez?"

"He didn't mention a name." Her brows drew together. "But something went awry and he did not get the seal."

"Which doesn't mean Gutierrez didn't steal it."

"Do you know where he is?"

"No idea whatsoever."

"But, as everyone else is in London," she began, excitement in her voice, "it stands to reason that Gutierrez—"

"No." He shook his head. "Gutierrez has no legitimate standing with the society or anyone else. He masquerades as an archeologist but he is a thief, nothing more than that. Admittedly, he is knowledgeable about the artifacts he procures for whoever will pay his price, but he will not show his face here. He is far too clever for that."

"Nathanial." Her forehead furrowed. "Why would my brother show the seal to a man like that in the first place?"

Because they were two of a kind. Because he was already touched by madness. Which only begged the question, then, of why he had shown it to Nate and Quint.

"I don't know," he said simply.

She paused. "Have you considered the possibility that perhaps my brother was mistaken about those he suspected? That the seal might have been taken by someone unknown to him? By someone whose name we might never know?"

His gaze searched hers. She wanted reassurance that their efforts would not be for nothing. He couldn't give her that. He drew a deep breath. "Are you prepared to end it, then? To put this behind you and go on with your life? To admit defeat?"

"No." She shook her head. "Not yet."

He smiled. "Well, then."

"I should be getting back." Renewed determination sparked in her eyes and she started toward the court-yard door.

"Where are you going?"

"I am returning to the ballroom. I don't often have the chance to dance, and it is one of the few things I have always done simply for the joy of it. Besides, one never knows what kind of information one might acquire during a dance." She glanced back at him. "And don't think I have forgiven you for your high-handed manner or the vile things you have said."

"The truth is often vile."

She ignored him. "I simply have other matters that concern me at the moment."

"And my manner is in your best interest!"

"Hah." She scoffed and stepped into the corridor.

He started after her and pulled up short. Damnation, he was too late.

"Miss Montini?" A tall, handsome man stood in her path.

"Yes?" she said coolly.

"I was afraid you had decided to leave before we had our dance," he said. Bloody hell. He would have recognized that accent, if not the face, anywhere.

"Our dance?" She shook her head. "My apologies but I fear I don't remember promising you a dance."

"Then my heart will surely break." The American chuckled. "Last year we only danced once, and you promised to save a dance for me this year. Unless, of course . . . " He paused. "You're not married, are you?"

She laughed. "No, I am most certainly not married."

Not yet!

"Excellent." He offered his arm. "Then shall we?"

"Yes, of course. But I am sorry. This has been a very long year and I'm afraid I don't recall your name."

"Yet another wound to my heart, but in truth, I'm not surprised. I was only one of a multitude of partners you favored last year." He tucked her hand into the crook of his arm, and Nate resisted the urge to leap after them and wrench the intruder from Gabriella's side. "Allow me then to introduce myself once again. I am Alistair McGowan."

"Mr. McGowan." Surprise sounded in her voice, and she cast a smug smile over her shoulder at Nate. "There is no one I would rather dance with."

Nate clenched then relaxed his fists at his sides. He certainly wasn't jealous of Rathbourne, but the viscount's attentions to Gabriella were a cause of great concern. The man had enough money and power to do precisely as he pleased. The very idea of Gabriella going to his house alone, being in his employ, sent tremors of fear through him. There was little he could do to protect her there. Admittedly, there was probably little he could do to keep her away.

But Alistair McGowan was a different matter entirely. From what he knew of the man, and the few times they'd crossed one another's path, he was a decent enough sort. For an American. He no more seriously considered McGowan a suspect in the theft of the seal than he did Quint. If McGowan had the seal, he probably came by it in a relatively honest manner.

He stared after Gabriella and McGowan. The American inclined his head toward her, and a faint ripple of laughter drifted back to him. He was making her laugh? Damned colonist.

Didn't McGowan realize she was taken? Didn't *she* realize she was taken?

Of course not. He had barely begun to realize it himself.

Sixteen

*M*y apologies once again, Mr. McGowan." Gabriella smiled up at him, which wasn't at all difficult.

He was an adequate dancer, or at least she was in no fear of having her feet trampled, as so often happened at this particular gathering. McGowan was handsome as well, with blond hair and broad shoulders. He had the greenest eyes she'd ever seen, crinkled at the corners, no doubt from staring across the desert sands. Wickedly attractive, was the phrase that came to mind. Good. When Nathanial watched her dance with this man, perhaps he would indeed be jealous. Not that she cared. "I can't imagine how I might have forgotten you."

"It has been a long year," he said with a smile. "I would have been surprised if you had remembered. It was, after all, only one dance and not as if we had shared a kiss in the moonlight."

She stared at him. "Why did you say that?"

"Because, Miss Montini," he grinned, "you make my thoughts to turn to things like kisses in the moonlight."

"Are all Americans this forward?"

"Yes," he said in a somber manner, though amusement twinkled in his eyes. "As well as charming, each and every one of us. Even the ladies." He thought for a moment. "Although they do, all in all, tend to be prettier than the gentlemen." He leaned toward her ear in a confidential manner. "We much prefer it that way."

She laughed. "I must confess, I didn't expect you to be so dashing."

"No?" He held her a bit firmer and performed a complicated step to avoid another couple who appeared to be careening out of control. She followed him easily. Perhaps he was better than adequate. "You didn't expect a man you think might be a thief to be enjoyable company?"

Caution edged her voice. "How did you know about that?"

He shrugged. "Word does tend to travel, Miss Montini. And while you have my condolences for your brother's death, I assure you I had nothing to do with the disappearance of his seal."

She wasn't sure what to say. It was one thing to accuse Lord Rathbourne of misdeeds. He was, after all, a not especially pleasant person. And quite another to voice her suspicion of Alistair McGowan to his handsome, smiling face. Still, she had no reason to trust him.

"And why should I believe you?"

"I don't know. It's harder to prove one's innocence than one's guilt, I suppose." He heaved a frustrated sigh. "Forgive me, Miss Montini. You should know there is nothing I would like better than to continue this dance, but I fear I am not especially good at dancing and talking at the same time. One takes all my concentration, leaving the other lacking in substance if not style. And

I suspect you have a great number of questions for me. Would you mind if we stopped dancing to talk?"

"Not at all." She smiled, and he escorted her off the floor, to chairs arranged by a potted palm. While in plain view, the plant still provided a modicum of privacy. She took a seat and he settled in the chair beside her.

"I ran across your brother more than a year ago now." McGowan began without preamble. "You should be aware, although we had known each other for years, it was in no more than a casual manner. We were nothing more than acquaintances, really. We would cross paths on occasion, share a meal together, trade a story or two, that sort of thing."

"Go on."

"He had recently found the seal, and needless to say, was extremely excited about it."

She leaned forward. "Where exactly did he find it, Mr. McGowan?"

"He never said." He thought for a moment. "At the time, that struck me as somewhat odd, but your brother always did keep things like that to himself. At least that was my experience with him."

She nodded. "He was always reticent to give specific details about his finds."

"Yes, well, many of us are." McGowan shrugged. "It's a very competitive field, Miss Montini. It's not at all unusual to hear of someone who has lost a find because they opened their mouth to the wrong person. Still, it's often hard to keep one's enthusiasm to oneself. The Ambropia seal was the kind of discovery that elicited that type of excitement."

"I fear I am somewhat confused. If you and he were not especially close, why did he show you the seal?"

"Proximity played a part. We happened to be in the same place at the same time. The thrill of discovery is often greater when one can share it with someone who will appreciate its magnitude. We all have a tendency to brag about such things. There's little that warms a competitive heart more than seeing a flicker of envy in the eyes of a colleague." He paused for a moment. "Beyond that, your brother and I shared a similar passion. I too wish to find a city lost to the ages."

She raised a brow. "Ambropia?"

"No, although if a clue to its location fell into my hands, I certainly wouldn't walk away from it." He chuckled. "No, Miss Montini, there are men who search for Ambropia and Hattusha and Knossos today much as they once searched for Babylon and Troy and Ephesus. They do so because there is something about a city lost in time, abandoned, forgotten, relegated to myth and legend, that grabs one's imagination. And buries itself in one's soul." He glanced at her. "Are you familiar with Shandihar?"

She nodded. "It was on the silk route in southern Turkey, Asia Minor, the crossroads of the world at one time. Reputed to be a city of great wealth and glory, it was described in writings from the sixth century. It is believed the people of Shandihar worshiped only one god, or rather, goddess—Ereshkigal, the queen of the night."

He stared at her. "How do you know all that?"

"I remember everything I've ever read." She smiled. "It's a useful skill."

"I can well imagine," he murmured, studying her with a mixture of admiration and possibly envy.

"About Shandihar?" she prompted.

"Ah yes. The discovery of Shandihar, Miss Montini, is the quest that has captured my heart. And I will find her one day." Absolute confidence shone in his eyes. "It is my destiny, I have no doubt of that."

"At least you know Shandihar did indeed exist." Gabriella blew a long breath. "The writings about Ambropia are so obscure, the very name of the goddess who protected it is still as yet unknown. She is only known as the Virgin Goddess."

"And the location of the city is the Virgin's Secret." He nodded. "Which is why your brother's find was so important a discovery. Never before has there been reference either to Ambropia or the Virgin's Secret on so ancient an artifact."

"No, Ambropia was only mentioned by the Greeks, and those writings are vague and minimal."

"That the symbols for both the city and the Virgin's Secret were found on an Akkadian seal would seem to indicate that the city was more than mere legend."

"One would hope, but quite honestly, Mr. McGowan," she met his gaze firmly, "that does not concern me. If my brother were still alive, I am certain he would want to pursue the search for the city itself. I want only to recover the seal and give my brother the credit due him. I don't want him to be remembered as . . . " She paused to find the right words. "I want to restore his reputation. His good name."

"His good name. Yes, of course," McGowan murmured. His gaze slid past her, then returned to meet hers. "Your quest strikes me as both noble and honorable, but I do hope you understand there are others to whom those words do not apply. Miss Montini." He stared into her eyes. "Ambropia would be a find that would bring untold fame and fortune and glory to its discoverers. Your brother's seal is the first step toward that discovery. There are those who would not hesitate to use whatever means possible to acquire it."

"I am well aware of that, Mr. McGowan."

"Then you are aware as well that your journey could be a dangerous one."

"I am." She nodded. "But I'm not worried."

"Perhaps you should be. I wish I could be of further help." He grinned. "Indeed I can think of nothing I would like better than to help you."

"Why, Mr. McGowan." She widened her eyes in an innocent manner. "Are you trying to sway me with flirtatious banter?"

"I am trying." He smiled, then sobered. "You have no reason to believe me, but I do not have the seal." He paused. "Nor do I know who does."

"And would you tell me if you did?"

"Ah, Miss Montini." He took her hand and raised it to his lips, his gaze never leaving hers. "I daresay I would tell you very nearly anything to see gratitude light up those lovely blue eyes of yours."

She laughed. "Mr. McGowan, you are past trying now. I think you have succeeded."

"Good." He grinned. "I find all this talk has left me parched." He got to his feet. "May I fetch you a cup of punch?"

"That would be lovely." She smiled, and he took his leave. She watched him circle the room, heading toward the alcove where refreshments were arranged.

Blast it all, she did believe him. Not that she was swayed by his flirtatious manner or his handsome face, but there was an air of honesty about him. And his manner struck her as forthright. He seemed the kind of man who would not lie well. She did not consider herself a particularly good judge of character, but there was something about McGowan that elicited trust. She could be wrong but didn't think so.

If she eliminated McGowan as a possibility, as well as Rathbourne—although he'd admitted he had tried to acquire the seal—that left only Gutierrez. Who may or may not have stolen it for Rathbourne, although his lordship claimed he didn't have it. And was willing to let her view his collections to prove it. Which might be rather pointless, all things considered. Still, it would be interesting to see the seal Rathbourne said might match her brother's, as well as his other artifacts.

Which left only Nathanial and Quinton of those her brother suspected. She still wasn't sure she entirely trusted Quinton, and in truth, what woman would? As for Nathanial, she'd had no choice but to trust him. Now, without quite noticing how or when it had happened, she did trust him. Certainly with her quest. Perhaps with her heart as well, although that was not possible.

She shook her head to clear the absurd thought. Even if she had her heart to give, she would think long and hard about giving it to a man who thought she was a mere woman. Women were doing all sorts of things these days that men didn't think they should or could. Why, hadn't Amelia Edwards traveled Egypt for years and then written *A Thousand Miles up the Nile*? A book archeologists—men—found praiseworthy and most helpful in their own pursuits. Indeed, she'd read several different memoirs, written by women, that were their accounts of traveling in remote parts of the world. There was nothing *mere* about those women. The fact that she couldn't think of a woman actively engaged in archeological pursuits didn't mean there wasn't one somewhere. Perhaps she could be the first? It was an intriguing idea. A new hope for the future, possibly to replace the one that had vanished with her brother's death.

I would never abandon you.

Enrico had died, he hadn't abandoned her. At least, not with his death. Regardless, Nathanial had no right to imply otherwise.

And I would give up my own life before I would allow you to come to any harm.

How could one stay angry at a man who would say things like that? Still, anger was one way to keep him at arm's length. But with each passing day spent in his presence, she wanted to be in his arms. She wanted to be in his life for the rest of her days, and that simply was not going to happen. Even dwelling on it was absurd.

One way or another, their time together would soon be at an end. Then she would disappear from his life. It was for the best, really. He was obviously beginning to feel some affection for her. And she . . .

She shoved the thought aside.

It scarcely mattered at the moment. The only important thing now was finding the seal. Before it was too late for her brother's redemption. Before Nathanial's offhand talk of what he loved about her became something more significant. Before she lost her heart to him and it was too late to save herself.

If it wasn't already too late.

Seventeen

*N*ate casually stepped up to the refreshment table beside McGowan.

"Harrington," McGowan said coolly.

Nate nodded. "McGowan."

"I'm surprised to see you here. I find myself indulging in this nonsense every year, if only to make certain the society realizes I am still alive and have not abandoned my work and returned permanently to America." McGowan raised a brow. "Yet I cannot recall the last time I saw you in attendance."

"I have no need to let anyone know of my continuing existence on this earth," Nate said in a lofty manner, then grinned. "Besides, I have always found this event to be somewhat deadly in and of itself."

"You're late, by the way." McGowan helped himself to a glass of punch.

"What do you mean, I'm late?"

"I've been here for a good minute now. I expected you, oh, at least thirty seconds ago."

"Don't be absurd." Nate paused. "Why would you expect me?"

"Why? Excellent question." McGowan slanted him an amused glance. "Perhaps because when I encountered Miss Montini, you were right behind her in the courtyard, glaring at me. Or perhaps because you then proceeded to follow us into the ballroom, again glaring at me. Or it might be because when Miss Montini and I were dancing you continued to glare."

Nate scoffed. "I do not glare."

"Harrington, you looked at me as though I was about to steal an artifact of great worth and rare value from right under your very nose."

"I do not glare," Nate muttered.

"And you looked at her as if she was of great worth and rare value."

"We are . . . " Nate paused, then said the first thing that came to mind. "Colleagues."

McGowan snorted. "That's what I thought." He sipped his punch and studied Nate. "Do you have questions for me as well?"

"Did she?"

McGowan chuckled. "She did indeed. She's very knowledgeable and quite determined."

"You noticed that, did you?"

"It would have been impossible to miss." McGowan paused for a moment. "I had the distinct impression she doesn't realize the kind of man her brother was."

Nate shook his head. "I don't think so.

"I knew Montini for probably, oh, a dozen years or so. Not well, of course, no one knew him well. He was too . . . " McGowan thought for a moment. "Competitive, I think, to make friends. He didn't really trust anyone. When I first knew him, he had a boy who traveled with him. Perhaps a brother but I'm not certain."

"I've met the brother," Nate said.

McGowan considered Nate closely. "Might I ask you a question?"

Nate nodded.

"Miss Montini asked me why her brother had shared his find with me. I think it was more than likely because I was available. He told me about the seal and showed me the impression in Cairo. I believe it had just come into his possession. That was in January of last year." Curiosity glittered in McGowan's eye. "I was wondering when he shared the impression with you and your brother. And why."

"It was a few weeks later, if I recall correctly." McGowan's question had already occurred to him but it wasn't something he wished to dwell on or examine. It was somewhat disquieting to consider, but he hadn't voiced his unease to anyone. Not to Sterling, definitely not to Gabriella, nor had he talked about it to Quint. Still, it was a minor detail. Scarcely worth mentioning. "I think he showed it to us because of my brother's work years ago with Professor Ashworth."

"Isn't Ashworth an expert on Ambropia?"

Nate nodded. "He was Quint's mentor once. My brother idolized him, and he taught Quint everything he knew. At some point they had a falling out. Quint never said what it was about and they went their separate ways."

"You think Montini just wanted to flaunt his find?"

"To be honest, I don't know." Nate shrugged. "That was Montini's nature. It might also be that, because of Quint's history with Ashworth, Montini thought he would be more likely to recognize the validity of the seal." Nate drew his brows together. "I have tried over and over to recall the exact details of that meeting. What was said and by whom. It seems to me Quint showed little interest in the seal."

"Given his background with Ashworth," McGowan said slowly, "didn't that strike you as odd?"

"Not at the time." In fact, he hadn't paid much attention to Quint's relative lack of enthusiasm for Montini's find. It hadn't seemed important. Now, with all that had happened, it did indeed seem more than odd. Perhaps it was time he had a long chat with his brother.

McGowan sipped his punch and considered Nate thoughtfully. "There's something I didn't tell Miss Montini that might have some bearing on all this. Or it might be nothing at all." He lowered his voice. "It was some time ago—autumn, if I recall correctly. I was in Crete, near the Kephala mound. I didn't see him myself but I heard your brother was in the region as well."

"Go on." Nate and Quinton often went their separate ways for reasons of expediency or personal interests, or simply because on occasion they preferred to travel alone. Quint more so than himself.

"I heard a rumor—and mind you, it was nothing more than that—about a game of chance—cards, I believe. Gossip had it that your brother had won an antiquity of great value."

"How intriguing."

"The loser in that game was a Spaniard." McGowan's brow furrowed. "A man named—"

"Gutierrez?"

"Yes, that's it. I heard Gutierrez was furious. Nasty sort, from what I know of him, and dangerous as well no doubt. He accused your brother of taking advantage of his inebriated state." McGowan paused. "I assume you know Gutierrez often procured antiquities for Lord Rathbourne?"

Nate nodded.

"I heard about Montini's death a few weeks later." He shrugged. "As I said, I don't know if it's significant or of any interest at all in terms of the missing seal."

"Neither do I." Nate shook his head. "I suspect it's not, but I do appreciate it nonetheless."

"There's one other thing."

"Yes?"

"Does Miss Montini know how her brother died?"

"She was told he died of a fever."

"I see. My information is probably inaccurate then." His gaze met Nate's directly. "I heard he was killed. That his throat had been slit." McGowan grimaced. "You might wish to keep that to yourself."

Nate nodded. "She doesn't need to know."

"I'm not sure she realizes how dangerous this game is. But I thought you should know."

"I do appreciate your candor."

"Well, as I have no real way to prove my own innocence, it seemed the thing to do."

"You could simply be trying to steer us in another direction."

"I suppose I could." McGowan grinned. "Would that I were that clever." He filled another glass and offered it to Nate. "I was supposed to be bringing Miss Montini a glass of punch but I assume you'd prefer to do that yourself."

"Yes, thank you," Nate said absently, accepting the glass, his thoughts returning to McGowan's comments.

Was it possible that Quint knew far more about the missing seal than he had let on? Surely not. Quint might have been many things, but he would never steal another man's discovery for himself. No, he knew his brother better than that. But it was indeed past time to have that long chat.

"Does she know?" McGowan asked in an offhand manner.

Nate jerked his attention back to the American. "Does who know what?"

"Does Miss Montini know you're in love with her?"

"I'm not . . . " Why continue to deny it when even a stranger could see it? Nate blew a long breath. "No, she doesn't."

"You might want to tell her." McGowan chuckled. "Before someone else realizes what a prize she is."

"I am surprised no one has noticed before now."

"Oh, I imagine many have noticed. She is hard not to notice. And now that her brother is dead . . . " McGowan paused for a long moment as if debating his words. "She did all of his research for him, you know, prepared all of his paperwork, maintained his correspondence, that sort of thing. From what I understand, he was extremely possessive of her. I saw something of that here last year. He was most intimidating toward any man who showed her the least bit of continued attention.

"He used to have a manservant, a big, powerful sort, rather on the exotic side in appearance, who traveled with him for years. Then I heard Montini had left the man here in London as protection for his sister. To be honest, up until then I hadn't known he had a sister. Only the boy, who I assumed had gone to London as well."

"I see." The description sounded familiar. Nate narrowed his eyes. "Was his name John?"

"No, it was Greek, I believe." McGowan frowned. "Or possibly Irish."

"Xerxes Muldoon," Nate said slowly, also known as John, no doubt. How very interesting.

"That's it. At any rate, now that her brother is dead, she is free." McGowan chuckled. "I know if I were looking for a wife—"

"I'm not looking for a wife."

"And that, Harrington, is exactly when you tend to find one." McGowan nodded in Gabriella's direction. "I would go now, if I were you. Before anyone else realizes the delectable and brilliant Miss Montini is now available."

Nate stared at the American. "Excellent advice, McGowan." He grinned. "I shall take it to heart."

McGowan raised his glass. "See that you do." His gaze sobered. "And do not let your guard down."

Nate nodded and started back toward Gabriella.

The American had certainly been full of unexpected revelations. Most significantly, of course, about Quint. But about Montini and Gabriella as well.

He had suspected from the first that she was not being completely honest with him about her life. As for that other brother of hers, it was more than a little odd that she wasn't more concerned about his whereabouts. Indeed, she'd scarcely spoken of him. She'd only said they were close. As one, if he remembered right. And he looked so very much like her . . .

She stood up when he approached. "Your mother says we should be leaving now."

"I'm surprised Sterling agreed to stay this long," he

murmured, and handed her the punch. "McGowan sends his regrets along with refreshment." She was exactly the same height as the brother who had accosted him in Egypt. The brother she rarely mentioned.

"How very kind." She sipped at the punch.

And her eyes, that unique deep blue, could of course run in the family. Her brother had worn a hat pulled low, but Nate had noticed his eyes. They were the same in hue and shape.

"Why are you staring at me?"

And the same fire flashed in them when angered.

"Am I?" he said coolly.

"Yes you are." Her brows drew together.

What he was thinking was absurd.

She huffed. "It's most disconcerting."

If he'd had the same thought about another woman, it would have been ridiculous.

"My apologies."

Absolutely impossible.

Unease shaded her eyes. "Nathanial, what are you thinking?"

But when it came to Gabriella, it wasn't the least bit improbable. Stupid and reckless perhaps but not out of the realm of possibility.

"Nathanial?"

It was exactly the sort of impulsive, dangerous, foolish thing she would have done.

"It's nothing of any importance." He plucked the glass from her hand and set it on a chair, then tucked her hand in the crook of his arm and started toward the door. "I was just thinking about family resemblances and how very much you look like your brother."

"Really." She shrugged. "I never noticed any similarity at all."

Indeed she looked nothing like Enrico Montini, the only brother Nate now suspected she had. And he knew exactly how to confirm it.

Eighteen

*L*ord Rathbourne will be with you shortly." His lordship's stern-faced butler nodded a bow and took his leave, closing the library doors behind him.

Gabriella resisted the urge to shift from foot to foot nervously, although she would have happily slit her own wrists before letting Nathanial know she was the least bit apprehensive. He looked somewhat uneasy himself. He hadn't wanted to come; no, in truth he hadn't wanted *her* to come. And he certainly hadn't hidden his feelings.

They had discussed it yesterday morning, which was a continuation of the discussion they'd had the night before, upon their arrival home from the ball. And they'd been discussing it in the afternoon when the note arrived from Lord Rathbourne inviting them here this morning. She suspected there were any number of people in the household, Xerxes included, who might have called their exchanges something more akin to argument than discussion. But arguing with Nathanial kept him at arm's length, which was exactly where she wanted him. No—not where she wanted him—where she needed him.

Aside from their differing opinions regarding Lord Rathbourne, Nathanial seemed somewhat cross over-all. She had caught him studying her when he thought she wasn't looking, as if to determine the answer to a question he hadn't asked. Or to learn her secrets. It was most unnerving. In addition, it seemed that Quinton had vanished, which apparently wasn't at all unusual. Xerxes heard from the other servants that Master Quinton often disappeared for days at a time, which everyone attributed to dissolute living, to drink and gambling and women. Regardless, Nathanial was obviously not pleased by his brother's absence.

"Good day, Miss Montini." Lord Rathbourne stepped into the room and crossed the floor to her, nodding at Nathanial in passing. "Mr. Harrington."

"Good day, sir," Nathanial said in a remote but none-theless polite manner.

"Miss Montini." Lord Rathbourne took her hand and raised it to his lips. His gaze bored into hers, and a chill ran up her spine. "You have no idea how delighted I am that you could join me today."

"Thank you for the invitation, my lord." Gabriella cast him a reserved smile and pulled her hand from his. "Will Lady Rathbourne be joining us?"

"She has already returned to the county," he said in a dismissive manner. "She has no interest in my collections, but I am hoping you will find my acquisitions so intriguing you will not hesitate to accept my offer of employment."

"I am somewhat busy at the moment."

"Very busy," Nathanial said pointedly.

Lord Rathbourne ignored him. "Ah yes, your search for the missing seal. Come now, Miss Montini, it cannot possibly take up all your time. And I must confess that when I have a pressing problem, I find doing something entirely different clears my mind, thus paving the way for a solution. And one way or another your search will soon be over."

"What makes you think that?" Suspicion sounded in Nathanial's voice.

Lord Rathbourne cast him a long suffering look. "My dear boy, everyone knows a request for validation of any artifact has a life span of one year, from the start of one committee meeting to the end of the meeting on the following year. As the Verification Committee began its meeting yesterday and will conclude eight days from now, the clock is ticking, as it were."

He returned his attention to Gabriella. "Once you have given my proposal due consideration, Miss Montini, I am confident you will find it irresistible." He stepped to a wall of shelves and glanced at Nathanial. "You will find this interesting, Harrington."

"No doubt, sir."

The older man reached inside a bookshelf. "There is a lever here that is released by a combination lock. I dialed the combination a few minutes before you arrived." He flipped the unseen lever and a wall of shelves slid to one side, revealing a large opening. "The lever releases a spring which opens the door. I had the system designed expressly for my needs." He bowed to Gabriella. "After you, my dear."

She took a deep breath and stepped through the opening, his lordship a step behind her, leaving Nathanial to trail after them.

"Welcome to my treasure room."

It seemed at first a small room, lit only by the light from the library behind them. There were no windows and no daylight whatsoever. Gabriella had a disturbing sense of solidity, as if she were in a tomb, the last resting place of a pharaoh. Lord Rathbourne quickly lit gas sconces positioned on either side of the opening on the wall behind her, and she saw that the room was much larger than she had at first thought. In front of her, what she'd assumed was a wall, in fact was a series of narrow panels, each about a foot wide. They extended from the floor to a few inches below the ceiling, an ornate brass knob positioned in exactly the same place on each panel. Lord Rathbourne moved to one, grasped the knob and pulled. The panel was actually one end of a long glass display case that slid outward into the room, revealing narrow shelves filled with Egyptian antiquities.

Gabriella gasped and moved closer. Even Nathanial stepped up to get a better look.

"Here we have the funerary urns of the ancient Egyptians . . . "

It was indeed a collection to rival any she'd seen in a museum. His lordship pulled out case after case of artifacts. The assortment of Egyptian sepulchral items alone was varied and endless. Here were the figures of deities carved from carnelian and lapis lazuli and jasper, or fashioned out of blue porcelain. She recognized treasures unique to Thebes, Abydos, and Karnac. There were amulets and scarabs cut of stone or semiprecious gems, originally intended to be tucked inside the folds of a mummy's wrappings. And jewelry of gold and silver and bronze from long dead pharaohs and their queens.

There were cases filled with the remnants of other civilizations as well, from the Etruscans, the Lycians, and the Assyrians. There were artifacts of Greek and Roman origin, black and red vessels and sculpted marble remnants, along with coins marked with the likeness of caesars and emperors and kings. At first glance it seemed there was little of the ancient world that was not represented in the varied and extensive collections of Viscount Rathbourne. It was the work of a lifetime, and indeed it might take a lifetime to examine it all. It was extraordinary, and her heart sped up at the sight of it all.

There was as well a case filled with cut and natural gems. Large diamonds, rubies, emeralds. A king's ransom in precious stones.

"These are some of the finest and rarest stones in the world." A note of pride sounded in Lord Rathbourne's voice. "They are as fine as the crown jewels themselves."

"One could support a small country with these," Nathanial murmured.

"A large country, Mr. Harrington," Lord Rathbourne corrected.

"But where—"

"Here and there, Miss Montini. A true collector does not reveal all his secrets." His lordship chuckled dryly. "In addition, there is a room similar to this one on the floor directly above us that is strictly for the storage of my paintings. Renaissance masters, primarily." Rathbourne smiled in a satisfied manner. "I have a fondness for such things and I have the means to indulge myself." He raised a questioning brow. "Would you care to see those as well?"

"Our time is limited today," Nathanial said sharply.

"Nonsense," Gabriella murmured, her gaze darting from one treasure to another. "We have plenty of time."

Lord Rathbourne chuckled. "Perhaps another day would be best." He pulled out one more case. "I think this will be of particular interest to you."

This case held ancient cylinder seals, dozens, perhaps as many as a hundred. Made of stone or clay, they were in no particular order and looked to be Babylonian and Assyrian, Akkadian and Egyptian.

"This one, I think." He pointed at a cylinder carved of greenstone toward the middle of the case.

She stepped closer and peered through the glass. Her breath caught. It did indeed resemble the impression she had seen of her brother's seal. Still . . . She shook her head. "It's made of the same material and looks similar in size. But without comparing an impression with my brother's, it's impossible to say."

"I can arrange for an impression."

"This is all quite remarkable, my lord, but we should be leaving," Nathanial said.

"I've never seen anything like this in other than a museum." Gabriella met Lord Rathbourne's gaze directly. "It's a pity not to share it with the world."

"I am a selfish man, Miss Montini. I make no apologies for my nature." He shrugged. "When we spoke at the ball, I told you I wished to have my collections put in order so that when I am no longer here, what I have accumulated will be acknowledged. However, since we last spoke I have had further thoughts."

"Yes?" Gabriella said.

"It seems something of a shame to have my life's work relegated to a shelf here and there in a museum full of such things, with only a brass plate as recognition of my achievement. I would much prefer to have all that I have accumulated remain as one. I am considering keeping my collections together in one place, in this very house, displaying them here after I'm gone." His eyes took on a far off expression, as if he were seeing into the future. "The Rathbourne Collection at Rathbourne House. It has a nice sound to it, don't you think?"

Nathanial looked as though he were about to say or do something embarrassing. Gabriella shot him a threatening glance.

"And I will need a curator." Lord Rathbourne's cool gaze met hers. "You, my dear."

She widened her eyes. "Surely you can't be serious."

"I am never less than serious."

"She's not qualified for something like that," Nathanial said quickly.

"She most certainly is," Lord Rathbourne said to him, but his gaze stayed on her. "She has spent years studying antiquities, ancient civilizations, history, languages—"

"How did you know that?" Gabriella drew her brows together.

"I made it my business to know." He shrugged. "It was not difficult information to uncover. You have not lived in secrecy. In addition, you are familiar with current finds and discoveries and research. While you are not well known, you have crossed paths through the years with scholars and collectors, museum directors and archeologists."

"But she's a—" Nathanial started, then obviously thought better of it.

"If you were going to say she's a woman, I commend

you for your restraint in not pointing out the obvious. Indeed she is a woman." Lord Rathbourne's tone was deceptively casual. "Surely you are not suggesting her gender should preclude her from consideration for this position?"

Nathanial had the faintest look about him of a rat caught in a trap. Good. Perhaps he would have to chew his leg off to escape. "No sir," he said weakly. "Of course not."

"That's very kind of you, my lord, but—"

"Kindness has nothing to do with it, Miss Montini. I am rarely if ever kind. I find the idea of a beautiful and brilliant woman being the curator of my collection—the public face, as it were—of the Rathbourne Collection, to be a stroke of genius."

"Admittedly," she said choosing her words with care, "it is an intriguing—"

"Allow me to be blunt, if you will," Lord Rathbourne interrupted. "Your life to this point has been filled with your studies and the work you did for your brother. He is now dead. If you were a man, you would have worked by his side. Even a cursory examination of your life up to now would indicate that is something that surely has crossed your mind. An intelligent and imaginative creature such as yourself cannot immerse herself in the legacy of the past without some desire to see where it all began. To have a hand in its rebirth."

"My lord, I—"

"You might well have aspired to follow in your brother's footsteps, even though that aspiration was absurd given the restrictions of your gender. If such desires have indeed occurred to you, it is time to put them to rest and move forward." He leaned closer and his gaze trapped hers. "I am offering you an opportunity that will never come your way again, Miss Montini. The chance to create a prominent, if not preeminent, private museum. Unfettered by the meaningless tyrannies of a board of trustees who can't tell the difference between an exquisite twenty-four-hundred-year-old Greek amphora and a worthless flower vase. You would have unlimited funds at your disposal to acquire new pieces, to complete what I have only begun.

"Think of it, Miss Montini." His voice lowered in a seductive manner, and in the back of her mind she wondered if this indeed was what it felt like to be seduced by a man, not a boy. To feel your resistance fade with every word. To feel an ache, a longing build slowly but inevitably toward surrender. To know, even as you denied it, even as you knew it was a dreadful mistake, that you would succumb. "You will never be among those who search for treasure, but you could be the one who brings those treasures to the world. With your knowledge and my fortune, you and I together could—"

"But won't you be dead?" Nathanial blurted.

"Nathanial," Gabriella snapped.

"He said he wanted this to happen after his death." Nathanial shrugged. "Which would indicate to me there would be no 'together' in any way unless he plans to oversee this from beyond the grave."

"Quite right, Mr. Harrington," Lord Rathbourne said in a cold, clipped tone. "However, while I am increasingly aware of my own mortality, I do not intend to depart this earth in the immediate future." His gaze returned to Gabriella. "As much as I have implicit faith in leaving my acquisitions in Miss Montini's capable hands, I would like to begin planning my legacy while I am still able to do so. And I would like you to begin cataloguing my collections as soon as possible."

She thought for a moment. It was, as he had said, irresistible.

"Gabriella?" Nathanial said.

And what else was she to do with her life? She squared her shoulders. "How soon?"

Nathanial's brow furrowed. "Surely you're not thinking of accepting this offer?"

The older man ignored him. "You may begin as early as tomorrow if you wish, at least to get some idea of the immensity of the job. I do not expect your complete attention until you have resolved the matter of the missing seal."

Nathanial stared. "Gabriella—"

"That is most gracious of you, my lord." She narrowed her eyes thoughtfully. "I imagine the salary would be commensurate with the position?"

"Not at all, Miss Montini. I had planned on paying you an exorbitant amount, far more than any comparable position anywhere." Lord Rathbourne smiled. "I find nothing ensures loyalty better than overpaid employees. We can discuss specific terms now if you wish or later if you prefer."

"Another day would be fine, there is no particular hurry. Indeed, until the matter of my brother's seal has been put to rest, I would be reluctant to accept any monetary compensation. Let us consider anything I do until then to be no more than preparatory." Gabriella extended her hand. "I shall return tomorrow, then."

Lord Rathbourne took her hand in his. "I foresee nothing but success in this venture we are engaging upon, Miss Montini."

She had the distinct impression this was a man who would permit nothing but success. His touch still triggered distaste, but then he didn't want her in the manner in which other men might. He wanted her skill, her knowledge, her mind. Nonetheless, it would be an uneasy alliance. She certainly didn't trust him, and she suspected he didn't trust anyone.

"Good day, Miss Montini." He released her hand. "Mr. Harrington."

"Sir." Nathanial nodded and they took their leave.

They didn't say a word to one another in the carriage ride back to his house, which suited her perfectly. She didn't wish to hear his admonitions, his warnings, his arrogant insistence that he knew better than she how she should live her life. He had no right to do so. Besides, she fully intended never to see him again when the matter of her brother's seal was resolved. It would be better that way. For them both.

The moment they entered the house, he took her elbow and steered her toward the library. The line of his jaw was tight with tension.

She huffed. "Where are we going?"

His voice was low, barely under control, and she realized she might have pushed him just a touch too far. Not that it wasn't his own fault.

"Short of taking you to my rooms, which I would dearly love to do—"

"What? And turn me over your knee?"

"That too," he snapped. "The only place in this house

that I can ensure privacy that would not be considered highly improper—"

"And we wouldn't want that."

"No, Gabriella, we wouldn't. I have the sensibilities of my mother and my sister to consider, as well as your reputation. Not that you seem to be giving it any thought whatsoever."

"When did you become so concerned with propriety?"

"When I met you." He kicked open the library door and fairly hauled her into the room.

Mr. Dennison jumped to his feet behind his desk. "Master Nathanial! Is something amiss?"

"You might say that, Dennison." Nathanial jerked his head toward the door. "Now, get out."

Gabriella folded her arms over her chest and glared.

Mr. Dennison's gaze skipped from Nathanial to Gabriella and back. "If there is something I can do to be of assistance—"

"I will call you." Nathanial blew a long breath. "My apologies for my rude behavior, but—"

"None necessary, sir." Mr. Dennison gathered up some papers on his desk, then quickly crossed the room to the door, casting a curious glance at Gabriella as he passed. She didn't doubt there would a note on its way to Florence within the hour. "I will be in the back parlor, sir, if you have need of me."

"If you will simply make sure we are not disturbed." Nathanial mustered a weak smile. "I would be most appreciative."

"Of course, sir." Dennison took his leave, closing the door firmly behind him.

Nathanial narrowed his eyes and stared at her in

silence. One minute stretched to a second and then a third. She resisted the urge to stamp her foot on the floor.

"Well, go on. Say it."

"Say what?" He practically growled the words.

She shifted uneasily. "Whatever it is you have to say."

His eyes narrowed even more, if possible. "What makes you think I have anything to say?"

"Come now, Nathanial. You are very nearly about to explode." She sniffed. "Your restraint is not that good."

"My restraint." His voice rose. *"My restraint?"*

"Yes, your restraint," she said in a lofty manner, and started toward the door. Perhaps this was not a good time to talk about Lord Rathbourne or anything else. Besides, there wasn't anything he could say that hadn't already crossed her mind.

"Oh, no." He stepped directly in her path. "We are going to discuss this and we are going to discuss this now."

"Very well." She turned away from him to take one of the chairs in front of the desk, sitting pointedly with her back to him. And realized it was not a good idea. "If you're going to ask if I'm insane again—"

"Oh, I no longer think there's a question about your sanity."

"I wasn't mad the last time you asked and I daresay I am not mad now."

She heard him behind her, and without warning he grabbed the chair she was in and spun it around to face him. "I won't allow it."

"You have no say in the matter."

"As you are in my home—"

"And I needn't be! I have my own— I have elsewhere I can reside and do so precisely as I think best."

He ignored her. "Nonetheless, I promised to protect you and I cannot do so if you are in that house. Rathbourne is a dangerous man." He leaned closer and braced his hands on the arms of the chair. His eyes blazed with anger. Without thinking, she shrank back. "He wants to add you to his collections the same way he has added his wife."

She scoffed. "Don't be absurd."

"He wants you to be the beautiful and brilliant curator of his collections. As much an acquisition as his art and his artifacts."

"Even if you're right . . . " She pushed him aside and got to her feet. " . . . why shouldn't I do this? I am more than qualified. Lord Rathbourne said it and he was right. I have indeed been training for this very position most of my life. Why shouldn't I be the curator of his collections?"

"It's not something that a woman—"

"I am so tired of that argument!" She crossed her arms over her chest. "And what am I supposed to do? I cannot—no—I will not spend the rest of my days with my nose in a book gaining knowledge I will never put to any useful purpose. It's all very well and good for you to stand there and say I cannot do this and I cannot do that because I happened to be born female. You can do whatever you want simply because you're a man. So you tell me, Nathanial, with the benefit of your male wisdom, what am I to do with the rest of my life?"

"You could do what other women do." He stared at her as if she had indeed lost her mind. "Get married and have children."

"No," she said sharply. "I can't."

"That's right because you're not like other women!"

He shook his head. "You certainly can't if you work for Rathbourne. Gabriella, your reputation will be ruined."

"I don't have a reputation."

"You will. Do you know what people will say?"

"Bloody hell," she said for the first time in years, the outburst as startling to her as it was to him. Regardless, she was past reason now. She raised her chin and lied. "They'll say what a clever, competent woman she is."

"They'll say you were bought and sold!" His tone was grim. "They'll say that you were as much an acquisition and are as much a possession as everything else in his collection. And such talk would inevitably include speculation about your personal duties with regard to Rathbourne."

She gasped. "There will be no personal duties!"

"No one will believe that!"

She shrugged. "I have never particularly cared what people have thought of me."

"I have always thought it absurd that we care so much about what other people think at all." Nathanial's gaze locked with hers. "And yet, despite what you say—which I don't believe, by the way—you will care."

"All right, then." Her voice rose. "I admit it! Yes, I know exactly what people will say. And yes, I understand it won't be especially pleasant. And yes, it will concern me and I will care!"

"Your reputation will be shattered!"

"No more so than—"

"You will be ruined!"

"I'm already ruined!" The words were out of her mouth before she realized what she'd said. "And that is why I will never marry."

He stared at her. "What do you mean by ruined?"

She widened her eyes in disbelief. "Surely you don't need me to explain? This is difficult enough as it is."

Realization dawned on his face and he paused. "How ruined?"

She choked. "I didn't know there were degrees!"

"Certainly there are degrees." He huffed. "Was it a single indiscretion or were you . . . "

"What? A whore in a brothel?" How could he possibly ask such a question? "Now who is insane? And furthermore it's none of your concern!"

"Of course it's my concern. I want to know how many men have come before me."

"Before you?" She scoffed. "There has been no *you*. Nor will there ever be!"

"I wouldn't wager on it!"

"Your confidence, Nathanial . . . " She strode to the door, yanked it open, and stepped through. " . . . is exceeded only by your arrogance." She slammed the door behind her.

And almost at once regretted it.

Nineteen

She slammed the door in his face? How dare she? How could she?

Not that he didn't deserve it. His heart sank. Asking just how ruined she was might not have been the wisest thing to say.

But he'd never been in this situation before. He ran his hand through his hair. What in the name of all that was holy was a man supposed to say when the woman he loved, the woman he fully intended to marry—even if he hadn't quite accepted it yet himself or mentioned it to her—told him she'd shared someone else's bed? It wasn't the kind of thing a man wanted to hear. One wanted—no, expected—to be the only man to ever share the bed of the love of his life.

He should have said he didn't care.

Damnation! If he'd taken a minute to think, perhaps his brain would have come up with just that, or at least something considerably better than his mouth had. He should have said it didn't matter to him if there had been a hundred men or just one. That no matter what had happened in her life before him, it was of no significance. He should have said the only thing that mattered was here and now and forever after.

Blast it all, that's what he should have said. Well, he would say it now if it wasn't too late.

He took a step toward the door and it swung open.

Gabriella stepped into the room, closed the door behind her and pressed her back against it. "I am not used to running away in a cowardly manner. I find I don't like it." Resolve lit her eyes. "When I was fifteen, I met a boy not much older than I who, for want of a better word, seduced me. I was young and foolish. And that, Nathanial, is the *degree* of my ruin."

Relief washed through him, and guilt. "You didn't have to tell me."

She studied him. "I know."

"Why did you?"

She shrugged, "I suppose I didn't want you to think even worse of me than you do. Now . . . " She folded her arms over her chest. " . . . it's your turn."

"My turn for what?"

"I made any number of assumptions about you before we even met. I must confess that in most of those I have been proved wrong. However, I am fairly certain that you too are not a virgin."

He sucked in a sharp breath. "Gabriella!"

"I simply want to know what the *degree* is when it comes to your own fallen status."

He huffed. "Men do not fall!"

"I know, Nathanial." She heaved a resigned sigh. "And I consider it a great pity. Another example of the inequities in this world." She paused. "I am going to my room now. I have quite a lot to think about, what with the question"—she gestured with her left hand—

"of Lord Rathbourne's offer of employment and"—she waved in his direction with her right—"you." With that, she nodded, turned, and swept from the room.

He stared after her. She didn't have to tell him about her past, and if he hadn't been such a fool, she wouldn't have felt compelled to do so. It was obviously something she didn't want to discuss. He'd always considered himself fairly successful with women. Probably not as successful as Gabriella imagined but successful nonetheless. But with her, his foot was lodged firmly and permanently in his mouth and he was a complete and total idiot.

And again he had missed the opportunity to tell her it didn't matter. He resisted the urge to smack his hand against his forehead and started after her.

Without warning the answer struck him and he pulled up short. She didn't have to tell him, but she had. She trusted him! She cared what he thought! He grinned. She couldn't live without him.

Thank God.

He hurried along the corridor to the main staircase. First he would tell her that he didn't care about anything that had happened before the moment they met. He started up the stairs. What she'd done or—he snorted to himself—who she'd pretended to be was of no consequence to him. He turned into the wing that housed their rooms. Then he'd tell her he loved her. He reached her door, was about to knock, instead grabbed the handle, flung it open, and said the first thing that came to mind.

"Did you love him?"

She stood near the window. Her eyes widened with indignation. "What are you doing here? You can't just come in here without my permission. And why didn't you knock?"

He started toward her. "I want to know if you loved him. This . . . this . . . *boy*. Not that it matters," he added quickly. "I simply want to know."

"Very well, then." She rolled her gaze toward the ceiling. "As I said, I was quite young. I knew nothing about love. I cannot say I know anything about love now, to be honest although I do know—" She shook her head and continued. "It was exciting and dangerous. As stupid as it sounds, I didn't even understand it was wrong. But I can say no, I was not in love with him. I've never been in love before. It was . . . " She thought for a moment. "Oh, I don't know, a first taste perhaps, of desire or passion."

"A first taste?" He moved closer.

She eyed him suspiciously. "What are you doing?"

"I'd like to discuss passion." He stepped toward her. "And desire."

A flicker of panic showed in her eyes. "I've never talked to anyone about this, Nathanial. Never. I don't know why I did so now."

"Because you trust me." He cast her a smug smile.

"Yes I suppose, but . . . " She shook her head. "Trust is a fragile thing that can be easily shattered." She stepped back. "I do hope you don't think you can now take advantage of me because I am—"

"I don't think that at all. I would never think such a thing." Indignation sounded in his voice, and before she could bolt he caught her and pulled her into his arms. "And I resent you thinking that I would. And I further think there is an excellent possibility that you will take advantage of me."

"Do you indeed?" She raised a brow. "And yet it is your arms that are around me."

"Convenient, isn't it?"

"If I intended to take advantage of you." She pushed against him in a token and ineffectual manner. "And I can't imagine why you would think such a thing is even possible."

"I don't." He gazed into her eyes and smiled slowly. "I simply hope."

She stared at him and heaved a sigh of surrender. "You are so annoying," she muttered, threw her arms around his neck and pressed her lips to his. He gathered her closer, slanted his lips across hers.

Her mouth opened to his, and his tongue met hers. She tasted exactly like she smelled, of spice and heat and all the things he'd ever loved. Desire welled within him and hunger deepened his kiss. And she responded in kind, sharing his hunger, his greed, his need.

Abruptly, she wrenched her lips from his. "This is a dreadful mistake, Nathanial."

"And yet it seems so right," he murmured, his lips trailing along the side of her neck. "We are made one for the other, Gabriella. I cannot imagine why it would be a mistake, but do feel free to tell me."

"Because I have grown to like you, and yes, to trust you and possibly . . . " She sighed, and he nuzzled that lovely spot where neck met shoulder. "I am not a fool, Nathanial. Anything more between us and I shall surely lose my heart. And you will most certainly break it."

"Nonsense." She could scoff all she wanted but she did indeed smell like a summer day. And he'd always loved summer.

"There isn't a doubt in my mind." She pushed out of

his arms and moved away. "I have never experienced heartbreak, except the kind one feels at the death of a brother. I never knew my mother. I was too young at the death of my father to understand the depth of my loss. I have always thought of myself as a person of strength, but this, you . . . " She waved at him. "I find it terrifying and therefore best avoided. I suspect my heart is a fragile thing."

"I would never hurt you." He reached for her but she stepped out of the way.

"You would never mean to hurt me, but you would. It's inevitable."

"I don't believe that."

"What you believe isn't nearly as important as what I know about . . . the way the world works, if you will. There is no future for us." She raised her chin. "Now, please leave."

"Do you really want me to go?"

"Yes, I do." She waved at the door. "Go. Now. Please."

"Very well." He studied her for a long moment. "But this isn't over between us, Gabriella."

"Of course not." She brushed an escaped tendril of hair away from her face. "We still need to find the seal."

"In addition," he said firmly, "there is much that remains unsettled. The question of Lord Rathbourne's offer has not been resolved—"

"Oh, I do think—"

"Nor has the matter of your future."

"I daresay, my future has nothing to do with—"

His gaze met hers directly. "I have a great deal I need to say to you, and I'm not sure this is the best time. You're not especially rational at the moment—"

She huffed. "I am unfailingly rational."

"Yes, that is yet another thing I love about you." He grinned and left the room, leaving her staring after him with something that might have been confusion or apprehension or . . . hope.

He still hadn't told her he didn't care about her past. He'd probably care even less when he knew all there was to know. But right now he knew the only thing that really mattered.

She'd never been in love before. *Before*. What a glorious word. His grin widened.

Until now.

He strode down the hall with a swagger in his step he would have considered obnoxious in another man. Certainly there were problems to overcome beyond the question of the seal. First and foremost was that nonsense about Rathbourne and his ridiculous position. Still, given her education and intelligence, he could see why she might find it appealing. And then there was the question of money. With the death of her brother, it was obvious to him she didn't have any. Aside from that apricot gown of hers, the rest of her clothes, though well cared for, were decidedly worn. Rathbourne's offer would tempt even the most financially sound.

Nate passed Quint's door and heard sounds of occupation inside. He clenched his jaw. Good. His brother was back. It was past time he and Quint had a long talk, not that he thought Quint knew anything about the missing seal. Still, the queasy feeling that had settled in the pit of his stomach with McGowan's disclosures continued to linger.

Nate rapped sharply on the door. A faint voice sounded from the other side. He pushed opened the door and didn't see his brother in the sitting room that opened on one side of his bed chamber, a mirror image of his own rooms.

"Quint?"

"Here." His brother sauntered out of the adjoining dressing room, half dressed, drying his face with a towel.

Nate raised a brow. "Just now shaving for the day?"

Quint grinned.

Nate studied him. Quint was the only person he'd ever met who could spend two days drinking and whoring and who knew what else, and look more refreshed than tired.

"We have to talk," Nate said firmly.

"Do we?" Quint tossed the towel onto a chair. "I don't like the sound of that." He moved to the wardrobe and perused its contents. "What do you wish to talk about, little brother?"

"Miss Montini—"

"Ah yes, the delectable Miss Montini." He selected a shirt, moved to the cheval mirror, and pulled it on. Both brothers had long ago dispensed with the services of valets, even in London. "Have you kissed her yet?"

"That's neither here nor there and none of your concern."

Quint caught his brother's eye in the mirror and raised a brow.

"Once or twice perhaps," Nate muttered.

"And just a few minutes ago, no doubt."

Nate narrowed his eyes suspiciously. "Why would you say that?"

"I heard you go into her room." Quint chuckled. "It has been my experience that when there is a discussion between a man and a woman that involves screaming at the top of their lungs and then silence, it means either they have killed one another or fallen into each other's arms. You don't appear to be dead."

"No, well . . . " Nate grinned in a sheepish manner, then paused. "We weren't screaming."

Quint grinned.

"So you couldn't have heard us."

Quint's grin widened.

"Yes, I kissed her," Nate said, his tone harder than he had intended.

"And you're in love with her."

For a moment he considered denying it, but to what purpose? He drew a deep breath. "Yes, I am."

Quint chuckled. "I knew she would do for you."

"I've never met anyone like her."

"There's never been anyone like her."

Nate ignored him. "She is equal parts intelligence and foolishness, honesty and secrets. From the moment I first saw her at Reggie's ball," he shook his head, "I have not been able to get her out of my mind."

Quint raised a brow. "So this is a permanent state?"

"Yes it is." Nate nodded. "Although convincing her of that . . . "

"How difficult can it be? You say, 'I love you, marry me, and I shall spend the rest of my days doing everything in my power to make you blissfully happy.' "

Nate shook his head. "It's not that easy."

"Have you tried it?"

"Admittedly, I haven't—"

"Then you should."

Nate eyed his older brother. "Should I be taking

advice from a man who has never uttered such words himself?"

"The fact that I haven't doesn't mean I don't know the proper way to go about it. Besides, she already knows how you feel."

"How could she—"

"Everyone in the house knows how you feel."

"Still." Nate shook his head. "I don't know that it matters."

"Make it matter." Quint rolled his gaze at the ceiling. "It's obvious she feels the same way about you."

Nate grinned. "I hope so." He blew a long breath. "She has come to trust me to a certain extent but not completely. She has secrets. There is much she has not told me."

Quint shrugged. "We all have secrets."

"Yes, we do." He studied his brother carefully, then drew a deep breath. "Did you steal her brother's seal?"

Quint met his gaze directly. "No."

"Very well," Nate said slowly. "Let me rephrase that. Do you have Montini's seal?"

Quint paused for a long moment. "Not on me."

"Did you win it from Javier Gutierrez in a game of chance in Crete?"

Quint's eyes narrowed. "Lucky guess, brother?"

Nate grimaced. "Unlucky, I would say."

Quint heaved a sigh of surrender. "Yes, I wrested the seal away from Gutierrez." He snorted in disgust. "The man is an idiot."

"The man is dangerous."

"So am I when necessary." He waved at a nearby chair. "You might as well sit down. It's a long story."

Nate sat in the indicated seat and stared at his brother. "Then you should begin."

"Very well." He thought for a moment. "First you should know it's not Montini's seal."

"Oh?" Nate raised a brow.

"Years ago, when I was working with Professor Ashworth, he purchased a crate in Athens of . . . well, mostly trash. Bits and pieces of pottery, marbles, ancient tools, that sort of thing. There were several cylinder seals in the crate as well. One caught my attention." He met his brother's gaze. "It looked Akkadian and was carved from greenstone."

Nate held his breath. "And?"

"And, from a cursory examination it appeared to have the symbols for Ambropia and the Virgin's Secret. However," he clenched his jaw, "to my eternal regret, I put it back in the crate intending to study it further at a later time. I never saw it again. The crate was stolen."

"What did the professor say?"

"I didn't tell him." Quint shook his head in disgust. "It was what he'd spent much of his life looking for. I wanted to surprise him with it. I was such a fool. I never should have let it out of my sight."

"You think Montini stole it?"

"No, although I wouldn't have put it past him. Besides, if he had stolen it then, it wouldn't have taken him years to announce his find. I have no idea who took it originally, nor how many hands it might have passed through before it came into Montini's possession." He shook his head. "But I knew it was the seal I'd seen—had in my hands—the moment I saw Montini's impression."

"And?" Nate prompted.

"And." His gaze met Nate's without so much as a glimmer of remorse. "And I had every intention of stealing it from him."

Nate drew his brows together. "But you didn't?"

"No." Quint blew a long breath. "I was about to, but Gutierrez did so before I could."

"You saw Gutierrez take the seal?"

Quint chuckled. "He didn't see me but I was practically right behind him. It was no secret how superstitious Montini was about his finds. I knew, I'm assuming Gutierrez knew as well. There was every reason to believe that Montini wouldn't unwrap the cloth around the seal until it came time to present it to the Verification Committee. Which meant he wouldn't discover the theft until then."

"We think Gutierrez might have been in the employ of Lord Rathbourne," Nate said. "His lordship admitted to Gabriella that he had tried to acquire the seal." He thought for a moment. "But why didn't Gutierrez bring the seal to Rathbourne as soon as he had it?"

Quint shook his head. "Who knows why a man like Gutierrez does what he does? Besides, that would have meant a trip to London, and I wouldn't be surprised if Rathbourne isn't the only one employing Gutierrez for less than legitimate purposes. But it worked in my favor. I watched Gutierrez carefully, waiting for the opportunity to take the seal." He glanced at his brother. "Didn't you wonder at the somewhat meandering path our travels have taken this past year?"

"Not really." Nate grimaced. "It didn't seem out of the ordinary at the time."

"At any rate, my opportunity arose in Crete. From my observations of Gutierrez, I knew he was an insatiable gambler and had as well a taste for drink. He is the kind of man who does not know his own limits when it comes to spirits and thinks he is in control of his faculties when he is not." Quint shrugged. "It was remarkably easy to get him inebriated, engage him in cards, and win the seal from him." He chuckled. "I think it took him a few days to realize what he had lost."

"I heard he was furious."

"Yes, I suppose he was." He paused. "I understand Montini had an encounter with him in Crete as well. Shortly after that I heard Montini had been killed, his throat slashed."

Nate stared. "You never mentioned that."

"You didn't want me to talk about the kind of man Montini was. I assumed you wouldn't want me mentioning how I had heard he'd died either."

"You could have told me. Although it scarcely matters now, I suppose. So . . . " Nate chose his words with care. "Where is the seal?"

Quint hesitated for a long moment, then sighed. "It's in the attic."

Nate got it his feet. "Let's go, then."

"May I at least finish getting dressed?" Quint tucked his shirt into his trousers.

"No." Nate started toward the door.

"Mother will not like it if she sees me without a coat," Quint warned.

"Then we'll take care that she doesn't see you."

Nate led the way up the stairs to the servants' quarters and to the final flight of stairs to the attic, Quint a few steps behind him.

"What did you intend to do with the seal? Try and find Ambropia?"

"No," Quint said in a tone that indicated that was all he would say on the subject.

Nate opened the attic door and turned to his brother. "Well?"

Quint brushed past him. "I put it in the trunk with Great-grandmother's things." He chuckled. "It seemed appropriate."

Nate trailed after him. His heart sped up with excitement. He'd give the seal to Gabriella, she'd give it to the Antiquities Society, and he could then proceed to convince her that her future from this point on was with him. And why not? After all, he'd be her hero.

"I hid it up here the day I got home."

"The day of Reggie's ball?"

Quint nodded. He skirted around the leavings of generations of Harringtons, furniture discarded in favor of something more in style, only to be pushed farther back into the recesses of the massive attic when its replacements were in turn discarded. Paintings were stacked against the walls, trunks and crates and boxes hindered their path. He reached the trunk in question in very nearly the same spot it had occupied since they'd last played up here as children. He flipped open the lid, bent down, and fished around inside it.

"Here it is." Quint pulled out a small, cloth-wrapped bundle tied with a string. He pulled off the string, unwrapped the seal and stared. A moment later his wry laughter rang through the attic.

Nate stared at him. "What do you find so amusing?"

"Irony, dear brother. The world is full of irony. And jokes perpetrated by a god far more whimsical than I. This." Quint thrust the bundle at him and grinned. "This is not Montini's seal."

Twenty

What do you mean this is not Montini's seal?" Disbelief twisted Nate's stomach.

"Here. See for yourself." Quint handed the seal to him. "It's not greenstone."

Nate held it up to the faint light from the far off attic windows. "It's chalcedony. And it looks . . . " His heart sank. "Late Assyrian."

"The one we're looking for, the one I took from Gutierrez, was Akkadian, a mere fifteen hundred year difference."

Nate glared at his brother. "How could this happen?"

"How would I know?" Quint snapped.

"The seal was in your possession!" Nate narrowed his eyes. "Wasn't it?"

"It was when I took it from Gutierrez! I examined it thoroughly. Bloody hell." Quint stalked back and forth across the attic. "I've done it again. I had it in my hands! And I lost it! Again! How could I have been so stupid? How could I have—"

"How did you lose it?"

Quint stopped in mid-step and glared at his brother as though he was an idiot. "I didn't *lose* it."

"You just said—"

"I didn't lose it! Somebody must have stolen it from me and substituted that one. The same way Gutierrez stole it from Montini. And someone else stole it from Ashcroft, and God knows how many other people stole it from who knows how many other people through the years. Through the centuries!" He gritted his teeth. "It's the curse, that's what it is."

Nate shook his head. "The seal isn't cursed."

"No, but the city is, remember? The Curse of the Virgin's Secret? 'He whosoever disturbs the sleep of the Virgin's city,'" he gestured in a wild manner, "and so on and so forth?"

Nate scoffed. "You don't believe in that."

"I'd rather believe in a curse than my own stupidity." Quint sank down on top of a crate, rubbed his forehead and muttered more to himself than to his brother. "But I cannot believe this. I had it in my hands."

Nate stared. His brother's distress was not only foreign to his nature but struck Nate as out of all proportion to the loss. They'd lost far greater treasures before. There was more here than Quint had admitted thus far. Damnation, did everyone around here have secrets but him?

Quint's brow furrowed in thought. "I examined the seal after I won it, then I wrapped it back up and tucked it in my bag." He got to his feet and paced. "Every now and then I would check to make certain it was still there, but I never unwrapped it again."

"Could Gutierrez have taken it?"

"It's a definite possibility." Quint paused and looked pointedly at his brother. "As is Montini." He blew a long breath. "As are any number of other people."

"It doesn't make any sense." Nate shook his head. "If Montini had it, he would have mentioned it in his letters. Probably his last, given you had the seal not long before his death."

"One would think."

"His last letter . . . " Nate thought for a moment. "While not incoherent, it was little more than ramblings."

"If Montini had it, wouldn't he have wanted to let his sister know?"

"The more I learn of Montini, the more I hesitate to assume anything he might have done. It is a possibility, though. You said he was in Crete when you were."

Quint nodded.

"Then if indeed Montini was the one who switched the seals . . . " Nate blew a long breath. "Where is the seal now?"

Gabriella stared at the door that had closed behind Nathanial and finally sank down on the bed. Nathanial Harrington was a constant surprise.

She'd never imagined that any man, upon hearing of her ruined state, would act as if it was of no real consequence. Surely he must care somewhat, as evidenced by his stupid question about the degree of her ruin. Regardless, it was probably no more than curiosity on his part. It wasn't as if he planned to marry her. He'd said her future was still unresolved and hadn't corrected her when she told him they had no future together. Of course not. The brothers of earls did not marry the ruined sisters of treasure hunters. It might well happen that way in fairy tales, but life was a far different matter.

She'd fully intended to disappear from his life when their search had ended. To perhaps travel. But now Rathbourne had presented her with another possibility. And disappearing from Nathanial's life didn't mean she had to leave London. Besides, he would no doubt soon be off on his travels with his brother, back to those parts of the world where man had lived eons ago and left remnants of those lives behind. Their own lives would take different directions, and it was entirely likely they would never cross paths again. An awful ache welled up inside her at the thought.

How different her life might have been. As pointless as it was to consider it now, her thoughts couldn't help but stray to her mother and the family she had never known. She got to her feet and paced the room. It was too late. One couldn't go back and start one's life anew. She was who and what she was and nothing could change that.

Despite what she'd said to Rathbourne and Nathanial, she wasn't nearly as confident about the wisdom of accepting his lordship's offer as she knew she sounded. There wasn't anything Nathanial had said that hadn't already crossed her mind. If one wished to speak in terms of degrees of ruin, being in Rathbourne's employ would certainly put her past any hope of true respectability, even though the position would increase her stature in the rarified world of antiquities. She would be what no other woman had dared to be before. And she would pay the price. But it would give her life purpose, and put to some practical use all the knowledge she had worked so hard to acquire. And if, with the passage of the years, her heart became no different than the relics in Rathbourne's collections, brittle and fragile and ancient, who would notice? Who would care?

It was a distressing thought, and she brushed it from her mind. Time enough to deal with the rest of her life later. She and Nathanial still had the seal to find. She'd known from the start that recovering it would be difficult if not impossible, even if she hadn't wished to accept it. But perhaps it was time to face the truth. They'd found no significant information as to who might have taken the seal or where it might be now. Tomorrow she would have complete access to Rathbourne's collections and could verify for herself his claim that he didn't have it. She blew a long breath. Other than that, she was simply out of ideas.

Still, admitting defeat, giving up the search, would mean it was time as well to give up Nathanial. She knew that day was fast approaching. Somehow, she knew as well this longing inside her—this sense of inevitability when she looked into his eyes, the feeling of perfection when he held her in his arms—surely this was love. If not for a youthful indiscretion . . .

No, it wasn't just her ruin that kept them apart. They were from different worlds and nothing could change that. She moved to the window and gazed unseeing over the street below. Once, she had been seduced by a boy, a cursory, not especially pleasant experience that was over very nearly as soon as it had begun. Today, Rathbourne's words and promises had seduced her as well. Now, she wanted yet another seduction.

If she was to live the rest of her life alone, it seemed a shame not to have at least one memory to sustain her through the long years ahead. One night of passion and desire and lying in the arms of the man she loved. One night of imagining it was not the end but merely the beginning.

One night would never be enough. But if she couldn't have Nathanial forever, one night would have to do.

Dinner had been an odd affair. Everyone seemed preoccupied by their own thoughts. Quint was obviously annoyed at himself for losing the seal. Gabriella had been even more reticent than usual; probably Rathbourne's offer dwelled on her mind. Sterling was always somewhat reserved. Mother continued to study Gabriella in a thoughtful manner. And he didn't know what his next step should be. He was certain if he did not tread warily, he would surely lose whatever hope he might have of winning Gabriella's heart and her hand. If not for Reggie's constant and excited chatter about the season and who she had met and the endless social activities ahead, dinner would have been a dismal and disquieting affair.

Now, Nate paced his room, his dressing gown thrown over his nightclothes, a glass of brandy in his hand. Sterling had insisted that Quint accompany him and Reggie to a musicale that had sounded rather dreadful to everyone but his sister. Mother said she had correspondence to attend to and retired to her rooms. Gabriella refused to meet his gaze throughout dinner and then retreated to her room, claiming it had been an eventful day and she was tired. He had fully intended to retire as well but found himself too restless to even attempt to sleep.

He hadn't had a chance to speak privately with Gabriella, to tell her what he'd learned from Quint. In truth, he wasn't sure exactly what he would say. He now knew who had taken the seal from her brother, and knew as well that it had been in his own brother's possession. But where the seal was now—that was still an unanswered question. A question that might never be answered.

And that wasn't the only question. He took a sip of the brandy. There was still much he didn't know about Gabriella. He was fairly certain now that she was indeed the brother he had met in Egypt. He was a fool not to have realized it sooner. And he was certain as well that "John," the footman, was in truth Xerxes Muldoon. But since the Antiquities Society Ball he'd had no opportunity to question the big man. No, he'd been too busy trying to convince Gabriella of the folly of working for Lord Rathbourne. Or too busy getting the truth from his brother.

Beyond that, he still hadn't told her of his feelings, and in that too he wasn't sure what to say. Did one just blurt out declarations of love? Proposals of marriage? In the back of his mind he had the most awful conviction that if he didn't say something soon, it would be too late.

He blew a long breath. He'd never considered himself a coward, but the fear of not having her by his side for the rest of his days lay like a heavy weight in the pit of his stomach. No, it was better to put off saying anything at all than to run the risk that she didn't share his feelings. Still, Gabriella had said that she'd never been in love *before*. Which did seem to indicate she was in love now. He clung to the word like a shipwrecked sailor hanging onto a floating spar.

This was absurd, he told himself. All that was unresolved between them was driving him mad. He downed the last of his drink and set the glass beside a decanter. It needed to be settled and it needed to be settled now.

He stalked to his door and flung it open.

To his surprise, Gabriella stood in the corridor, a wrapper worn over her nightclothes, eyes wide, hand poised to knock.

Twenty-one

"What are you doing here?" Nathanial asked sharply.

At once her confidence faltered. She squared her shoulders. "I wish to . . . " Wish to what? Experience true seduction by a man? By him? "Talk to you."

"You do?" His gaze slid over her. "Dressed like that?"

She ignored him. "You said today there was much that remained unsettled. I am here to . . . to settle it."

"It?"

"It. Everything." She pulled her brows together. "Are you always this obtuse or is there something about me that encourages you to be annoying?"

"There's something about you." He chuckled. "Did you wish to come in?"

"No," she said in a sharper tone than she'd intended. "I wish to stand here in the corridor."

"It would be most improper, you know, for you to be in my rooms, especially dressed as you are. Most of my family is gone, Mother's rooms are in the other wing, and the servants are all abed. We shall be quite alone."

"I am aware of that."

"Very well, then." He stepped aside and waved her in. "Do come in."

She stepped into the room. He closed the door behind her with a snap and she jumped.

"Are you nervous?"

She scoffed, belying the churning in her stomach. "Not at all."

His quarters consisted of a small sitting room with a writing desk and two comfortable looking wing chairs that flanked a love seat, the chairs positioned before a fireplace. An archway off to one side revealed a bedroom and a bed of massive proportions. Obviously Jacobean, it was dark and heavy and masculine and, she swallowed hard, most appropriate for seduction.

"Would you care to sit down?" He waved at the love seat.

"I would prefer to stand at the moment." She clasped her hands together and drew a deep breath. "First of all, you should know, I have no intention of marrying you."

He grinned. "I don't recall asking you."

"I realize that, but should you decide, out of some misplaced sense of honor, to do so, you should know the answer would be no."

"Thank you for settling that." He studied her curiously. "Why exactly are you here?"

"I have been giving . . . that is, I have been thinking . . ."

He shook his head. "Oh, that's never good. Please don't tell me you have a plan."

She glared at him. "You are making this most difficult."

"Making what most difficult?"

"This." Without thinking, she waved at the bed in the next room. "All of this."

"All of what?"

"I want you to seduce me," she blurted, then winced. She hadn't planned to simply announce it, but then her plans never seemed to go well anyway.

His eyes widened. "Do you?"

"Yes, I do." She paused. "You seem surprised."

"I suppose I shouldn't be, given your state of undress, but yes, I am surprised."

She shrugged. "I wasn't sure what to wear to a seduction. I've never been seduced by . . . "

"A man?"

"Yes, a man before. It seemed to me the fewer clothes I had on, the more . . . expedient it would be."

"Yes, well, expediency is always a consideration in seduction." He snorted back a laugh.

"Do you think this is amusing?"

"No." He smiled. "I think it's delightful."

"Excellent. You should probably begin by kissing me." She raised her chin and closed her eyes. And waited. And waited. She opened her eyes. "Well?"

He grinned. "Well what?"

Heat rushed up her face and she started for the door. "If you don't wish to—"

He moved to block her way. "There is nothing, Gabriella, absolutely nothing, I wish to do more."

"Well, then." Again she raised her chin and closed her eyes. And again waited.

"Open your eyes." He sighed. "I am not about to

seduce a woman who looks like she's bravely going to the gallows."

"My apologies. I don't intend to look like I'm going to the gallows, bravely or otherwise. I am, in truth . . . " She thought for a moment. "Eager—yes, that's what I am. Perhaps we should . . . " She took a step toward the bedroom.

"Good Lord, Gabriella, I am not going to throw you on the bed and have my way with you." He cast her a disgusted look, crossed the floor to a decanter, filled a glass and brought it to her. "Here, drink this."

She took the glass and eyed it with suspicion. "What is it?"

"It's an ancient elixir that will cause you to fling yourself at my feet, begging for my very touch."

"It's seems to me I have very nearly done that already," she murmured, and took a long sip, the liquor burning a path down her throat, washing her in an immediate sensation of warmth. "It's brandy."

"Disappointed?"

"No, I like brandy. I don't have it very often but I do like it." She took another sip. "It's quite tasty and very warming."

"It's also very potent." He plucked the glass from her hand and eyed it. "And already half gone."

"Then you should refill it." She did feel more relaxed. And she hadn't lied to him, in spite of some apprehension, which was to be expected after all—she was indeed eager.

He refilled the glass and handed it to her. "Only one more sip. I don't want you inebriated."

"Really?" She took another long sip and gave him back the glass. "Why not?"

"Because while it might be 'expedient,' it won't be nearly as much fun for either of us if one of us isn't aware of what is happening."

"Oh." She drew her brows together. "That makes sense. I do wish to be aware." She met his gaze firmly. "I fully intend for the memories of tonight to sustain me through the rest of my life."

He swirled the brandy in his glass and studied her, his expression unreadable. "I do hope it lives up to expectations."

"I can't imagine otherwise." She smiled. "Seduce me, Nathanial."

"Oh, I have every intention of doing so. But seduction, my dear Gabriella, is an art. And like any art, cannot be rushed."

"Are you an artist, then?"

"Tonight I am," he murmured, and circled around behind her. She held her breath. The lightest kiss fluttered against the back of her neck, and she sucked in a sharp breath. His voice was low and enticing. "There are especially sensitive places on a women that I suspect most women are not even aware of."

"Are there?" she said weakly.

"There are indeed. The back of the neck." Again she felt the barest whisper of a kiss. His arm curled around her and he pulled the tie of her wrapper free, then pushed the garment off her shoulders and it fell to the floor. His hands rested on her shoulders. "The curve where neck meets shoulder." His lips caressed that very spot, and she tilted her head to one side and sighed.

"Oh my . . . " Her eyes closed. He gently turned her to face him.

"The base of the throat." His lips murmured against

her throat, the sensation delightful and thrilling. She felt him fumble with the ties that closed her gown, and a drift of cooler air when it opened. He slid the gown off her shoulders and down her arms until it too joined the wrapper on the floor. And she stood completely naked in front of him.

She opened her eyes. He framed her face with his hands, and his lips met hers in a kiss soft and gentle. A prelude. She opened her mouth to his, and his tongue traced the edges of her lips, slowly and deliberately. She heard a faint moan and realized it had come from her.

She rested her hands on his chest, feeling the heat of his body through the silk of his dressing gown. His hands released her face but his mouth lingered on hers. He skimmed his hands lightly down her arms, then wrapped his arms around her and pulled her closer.

His mouth slanted over hers, demanding now, insistent. Heat gathered in her midsection and lower. She responded to his kiss with a heretofore unknown need, an urgency that seemed to come from somewhere deep inside her. Her tongue dueled with his and she reveled in the taste of him, of brandy and desire and everything she'd ever wanted.

One hand splayed across the small of her back, the other drifted to caress her derriere, and she pressed herself closer to him. The evidence of his arousal was hard against her, and without conscious thought she ground her hips against him.

He groaned. "Good God, Gabriella."

"Nathanial." She fairly sighed his name. "I want . . . "

"I know, my love." He scooped her into her arms, carried her to the bed, and laid her gently down. As if she were a fragile, delicate treasure.

She watched him quickly strip off his clothes through eyes half closed with desire. Her gaze drifted from broad shoulders to firmly muscled chest and lower, over his taut stomach to his erection, swollen and enormous. Heat flooded her face and she thought her blush odd, since she wasn't the least bit embarrassed at seeing him naked. Or at him seeing her naked. Nothing mattered but the longing for his body to join with hers.

Nathanial lay down beside her, kissed the base of her throat and trailed kisses lower to a point between her breasts. His hand cupped one breast and his fingers grazed her nipple. She gasped with unexpected pleasure. His mouth moved to her other breast and he ran his tongue in a circle around her nipple until her breath came faster. He took her nipple carefully in his mouth and sucked, his hand still toying with her other breast until she writhed with the sheer pleasure of the sensations he produced with his teeth and his tongue and his hands. Moisture gathered between her legs and she shifted her hips upward wanting . . . more.

"Oh . . . yes . . . "

He shifted his mouth to her other breast and slowly ran the tips of his fingers over her stomach in easy circles. His hand drifted lower, the touch of his fingers igniting a blaze deep inside her. He caressed the tops of her thighs, then slipped his hand between her legs, and they fell open as if of their own accord.

He touched her then, in that most intimate spot, and pleasure she'd never suspected shot through her. And she moaned and wanted more. Much more.

"You are so beautiful," he said softly.

He slid his fingers over her, over that point of exquisite pleasure. And toyed with her and teased until her hands clutched at the bedclothes and she squirmed with unbridled need.

Her hips arched upward and she moaned. "Please."

She wondered if she'd lost her mind and thought if this was madness, what a glorious thing it was. She scarcely noticed when his mouth left her breast and followed the path taken by his hand, lower across her stomach and lower still. Until his fingers parted her and she felt the touch of his tongue.

"Dear Lord." She gasped under his touch. "Nathanial." She could barely choke out his name. "You can't. You shouldn't. You—"

"Seduction, my sweet . . . " His raised his head and looked at her, his eyes dark with passion. " . . . is a complicated art."

His head nestled back between her legs and his tongue continued what his fingers had begun. And she was lost. Any reluctance to allow what was surely most depraved was dashed aside by never imagined delight. She knew only the pleasure, the sweet sensation of his touch. And it was not enough. A yearning ache built inside her as if she were struggling toward something just out of reach. She needed . . . she wanted . . .

Abruptly, Nathanial moved, and she gasped. Surely this wasn't all he intended? She knew full well there was more to seduction. Although, thus far it had been so much more than she'd ever dreamed. Still, surely it couldn't end like this with her needing, wanting, something more.

He positioned himself between her knees and she bit back a sob of relief. She lifted her hips up to meet him, a whimper of need escaping from her lips. His arousal nudged her and she tensed. She wanted this . . . no, she needed this. Still, she'd only done this that once and it was so long ago. She couldn't recall the boy's erection but certainly it was far smaller and insignificant than this massive implement that was about to impale her.

He nuzzled the side of her neck. "Gabriella, my love."

He eased himself into her. It was an odd sensation, She didn't remember this feeling at all. He entered her slowly and she felt tight around him and stretched and filled. He lay quietly for a long moment then began to move, with an easy, measured stroke. And the strangeness of it faded to a new and unique pleasure. She moved with him and her body throbbed with his.

She clutched at his shoulders and urged him on. His thrusts came deeper, faster, harder, and she wanted more. Her legs wrapped around his. Tension, odd and insistent and unyielding, coiled within her. With every stroke of his, her need built, until she wondered if she might burst with the intensity of the growing pressure. And longed for it. Her hips rose to meet him, welcome him, take him.

Without warning her body exploded around his. She arched upward and dug her fingers into his flesh. Wave after wave of unexpected pleasure coursed through her. Vaguely, through a fog of sensation, she heard someone cry out and realized it was her. He gripped her tighter and pumped faster. With a groan, he thrust deeply into her and shuddered. Warmth filled her and he moaned against her ear and stilled.

For a long moment they lay together, still joined, legs entwined, hearts beating in tandem. It was quite the most extraordinary thing she'd ever experienced. The intimacy of his body joining with hers, the spiraling desire, the joy of release. And now, still together as one, her breathing in rhythm with his, utter peace and complete contentment enveloped her. She could stay like this, with him, forever.

At last he shifted and pulled out of her. A sense of loss gripped her, but he drew her close against him, as if never to let her go. She reveled in a satisfaction she'd never known, never expected to know. She rested her head on his chest, his hand stroking her hair.

"So." A smile sounded in his voice. "Was your seduction acceptable?"

"Yes, Nathanial, it was acceptable." She smiled. "More than acceptable." She sighed against him. "It was delightful."

Indeed, she'd never felt quite so delighted in her life. And cherished. And even, at least for the moment, loved. That, no doubt, was an illusion brought on by intimacy. Still, even an illusion could be enjoyed, as long as one accepted that it was nothing more than fantasy.

"Now you are truly ruined, you know."

"And I wasn't truly ruined before?"

He chuckled. "Degrees, Gabriella, it's all a question of degrees."

"Well, then I suppose I am." She snuggled against him. Against the solid warmth of him. There was something about laying pressed against a naked man who had just made you feel things you'd never suspected possible that was unlike anything she'd ever imagined. There was obviously something to be said for being truly, gloriously ruined. "I certainly feel truly ruined."

"Gabriella . . . " His voice was deceptively casual. "About this offer of Rathbourne's . . . "

At once the feeling of contentment vanished. She

pulled away from him, sat up and clutched the covers around her. "Yes?"

He sat up, resting his back against the pillows. His gaze met hers directly. "I think it's a mistake."

"I think it's an opportunity," she said slowly. "And aside from other considerations, I now have the chance to make certain Rathbourne does not have the seal."

"I don't care. He's a dangerous man."

"I'm not concerned."

"That in itself is a problem." His eyes narrowed. "You should be concerned. And wary."

She studied him carefully. "Do you now plan to forbid me to accept his offer? Again?"

"If I have to." His voice was grim.

"I thought we had established that you had no right to forbid me to do anything."

"This," he gestured in an angry manner, "gives me the right."

"This," she mimicked his gesture, "doesn't give you any rights whatsoever. I was already ruined, remember?"

"I can scarcely forget," he snapped.

Of course he couldn't forget, what man could? "This discussion is at an end," she said in a cold manner. "I need to return to my room. My clothes—"

"I'll get them," he said through gritted teeth, threw off the covers, slid out of bed, and strode into the sitting room.

"You're naked!" She clapped her hands over her eyes, the annoying feeling of heat again flushing her face.

"I was just as naked a minute ago," he muttered from the sitting room. "It didn't seem to bother you then."

"A minute ago it didn't!"

"You can uncover your eyes." He had slipped on his

dressing gown. "Here." He dropped her nightclothes on the bed.

"Turn around."

"Whatever you want." He turned around. "Because everything is apparently about whatever you want."

"That's absurd." She scrambled out of bed and quickly slipped on her gown. "I have no idea what you are talking about."

"*You* want to find the seal! *You* want to restore your brother's name! *You* want to work for Rathbourne! And tonight," his voice hardened, "*you* wanted *me*."

"I apologize if it was an inconvenience for you." She pulled on her wrapper and tied it. "I shall not bother you again." She started for the door.

"Damnation, Gabriella, do not put words in my mouth." He grabbed her and pulled her into his arms. "It wasn't an inconvenience and only you would say something like that."

She struggled against him but he held her tight.

"I have wanted you from the first moment I saw you. You should know that if you don't already. But I want more. And one of the things I want is to keep you safe."

"I can't imagine any harm will come to—"

"I can!" he said sharply. "I can imagine all sorts of harm that might come to you." He drew a deep breath. "If you insist on going to Rathbourne's, I would insist—"

She narrowed her eyes. "Insist?"

"Fine, a request, then."

"And if I don't agree, will you threaten to have me arrested again?"

"Perhaps! Or maybe I'll just tie you to a chair and keep you right here until you learn some sense!"

"Oh, you'd like that wouldn't you?"

A hint of wicked amusement glinted in his brown eyes, and the most inappropriate frisson of desire shot through her. She ignored it. "Probably." He shook his head. "I don't want you to go to that house alone."

"You're not—"

"No, I'm not. I would like you to take one of the footman along." He studied her intently. "The new one, I think. John Farrell."

Xerxes? She nodded. "Very well."

He raised a brow. "What? No argument?"

"It seems a reasonable enough request. Now . . . " She pushed against him. "Are you going to release me?"

"For the moment." He gazed into her eyes and her breath caught. "But only for the moment." He kissed her hard and released her from his embrace. "You should go before someone sees you."

She nodded. Why was it that when he kissed her, she forgot everything else? And she wanted nothing more than to stay in his arms forever? She stepped out of Nathanial's room, crossed the corridor, and opened her door.

Before she could go in, the door to Quinton's room opened. "Miss Montini?"

She winced to herself but adopted a pleasant smile. "Mr. Harrington. I trust you had a pleasant evening."

"It was a thrill beyond measure," he said wryly, then paused. "I have a favor to ask of you."

"Oh?" What on earth would he want from her?

"My brother has never been in love, and I suspect his heart could be easily broken. I watched Sterling's heart break and should prefer not to see the same thing happen to Nate. I would appreciate it if you would take care that such a thing does not happen."

"I have no idea what you're talking about, Mr. Harrington."

"No? My mistake. Apparently you are not as intelligent as I have heard." He nodded. "Good evening, Miss Montini."

"Mr. Harrington," she murmured, and stepped into her room, closing the door behind her.

Surely he was wrong. Oh, it was obvious Nathanial did indeed have some feelings for her. He wished to protect her, of course, but that was part and parcel of the obligation he had taken on to help her find the seal. He couldn't possibly . . . Her heart fluttered at the thought.

No! She thrust the idea firmly aside. He would have said something by now. He'd had every opportunity. And Nathanial was not the type of man to keep something like that to himself.

She climbed into bed and tried to sleep. But she couldn't get the question out of her head.

What if Quinton was right?

Twenty-two

You asked to see me, sir."

Nate sat in his brother's chair behind the desk in the library and studied the footman. Xerxes Muldoon was a big, broad-shouldered man, probably some twenty years older than himself, with a slightly exotic appearance about the eyes. He looked nothing like a footman. Nate wondered why he hadn't noticed before.

"Miss Montini insists on doing something I think is exceptionally foolish," he began.

Muldoon waited expectantly, the perfect footman.

"This morning, she is to begin cataloguing the collections of Lord Rathbourne. There have long been rumors about Rathbourne, some of the most vile nature. Whether they are true or not, I don't know." He shook his head. "And frankly I don't care."

"Sir?"

"I think he's dangerous. I don't want her at his house without protection." He met Muldoon's gaze directly. "I want you to accompany her."

"Yes sir." Muldoon shifted uneasily. "Does Miss Montini know?"

"She does. She's not especially happy about it but she's agreed." He blew a long breath. "She is the most independent female I have ever met."

"She does appear so, sir."

"And she thinks nothing of the consequences of her actions."

"No sir."

"She is probably the most brilliant woman I have ever encountered as well."

"Yes sir."

"And stubborn." Nate huffed and shook his head. "Has she always been this stubborn, Muldoon?"

"Yes sir, she—" Realization dawned in Muldoon's eyes. "I beg your pardon sir, I . . . " Muldoon sighed and crossed his arms over his chest in a most unfootman-like manner. "How did you know?"

"I didn't until a few days ago. Then I put two and two together. I am not as stupid as I might appear."

"You couldn't possibly be," Muldoon said mildly. "I have heard of Rathbourne on occasion, when I traveled with Miss Montini's brother." He raised a brow. "I assume you know that as well."

Nate nodded.

"I think you're right to be concerned. You needn't worry. I won't let her out of my sight. I have always protected her." His eyes narrowed and an implicit threat sounded in his voice. "From everyone."

"I love her," Nate said simply.

"Good." Muldoon's voice softened. "I suspected as much. She needs someone to love her."

"Didn't her brother?"

"In his own manner, I think. He didn't mistreat her in any way." Muldoon paused to choose his words. "No doubt you're aware of Montini's reputation, the kind of man he was?"

Nate nodded.

"He was a very selfish man. He had his work and his own needs. There was nothing left for a little girl." He shook his head. "He never even noticed when she stopped being a little girl, but others did."

"And that's when . . . "

Muldoon shot him a sharp glance. "She told you about that, did she?"

"Yes."

"How interesting." He studied Nate thoughtfully. "I knew, of course, and my wife and Miss Henry, but to my knowledge she has never told anyone else."

"I see." Nate couldn't quite hide a smile.

"I wouldn't be too confident if I were you." Muldoon shook his head. "I have known Gabriella much of her life. Even so, I find her to be one of the most confusing people I have ever met. She is convinced that because of the incident she will never marry."

"I gathered as much."

"She has, as well, a suspicious nature. Trust does not come easily to her."

Nate nodded. "I noticed that too."

"Nor does love." Muldoon paused. "My wife and I have often discussed this. We have long been concerned about her." He cast Nate a wry smile. "We may be in her employ but we have always thought of her with the fondness one feels for a daughter." He fixed Nate with a hard look. "With the exception of my wife,

Miss Henry, and myself, everyone Gabriella has ever truly trusted or loved in her life has left her. It is not a great leap of the imagination to understand that is why she does not trust or love easily."

"I would never hurt her." Nate met the other man's gaze. "Nor would I ever abandon her."

"See that you don't."

"There is another thing that puzzles me."

Muldoon chuckled. "Just one?"

Nate grinned. "No, but I am curious. About her trip to Egypt?"

"You figured that out too."

Nate shook his head. "Again, not until recently."

"It wasn't as difficult as you might think. As pretty as she is, she still makes a passable young man." Muldoon grinned. "And then of course she had me to make sure nothing went awry."

"Even so." Nate shook his head. "It was a dangerous venture."

"As well I know. She threatened to go by herself if I didn't accompany her." He shrugged. "And I wouldn't put it past her to do just that."

"I have a number of other questions."

"No doubt you do, but I've probably said too much already. Anything else you will have to ask her yourself." Muldoon paused. "Am I to assume I will be allowed to stay here, then? In my position as John Farrell?"

"For as long as necessary." Nate nodded toward the door. "Gabriella is probably ready to go. You should join her."

Muldoon nodded.

"Oh, before you do, might I ask what you did with the other John Farrell?"

Muldoon grinned. "Paid him handsomely to take a holiday and visit his family in the country."

"Excellent." Nate laughed, then sobered. "It might be best, as well, if you don't tell Gabriella about this chat of ours."

"I would never lie to her," Muldoon said firmly. "However, if she doesn't ask me directly, I would see no need to say anything. For the moment," he added pointedly.

"Agreed." Nate paused. "Watch out for her, Muldoon."

"I always have." The older man smiled and took his leave.

Nate chuckled to himself. Secrets, everywhere he looked someone had secrets. He suspected he had only scratched the surface of Gabriella's. But his talk with Muldoon explained a great deal. If he was going to keep Gabriella in his life—and after last night there wasn't a doubt in his mind that he wanted to do exactly that, not that he'd had any doubts before—he would obviously need all the help he could get. Muldoon might just turn out to be an unexpected ally. The big man had only her best interests at heart. After all, he had known her much of her life and was currently in her employ—

Her employ?

Surely he meant her brother's employ.

But her brother was dead. What did Muldoon mean?

Nate got to his feet and started after him.

The library door swung open and his mother stepped into the room. "Oh, good, Nathanial, you're here."

"I was just about to leave."

"No, you're not." Sterling appeared behind her, stepped into the library and closed the door behind him in a resolute manner. He had his earl's face on, which usually meant someone had done something to annoy the staid, controlled structure of his existence.

"Do sit down, both of you," Sterling said coolly. He carried a sheaf of papers in his hand and moved to stand behind his desk.

Nate leaned toward his mother. "What have we done?"

"I have no idea, dear. My conscience is clear." She thought for a moment, then nodded. "Yes, completely clear."

"As is mine," Nate murmured. Not that it was ever completely clear, but he couldn't think of anything he had done recently to which his brother might take umbrage. Of course, Sterling might wish to chastise him for having Gabriella in his rooms last night, but then, Nate knew Sterling would never involve Mother in a discussion of that nature.

"This . . . " Sterling tossed the papers on his desk. "Is a report."

"How nice, dear," Mother said with a pleasant smile. "What does that have to do with us?"

"It's a report about Miss Montini."

Nate and his mother exchanged glances.

Sterling seated himself behind the desk. "Might I suggest in the future, when each of us feels the need to hire an agency of investigation in regards to the same person, we do so together. Thus incurring only one bill rather than three."

"You needn't take that tone, Sterling." His mother fixed her oldest son with a firm look. "I had no idea that you would take it upon yourself to investigate Miss Montini."

"Regardless of whether or not you knew her mother, did you think I would simply allow a woman who was caught breaking into the house to reside with us without wanting to know more about her?" Sterling drummed his fingers on the desk.

Mother sniffed. "When you put it that way, it makes a certain amount of sense."

He picked up the papers and shuffled through the report. "It seems each of us requested information in a slightly different area. Mother wished to know more about family. You, Nate, wanted her past. And I wanted her current state of affairs."

Nate grinned. "We are nothing if not thorough."

Sterling glanced at the report. "This paints an interesting picture of Miss Montini. I would say some of it is not unexpected, although much of it is quite surprising. Don't you think so, Mother?"

"I don't know dear," she said in an offhand manner. "I haven't seen the report yet."

Sterling's eyes narrowed. "But you know more about Miss Montini than you have thus far mentioned."

"She knew Gabriella's mother." Nate's gaze slid from his brother to his mother. "But she told us that."

"Well, perhaps one of us should have thought to ask who her mother was, or why Miss Montini looks so much like Emma Carpenter."

"There was no need for that to be in the report," their mother said under her breath. "I knew all that." She cast her oldest son a stern look. "You should not let them charge you for that."

"Well, I don't know what you're talking about." Impatience sounded in Nate's voice.

"Allow me to explain, dear," Mother said. "As you know, Emma's mother, Lady Danworthy—Caroline—

has been a friend of mine since we were girls. She had two sisters, one older, one younger. The younger of the two, Helene—a lovely girl, by the way—was disinherited when she married against their father's wishes. She married a wealthy man, significantly older than she and, God forbid, Italian."

"Montini?" Nate said slowly.

Mother nodded. "The situation was most distressing. Her father declared that as far as he was concerned, he had only two daughters. He relented rather quickly after Helene married and left for Italy, but what with the distances involved and whatnot, it was too late by then. Helene died giving birth to Gabriella. The family tried to maintain contact with Mr. Montini, but from what Caroline has told me through the years, he had little interest in keeping in touch with them. He died when Gabriella was eight years old and somehow she was lost."

Nate drew his brows together. "What do you mean, lost?"

"By the time Caroline's family learned of his death, the little girl had vanished. They tried for years to find her. Ultimately they were told the girl had died." Mother heaved a heartfelt sigh. "Needless to say, they stopped all efforts to find her. It has been one of the great sorrows of Caroline's life that she wasn't able to save her sister's child. And that," she turned a firm gaze to Sterling, "is why I insisted Gabriella stay here. I did not want her lost again."

"Why haven't you simply told Lady Danworthy that you've found her niece?"

"I had my reasons," Mother said in a lofty manner.

"And those are?" Sterling prompted.

"I am not used to being quizzed like a common criminal by my own son."

"My apologies, Mother," Sterling muttered.

"You don't sound the least bit sincere, dear. You need to work on that. First of all, Caroline is in Paris with her sister, and Emma as well. In her most recent letter she said they will be returning in a few days. Secondly, I was not entirely certain of Gabriella's intentions. After all, we did meet her when she was caught breaking into the house. There is also a sizable inheritance involved. Quite frankly, I didn't want to tell Caroline about her niece's existence if Gabriella's motives were less than honorable. It would quite break her heart.

"However . . . " Mother smiled in a satisfied manner. "Aside from a certain penchant for what might be called impulsive, even illegal, behavior, I am quite impressed with Gabriella's character." She turn a steady eye on her youngest son. "You could do far worse."

Nate grinned. "But I could not do better."

"No, darling, I don't think you could."

"According to this," Sterling waved at the report, "after her father's death, Gabriella was literally passed from one distant relative of his to another." His expression darkened. "From what I've read here, it was not a pleasant experience for her. She was not especially wanted and was treated more like a servant than a relative."

"Oh dear," Mother murmured.

"Approximately two years later, Enrico Montini, her half brother from her father's first marriage, found the girl." Sterling glanced at his mother. "I assume that's when Lady Danworthy's family was told she was dead?"

Mother nodded. "That sounds accurate."

"The trail would appear to end there. However, the report says Montini was thereafter accompanied by a young boy that he claimed was his brother. However . . . " Sterling's gaze met Nate's. "Gabriella has no other brother."

Nate nodded. "I had come to much the same conclusion, but I hadn't put this particular piece of the puzzle together."

"So you're saying that Enrico Montini hauled his sister around to all those dreadful, dangerous places you and Quinton frequent on your search for antiquities and pretended she was a boy?" Anger flashed in Mother's eyes. "How could he? Had he no thought for the consequences of raising a girl that way?"

Nate shook his head. "Apparently Montini had no thought for anything other than his own concerns."

"And there was a significant fortune involved," Sterling added.

"Yes, of course," Mother said thoughtfully. "The inheritance from her mother's father."

"I doubt that he knew about that." Sterling tapped the report with his finger. "Apparently, Gabriella's father left her a sizable fortune and it was entirely in Montini's hands." He shrugged. "According to this, Montini's father was not pleased with his son's choice of vocation and left very nearly everything to his daughter. As long as Montini had Gabriella, he had the means to support his work." He looked at his brother. "Your Miss Montini is a very wealthy woman, although I suspect she didn't know that until her brother died."

"That explains a lot," Nate said. "Go on."

"Nine years ago, the alleged younger brother vanished and Miss Montini began attending school here in London. She is remarkably well educated for a woman—"

Nate snorted. "Don't let her hear you say that."

Sterling continued. "She owns a small house in a respectable if not particularly fashionable section of the city and employs . . ." He flipped through the pages. "A Miss Florence Henry as a companion and—"

"Xerxes Muldoon and his wife." Nate nodded. "I recently discovered that."

"Well, this is all very interesting," Mother said.

"Indeed it is." Sterling clasped his hands together on the desk, his gaze shifting between his mother and his brother. "Now that I am confident we know very nearly all there is to know about Gabriella, what do the two of you intend to do?"

"I intend to reunite Gabriella with her family," Mother said firmly.

"I intend to make her a member of this family." Nate grinned.

Sterling raised a brow. "Because she has a fortune and a respectable family?"

"No," Nate said sharply. "Because she is the most remarkable woman I've ever met. Because I cannot imagine living my life without her. And because regardless of who she is or what she has or doesn't have, she holds my heart in her hands."

Mother beamed. "Wonderful, Nathanial."

Sterling cast him an approving smile. "Best wishes, little brother. Now . . ." He leaned forward and studied Nate. "What is the progress regarding the Montini seal?"

Twenty-three

ven the vast number of treasures that might well take as long to document as Lord Rathbourne had taken to collect could not diminish the unease that settled more firmly about Gabriella with every minute in his house.

Now, she sat on a wrought-iron bench in the tiny walled garden off the library. When the butler, Franks, had shown them in, he pointed out the French doors, hidden behind velvet drapes, that led to the garden. He had said as well that Lord Rathbourne suggested she might like to make use of the garden to avail herself of fresh air should the treasure room become too stuffy. It was unexpectedly thoughtful. A gravel path led from the door to a tall hedge. On the other side of the hedge, hidden from the house, the wrought-iron bench faced a small tiered fountain.

Sitting here, one might well imagine they were somewhere far from the dark, brooding house looming behind them. Gabriella wondered if Lady Rathbourne ever sat here and imagined just that.

She wasn't sure she could spend day after day in this house, in the windowless room she couldn't stop comparing to a tomb. Lord Rathbourne was not at home today and she was grateful for his absence. When she'd been in the treasure room, Xerxes positioned himself just outside the opening in the viscount's library. Right now he stood behind her in the doorway, vigilant and watchful. Even though the hedge obscured her view, she knew he was there. Any other time, she would have found his protectiveness annoying. Here and now, it was a comfort.

Today, she had planned to start making a preliminary list of the separate and varied collections, if only to begin to determine the enormity of the job. Instead, however, she'd spent most of her time studying the seal that was so similar to the one her brother once had. While she was certain it wasn't the same, she would very much have liked to see an impression and compared it with her brother's. Which reminded her, she needed to stop by her own house to see if Florence had found the impression on her way home.

Home. When did she start thinking of Harrington House as home? It wasn't that it was grander than anything she'd ever known; size and affluence had nothing to do with it. There was a sense there of family and tradition and belonging. An air of continuation. The feeling that no matter what else happened in the world, regardless of where family members might wander, this would always be a place that welcomed them.

Perhaps if she hadn't experienced the easy affection in that house, Rathbourne's might not seem as grim, although she doubted it. The few servants she had met thus far, while not overtly unpleasant, were not particularly friendly either. She couldn't quite put her finger on why, but it struck her that there was no warmth in this house. No feeling of occupancy. No sense that this was something other than a showplace, a display cabinet. She shivered at the thought.

In spite of the opportunity Rathbourne's collections offered for her future, she knew now she had to reconsider her decision to accept the position.

That would please Nathanial. Not that she cared. She blew a long breath. Of course she cared. She was lying to herself if she thought otherwise. At least being at Rathbourne's house took her mind off Nathanial. And off Quinton's comments.

Was it at all possible that Nathanial's heart was at stake? Some of the things he'd said—and so much that he'd almost said—might lead one to believe, if one were silly and foolish—

"What are you thinking, girl," Xerxes said, rounding the path.

"Nothing of significance." She shrugged.

"I thought you might have been thinking about Mr. Harrington."

She started to deny it, then couldn't. Besides, Xerxes always seemed to know when she was less than truthful.

"Perhaps you should—think about Mr. Harrington, that is."

"Thinking about Mr. Harrington in any manner whatsoever is pointless."

"Why?"

"Why?" She stood and turned toward him. "Because he and I . . . " She shook her head. "We would never suit."

"Oh?" Xerxes raised a brow. "From my observation, there is no one who would suit you better."

"Regardless." She shook her head. "It's really not possible."

"Not if you won't let it be possible." He studied her carefully. "It's up to you, girl. It's all in your hands. I would hate to see you let happiness slip through your fingers."

"Happiness?" She thought for a long moment. She wasn't sure she'd ever been truly happy, and not sure she'd know happiness if it came her way. She'd been content enough, she supposed, although now it struck her that most of her life thus far had been spent in preparation for something that would never come. Had been spent waiting. "Do you really think so?"

"I think," he chose his words with care, "Nathanial Harrington is the best thing that has ever come into your life. And I think you are the best thing that has come into his. I further think if you don't understand that and accept it, then you are not as intelligent as I have always known you to be. However," he shrugged, "what I think isn't nearly as important as what you know."

"What I know?" What did she know? She knew she loved Nathanial. She knew she didn't want to leave him. As for his feelings . . . Didn't she know those as well? Didn't she know when he called her "my love" or when he tried to protect her or when he held her in his arms or when she gazed into his brown eyes—didn't she know then that he shared her feelings? She met Xerxes's gaze. "What if I'm wrong?"

"What if you're not?" Xerxes smiled. "You should talk to the man. I suspect you haven't done that."

She shook her head. "We talk all the time."

"About how you feel? What you want?"

"Nathanial says everything is about what I want."

"And?"

"And." She drew a deep breath. "And Nathanial Harrington is what I want."

"Then perhaps it's time to do something about that."

"Perhaps . . . you're right, it is indeed." She smiled. "And I will. Now, it's time to go." She started back into the house, her voice brisk, her tone decided. "We need to stop at my house. I must speak to Florence and you should probably see your wife."

Xerxes chuckled. "Your Mr. Harrington doesn't stand a chance."

"He's not my—" Resolve washed through her and she grinned. "But he will be."

She would talk to Nathanial as soon as possible. Confess her feelings and pray he felt the same.

By the time their carriage rolled to a stop in front of her house, the most intoxicating sense of hope bubbled within her. She had learned to trust him, she loved him, and it was past time to take the greatest leap of faith of all.

"I was just about to send you a note." Florence hooked her arm through Gabriella's and steered her into the parlor. "Miriam and I are going to take the first train north in the morning. We have received word that her mother is ill."

"Oh dear," Gabriella murmured. "How bad is it?"

"We're not certain. The note we received was rather vague." Florence seated herself and indicated Gabriella should sit beside her. "But it did say we should waste no time. Miriam is quite concerned."

"I can well imagine." Gabriella frowned. "But shouldn't Xerxes go with you, then?"

"Absolutely not," Florence huffed in indignation. "He needs to stay here with you." Her eyes narrowed. "Especially as you insist on working for that dreadful viscount."

"I see you have been talking to Mr. Dennison."

Florence's expression remained firm but a smile lit her eyes. "Why yes, I have. Now about this position of yours with Lord Rathbourne—"

"You needn't worry about that." Gabriella blew a resigned breath. "As great as the opportunity is, I have decided not to accept his offer. Being there today, however, did give me the chance to look for the seal."

"And?"

"And he has one that might well be its mate, but I found nothing more than that. Nor did I really expect to. Lord Rathbourne's arrogance is such that if he had my brother's seal, I doubt that he would hesitate to tell me." She shrugged. "Unless I could prove it was Enrico's—have you found the impression yet?"

Florence shook her head.

"I doubt it will matter. I am afraid we might never recover the seal. As for Lord Rathbourne, I intend to tell him tomorrow that I will not accept his offer."

"Excellent." Relief washed across Florence's face. "I cannot tell you how worried I have been. As has your Mr. Harrington."

"Mr. Dennison again?"

"He is a fount of information as well as . . . "

Gabriella raised an amused brow. "As well as?"

"Gabriella." Florence took the younger woman's

hands. "I suspect Mr. Dennison may soon ask me to marry him."

Happiness for her friend washed through her. "How wonderful."

"Yes, it is," Florence said slowly. "However, I am not certain what my answer will be."

"Why ever not?"

"If I marry Mr. Dennison . . . " Florence paused. "I am concerned as to what will happen to you."

"To me?" Gabriella widened her eyes with surprise. "You should not concern yourself with me."

"Your welfare has concerned me for nearly a decade," Florence said firmly. "I do not intend to abandon you now."

"Don't be absurd." Gabriella scoffed. "You wouldn't be abandoning me at all. Besides, you and Xerxes and Miriam are my family. Even if we no longer reside in the same house, that will never change. And we are not so large a family that we cannot include one more."

"But things will change."

"For the best," Gabriella said firmly. "You must follow your heart, my dear friend. You have always told me to do so."

"And are you following it now?" Florence's gaze searched hers.

"I think I always have really." Gabriella thought for a moment. "I followed my heart when I studied to make myself indispensable to Enrico. In many ways the search for the seal was following my heart. As for anything else . . . yes, Florence." She cast her friend a brilliant smile. "I am going to follow my heart."

But it seemed the moment she had decided to confess her feelings, there was no opportunity to do so. It was late afternoon by the time she arrived back at Harrington House, and Nathanial was nowhere to be seen. Still, his absence gave her time to decide exactly what she would say. Simply blurting out her feelings didn't seem quite right. She'd never been especially good at being coy, so anything other than a forthright approach might be even more awkward than necessary. She should tell him as well that she wasn't impoverished, and perhaps it was also time to mention her childhood . . . and oh, yes, the fact that she was the brother he had met in Egypt. She cringed at the thought of all she had kept from him. Still, if he did love her, it might not matter. If he didn't, then it wouldn't make any difference at all.

She was hopeful that after dinner there might be time for a moment alone. But Nathanial and his brothers had again gone to the earl's club for the evening. Lady Wyldewood had invited her to accompany her and her daughter to some event or other, but she'd begged off. Instead she retired to her room with a book. She had selected, of all things, a work of fiction from the library, something about a young woman attempting to find the perfect matches for her friends. Utter nonsense, really, but surprisingly engrossing. She had intended to read until she heard Nathanial in the hall, and left her door open a crack to ensure that she would. Then she'd talk to him.

And if her visiting his room again led to something other than conversation and confession, well, apparently once one was truly ruined, one wished for nothing more than to be truly ruined again. And again.

But before long the words swam before her eyes and

the book fell from her hand and she slept, to dream of dark-eyed men with hair streaked by the sun, and kisses in the moonlight, and leaps of faith.

Nate made his way along the corridor to his rooms. Even though he, Sterling, and Quint had spent a long evening at Sterling's club, he wasn't the least bit inebriated. Well, perhaps he was the least bit inebriated, but certainly not extensively.

He glanced at Gabriella's door and pulled up short. It was slightly open and a light still burned inside her room. Was she waiting for him? He grinned. What a delicious idea. Even before last night he knew he wished to share her bed every night for the rest of his life, but he hadn't expected to do so quite so soon. Not that it wasn't an excellent idea.

"Gabriella," he said softly, pushed open her door and slipped inside the room.

She lay curled on her side, one arm flung off the bed, a book she had been reading on the floor beneath her hand. She was obviously asleep. Disappointment stabbed him. As much as he would like to do so, he wasn't going to wake her up. He moved quietly to the side of the bed, picked up the book, glanced at the title and smiled. Fiction. And romantic fiction at that. She had certainly come a long way since they first met. It was such a short time ago and yet it seemed he had known her forever. In his dreams perhaps or in his heart.

He set the book down on the table by the side of the bed, started to extinguish the lamp, then paused to look at her. He would never tire of looking at her. Not if they lived to be as old as the relics he hunted. And one day there would be children and . . .

And he certainly couldn't continue hunting for antiquities if he had a wife. The thought pulled him up short. How could he leave her? Regardless of what Gabriella had hoped for her life, he couldn't possibly drag her around with him. Not now that he knew how she had grown up. It wouldn't be right, and it wouldn't be what she deserved. She deserved something . . . well, better. If he wanted Gabriella in his life, his life was going to have to change.

He looked at her once more, then extinguished the lamp. It was a small enough price to pay. Indeed, it was well worth it.

Twenty-four

*W*ould you be so good as to tell Lord Rathbourne I should like to see him," Gabriella said to his lordship's butler. Today as yesterday, Franks had greeted them with as few words as possible, and then escorted Gabriella and Xerxes into the library.

"As you wish, miss." The butler hesitated. "I have not yet spoken with his lordship this morning but, as the treasure room has been opened, I assume Lord Rathbourne is occupied elsewhere in the house. I shall inform him of your request as soon as I see him."

"There's nothing to be done about it, I suppose," Gabriella said to Xerxes when the servant had left the room. "I might as well finish the list I began yesterday. It's the least I can do."

Xerxes frowned. "You don't owe this man anything, girl."

"Aside from an apology, you mean?" She shook her head. "I agreed to take this position and now I am about to renege on that agreement. It does not sit well with me but . . . " She glanced around the library and shivered. "I think it's best."

"We all think it's best," Xerxes said firmly.

No doubt Nathanial would agree, if she ever again found the opportunity to speak with him. Today, she thought. She would definitely tell him everything today.

She took up where she'd left off yesterday, filing page after page with notes on the various collections. By late morning Lord Rathbourne had still not made an appearance.

"We could simply write him a note and leave," Xerxes suggested hopefully. He didn't wish to remain there any longer than she did.

"No," she said firmly. "However, I am going to step outside for a moment."

She pulled open the drapes that covered the French doors to the garden, sunlight flooding the dark room. What a pity, this could be such a pleasant house. She opened the doors and stepped down two steps onto the pathway. As he did yesterday, Xerxes stood in the doorway, leaning against the doorjamb, her guardian. And like yesterday, his presence was reassuring.

She walked the few steps around the hedge and stopped short. Lord Rathbourne sat on the end of the bench closest to her, his back to her, his head tilted to one side as if he were listening to something. In all honesty, lord or not, it was insufferably rude to have ignored her request to speak to him. She had no idea how he might have slipped out there without either she or Xerxes seeing him, and yet obviously he had.

"My lord," she said firmly and stepped closer. "I should like to have a word with you." It would be best just to say it quickly and get it over with. She drew a deep breath and released the words in a rush. "As much as I appreciate the opportunity the position as your curator affords me, I do regret that, after further and due consideration, I cannot accept the position."

Surely he'd want a reason? Surely she had one that would sound better than she couldn't work with the unease that surrounded her in this house, in his presence? She stepped closer. "My plans for the future— my future, that is—have changed." That wasn't exactly the truth but it wasn't a complete lie either. Her plans had changed, or at least, if she were lucky, they would. "Well then, my lord, you do have my eternal gratitude for your faith in me, and my apologies, of course. So, that said, I shall take my leave." She turned on her heel and started off. And stopped in mid-step.

This was certainly the height of cowardice. Why, she hadn't even allowed the man to get a single word in. She at least owed him the courtesy of listening to his response. She braced herself and turned back. "My lord?"

He still didn't respond. He was no doubt furious.

"Lord Rathbourne." She squared her shoulders and approached him. "I fully understand—" And froze.

Shock clutched at her throat. It was obvious the man was dead. The glassy unfocused look in his eyes would have told her that even if it weren't for the slash that stretched from one side of his throat to the other and the drying reddish-brown blood that had soaked his clothes and settled in a thickened puddle at his feet.

Gabriella couldn't pull her gaze away. His face was ashen, drained of color. The thought occurred to her that any other woman would have swooned or at least screamed. She, however, was made of sterner stuff. She had seen and studied more than a few mummies over the years. Still, it was one thing to look at a three-thousand-year-old Egyptian and quite another to look at a newly dead British lord. Her stomach heaved. She turned on her heel, stumbled a few steps to the nearest flower bed, bent over and retched.

Almost at once she heard Xerxes hurry up behind her. "Gabriella, are you—"

"I'm fine." A slight touch of queasiness lingered but she did feel much better. She wiped her mouth with the back of her hand, straightened, and turned back toward the grisly scene.

"You shouldn't look at him, girl," Xerxes said grimly, handing her his handkerchief.

"I've already seen him." She dabbed at her mouth. "I can't imagine he looks any more dreadful now than he did a moment ago." She studied the dead man. "His throat's been cut, hasn't it?"

"It would appear so." He grabbed her arm and steered her back along the path and into the house. "If you've seen enough . . . "

"More than enough." She shook her head. "It's not the type of thing one expects to see in the middle of London. In more uncivilized parts of the world, of course, this sort of thing is not unexpected. I daresay it happens all the time in places like Asia Minor or Egypt. Why, one might not even be surprised to see a man with his throat slit sitting in a garden on a pleasant spring day," she said brightly.

Xerxes stared at her. "You're babbling, girl." He set her down on the sofa, strode to the doorway and called to the butler.

"Utter nonsense," she said under her breath. "I don't babble. I'm not the type of woman who babbles." She was simply keeping up a steady stream of observation. After all, she'd never seen a dead man before, and never imagined she'd see one with his throat cut. In the back of her mind she had the oddest conviction that if she stopped making relatively rational comments, she'd start screaming and never stop. Regardless, at the moment she couldn't stop talking.

Franks sent for the authorities, and it seemed as though the library was filled with people in no time at all, although it could have been hours. She'd lost all track of time. She wished Xerxes would stop looking at her as if she were mere seconds away from insanity. She was fine. Perfectly fine. Why, even her stomach had settled down. And that nice constable who was the first to arrive hadn't seemed the least bit annoyed by her observations as to his lordship's nature and her opinion that very nearly anyone who had ever met him might have a certain desire to slit his throat. Not her, of course, she had no reason to wish him dead. After all, he had offered her an opportunity few women would have imagined. And an exceptionally fine salary as well. No, no, it wouldn't have made any sense for her to have killed him.

The constable had asked where they could be found if it was necessary to speak with them further, then sent them on their way, but not until he and Xerxes exchanged knowing glances. The kind of looks men traded when dealing with an irrational woman. It was most annoying. She might well be babbling, although it did seem to her that every word was significant, but she was certainly not irrational.

She kept up a steady stream of chatter in the carriage on the way home. Had Xerxes noticed the expression on Rathbourne's face? Admittedly it might be in her own mind but she thought his lordship looked somewhat surprised. Although she supposed surprise was to be expected unless one had known one's throat was about to be slit like a pig's. In which case one would certainly take steps to prevent such a thing. Didn't he think so? And didn't Xerxes think as well that the viscount had been dead for some time? After all, she and he had been in the house for a good three hours and they certainly would have seen his lordship and whomever might have been with him go into the garden. Even if they hadn't, surely they would have heard something. A man probably couldn't have his throat cut without making some sort of sound. Gurgling or something of that nature.

The moment they crossed the threshold of Harrington House, Xerxes ordered a footman to send for Nathanial, then took her into the parlor. Apparently, the older man's tone left no room for hesitation, as Nathanial arrived within minutes. Xerxes joined him outside the parlor doors, obviously warning him about her state of mind. Which was absurd. Her state of mind was perfectly fine, even excellent if one considered it had only been a short time ago that she had found a blood-soaked, surprised-looking, very dead viscount in a garden.

"Gabriella?" Nathanial stepped into the room, Andrews right behind, bearing a tray with a decanter of brandy and glasses. Probably the very one he had brought on the very first night she was there. How appropriate, or perhaps ironic; she wasn't sure. Nathanial nodded at Andrews, and the butler left the room. Nathanial looked as if he wasn't sure what he should do now. "Brandy?" he asked her.

"I would think tea would be more appropriate at this time of day." However, in spite of the pleasantness of the day, the tips of her fingers were icy. "But I am a bit chilled. I find brandy to be excellent when one is chilled. Or nervous. Don't you? It does seem to soothe the nerves."

He filled two glasses and handed her one. She took it and noticed that her hand shook. He raised a brow.

"You needn't look at me that way." She took a long sip of the brandy, its warmth comforting and welcome. "I am fine. Perfectly fine. Admittedly, my hand is shaking, but then it's been that sort of day. I suspect anyone would shake a bit upon finding a dead viscount in a garden."

"Yes of course."

"Lovely garden," she murmured. "Quite peaceful." Except of course for the dead, blood-soaked man with the staring eyes and the surprised expression.

He sipped his own drink and studied her warily.

"I am not a delicate, fragile flower, you know."

"I know." He moved closer. "You are not like most women."

"I most certainly am not." She shrugged. "Most women, at the very least, would have screamed at coming upon a scene like that. I simply . . . "

He nodded. "John told me."

"John?" She pulled her brows together. *Xerxes.* "Yes, of course, John."

"He sent word as to what had happened but it only arrived a few minutes ago. I was about to come after you."

"It wasn't necessary." She cast him a bright smile. "I am fine."

"Are you?"

She laughed, and even to her own ears it had a strange, vaguely hysterical sound to it. "Perfectly fine. And the brandy is much better than tea."

"Do you feel better now?"

"Much."

He studied her cautiously. "It is understandable, you know . . . your reaction, that is."

"I would think so," she huffed. "Why, the contrast alone between the serenity of the garden and the—" She shivered in spite of herself. "—violence of what must have happened was enough to make anyone ill."

"Are you sure you're all right?"

"Perfectly." She took another long drink. "He must have been dead for some time, you know. We'd been there all morning so it must have happened last night." She nodded. "He looked quite . . . dead."

"Gabriella."

"Not recently dead." She shook her head. "Not that I know what someone recently dead would look like, but he looked, well, rigid. Quite, quite dead I would say."

Nathanial's brow furrowed in concern. "Gabriella."

"Am I babbling?"

"Yes."

"Don't be absurd." She took another bracing swallow. "I never babble."

"And yet—"

"I don't think it was a robbery," she continued, as if he hadn't said a word. "There was nothing disturbed in the treasure room. At least not that I noticed. And I would have noticed. I notice such things. I am nothing if not observant."

He stared at her.

She ignored him. "And if one were to rob the viscount, there are any number of things—priceless things—one could quite easily abscond with simply by slipping them in a pocket." She shook her head in an earnest manner. "No, it wasn't robbery, but then he wasn't a very good man, was he? I imagine there are all sorts of people who would have gladly slit his . . . " She tossed back the rest of her brandy and held the glass out to him. Her hand shook uncontrollably and she noted it with a strange sort of detachment. As though she wasn't the one looking at her hand and it wasn't her hand.

"But you are still shaking." He took the glass from her and set both their glasses on a table.

"It's nothing."

"And your hands . . . " He took them in his. "Are very cold."

"They are, aren't they?" Her voice was oddly detached, as if it were someone else's voice. "How very unusual."

"You are not fine at all." He pulled her into his arms, and she rested her head against the solid protection of his chest. "You have been through an ordeal."

"I am fine." A sob rose up inside her. Where on earth had that come from? She didn't sob. Or weep. Or cry. She couldn't remember the last time she had. She swallowed hard. "Perfectly . . . "

"Yes, of course, perfectly fine." He chuckled. "And have you at last run out of things to say?"

"No," she muttered against his chest, but it did sound somewhat like a sob and his arms tightened around her.

She closed her eyes and listened to his heart beat. The warmth of his body coupled with the heat of the brandy washed through her, and with it the most remarkable understanding and acceptance. Nothing in the world could hurt her if she was in his arms. She closed her eyes and sagged against him, abruptly too weary to stand.

He scooped her into his arms and carried her out of the room.

"What are you doing? Where are we going?" she murmured, but she didn't really care. He could take her anywhere and she would go willingly.

"I'm taking you to your room." His voice sounded very far away.

"Mmm." She snuggled against him. "How lovely."

He said something she didn't quite hear, and scarcely cared. In some distant still functioning part of her mind she realized she'd be asleep long before they reached her bed. And wasn't that a pity? She had so very much to tell him. About who she was and what she wanted. And that what she wanted most of all was him.

Twenty-five

"Well?" Nate demanded the moment Quint stepped into the library. It was already evening, and his brother had been gone for hours. Sterling and Mr. Dennison had been waiting with him for Quint. They each sat behind their respective desks.

"Did you learn anything of value?" Sterling asked.

Sterling had sent Quint to find out what was known thus far about Rathbourne's death. And only did so because of the possibility that the murder might be connected to Gabriella's search for the Montini seal, not because Sterling still harbored some feelings for Lady Rathbourne. He hadn't actually said that, and no one had dared to ask.

Quint grinned. "It's amazing what one can learn when bandying about the name of the Earl of Wyldewood."

Sterling shrugged. "It can be useful on occasion."

"The inspector in charge practically fell all over himself to help me."

Sterling raised a brow.

"Well, perhaps not all over himself but he was helpful." Quint plopped into a chair. "They don't know much at the moment." He glanced at Nate. "I don't have much more than what John told you."

Nate clenched his jaw impatiently. "Blast it all, Quint, just tell me what you do know, then." If Gabriella was in danger, he needed to know. "And his name is really Xerxes Muldoon. He is employed by Gabriella."

"My, she is full of surprises," Quint said under his breath.

"Quint!"

"Very well." Quint thought for a moment. "Nothing appears to have been taken. The servants said there was nothing missing in the rest of the house, and Miss Montini told the police nothing appeared to have been disturbed in his treasure room." He cast Nate an incredulous expression. "Did you know he had a treasure room? The inspector said it was on the order of a vault."

"You knew he was a collector of rare antiquities," Nate replied. "He was also very protective. He didn't display them as most collectors do but kept them locked away, for his enjoyment alone." He shrugged. "Most of his collections were antiquities, but there were gems and paintings as well. The sum worth must be in the millions." He glanced at Sterling, who displayed no particular reaction. Rathbourne's death would leave his wife a very wealthy woman, which might well come as a relief to anyone who might be concerned about her welfare.

"The police are using lists Miss Montini compiled to make certain nothing is missing, but at this point they are fairly certain robbery was not a motive." Quint paused. "It's believed from the state of the body that he had been dead ten to twelve hours." He met Nate's gaze. "Which means he was killed last night. It also means . . . " Quint winced. "When Miss Montini found him it was not a pretty sight."

"I know." Nate had talked to Xerxes again after Gabriella fell asleep. The older man had been quite detailed in his description of the morning's discovery.

"Excellent." Sterling nodded. "Then there is nothing to indicate any connection between Miss Montini's search and Rathbourne's murder." His younger brothers traded glances. Sterling narrowed his eyes. "Is there?"

"Rathbourne's throat was cut." Nate drew a deep breath. "As was Montini's."

"What?" Surprise crossed Sterling's face. "I thought Montini died of a fever."

"Not according to what Quint heard in Crete," Nate said. "I suspect Gabriella was only told that to protect her."

For the first time, Dennison spoke. "It is somewhat awkward for foreign officers to inform a relative, particularly a young lady, of a loved one's death, when that death has been violent, sir," he said. "It's often believed kinder to conceal the fact of a violent death, as nothing can be done about it. I have heard about such things happening before."

"And she still doesn't know?" Sterling asked.

"I don't see any reason why she needs to know," Nate said simply.

Quint glanced at him. "Have you told her the rest of it yet?"

Sterling frowned. "The rest of what?"

"About the seals," Quint said.

Nate shook his head. "I haven't had the chance. I fully intend to tell her, but the opportunity has not yet presented itself. I need to find the right time."

"Perhaps," Gabriella's voice sounded from the doorway, "that time is now."

For a long moment none of the men said a word. Then Quint jumped to his feet. "If you will excuse me, I have an errand to attend to."

Sterling stood. "Mr. Dennison and I were just on our way out as well."

His brothers and the secretary hurried out of the room, murmuring polite greetings to Gabriella as they passed by. So much for brotherly support, Nate thought. Gabriella stared at him, stone-faced. They were rats deserting a ship that was not only sinking fast but on fire.

"Do you feel better?" he asked cautiously. Just how much had she heard?

"I'm fine."

He smiled. "Perfectly fine?"

She ignored him. "What haven't you told me about the seals?"

"Perhaps you should sit down."

Her jaw clenched. "I prefer to stand."

"Brandy, then?"

"No, thank you."

"Whisky?" Nate strolled to the whisky decanter and poured himself a glass.

"No." She crossed her arms over her chest. "What haven't you told me about the seals?"

"Quite a lot really." He took a long sip of his drink. "Are you sure you wouldn't rather sit down?"

Her eyes narrowed.

"Very well, then." He wasn't exactly sure how to say this. It did not cast Quint in a good light. Although, on the other hand, at least Quint hadn't stolen the seal. He drew a deep breath. "Quint saw Gutierrez steal the seal from your brother. Some months later, he managed to wrest it from Gutierrez in a game of cards."

"Then Quinton has the seal?"

"Not exactly." He shifted uneasily. It had been awkward enough to tell her of the path the seal had taken, but to tell her now that its whereabouts were still unknown, might always be unknown, was even more difficult. "When Quint unwrapped the seal the other day, right here in the house, he discovered someone had taken it and substituted a different seal."

She stared at him. "That's exactly what happened to my brother."

"Ironic, isn't it?" Nate pulled the seal Quint had found in the attic from his waistcoat pocket and handed it to her. "This is the seal Quint had."

She turned it over in her hand, glancing at it briefly. "This is chalcedony. My brother's was greenstone." She met his gaze firmly. "Where is it?"

He shook his head. "I don't know."

"Does your brother know?"

"No."

Suspicion flashed in her eyes. "Are you sure?"

He drew his brows together. "Yes. Quint wouldn't lie to me."

She shrugged. "He said he didn't steal the seal."

"And he didn't." Nate frowned. "He came by it in a relatively legitimate manner."

She snorted. "Relatively."

"Nonetheless, he didn't steal it."

"He could have told us all this at the beginning." She put the chalcedony seal on the desk. "It would have saved us a great deal of trouble."

"It would have made no difference at all. And yes, he could have told us." Nate paused. "He should have."

"And you trust him now?"

"Yes, I trust him. He would never lie to me."

"Do you know that?"

"I haven't a doubt in my mind."

"Well, I don't trust him."

"You don't have to."

"His reputation is not one that engenders trust."

"His reputation is not nearly as bad as—" Nate caught himself.

"Not nearly as bad as what?" Challenge flashed in her blue eyes.

"Nothing," Nate muttered.

"Not nearly as bad as my brother's?" Her voice was hard. "Is that what you were going to say?"

He tried to deny it. "No, of course not."

"Come now, Nathanial, there's no need to protect me. I know exactly the kind of man my brother was."

Nate stared. "I didn't—"

"My brother, Nathanial . . . " She met his gaze directly. In spite of the cool tone of her voice, there lingered an undercurrent, the merest hint, of despair. "Was the kind of man one would expect to end his days with his throat cut in some foreign land."

"You heard that as well?"

"Yes." She sighed and brushed a stray stand of dark hair away from her face. "I heard that."

"I am so sorry."

"What? Sorry that I heard it? Or sorry that it happened?"

"Both."

"You needn't be." She studied him for a moment. "I didn't know how he died, but it comes as no surprise."

"Still, surely it's upsetting."

"Upsetting?" She scoffed. "Of course it's upsetting, especially after finding Lord Rathbourne." She shuddered. "Although I suspect it's a rather quick way to die."

"Gabriella, I—"

"But I did know what kind of man Enrico was. I have always known. It was simply difficult to acknowledge aloud. He was all I had, all the family I've ever known." She paused for a long moment. "I watch you with your brothers and your mother and sister. There is a bond between you all that is . . . quite remarkable. And I confess I am envious.

"My brother and I," she shook her head, "we did not share what I see between you and your family. I was an obligation for Enrico. Not that he treated me badly," she added quickly. "He saw to it that my needs were met."

"You needn't say anything more."

She ignored him and paced the room. Her words seem to come of their own accord. "It wasn't until he died that I learned we weren't in the financial straits he had always led me to believe we were. I discovered I had a significant fortune that had supported me and my brother's work. Enrico had never mentioned it."

He nodded. "I know."

She continued as if he hadn't said a word. "When Enrico found me, a few years after my father's death, my circumstances were dismal. He rescued me, Nathanial. He was my savior and I adored him.

"He dressed me as a boy and took me with him on his excavations and his hunts for treasure." She paused in mid-step and met Nate's gaze defiantly. "I loved every minute of it. It wasn't until he left me in England that I came to realize that what I had thought was his brotherly desire to keep me by his side was really no more than a convenience. It was easer for him to keep me with him than to arrange for my upbringing elsewhere. As much as I loved it, it was not in my best interests. Somewhere in the back of my mind, I think I have always known my brother's concerns were always and only for himself, for his work, even if I have not dared admit it even to myself until recently."

"I know."

"You know?" She jerked her gaze to his. "You know about my childhood? My fortune?"

He nodded.

"How could you possibly know any of this?"

He winced. "I had some inquires made."

"Inquiries?" Her eyes widened. "You had me investigated?"

"Can you blame me?" He glared at her. "You lied to me, to my family. Bloody hell, Gabriella, you broke into my house!"

"How long have you known?"

"Only since yesterday."

She studied him carefully. "And when did you know of Quinton's part in all this?"

He hesitated. She would not take this well. "A few days ago."

"Before I came to your room?" she said slowly.

He braced himself. "Yes."

"And you did not think to tell me then?"

"I had other things on my mind?" he said weakly.

"Yes," she said simply. "I suppose you did."

Long moments ticked by in silence.

"So." She met his gaze. "It's at an end, isn't it?"

Panic flickered through him. "What's at an end?"

"The search for the seal. We are no closer now than when we started." She cast him a wry smile. "So ends my efforts to give my brother the acknowledgment in death that he didn't have in life. That he might not have deserved. I owed him that much."

"You didn't owe him anything," Nate said in a harsher tone than he'd intended.

"Oh but I did." She shook her head. "My brother gave me a purpose and a love for all things ancient. He did not prevent me from achieving far more in terms of my studies than most women ever dream of. He gave me as well Florence and Miriam and Xerxes, an odd sort of family admittedly, but a family nonetheless. My life has not been a bad one, Nathanial, and for that I do indeed owe him. Besides, he was my brother and I loved him. No matter how he regarded me." She blew a long breath. "I was told recently that no matter what I did, how hard I worked, he would never love me. I hadn't even realized that was what I'd wanted."

His heart twisted for her. He should tell her that *he* loved her, that *he* wanted her in his life for the rest of his days. That *he* would never leave her. But telling her now might seem as though he was simply trying to ease her pain. No, his feelings could wait.

"Gabriella." He started toward her.

She stepped back. "Please don't." She drew a deep

breath. "If you take me in your arms, I will let you. If you take me to your bed, I will allow that as well." Her blue eyes were shadowed with emotion. "I have a great deal to think about. The rest of my life. You."

"Me?" Hope rose within him.

"Yes, you." She shook her head and started out of the room. She paused at the doorway and looked back at him. "I trusted you."

He shook his head. "I never betrayed your trust. I didn't tell you everything but I fully intended to. I never lied to you." He paused. "And trust, Gabriella, as well as honesty, has to go both ways."

"I know, Nathanial." She stared at him for a long moment. "As do leaps of faith."

When had finding the seal become less important than what she might have found with Nathanial?

She'd spent the rest of the evening alone in her rooms trying to sort out her thoughts and emotions. Now she tossed and turned and tried to sleep, with no success. Not surprising, really. She had entirely too much on her mind to sleep.

It was most annoying that he'd had her investigated, but she couldn't blame him. She had lied to him from the beginning. She had expected him to trust her but gave him little reason to do so. She wanted to be angry with him for keeping the information about Quinton's involvement from her, but didn't doubt that he would have told her. She couldn't fault him either for loyalty to his brother, loyalty that was no doubt returned. Nathanial was that sort of man. Honorable and honest. And she was a fool not to have realized that before now.

She had indeed trusted him. She groaned and punched the pillow. Obviously, she still did. What other reason could there be for confessing to him all the things she had? All those feelings about Enrico she had never admitted to herself, let alone to anyone one else.

And she loved him. She should have told him, but after talking about Enrico it would have sounded . . . well, pathetic. Obviously she was more of a coward than she had ever imagined. Now, she feared telling him. Feared he wouldn't feel the same, and feared as well the look of pity in his eyes. She could accept almost anything but that.

It was past time to face the reality that the search for the seal was over. And hadn't she told Nathanial yet another lie? Deep in her heart, didn't she want to find the seal as much to justify her own life as well as her brother's? Wouldn't it have been her own triumph as well as his? Wouldn't his moment of glory been hers too?

Still, it scarcely mattered now. There was nothing to show for her efforts but the seal Quinton had had. She'd paid it scant attention. Carved of chalcedony, it appeared Assyrian . . .

Good God! She bolted upright in bed. How could she have been such an idiot?

Gabriella flung off the covers, leapt out of bed, and headed for Nathanial's room. She forced herself to knock quietly on his door; it wouldn't do to wake up the entire household. She tried the handle and grinned. The man didn't lock his door. Stepping into his room, she snapped the door closed behind her.

She crossed the dark sitting room, grateful for the

faint light from the window. Silly man didn't even close his drapes. She felt her way to his bed and reached out to shake him.

"Nathanial," she whispered.

"Wha . . ." he groaned.

Laughter bubbled up inside her. "Gracious, Nathanial, how can you sleep when I can't?"

"Gabriella?" he said, his voice rough with sleep.

"Were you expecting some other visitor?"

"I wasn't expecting anyone." He grabbed her and pulled her onto the bed. "But I am nothing if not a grateful host."

Before she could protest, he pressed his lips to hers and kissed her long and hard, a kiss to melt even the sternest resolve. A kiss to steal a heart or seal a promise.

He pulled away. "Am I to take this to mean you are no longer angry with me?"

"I wasn't angry with you."

He chuckled. "Then I would hate to see you when you are." He paused. "Why are you here?"

"First . . ." She kissed him again. She couldn't see his eyes in the dark, and that was for the best. For good or ill . . . she drew a deep breath. "I love you, Nathanial, and I thought you should know."

"Gabriella—"

"No, you needn't say anything right now. But that's not all I have to tell you." She kissed him once more, then grinned. "I know where the seal is."

Twenty-six

"Y ou what?" At once he was wide-awake.

"I know where the seal is." She laughed and rolled off the bed. "Get dressed and I'll meet you in the hallway."

"Why am I getting dressed?"

"We have to go find the seal." Her shadow moved away and disappeared into the sitting room.

"Now?" he called after her in a stage whisper. Excitement sparred with disappointment. Couldn't they go in the morning? After a long night in his bed?

"Yes, now."

He heard the door close behind her. She knew where the seal was? He grinned. Wasn't that incredible? Wasn't she incredible? And she loved him. Damnation, he hadn't expected that. Not tonight anyway. He had hoped, of course. He quickly threw on clothes and stepped into the hallway. She was already waiting for him.

He raised a brow. "I see you're wearing your house-breaking clothes."

Even in the scant light shed by the lone lamp in the

hallway he could see her blush. He loved making her blush.

"They were . . . expedient." She shrugged. "And they seemed appropriate."

"For treasure hunting perhaps." He grabbed her and pulled her into his arms. "Does this mean we will be breaking into any houses?"

"Absolutely not," she said staunchly.

"Good." He rested one hand on the small of her back, his other hand drifting lower to caress her buttocks. "I love it when you wear men's clothes."

"Stop it, Nathanial." Her smile belied her words. She pulled out of his arms and started toward the stairs. "Come along."

"Why can't this wait until morning?"

"It can, I suppose, but I can't." She hurried down the stairs.

"Where are we going?"

"I have a small house." She glanced back at him. "I assume you know that?"

He grinned. "Will we be taking Mr. Muldoon with us?"

"I see no need to wake . . . " She heaved a resigned sigh. "You know about him as well."

"Gabriella, my love." They reached the front door. He opened it and they stepped outside. "I know everything."

She snorted. "We'll need a carriage, it's too far to walk. Can you harness one yourself?"

"Yes, but I know where we can get a cab." He took her elbow and they started off at a brisk pace.

"At this hour?"

He nodded. "It's not far from here." He paused. "It's a . . . business establishment."

"What kind of business has cabs waiting at this hour?"

"A very discreet business," he said firmly. "Which is all you need to know."

"Oh," she murmured. "I see"

A quarter of an hour later they reached their destination, and as he had thought, there were several cabs waiting for fares. He held his questions until they settled in one and were on their way.

"You think the seal is in your house?"

She nodded. "And has probably been there all along."

"Why?"

"The seal you showed me last night, the one Quinton had." She leaned toward him, excitement underlying her words. "It's the same one Enrico showed to the committee. The one that was substituted for his."

"You're certain it's the same one?"

She hesitated. "Yes. Yes, I am."

"So you're saying—"

"Enrico must have been the one to take it from Quinton." A smile sounded in her voice. "He would have liked the irony of that, of replacing his seal with the one that had been traded for his. As though it had all come full circle."

"But why didn't he tell you that he had recovered the Ambropia seal?

"I'm not sure he didn't." She thought for a moment. "You read his last letter. It was rambling and convoluted but there was an odd sense of victory to it. I paid no real attention to it at the time. But now . . . " She nodded. "Now, it makes sense.

They pulled up in front of her house and he asked the

driver to wait. She hurried up to the front door, inserted a key and turned the lock easily. Too easily perhaps. Unease drifted through him and he ignored it. It was probably nothing more than the circumstance of being at a house unknown to him late in the night.

She stepped inside and glanced back at him. "Florence and Miriam were called away so there is no one here." She lit a lamp in the front entry, stepped into what he assumed was a parlor, and came back with a second lamp. She lit that one and started up the stairs. He trailed after her, unable to shake a sense of unease.

She turned at the top of the second flight of stairs, led him down a narrow hallway and pushed open a door.

"Hold this, please." She thrust the lamp at him.

He glanced around. They were in a bedroom sparsely furnished with only a bed and a dresser. A small wooden crate sat in one corner. Gabriella moved to the crate and shoved off the top. It clattered to the floor, the noise resounding in the dark house.

He drew his brows together. "Did you hear something?"

"No." She stared at the crate.

"I thought I heard something," he muttered, and strained to listen. It was probably nothing more than the sound of the top of the crate echoing in the house. Still, he could have sworn he had heard something else.

"This was sent to me after Enrico died. We opened it but. . . " She paused for a moment. Regardless of Enrico's character, he was still her brother and she had obviously cared for him. "But I haven't yet looked in it."

She drew a deep breath and knelt down in front of the crate. He positioned the lamp to give her better light, moving it farther away from his nose. It had an odd scent of smoke, and he wondered if it had been some time since it was used.

Gabriella reached into the container and began pulling out the odds and ends of Enrico Montini's life. A few articles of clothing, several books and bound notebooks, some interesting but not particularly important artifacts, a well-worn pair of boots. She started to set the boots down then hefted one in her hand and glanced at Nate.

"What?" He moved the lamp closer.

She reached into the boot and pulled out a cloth-wrapped bundle. She dropped the boot and started to unwrap the bundle but her hands shook. She grimaced. "I don't recall my hands ever shaking before yesterday."

"Here." He grabbed her free hand and pulled her to her feet, then traded her the lamp for the bundle. Quickly, he unrolled the wrappings to reveal an ancient cylinder seal. She moved the lamp closer. It was greenstone. He met Gabriella's gaze. "I think we've found your seal."

She grinned. "Thank you, Nathanial."

"No, it's I who should thank you." He leaned closer and kissed her. "I can think of nothing I'd rather do than hunt for treasure with you."

She laughed, and for the first time since they'd met it struck him as carefree and happy. The sound of it wrapped around his soul.

"Do you want this?" He held out the seal.

"No, you keep it." She brushed her lips across his. "I trust you."

He smiled, slipped the artifact into his pocket, and took the lamp from her. "As much as I would like to linger here, we should be on our way. We have a driver waiting and it is nearly morning. Besides, now that you have the seal, you obviously need to prepare your presentation to the Verification Committee. You haven't much time left."

Her eyes widened. "My presentation?"

He raised a brow. "Who else?"

"I hadn't considered that. I really hadn't thought beyond recovering the seal. But of course." She lifted her chin and cast him a satisfied grin. "It will be my presentation."

"You are going to be a handful," he said under his breath.

"What?"

"I said we should probably get the impression while we're here."

"That's not what you said."

"Nonetheless, we should still get the impression."

"I'm afraid that's a bit of a problem," she said slowly.

"Oh?"

"I don't actually have the impression."

"But you said—"

"Yes, well." She winced. "It sounded so good at the time. But I am confident it's in the house. Somewhere."

He narrowed his eyes. "Are there any other lies you wish to confess?"

"Not at the moment," she said in a somber manner, but her eyes twinkled with amusement. "But if something comes to mind I shall be sure to tell you. Although didn't you say you knew everything?"

"Hmph."

He led the way into the hall and stopped. The hairs

on the back of his neck prickled. There was a distinct odor of smoke. "Do you smell that?"

"What?" She stopped and her eyes grew wide. "Smoke? But how?"

"It doesn't matter. We have to go." He grabbed her hand and started for the stairs. Smoke drifted up from the lower floors. "Is there a back stairway?"

She stared at the smoke now billowing up the stairs. "My house is on fire!"

"A back stair, Gabriella?"

"My house . . . " She shook her head as if to clear it. "This way."

She dashed toward a door at the opposite end of the hall and reached for it. He yanked her back and carefully placed his hand on the door. It was cool. He pushed it open. "I have the lamp, I'll lead the way. Grab onto my coat."

"Why?"

"Because I said so!" he snapped, and struggled for calm. It wouldn't do either of them any good if he did not keep his wits about him. "Because if I can feel you holding on, I'll know you're still with me."

"Very well." Fear sounded in her voice.

He quickly led the way down the two flights to the ground floor. There was some smoke but not much. The fire was obviously in the front of the house. Again he paused to feel the door before pushing it open. The moment he did, acrid smoke billowed around him and he choked. "Is there a back way?"

She coughed. "Yes." She grabbed his hand and pulled him toward the back of the house, into a room that appeared to be a scullery, to a door on the outside wall.

She fumbled with the key. Panic rang in her voice. "I can't get it open!"

"Move!" He shoved her aside, set the lamp down, took aim and kicked the door with the flat of his foot. He tried again and the door gave somewhat. Smoke was filling the room, the lamp no longer any use. He braced himself and tried again. The door splintered. He grasped the door and yanked it free. Grabbing Gabriella around the waist, he hauled her out of the building. They stumbled a few steps away from the house, both struggling to catch their breath.

She gasped for air. "Come on."

She sprinted across a small garden to a back gate with him right behind her. The gate opened to a narrow lane. She ran down it, turned into the street and circled to the front of the house, Nate close on her heels. She skidded to a stop and stared.

The front door was wide open and smoke poured out. Flames could be seen in one window. Gabriella stared in shocked disbelief.

"Bloody hell." Quint's voice sounded behind him.

"What are you doing here?" Nate snapped.

Quint stared at the burning building. "I heard you in the hall. I thought you might need help. So I woke Muldoon. We just got here."

Gabriella gasped. "My letters!"

Nate peered around his brother. "Where is Muldoon?"

"He ran for the fire brigade as soon as we realized where the smoke was coming from." Quint's gaze shifted to a point behind his brother. "You might want to stop her."

Nate swiveled to see Gabriella dashing back to the house and through the open door.

"Damnation." He raced for the door, Quint no more than a step behind.

"Here." Quint thrust a handkerchief at him. "Cover your nose and mouth and for God's sake be careful."

Nate nodded, clutched the handkerchief to his face and stepped inside. Flames roared at the foot of the stairs, a good six feet or so from the front door. The fire had spread into a parlor to the right. Dear God, where was she?

"Gabriella!" he screamed, praying to be heard above the din of the flames. Fear for her clutched at his heart. The smoke was so thick, if not for the light of the fire itself he wouldn't have been able to see his hand in front of his face.

"Here." She staggered out of parlor, choking and gasping for breath. He started toward her. A loud crack ripped through the air. He reached for her. Her terror-filled gaze met his. A huge chunk of the ceiling collapsed, missing him by mere inches. Gabriella crumpled to the floor beneath it.

His heart lodged in his throat and he grabbed pieces of the ceiling and threw them aside. At once Quint was by his side. It took a moment or perhaps a lifetime to free her. Nate pulled her from the wreckage with his brother's help, scooped her into his arms, and the two men made their escape. A split second after they stepped out of the house, the rest of the ceiling collapsed and flames licked at their backs. They staggered away from the building and Nate noted the fire brigade had arrived.

Muldoon rushed up to them. "Is she . . . " Fear flickered in the other man's eyes.

"No." Nate could see the faint rise and fall of Gabriella's chest with her labored breathing. "But we have to get her home."

Quint nodded. "We have a carriage."

They settled in the carriage. Quint sent Muldoon to fetch their family physician to meet them at Harrington House. Nate had no doubt that despite the lateness of the hour, the big man would not take no for an answer.

He cradled Gabriella in his arms on the endless ride that probably took no time at all. There was a cut high on her temple but she didn't appear to have suffered any burns. She still clutched what looked like a packet of letters in her hand. Even though he knew head wounds tended to bleed a lot, there still seemed to be an inordinate amount of blood. And he did the only thing it was possible to do.

"Dear Lord," he prayed. "Don't let me lose her."

He had lost all sense of time.

Vaguely, Nate noted that the sun had risen. He wasn't sure how long he had sat here in the corridor in his mother's wing of the house. She had insisted they put Gabriella in one of the larger suites. Now she was in Gabriella's room with the physician while he waited. Fear had settled in a heavy lump in the pit of his stomach.

But as long as he had been there, Quint and Sterling remained by his side. As had Muldoon. Not appropriate perhaps for a footman, but Muldoon was as much a part of Gabriella's family as any blood relation.

"Is that what she went back in the house for?" Quint glanced at the packet of letters on Nate's lap.

He nodded.

"What are they?" Sterling asked.

"I have no idea." Nate shook his head. "But not worth her life."

"They are to her," Muldoon said quietly. "Although she'd probably deny it. They're letters to her mother. She found them after her brother's death." His expression hardened. "He never gave them to her."

Nate had never hated anyone in his life before, but at the moment he would have gladly slit Enrico Montini's throat himself.

"Do you have any idea what happened?" Sterling asked. "How the fire started?"

"There was someone else in the house. I thought I heard something but I wasn't sure." He blew a long breath. "I should have paid more attention. I should have . . ." *I should have stopped her from going back into that house.* "I don't know if the fire was deliberate or an accident, and I suppose it doesn't really matter."

"Do you think it was someone looking for the seal?" Quint said.

"Or possibly the impression that would prove the veracity of the seal. Without the impression, anyone could claim discovery of the seal." Nate shook his head. "But I don't know. Frankly, I don't care."

Quint paused. "Did you find it?"

"Find what?" Sterling looked from one brother to the other, then realization dawned on his face. "The seal? The Montini seal?"

"We did." Nate could still feel it in his pocket.

"Well that's . . ." Sterling searched for the right word. "Good?"

Nate's gaze met his older brother's.

Sterling's voice softened. "She'll be fine, Nate."

"Of course she will," Quint added staunchly.

The door to Gabriella's room opened and Dr. Crenshaw stepped out, a grim look on his face, followed by Mother. Nate jumped to this feet, the letters falling to the floor. "How is she?"

"The cut on her head was superficial. I doubt it will even leave a scar. However . . . " The doctor paused. "Her lungs are somewhat congested, as would be expected, given what she's been through. And she has a nasty bump on her head that concerns me."

Nate resisted the urge to snap at the man. "But will she be all right?"

"Quite honestly, Nathanial, it's too early to say for certain. I shall be back tomorrow morning. We should know a great deal more then, one way or the other." He turned to Mother. "Someone should stay with her. Send for me if there are any changes."

"Yes, of course. Thank you." Mother signaled to Andrews to escort the doctor out. "I shall stay with her."

"No." Panic gripped him at the thought of her waking up without him there. Or him not being there and Gabriella never waking up at all. "I'll stay with her."

"Darling." Sympathy shone in his mother's eyes. "I don't think that's wise."

"Let him, Mother," Sterling said.

Mother cast a quelling glance at Sterling then turned back to her youngest son. "Nathanial, you smell strongly of smoke. It's quite overpowering. As her house has just burned, I daresay that's not the aroma she should awaken to. In addition, you are exhausted. You cannot be of any help to her in this state. I want you to bathe and sleep, then you may sit with her for as long as you wish."

He didn't like it but knew she was probably right. "Very well."

She aimed a pointed glance at Quinton. "You smell no better than he does."

"Yes, Mother," Quinton murmured.

"As for you." She addressed Muldoon. "I am aware of your connection to Miss Montini. You are welcome to stay outside her room as long as you like, and we will inform you at once if there's any change at all."

"I do appreciate it, ma'am." Muldoon nodded.

"There is nothing any of us can do at the moment but wait. Nathanial." Mother laid her hand on his arm. "We have known Dr. Crenshaw for many years. He has cared for everyone in this family at one time or another. I trust him completely and I can tell you he is most optimistic."

Nate smiled wryly. "That was optimistic?"

"Yes," she said firmly. "Gabriella will be fine." She turned to go back into Gabriella's room then stopped and knelt down to pick up the packet of letters. "What's this?"

"It's why she went back into the house," Nate said. "They're letters written to her mother. Gabriella found them after her brother's death." His tone was grim. "He kept them from her."

"One can only hope he is burning in Hell." Mother turned the packet over in her hands. "One should do something about this."

"As Montini is dead, I believe someone has," Quint said wryly.

"Yes, of course," Mother murmured, and glanced pointedly at Nate. "Now, go."

Nate quickly bathed and donned fresh clothes, but

he had no intention of staying away from Gabriella. He couldn't leave her, couldn't abandon her. He returned within an hour to sit by the side of her bed. Mother joined him for a while, and Muldoon stayed outside her door as well. He was grateful to know the older man was there.

The food his mother sent up for him later, as he kept his vigil, sat uneaten through the long hours of the day and into the night. Occasionally, in spite of himself, he dozed, but those brief moments of sleep were filled with images of Gabriella dashing back into the house, flames licking at the stairs, and the terror in her blue eyes.

So he watched her too still form in the bed. And he listened to her labored breathing and thought it eased somewhat through the night, but he was too weary to know if he had heard some improvement or just hoped he had.

And he thought of all the things he loved about her and how she'd said that she loved him and hadn't asked for anything in return. And he thought of all the things he hadn't said to her, all the things he'd hadn't had a chance to say.

And prayed it wasn't too late to say them.

Twenty-seven

*D*r. Crenshaw stepped out of Gabriella's room the next morning, his expression as grim as ever.

Muldoon and Nate jumped to their feet. "Well?"

The physician met Nate's gaze directly. "She is much improved. Her lungs sound almost clear, although she will cough a bit for the next few days. Fortunately, Miss Montini is a very strong and healthy young woman."

"And her head?" Nate asked.

"She will have a dreadful headache but her eyes look good. I am confident she will be fine within a few days."

Relief washed through Nate, and Muldoon heaved an audible sigh.

"I have given her something to ease the pain and instructions to continue its use. It will also help her sleep." The doctor's firm gaze pinned Nate's. "What she needs now is rest. No excitement of any kind, and the fewer visitors the better." Dr. Crenshaw narrowed his eyes. "I have known you all of your life, Nathanial Harrington, and it is obvious to me that you care for this young woman. The body has a way of healing itself. Rest and sleep are the best things for her. Your mother or the presence of another female would be acceptable, but I would strongly advise that you limit your visits."

"But I—"

"I suspect you would provide excitement she does not need. Leave her be, Nathanial, for now. However," the doctor's expression softened, "she is awake now, although probably only for a few minutes. I should warn you, the medication will make it difficult for her to concentrate and she may not make much sense. You may see her now, but for no more than a minute," he added firmly.

"Thank you." Nate started into Gabriella's room but Muldoon stopped him.

"My wife and Miss Henry are in the country. I didn't want to fetch them until we knew Miss Montini would recover. Now, I must go, but we'll return as quickly as possible." The big man's gaze locked with Nate's. "Take care of her."

"Always," he said, the conviction in his voice straight from his heart.

Mother stepped out of Gabriella's room. "Only a minute, remember."

Nate nodded, walked into her room and directly to her bedside. Gauze covered the cut on her head, her face was deathly pale, and her blue eyes seemed enormous. Still, she was the most beautiful thing he'd ever seen.

She cast him a weak smile. "Are you going to chastise me?"

"No." He sat down beside her bed and took her hand in his. "Not today."

"Oh dear." She sighed. "Then I must be dying."

"You're not dying." His voice was rough with emotion. "You shall live a very long time. With me."

"How very nice." Her eyelids were heavy, her voice soft. "I'm so tired. And so sorry."

He smiled. "Nothing to be sorry about."

"You could have been hurt. I couldn't bear it if you were hurt." Her eyes drifted closed, then opened, but it was obviously a struggle for her. "But I found it, didn't I?"

"Yes, you did." He leaned closer and gently kissed her forehead. "You found the seal."

"No." The word was no more than a sigh, and her eyes drifted closed again. "I found the letters," she murmured, and was again asleep.

He watched her a few moments, then quietly took his leave. He paused outside her door and blew a long breath. Staying away from her now might be the hardest part of any of this. But if that's what was necessary, that's what he would do.

His mother hooked her arm through his and walked him down the hall toward the stairs. "I have an idea, Nathanial, and I'm not certain you're going to like it."

He ran a weary hand through his hair. "What is it, Mother?"

"I think it would be best—"

"Where is she?" A short blond woman with a determined air and fire in her eyes appeared at the top of the stairs, Mr. Dennison a step behind her.

"I tried to stop her," Mr. Dennison said in a helpless tone. He'd never known Dennison to sound the least bit helpless before.

"Where is she? What have you done with her?" the woman demanded.

"Lady Wyldewood, Mr. Harrington, this is Miss Henry," Dennison said.

"Of course." Mother smiled. "I have been expecting you. Miss Montini is asleep now but the doctor assures us she will be quite all right in no time."

"Thank God." Miss Henry's expression crumbled. "That's what Mr. Muldoon said, but regardless, I have to see for myself. We met him a few minutes ago right outside the house. We came here as soon as we arrived home and discovered—" She drew a deep breath and squared her shoulders. "As soon as we saw our house was in ruins."

"You poor dear." Mother took her arm and steered her into a sitting room off the hall. "We have a great deal to tell you, not all of it pleasant, and the hallway is not the place to do it." She glanced at Nate. "Coming?" It was a command more than a question.

Dennison leaned toward Nate. "I shall be in the library if she—if you—need me."

Nate nodded and followed the two women.

"I wish to see Gabriella," Miss Henry said staunchly.

"And you will." Mother settled her on a love seat and rang for tea. "Nathanial, if you would be so kind as to begin."

Nate quickly recounted the events of yesterday and last night, from Gabriella's finding Lord Rathbourne's body to the fire. Miss Henry listened, eyes wide with horror and concern. "This is all quite unbelievable." She twisted her hands in her lap. "You should as well know we were sent on a fool's errand. We received a note saying Mrs. Muldoon's mother was gravely ill. We arrived to find her mother is fine so we saw no need not to return."

"Then someone wanted your house empty," Nate said slowly. "To search it, no doubt."

"So it would appear." Miss Henry shook her head. "This is my fault. I should have expected something like this. I never should have condoned her search for that blasted seal in the first place."

"My dear, I haven't known her very long," Mother said in a kindly manner, "but I sincerely doubt that you could have stopped her."

"No, you're right there. But I have been concerned from the beginning that this might prove dangerous. Her brother was . . . " She shot Nate a questioning glance.

Nate nodded. "We are all aware of what kind of man Enrico Montini was." He paused. "As is Gabriella."

Miss Henry heaved a resigned sigh. "I have long thought so but she never said anything. And I never brought it up."

Nate studied her. "We found the seal."

Miss Henry's eyes widened.

"It was among her brother's things." He paused. "But we don't have the impression."

"Oh." She waved in an offhand manner. "I have that."

"You do?" Nate stared.

"I thought it would be safer for Gabriella if she didn't have it. After all, no one would expect me to have it."

"Safer?" His voice rose. "Whoever was in that house last night might well have been looking for it. And as Gabriella had claimed to have it, she was scarcely safer."

"Yes, well, that might have been a mistake on my part," Miss Henry snapped.

"I think," Mother cut in, "what Gabriella needs now, in addition to rest," she shot her son a pointed glance, "is her family."

Miss Henry shook her head. "Aside from myself and the Muldoons, she has no family to speak of."

"No, Miss Henry," Mother said firmly. "In truth, Gabriella has a very large and extensive family."

"Her mother's family, you mean?"

Mother nodded.

"They didn't want her."

"Quite the contrary. They tried to find her for years." Mother paused. "They were told she was dead."

Miss Henry stared for a moment, then her eyes widened with understanding. "Enrico." She looked at Nate. "To keep control of her money?"

Nate shrugged. "Probably."

"Gabriella's aunt is one of my oldest friends," his mother said. "She, along with her sister and her daughter, have been in Paris. According to the last letter I received from Caroline, they are to return the day after tomorrow and should arrive in Dover by afternoon. From there, they have planned to go to Caroline's estate in the country rather than return to London." She looked at Nate. "We can leave on a morning train. That will get us to Dover in time to catch them, and we can bring them directly here."

"We?" Nate scoffed. "I'm not going anywhere. Can't we telegraph them?"

Mother's brows drew together. "This is not the kind of news one imparts in a telegram."

"I'm not leaving Gabriella."

"You are not supposed to bother her, remember?" Mother turned to Miss Henry. "The doctor says she is to have as few visitors as possible and she is not to be overly excited."

"I have no intention of overexciting her." Nate glared at his mother.

"No doubt." Miss Henry sniffed.

"Well, you certainly can't if you aren't here. Besides, it's likely she will sleep for at least another few days. We'll be back probably before she knows we're gone," Mother said firmly. "She needs her family, Nathanial. She needs to know there are people who care about her."

"I care about her!"

"She has lost her brother, the only family she thought she had. Regardless of the kind of man he was, she obviously loved him. Now she has lost her home as well. This will help her. Not her body as much as her heart, I think. And I know you want that." She leaned toward him, laid her hand on his arm and gazed into his eyes. "Do this for her." She straightened. "Besides, I am certain Miss Henry will wish to stay with Gabriella."

"Without question." Miss Henry nodded.

"And as you and Mrs. Muldoon have lost your home as well, I suggest you both stay here for as long as is necessary."

"That's most kind of you." Miss Henry thought for a moment. "If we are to avoid excitement, I would suggest, if she awakens, she not be told what you are up to." She shook her head. "The truth will come as a shock to her. She has long said she has no interest in her mother's family, although I have never quite believed it."

"Miss Henry," Mother said gently, "she went back into that burning house to retrieve her mother's letters. I think that says a great deal about her true feelings."

Miss Henry nodded. "I agree."

"Then we are all agreed." Mother beamed.

"No." Nate's gaze skipped from his mother to Miss Henry and back. "We are most certainly not agreed. The Verification Committee ends its meeting at noon two days from now. If we miss that, the opportunity to present the seal will be gone forever. It's what she's worked for. What she wanted."

"She wanted her mother's letters. Which makes this—" His mother set her chin in a stubborn manner. "—more important."

Nate clenched his jaw. "Miss Henry?"

Miss Henry thought for a long moment. "Discovery of the seal would have made her brother's reputation. She very much wanted that. But she has always wanted to . . . well, belong somewhere, and she has never felt that she did. So yes." She nodded. "I agree."

"I don't," Nate said. "However," he rolled his gaze at the ceiling, "I can see how knowing there were people who wanted her might be the best thing for her. And I certainly can't let you go alone."

"Excellent." Again his Mother beamed.

"And, as this might well turn out to be quite disastrous . . . " He blew a long breath. "I have an idea of my own."

"You want me to what?" Quint stared at him as if he'd lost his mind.

Nate had asked his brothers to join him in the library. If he was going to fetch Gabriella's lost family, he was going to need help.

"Listen to him, Quint," Sterling said from behind his desk.

"As I was saying . . . " Nate drew a deep breath. "The Verification Committee ends its meeting in two days. Even if I were to get back in time to make it, and in spite of Mother's assurances, I am not confident of that, there will be no chance to prepare a presentation. With luck, Gabriella will be well enough to present the seal herself, but she will not be able to prepare anything either. I can begin tomorrow but but—" Nate met Quint's gaze firmly. "I need you to help me put a presentation in order. Indeed, I need you to do most of it."

Quint snorted. "I think not."

"You're more than qualified," Sterling said mildly. "Aside from Professor Ashworth, you probably know as much about Ambropia and the legend of the Virgin's Secret as anyone."

"I don't care," Quint scoffed. "I am not about to do anything to legitimize Enrico Montini's claim."

"You wouldn't be doing this for Enrico Montini," Nate said, "you'd be doing it for Gabriella. And me," he added pointedly.

"All things considered, it seems to me this is the least you can do." Sterling had been told of Quint's involvement with the seals and was not pleased with his brother's actions.

Quint glared at his younger brother. "If you're not back, I have no intention of presenting . . . " He gritted his teeth. "The Montini seal."

"If I'm not back, you'll have no seal to present." Nate

shook his head. "I'm not letting the seal out of my sight."

Quint crossed his arms over his chest. "How am I expected to prepare an argument for the validity of an artifact without the artifact in question?"

"You'll have it until I leave for Dover, and I can give you the impression."

Quint narrowed his eyes. "You don't trust me."

"I trust you with my life." He met his brother's gaze directly. "I always have."

Quint studied him for a long moment, then shrugged. "I'll do what I can."

"Nate, is there any other way we can be of assistance?" Sterling asked.

"We?" Quint muttered.

"Yes," Nate said. "I don't like leaving her, but apparently I'm not permitted to see her. The doctor says she will be fine physically. But even though we have the seal, I'm not certain she isn't still in danger. Muldoon will be here and he has protected her for much of her life. Still, I would feel better—"

"Of course." Sterling nodded. "We will make certain she is kept safe. Anything else?"

"I don't know." Nate absently paced in front of the desk. This wasn't enough. Regardless of what his mother and Miss Henry thought, if he missed that meeting, Gabriella would never forgive him. No reunion could ever make up for it. He would need to do something to make it right. Some sort of grand gesture. Something unexpected to absolve him and capture her heart. The vaguest of plans took shape with every step.

"Perhaps," he nodded thoughtfully. "But I shall need the help of . . . of an intrepid earl and a daring smuggler king."

Sterling grinned. "As ever we ever have and ever will be."

Quint looked from one brother to the other, then smiled reluctantly. "Brothers, one for the other."

"One for the other." Nate grinned.

It was still a very good pact.

Twenty-eight

"Caroline," Mother called with an enthusiastic wave.

Lady Danworthy stared for a moment, then smiled, and made her way toward them through the crowd on the Dover pier. "Millicent!" The two women embraced. "What on earth are you doing here? Are you on your way to Paris? Wait until you see the gowns we purchased. They are magnificent. But then if you're going to Paris, you'll be visiting Mr. Worth's establishment yourself."

"I'm not going to Paris," Mother said. "I have come here to meet you."

"Why how very kind of you, and most unexpected." Lady Danworthy's brow furrowed. "My apologies, Millicent, but I don't understand why you're here."

"Get on with it, Mother," Nate said under his breath.

The boat from France had, of course, been late. Not that he hadn't expected exactly that. Regardless of the arguments made by his mother and Miss Henry, he knew this was a bad idea. Still, he and Quint had the presentation well in hand, and he'd made other arrangements as a precautionary measure. Mother was right about one thing, though. While Gabriella had awakened briefly a few times yesterday, barely long enough to take the medication the doctor left for her, she had gone right back to sleep. They might indeed return before she realized he was gone.

"I have something of great importance to tell you that simply could not wait," Mother said. "There's a café I noted at the end of the pier. We can talk there."

"Oh dear." Lady Danworthy's eyes widened. "It's something dreadful, isn't it?"

"No, dearest, it's something quite wonderful."

Lady Danworthy studied Mother for a long moment. "Millicent, I have known you for much of my life. If you say this is important, then it is." She turned and gestured at two women who stood some distance away, surrounded by several servants amidst a virtual sea of baggage. Nate winced at the sight. Oh, wouldn't that make all this easier?

"Nathanial," Mother said when the two women drew near. "You remember Lady Danworthy's sister, Mrs. Delong? And of course you know Emma."

"Although we haven't seen one another for years." Emma Carpenter held out her hand to Nate. "How are you, Nathanial?"

"Very well, thank you." He could barely choke out the words. He took her hand as much to give himself a moment to regain his composure as anything else. No wonder Gabriella seemed familiar to him when they first met. It wasn't merely that he had met her *brother* in Egypt, but aside from differences in the shade of their hair and eyes, and a slight difference in the shape of their mouths, Emma and Gabriella could have passed for twins. "You are as lovely as ever."

She laughed. "And you are more charming than ever, I see."

"Nathanial." His mother raised a brow. "Time is of the essence, remember?"

"Of course." Within a quarter of an hour he had arranged for the servants to stay with the luggage, settled the ladies in a café with an excellent view of the channel, and resisted the urge to check his watch more than twice.

"Well?" Lady Danworthy said. "I am dying of curiosity. What is this matter of great importance?"

"Caroline." Mother took her hand. "We have some news for you about Gabriella."

"Gabriella?" Confusion crossed Lady Danworthy's face, then she sucked in a sharp breath and her free hand reached for her sister's. "Gabriella, our niece?"

"Yes, Gabriella Montini." Mother paused, and Nate wasn't sure if it was to find the right words or prolong the drama of the moment, although it did seem to him dramatic enough. "Caroline, she's alive."

Mrs. Delong gasped. "What do you mean, she's alive?"

"I mean she's not dead. She's never been dead." Mother huffed. "Goodness, of all the things I have to explain I didn't think alive would be among them."

Lady Danworthy stared. "But we were told—"

"Yes, well that was a lie." Mother's expression hardened. "Gabriella's life up to now has been somewhat unusual, but I can tell you she is a lovely young woman. A bit headstrong and prone to impulsive behavior perhaps—"

Nate snorted to himself.

"—but brilliant and really quite delightful in her own, independent way."

Mrs. Delong's brows drew together. "Are you certain of this?"

"We have confirmed her identity, and you will have no doubts yourselves the moment you lay eyes on her." Mother smiled at Emma. "She looks very much like Emma."

"Who strongly resembles Helene," Mrs. Delong said under her breath, a stunned expression on her face.

"Helene's daughter," Lady Danworthy murmured, unshed tears glistening in her eyes. "But how?"

"It's a very long story and somewhat complicated. I shall tell it all to you on the way to London. You should know as well that Gabriella has been injured, although she is expected to be fine," Mother added quickly. "But she needs her family."

"Ladies, we should be on our way," Nate said, trying and failing to hide his impatience.

"No," Mrs. Delong said. "We can't go to London."

Nate groaned to himself. "Why not?"

Caroline looked at her sister. "Why not indeed?"

Mrs. Delong met her younger sister's gaze firmly. "We cannot meet Helene's daughter without her necklace."

"Yes, of course," Caroline murmured.

"I had forgotten all about the necklace." Mother shook her head. "I should have thought of that."

Nate clenched his jaw. "What necklace?"

"Nathanial," Emma began in a soothing manner. "One of our ancestors made his fortune working for the East India Company. He gave his wife a Chinese gaming chip set in gold to wear as a pendant, for luck I believe. She passed it down to her daughter, who passed it to hers. My grandmother had two more made, as she had three daughters, and never revealed which was the original."

"When Helene left England, hers was somehow left behind." Mrs. Delong set her jaw in a stubborn manner. "I will not meet her daughter without her necklace. She would have wanted her to have it. It means, more than anything else could, that we welcome her as a part of our family."

"Can't you give it to her later?" Nate said hopefully.

All four women stared at him as if, being a man, he couldn't possibly understand, and indeed he didn't. And the look in each and every eye told him this was not open for debate. He groaned to himself. "Where is this necklace?"

"It's at my country house," Lady Danworthy said.

He shook his head. "We can't—"

"Or course we can, Nathanial," Mother said firmly. "And can still make it back in time."

"In time for what?" Emma asked.

"As I said, my dear, this is a very long story. I shall explain it all to you on the way." She glanced at her son. "Shouldn't we be on our way?"

"Yes," he said sharply. "Let's be on our way."

They still might be able to make it back to London before the committee adjourned. If not, he had made plans for that as well. He only hoped his plan worked better than any of Gabriella's.

Gabriella struggled to open her eyes.

She was lost in the thickest of London fogs. Tendrils of haze, like incessant fingers, plucked at her, wrapped around her, reached into her soul. Voices sounded far in the distance, fading and growing more distinct and fading again. She tried to go toward them but couldn't seem to progress, couldn't seem to move at all. The fog grew deeper, darker, nearly black. So thick she could feel it envelop her, press against her skin, push into her mouth, her nose.

She couldn't see anything at all save for an orange glow off to her right. Fire, of course, the house was on fire. She turned to flee and realized she couldn't, she had to go back. She held out her hands. They shook and were empty. Shouldn't she have something? But what? And why couldn't she remember? She turned again and Lord Rathbourne stepped out of the blackness, a vaguely surprised look on his face, his shirt crimson and dripping. Somewhere in the distance a woman screamed. A high-pitched, rasping, hysterical sound of terror and panic, and . . . it was her voice!

She bolted upright in the bed. Pain shot through her head. She doubled over and pressed the heels of her hands to her temples and groaned.

"Gabriella?" A comforting hand rested on her shoulder.

She turned her head and peered through half-opened eyes. "Florence?"

Florence sat by her side. "Yes dear, I'm here. How do you feel?"

"I'd have to feel better to die." She groaned again. "Am I dying?"

"No, darling, you're going to be fine." Florence shook her head in a chastising manner. "You were really very lucky."

"Yes, well I don't feel lucky." She gingerly lifted her head and sat up slowly. "What happened to me?"

"You don't remember?"

"I don't seem to remember anything at the moment." Save the insidious fog and flames and Rathbourne. "What . . ."

"There was a fire at the house. You and Mr. Harrington—"

"The seal." She groped for the memory. "We found the seal."

"Indeed you did."

"And the fire." She remembered the heat and the smoke and the fear. Her throat ached almost as much as her head. "And Nathanial." She caught her breath. "Is Nathanial—"

"He's fine," Florence said. "There isn't a scratch on him."

Relief washed through her.

"Do you remember going back in the house?"

"Going back . . ." She drew her brows together. She remembered a sense of urgency . . . She shook her head carefully. "No."

"You went back in the house to get your mother's letters."

"Did I?" Gabriella murmured. "How very foolish of me."

"Yes, it was," Florence said firmly.

She remembered now, some of it, most of it. "And did I? Find the letters?"

"Yes, you did."

"I can't imagine why I would," she said under her breath. It made no sense to her now. Still, she did recall the feeling of urgency. "When . . ."

"The fire was three days ago. You have been asleep since then. You have needed it and you continue to need it." Florence nodded. "Complete rest is what the doctor said and no excitement."

Excitement was the last thing she wanted, although the throbbing in her head had subsided somewhat. "Where is Nathanial?"

"He is not here right now and that's none of your concern at the moment. No excitement, remember." Florence's voice softened. "He has been quite concerned about you."

Gabriella settled back against the pillows and managed a slight smile. "Has he?"

"Indeed he has," she said with a smile of her own, "and you shall see him as soon as you are up to it."

Gabriella plucked at the covers. "I feel up to it now."

"Nonetheless, it's not advisable," Florence said in the no nonsense manner Gabriella recognized. There would be no getting around her on this point. Probably. Florence rose to her feet. "What you need now is something to eat. Broth and tea and toast, I should think."

"I am hungry," Gabriella murmured. A thought struck and she widened her eyes. "Three days did you say?"

Florence nodded warily.

"Then the Verification Committee ends its meeting tomorrow. I have to—"

"You have to do nothing at the moment but rest." Florence's look left no room for argument. She paused. "The doctor left something for the pain in your head and to help you sleep."

"I don't want it." She shook her head gently. "The dreams . . . " She shuddered. "The pain in my head is nothing compared to the dreadful dreams. No, I shall do without it." She forced a smile. "I do feel much better."

Florence considered her carefully. "Very well, then. I shall be back in a minute."

She took her leave, and Gabriella rested against the pillows. It was all coming back to her. Discovering the dead viscount, hearing how her brother had died, finding the seal, the fire, the letters . . .

Nathanial was safe and he had the seal. She glanced at the window. It was already afternoon. Still, she needn't worry, there was time. She closed her eyes and blew a long breath. Nathanial had the seal and all would be well. He would make certain of it.

She dozed on and off through the day but by early evening her mind had cleared considerably. Where was Nathanial? Florence seemed particularly evasive and finally refused to discuss Nathanial at all save to tell her that she needed to avoid excitement, which meant avoiding Mr. Harrington. It was a most convenient excuse, and Gabriella had stopped asking. Once, when Florence was out of the room, a maid came in to bring fresh linens. Gabriella had asked her to fetch Nathanial, but the maid said that Master Nathanial had left the city. She'd had no more information that that.

Where was he? Where had he gone? He had the seal. Surely he realized the meeting was to end tomorrow at noon. What if he didn't make it? What if he didn't come back at all? What if he had gone off to find the lost city himself?

No, she told herself, firmly trying to thrust the disquieting thoughts aside. She trusted him completely. Nathanial would never betray her like that. He would never betray her at all. It was simply the circumstances and her own suspicious nature that made her wonder otherwise.

But as the day wore on into evening and night, dread curled inside her. She wanted to trust him. No, she did trust him. Surely wherever he was, whatever he was doing, it was a matter of importance. He would never abandon her. She knew that, not merely in her mind but in her heart.

Nathanial Harrington was the one person in the world she could count on.

Still, as she fell into a restless sleep that night a voice in the back of her head nagged at her.

What if she was wrong?

Twenty-nine

T his was the final day.

The thought struck Gabriella the moment her eyes opened. She threw off the covers and slid out of bed. The ache in her head was nearly gone, and certainly no reason to stay abed. Was Nathanial back? A glance at the window told her it was already late morning. Damnation! She pulled on her wrapper, swept out of her room and stepped across the hall to his door. She paused, then turned the handle and stepped inside.

"Nathanial?" She crossed the sitting room to his bed-chamber. His bed was untouched. Surely it had already been made up. Unless, of course, he hadn't slept in it last night. Where was he? Not that it mattered. She trusted him.

She hurried out of his room. She should dress, it was most improper to wander about the house in her night-clothes, but it couldn't be helped. At this particular moment propriety was not uppermost in her mind. She sped down the corridor to the stairway and fairly flew down the stairs, where she met the butler's startled gaze.

"Andrews," she said without preamble. "Have you seen Mr. Harrington? Nathanial?"

"Not today, miss."

"Do you know where he is?"

"No, miss." Andrews shook his head. "I have no idea where he is at the moment."

She huffed. "What about his brother?"

"Which brother, miss?"

"Any brother," she snapped.

"Neither Master Quinton nor his lordship are at home, miss."

"And Lady Wyldewood." She raised a brow. "Has she vanished as well?"

"I would not say she has vanished, miss. But no, she is not at home. Lady Regina, however, is still abed," he added in a helpful manner.

She gritted her teeth. "So is no one else home?"

"Miss Henry and Mr. Dennison are in the library, miss."

"That's something, at any rate," she muttered, and headed toward the library. "Thank you, Andrews," she tossed back over her shoulder.

"You are quite welcome, miss."

She flung open the library door and stormed into the room, interrupting what looked to be a discussion of a somewhat intense nature between Florence and Mr. Dennison. "Where is he?"

Florence rose to her feet, Mr. Dennison a scant beat behind her. "What are you doing out of bed?"

"I feel fine, perfectly fine," she snapped. "The only thing that would make me feel better is knowing where Nathanial is."

"Quite honestly, Gabriella." Florence met her gaze directly. "I don't know."

Gabriella's jaw tightened. "Mr. Dennison?"

He shook his head. "I can't say, miss."

"Can't say or won't say?"

"At this moment, Miss Montini, I have no idea where Mr. Harrington might be."

Gabriella's gaze shifted back and forth between Mr. Dennison and Florence. "I don't believe either of you."

"Nonetheless, we are not lying to you." Florence's lips pressed together in a disapproving manner. "You do realize you are not appropriately dressed?"

"I had other things on my mind," Gabriella said sharply. She paused and drew a deep breath. "I am going to my room now to dress appropriately and then I am going to the Antiquities Society in hopes that Nathanial has brought the seal to the committee."

Florence and Mr. Dennison exchanged glances.

"And you are not going to stop me."

"We wouldn't think of doing such a thing," Florence said. "By all means, go to the Antiquities Society. I think it's an excellent idea." She nodded. "In fact, Mr. Dennison and I will be happy to accompany you."

"You will?" Gabriella narrowed her eyes. "Why?"

"Goodness, Gabriella, will you ever stop being such a suspicious creature?" Florence huffed. "First of all, it would be entirely improper for you to be unaccompanied. Secondly, as perfectly fine as you may feel, I am not especially confident that you will not collapse at any moment. And third . . . " She paused. "I've been with you at the beginning of all this and I'd rather like to be with you at the end. Now, do put on some proper clothing and we shall wait for you here."

"Excellent." Gabriella nodded, turned, and started

back to her rooms. She knew she shouldn't be annoyed at Florence, and in truth she wasn't. She could trust Florence. As she could trust Nathanial. And as long as she kept saying that to herself, she could keep this mounting sense of doom at bay. After all, he'd done nothing to earn her distrust. Not yet. She dashed the thought from her mind. Leaps of faith, Gabriella, she told herself firmly. Leaps of faith.

It was well past noon when they finally arrived at the Antiquities Society building. The Verification Committee had adjourned and the annual general meeting would begin in a few minutes.

The moment she realized they would be too late, a heavy weight had settled in the pit of Gabriella's stomach. Still, it was not yet time to give up. She spotted Mr. Beckworth amidst the crowd milling in the corridors and hurried toward him, Florence and Mr. Dennison hard on her heels.

"Mr. Beckworth," she called.

"Gabriella." The director addressed her with a concerned smile. "I heard about the fire. Nasty business. Are you all right?"

"Perfectly fine, thank you. Mr. Beckworth . . . " She held her breath. "At the Verification Committee meeting, did Mr. Harrington present my brother's seal?"

"I am sorry, my dear." Sympathy shone in the older man's eyes. "I haven't seen Mr. Harrington since I met with the two of you in my office."

"I see," she said slowly. A terrible sense of defeat and disappointment washed through her. Despair caught at her throat. Still, she preferred not to let it show. She managed a polite smile. "Thank you, Mr. Beckworth."

"As you are already here, I assume you will be joining us for the general meeting."

She shook her head. "I'm not actually a member of the society."

"I know that, my dear, but it seems to me you usually attend the meeting." Mr. Beckworth smiled. "In the upstairs gallery, of course, with the other ladies."

"I don't think—"

"Of course she will," Florence said in a gracious manner. "She wouldn't think of missing it."

"Excellent." Mr. Beckworth nodded and took his leave.

"Come along." Florence hooked her arm through Gabriella's and steered her toward the stairs that led to the observation galleries. "If we don't go now, we won't find good seats."

"I have no desire to observe the meeting," Gabriella said, but allowed Florence to lead her up the stairs nonetheless.

Mr. Dennison had disappeared, but then why should he be any different from anyone else today? In truth, she had no desire to do much of anything at the moment. It was as if she had stood out in the cold for a very long time and was now numb to the touch. She dimly understood that this feeling would fade and leave in its stead despair and anger. He had failed her. She'd trusted him and he had failed her. And in an odd way, she still did trust him. Perhaps because when she fully realized that she was wrong to do so, her devastation would be complete. And she was not yet prepared for that.

They managed to procure seats in the front row, right behind the railing. The meeting would begin any minute.

There was some sort of activity, apparently outside of the doorway near the dais. Florence leaned closer to the railing to see what was happening. Gabriella stared ahead unseeing. It simply didn't matter. Nothing mattered save this awful ache that was growing inside her, somewhere near her heart.

"Well?" Nate stared at his brother.

Sterling chuckled. "It's hard to turn down a request from the Earl of Wyldewood."

"Excellent." Nate breathed a sigh of relief.

Mr. Dennison hurried up to them and nodded. "She's in the gallery. It was an excellent idea to put this part in the hands of Miss Henry, sir."

"I shall have to thank her later, and you as well." Nate turned to Quinton. "And?"

"Here." Quinton thrust a thin open book at him. "These are the rules of the society. I've marked the one you want."

"Thank you."

"You *should* thank me," Quinton replied. "It goes against everything I believe in to look at rules of any kind." He cast his brother a reluctant grin. "One for the other."

Nate returned his grin, acknowledged Sterling's nod of support, and stepped into the room.

The director took his place behind the podium, banged his gavel, and called the meeting to order. The room quieted. Mr. Beckworth began the way he always began, welcoming the members, and then droned on, the way he always droned on, at the beginning of any meeting. Gabriella had rather enjoyed it in the past.

Even in the gallery it was as if she were truly a part of it all. As if she belonged.

She tried to focus on his words, tedious though they might be. Anything to keep from thinking her own thoughts.

Beckworth paused. "This year we have had a most unusual request, but as it comes from the Earl of Wylde-wood . . . "

The announcement caught her attention. Florence nudged her. "Are you listening to this?"

"Yes," she murmured, and stared at the dais. What on earth was going on?

"The board has agreed to allow Mr. Nathanial Harrington to address the assembly. Mr. Harrington."

The director stepped aside and Nathanial took his place, a sheaf of papers and a small book in his hand.

Nathanial?

"Good day, gentlemen. I am most grateful to be allowed the opportunity to speak to you this afternoon," Nathanial began.

Gabriella stared in shock. What was he doing? She leaned closer.

"According to the rules of the Verification Committee, an artifact presented and rejected can only be presented again before the end of the next year's meeting. Exceptions can be made only under extraordinary circumstances." Nathanial's voice rang out over the gathering, strong and confident. "I believe this particular case meets that criteria.

"Last year, Enrico Montini had in his possession an Akkadian cylinder seal. The carvings on that seal included symbols for the lost city of Ambropia and the Virgin's Secret."

Murmurs of interest washed through the crowd. Gabriella's heart lodged in her throat.

"Unfortunately, it was stolen from him and he lost his life attempting to reclaim it." Nathanial's gaze rose to the gallery and found hers. "It has now been recovered thanks to the courageous efforts of Miss Gabriella Montini, but unfortunately too late for this year's committee meeting. According to the rules of this august institution . . . " He paused and glanced down at the book on the podium. "The general assembly may, through a simple majority vote, call for the reconvening of the Verification Committee. I urge you to do so now.

"Aside from the unparalleled historical importance of the seal, it is to be donated to the society, thus its validation is especially important. In addition," his gaze again met hers, "I propose it be known from this point forward as the Montini seal, in recognition of the man who brought it into the light of public knowledge and the woman who risked all to return it to us. Thank you." Nathanial nodded and left the dais.

"Most unusual," Mr. Beckworth said, retaking his position. "We shall vote on that proposal at the end of the meeting when we vote on other matters. And now turning to the . . . "

She stared in shocked disbelief. Blood roared in her ears. Her heart thudded in her chest. Nathanial hadn't betrayed her. He hadn't abandoned her. How could she have doubted him? Even for a minute?

"Come along." Florence got to her feet. "We must be going."

Gabriella stared at her. "What?"

"Come along," Florence said firmly, took her arm and urged her to her feet. "Now."

Gabriella was fairly certain she was putting one foot in front of the other but had no knowledge of doing so. One minute they were in the gallery, and the next in the downstairs corridor.

"Miss Montini? Gabriella?"

Gabriella turned to find the Earl of Wyldewood standing behind her, a genuine smile on his face. She wasn't at all sure she'd ever seen him truly smile before. "Yes?"

"If all went as Nathanial had planned, I was to give you this." He handed her a folded note. "And then escort you to the director's office."

She stared at the note in her hand.

He leaned closer to her and lowered his voice. "You should read it now, Gabriella."

She nodded and unfolded the note. Why did her hands always seem to shake of late?

The note read:

My Dearest Gabriella,

A much as surprise might be nice, it seems to me it might be wise to introduce something of this magnitude in private. You should know that after your father's death, your mother's family tried to find you. They ended their efforts only when they were told you were dead. They have always wanted you and have loved you as they loved your mother. My mother has arranged for your reunion.

You should know as well that I too love you.

Always,
Nathanial

She stared at the words on the page. A lump rose to her throat and her eyes fogged.

"Gabriella?" the earl said softly.

She glanced at him. "Do you know what this says?"

He grinned. "I have an idea."

She smiled at him. "Why, you're not at all stiff and stodgy, are you?"

"Don't tell anyone." He offered his arm. "Shall we, then?" She nodded and he escorted her along the corridor.

"Where . . ."

They paused before the door to the director's office and he stepped aside. "They're expecting you."

"They? Who?"

"Go on, my dear," Florence said behind her.

Gabriella looked at the earl. "Aren't you coming in?"

He shook his head. "I think not."

She glanced around. "Where is Nathanial?"

"I'm not exactly sure." He smiled in a brotherly sort of way. "Go on now. I suspect your future and some of your past awaits you."

"Very well." This was entirely too much to comprehend all at once. Nathanial had proven to truly be her hero. The news about her family was something she'd never dared dream of. And he had declared his love. It was all she'd ever wanted. No, it was so much more. Why, then, was she hesitating? She drew a deep breath and opened the door.

The door swung open and Gabriella stepped into the room. She was as lovely as always, if still a bit pale. She appeared cool and serene and confident, and he knew her well enough by now to know she probably wasn't the least bit serene.

Mother bustled over to her, took her arm and brought her to her family. "Gabriella, I want you to meet your aunts, Caroline and Beatrice, and your cousin Emma."

For a long awkward second, no one said a word. Then Lady Danworthy burst into tears and threw her arms around Gabriella. Followed a scant moment later by Mrs. Delong and Emma, all of them crying and talking at once. In the midst of it, one of her aunts fastened her mother's necklace around Gabriella's neck. The only one not weeping was Gabriella herself, who looked stunned. But not unhappy. He had been right to warn her.

Even Mother sniffed back a tear. "Isn't it wonderful. See what you've done, darling?"

"I didn't do it, Mother, you did."

"Nonsense, Nathanial." Mother shrugged. "You could have refused to accompany me. You could have put your foot down and stopped me. I am, after all, a mere woman."

He laughed. "There is nothing mere about you."

"Nor is there anything mere about her," Mother said pointedly.

"Nothing mere about her at all," he murmured. Gabriella had family now, and her brother's reputation had been assured in death regardless of what it might have been in life. She had everything she'd ever wanted. Would she still want him?

After a few more minutes she turned away from her family and stepped toward him.

"Thank you." Her voice was barely more than a whisper, whether from emotion or the lingering effects of the fire, he didn't know. "For what you did today and this." She drew a deep breath. "I read your note.

Without it I would have said the wrong things entirely. I might have been, well, less than pleasant. I had no idea."

"I suspected that." He stared down at her. "I thought you should know."

"And the rest of it?" Her gaze searched his. "The part that had nothing to do with my family?"

"Oh that, yes, well . . ." He studied her for a moment. "I cannot ask you to join with me in my work, my travels, because there would always be a risk to you, to your safety. I cannot put you in the kind of jeopardy you experienced in your youth, and I cannot take you away from the family you have just found."

Disbelief sparked in her blue eyes. "Nathanial, I—"

"Therefore, I will stay here in England if you will stay with me as my wife."

"I—"

He took her hands. "You once told me you wanted to become indispensable to your brother. I find that you have become indispensable to me."

She swallowed hard.

"Not to my work, although you are brilliant and clever, but you have become indispensable to my life because I cannot imagine another day without you. And you have become indispensable to my heart because it would surely shatter if you were not by my side."

She stared up at him, tears glittering in her eyes.

An audible sob sounded from her aunts.

"Are you going to say anything?" He raised her hands to his lips. "Leaps of faith, Gabriella. Will you leap? I promise always to catch you."

"No." She shook her head. "I can't."

His heart twisted. "I see."

"No you don't." She smiled up at him with a radiance that caught at his soul. "I can't leap now, Nathanial—" Her voice faltered. "I already have."

At once she was in his arms, and he pressed his lips to hers and didn't care where they were or who was watching. He knew only that he would keep her by his side for as long as they lived. And knew as well that this love they shared was as timeless, as priceless, and as rare as anything left by the ancients.

And further knew that she was the greatest treasure of all.

Epilogue

"You should have taken the seal back from Montini when you had the chance. It would have made everything much easier. I assume there was a moment after you killed him."

"No." Javier Gutierrez's gaze slid from one of his employers to the other. "I was interrupted. And I was not about to risk a hangman's noose for the seal or for you." He settled back in his chair and narrowed his eyes. "You pay well but not well enough."

"It was a pity to have burned down the girl's house."

"An unfortunate accident." Gutierrez blew an annoyed breath. "No one was supposed to be there. In my haste to leave, I knocked over the lamp."

"And Rathbourne's death? Rather unnecessary, I would think, although I can't imagine he'll be missed. Another accident?"

"Let us say . . . a moment of passion. He owed me money." Gutierrez shrugged. "He refused to pay. What could I do?"

His employers exchanged glances. They were an unusual pair, in his experience. Cold, ruthless, and well matched. If he was the type of man to be easily scared, these two would have done it. As it was, merely being in their presence sent a chill of unease along his spine. Gutierrez shifted in his seat. He was not used to unease.

"Still, obtaining Rathbourne's seal from his wife will be far easier than wresting it from him."

The other nodded. "Then we will have three."

"And they will reveal the location of the lost city, the final resting place of Ambropia. And we alone will at long last know the Virgin's Secret."

Coming December 2009
from Avon Books
one of Victoria Alexander's
classic love stories

Believe

and coming 2010
the next in the series
about the Harringtons

*Desires of a
Perfect Lady*

*At Avon Books, we know your passion
for romance—once you finish one of our
novels, you find yourself wanting more.*

May we tempt you with . . .

- **Excerpts** from our upcoming releases.

- Entertaining **extras**, including authors'
  personal photo albums and book lists.

- Behind-the-scenes **scoop** on your favorite
  characters and series.

- **Sweepstakes** for the chance to win free books,
  romantic getaways, and other fun prizes.

- Writing **tips** from our authors and editors.

- **Blog** with our authors and find out why they
  love to write romance.

- **Exclusive content** that's not contained
  within the pages of our novels.

Join us at
www.avonbooks.com